To Shannon

InterWorlds

Seraphim Reigns

Deborah Anne Carter

Walk with
Angels! ♡

D. A. Carter

Thank you to my husband, friends and family who have encouraged and supported me throughout the writing of this book.

Dedicated to my three wonderful children

Wesley, Melissa and Abbey

Love always...

∞

Contents

1. Castillo Di Duomo
2. Castillo Di Duomo -The Dream
3. The Woman
4. The Crystal Palace and the Garden's of Sukra
5. Nastacia meets with Dracon
6. Celestial's Abduction
7. Celestial's Rescue
8. The Kingdom of Semiramis
9. The Manticore's Feed
10. Patience's Demise
11. The Abyss
12. Shimm-rae
13. Oze
14. The North-East Region of Venus
15. Calvor
16. Calvor's Temptation
17. Laviathan - The Dark Angel
18. Calvor's Return
19. Dracon's Bride
20. The Beginning of Destruction
21. The Kingdom of Semiramis
22. The Dungeon's
23. Ring of Fire
24. The Castle of Alvor
25. The Fortress of Deimos
26. The Portal
27. The Wrath
28. Return to Venus
29. The Forest of Alvor
30. Nastacia's Return
31. The Wrath of Dracon
32. The Gathering

33. The Temple of Immortality
34. Leviathan
35. The Sacred Chamber of the Temple of Immortality
36. A Battle Most Fierce
37. The Castle Syrtis
38. Escape from Mars
39. Return to Castillo Di Duomo

∞

There was a slight chill in the air, as night was approaching. The silver faced stars shone brightly in subdued and modest glory. Visions of time and space began to unfold in Celestial's mind. She looked up and could see her planet, the greatest brilliant star in the magnificent night sky, outshining all others. She felt pleased... yet sad. A shiver ran down her spine. She thought about her planet before... before...the swarms appeared.

∞

Chapter 1

Castillo di Duomo

Italy, Umbria, 2000...

Edwina sat at the large oak table in the morning room, looking frantically at her watch. It was half past seven in the morning. Aware that it was her powerful and hugely wealthy employer's big day, she was anxious that her charge had not yet come down for breakfast. Her employer's dark temper would soon rise if his daughter was not ready in time, and Edwina would no doubt get the flack.

At that moment, Wishbone rushed in through the double open doors, Patience hanging on to his white harness, trying desperately to slow him down. His tail twitched briskly in anticipation of his favorite food, thick chunks of sirloin steak in rich, juicy gravy.

Edwina stood up, relieved to see them. "Come on, Patience, hurry up! How long do you need to get yourself ready? I've made you banana pancakes dripping in lovely golden syrup...mmm, yummy," she said, licking the hot, golden liquid from her fingers with a loud sucking noise. Edwina placed the plate of pancakes and a glass of milk in the same familiar place as always on the large breakfast table.

"You know your father gets upset if he is late for anything, and today is especially important to him. Wishbone will you stop slobbering over everything. Your breakfast is here too."

As soon as Wishbone was content that Patience was safely seated, he could not get nearer to Edwina quickly enough, pushing against her legs as she placed his large terracotta bowl down on the carefully restored ancient stone floor tiles.

"OK...OK, you silly dog. I do wish Patience was as eager as you."

He attacked his food with voracity, devouring every morsel as though there would never be another meal again. Patience, on the other hand, ate slowly, moving the food around her plate despondently. "Do I have to go? After all, Papa hardly notices I'm here anyway. He's not going to notice if I am there either, so what's the point?"

Edwina stroked Patience's shoulder tenderly. "I know, pet, but he does have a lot on his mind."

Patience's lip curled. "Like what?"

"Oh...like saving the planet, for instance!!" Edwina shuffled uncomfortably. She knew that Roberto neglected his daughter in some ways, but he was a good provider. It often happened in aristocratic families.

"Today we should be proud of him. He is about to receive an accolade for his great contribution to science, and we must be there by his side. After all, Patience, you are the only family he has got left, and you need each other." Edwina shut the fridge door with her foot while balancing a tray in her hands. Wishbone looked up at her with doleful eyes, hoping for more.

"It's sad to think that one day Planet Earth may be gone, despite our best efforts to save it. We must heed the warnings nature sends us. It is important, Patience."

Patience grimaced, mumbling under her breath, "Don't remind me. I do not see particularly what we can do about it."

Edwina rambled on. "Your father thinks that as an intelligent species, we are possibly in a unique position to catalogue and preserve all life on Earth. I mean, with man's knowledge of genetics and DNA nowadays, we might one day restore the life we know today on another planet."

Patience licked the syrup off her fingers. "You have been

watching too many science-fiction movies, Edwina. Your head's in the clouds."

Edwina sighed deeply. "And where did you get that saying, lippy? It's not impossible. That's all I am saying, and try not to speak with your mouth full, young lady. Your father would have a coronary if he were to see your table manners."

Patience laughed. Edwina so believed her father—why, she could not comprehend. She wished for a brother or a sister instead of hanging around adults all her life; if her mother were alive, she might have stood a chance. Marissa had died of a heart attack when Patience was born. She had learned from an early age not to mention her mother's name in front of her father, or a great big black cloud would hang over him and his dark mood would pervade the house.

Lord Roberto Bellucci was not the kind of man to mess with. Born into fading aristocracy, he was still proud of his heritage and everything it stood for. After the tragic death of his wife sixteen years earlier, he had thrown himself into his work as an astronomer. His research into heavenly bodies was revered among scientists. He had won accolades for many of his literary achievements, and today was to bring him the highest honor yet, for his contribution to the study of global warming related to the study of Earth's sister planet, Venus.

Patience put on her new coat, which her father had insisted she wear for the occasion. She hated it. It just did not feel right. The material was not soft enough, and her father would not listen, as usual, more intent on what he thought she should look like for HIS big day. Why should she care about that? He should have known by now that a blind person thinks more about how things feel than what they look like. How could he be so clever and yet so dumb...uh?

She reluctantly followed Edwina, pulled by Wishbone down the long hallway. Roberto had brought Wishbone home for Patience when she was just eight years of age. Edwina had thought it very odd that he had chosen such a huge dog for so small a child. However, true to his breed as a Bernese mountain

3

dog, he proved to be intelligent and good natured and became her constant companion. She relied heavily upon him, and even Edwina, who was not exactly an animal lover, came to love him as her own when he was not annoying her with his constant salivation and knocking things over clumsily.

The exquisite crystal chandeliers sounded like wind chimes as a warm breeze swept through the broad, vaulted vestibule leading to the grand open doors. At least she was leaving the Venetian gothic castle behind for a short time. Her ancestral home always gave her the creeps. It was as if it absorbed her soul into its history. Frightening nightmares of things of the past invaded her sleep...visions gave her sight of things she had never seen by the naked eye; she could describe them so vividly...they seemed so real...she told no one, not even Edwina.

Rising above the Piazzetta San Marco, the Castillo di Duomo, a medieval complex with views commanding the idyllic Umbrian landscape, was constructed in 1278 to protect the town and its surrounding territory. High, vaulted, frescoed ceilings; antique furnishings; murano glass chandeliers; and silk carpets offered a glimpse into a residence of a former period alongside the sympathetically modernized changes for added comfort. A walk among the candle lit cloisters and porticoes contributed to a certain inspiring atmosphere. An unfinished abbey lay bare, adjacent to the castillo, a crumbling primitive church neglected over the centuries. Legend claimed that it was built in atonement for the sins of the noble forefathers; however, it was abandoned after many lost their lives while building it. A noble Lady of the Bellucci line threw herself to her death from the high tower in grief for the loss of her husband, who was killed by an avalanche of falling stones during the building of the cursed abbey.

Unlike the Castillo, which was surrounded by dense woodland on all sides, screening it from curious eyes, the surrounding district was pastoral and traditional, offering a superb landscape of snowcapped mountains and vast stretches of olive trees and vineyards. In springtime, wild flowers in every imaginable shade burst into bloom throughout the region, surpassed only by brilliant sunflowers when summer rolled in. It was that time of year, and the sun burned away the cold dread that filled Patience's veins with ice.

Wishbone jumped clumsily into the car next to Patience, wagging his tail fervently in anticipation of the journey. Her father was already seated opposite, next to Edwina. Carlo, their driver, set off in the black limousine in earnest, hoping that the traffic would not delay their journey to the airport.

They passed through the network of wonderfully preserved medieval towns of Umbria, highlighted by hilltop fortresses, grand Romanesque churches, and monasteries filled with art treasures galore.

Roberto sat in silence. Edwina felt uncomfortable sitting directly across from him. She twiddled her thumbs nervously. Looking in Patience's direction, she attempted to break the awful silence. "Have you got everything you need, Patience? I hope you have not forgotten anything! We don't want to be running around at the last minute when we get there, do we?"

"Of course I have everything. It's just too bad if I haven't; we can't go back now. Anyway, I've got Wishbone. That's all I need; isn't it, boy?" She stroked his glossy brown fur coat.

Edwina smiled fondly at Wishbone's reaction, his tail thumping heavily against the car door with excitement. He was such a charmer. If only Patience could learn from him, life would be a lot easier. Roberto had explained to her that he had been extensively trained from about six weeks old to become a guide dog for the blind, and, craving love and affection, was very loyal to Patience. She loved him more than any human—they had become inseparable.

The journey to New York was a pleasant one in Lord Bellucci's private jet; every convenience was available in comfortable surroundings, much like a boutique hotel. Edwina usually accompanied them on such trips, much to Patience's annoyance. She yearned for her father's attention and wanted to be alone with him. She could have liked Edwina in other circumstances, maybe, but she felt a certain irritation toward her for taking the place of her father—she didn't want a nursemaid. Edwina felt the tension but cared deeply for Patience and only wished they could at least become good friends. It seemed like a constant battle of wills, which was very tiring at times; however, Edwina was not the type of person to give up. In any case, she loved her position in the family and its added perks. It caused quite a stir among the townsfolk, who were intrigued with the Castillo di Duomo, its cursed history, and the mystery surrounding Roberto Bellucci and his blind but genius daughter.

Patience was a protégé of the highly acclaimed Italian Chamber of Music Society. Beside Wishbone, her piano was her constant companion. She was brilliant for one so young, particularly as she had been born blind. She could recite any piece of music just by listening to it a number of times; her favorite piece, Pathetique Symphony, evoked images of her solitary existence, much like that of Ludwig van Beethoven, who overcame his disability through supreme effort of creative will. As a result, she matured quickly in many ways yet retained a certain innocence that other youths of her age had already lost.

The thought of going to New York again aroused mixed feelings for Patience. She was excited at the new sounds, smells, and textures to be experienced, but the unfamiliar territory brought anxieties that could be difficult to deal with, leaving her vulnerable and at the mercy of others. She hated that feeling of being so dependent upon Edwina. That was the only life she had known so far, but she was determined that she would change things in the future. How, she was not sure!

New York

A standing ovation in the auditorium excited Wishbone, and he began to bark uncontrollably. Patience laughed as Edwina ushered them out into the hallway.

"It's not funny, Patience. Have some respect. We are now going to miss your father's speech."

Patience shrugged, holding her arms firmly around Wishbone's neck. "I can't help it if Wishbone decides to bark, can I? You go back in if you want; I don't care if I miss Father's speech. Don't worry. I will be OK here."

Edwina looked at her watch. "Well, don't go anywhere. I will be back shortly."

She grabbed hold of Patience's hand and led her to a leather armchair. "Sit here and don't move one inch until I return. Is that clear?"

Patience felt her way into the comfortable seat, the smell of the worn leather reaching her nostrils. "Yes. OK, don't worry. I don't know this place enough to go wandering about, anyway." Wishbone placed his head in her lap.

Edwina sighed, stroking his head gently. She took one more look at Patience, and, shaking her head, turned on her heels and walked speedily back to listen to the conclusion of Lord Bellucci's speech.

Edwina had saved for months for her Armani pantsuit, a smart navy blue with a white, crisp, collared blouse to complement it. She was not exactly a classical beauty—her nose was slightly sharp—but her dazzling topaz-blue eyes and long auburn curls falling past her shoulders gave her an ethereal quality. She so wanted Roberto to notice that she had made an effort for the occasion. She was intensely proud of her employer's many achievements, though she knew that this was just another formality to him. Nothing would bring Roberto back to life, figuratively speaking. She had known him for a long time; he had died inside with the death of his beloved wife Marissa. And though it was an unspoken thing, it was obvious to her that he partly blamed Patience for her death.

She looked at him addressing the crowd charismatically. Her heart went out to him. What a waste of a great man. He was certainly good looking. His Italian background had ensured him of a Mediterranean golden olive skin tone with a mass of dark curls, his hair so black that there were glints of blue shining through. He was tall with an athletic build and a smile to melt any heart wide open—a smile not often seen anymore, replaced by a deep sadness in his velvet-brown eyes.

Roberto's speech came to a close with another standing ovation. He walked from the stage, handshakes all the way to his seat next to Edwina. Not one smile escaped his lips. Edwina wasn't even sure if he had noticed Patience's absence; he seemed so far away and distant. Feeling that familiar uncomfortable feeling around him, she excused herself to join Patience in the hallway. She was relieved to find she was still sitting in the same place, talking to someone. She could not make out whether it was a man or a woman from a distance. She looked down at the floor for a fleeting moment, and when she looked up again, the person had disappeared. *How could that be?* She thought, quickening her steps.

"Who were you just talking to, Patience?"

"Uh...no one!"

Edwina felt irritated. "Come on, Patience, I saw someone talking to you. Don't play games with me because, quite honestly, I am not in the mood."

Patience lifted herself out of the seat. "And neither am I in the mood. I am telling you the truth. I have not talked to anyone but Wishbone all the time I have been sat here bored out of my mind, believe me."

Edwina didn't know what to think. *Was I seeing things?* "OK, let's say no more about it."

"You mean you don't believe me, Edwina. I am telling you the truth. Why would I to lie to you?"

Patience seemed so agitated that Edwina did not want to pursue the conversation. "Come on. Let's go and get your father. We could all do with dinner, and...I need a drink."

She grabbed hold of Patience's hand and pulled her along briskly, Wishbone by their side. By the following morning, the incident had been forgotten, and they had returned to the Umbrian Castillo and its uncertain mystery.

8

Chapter 2

Castillo Di Duomo

The Dream...

There was only one way to go: stepping across the shimmering threshold into the misty forest. Patience felt the presence of something skulking in the dark, thick bushes, an evil massing copiously all around. The night was full of their mutterings; their lascivious snickering; sudden, wild laughter; and unnerving screams. A sneering sprite leaped out like a toad, and strange flowers sprang from the turf.

Suddenly everything fell into an unearthly silence. Patience shivered as the temperature began to drop rapidly, wrapping her arms tightly around herself...and then...IT came with a freezing gust of wind that tore the leaves from the trees...an appalling consternation, lightning pouring from its eyes, half crouching, half standing as it stole along like a snake insinuating itself noiselessly and ominously.

Patience took flight, running swiftly, faster and faster, until she felt as though her lungs would burst, but she could not run fast enough. Her legs seemed to move slower and slower as she fought her way through the dark, unfriendly forest; each branch intent on grabbing hold of her.

She stopped to catch her breath and noticed the wind had dropped. Stillness filled the forest once more. She closed her eyes for an instant and then opened them slowly to find herself staring into the eyes of her assailant. She froze for a second, hearing every beat of her heart...she could smell its fetid breath. Both kept perfectly still for what seemed like minutes...then...its gray, elongated tongue slithered out of its cruel mouth. Patience cried out with a piercing shriek...

She woke with a start, wrestling with her pillows, sweat dripping off her brow, gasping for air. Wishbone was on her bed licking her face. Relief overtook her despair as she grabbed his head and held him tightly. She could hear the sound of the clock ticking and the normal creaks and groans of the ancient castle but nothing more...yet she felt a cold presence pervading the room.

She shivered, clasping her arms around herself. "Just a dream," she told herself out loud, steadying her breathing. It was the same fevered nightmare that revisited her regularly inside the castle walls. Deep down inside, she felt it was something more profound...something prophetic, or a warning, maybe. She dared not analyze it.

"I am glad I have you, my boy. I think I would go insane without you." She stroked Wishbone's fur genially. He slept by her side for the rest of the night in the large silver wrought-iron four-poster bed swathed in diaphanous white drapes.

When morning came, the nightmare nagged at her mind for the rest of the day. She never wanted to revisit that awful, dark forest again in her sleep, shuddering away from the images of her dream world. Fortunately, not all of her dreams were the same. Some were of an enchanting nature, beauty beyond compare— not that she had anything to compare it with, but if everything looked as magical as it did in these other dreams, oh how she wished she could see. The only problem was that even in those wonderful dreams, apprehension existed; fear of an unknown pursuer still felt strong, with the feeling of unseen eyes watching her every move.

Such strange and colorful visions swirled around her brain night after night; her dark eyes glistened with tears as she tried to make sense of it all. Despair momentarily vanished when she sat at her piano. She played a new concerto to her heart's content and thus spent the rest of the afternoon in the music room with her jet-black Steinway grand piano, her most prized possession. The room was magnificent, richly decorated and furnished true to a period long gone. The mahogany furniture had stood the test of time, some pieces restored to their former glory, a fine coating of dust waiting to be swept away at any moment, revealing its true grained beauty. Any modern additions had been added sympathetically to preserve its unique original style. Luscious heavy drapes adorned the large floor-to-ceiling windows, slightly faded in places by exposure to the sunlight over recent years, but, of course, Patience could not appreciate the beauty of her surroundings and cared only about her beloved piano.

In the evening...when it was quite dark...Patience played her interpretation of the great composer Beethoven with the upmost expressivity. Her ability to enter and illuminate his world was an inspiration to other gifted pianists.

She was so absorbed in her art that she did not notice immediately that she was not alone...until she felt the gentle hand upon her shoulder. Startled, she stopped playing abruptly.

"For God's sake, Edwina, is that you? You scared me to death! My God...don't creep up on me like that!"

An unfamiliar voice whispered softly in her ear, "Do not be alarmed, little one. You do not know me, but you have seen me in your dreams."

Patience's blood ran cold. "But...but that's just not possible!"

"Do not be afraid; I will not harm you. On the contrary...I have come to help you. Your life is in danger."

Patience immediately thought back to her dreams. Am I dreaming now? How can this be? It's not possible! She steadied her breathing, cleared her throat, and spoke with an air of confidence that belied her fear. "Firstly, I'm not little. I am almost sixteen and considered quite tall for my age. And secondly, I am very capable. Thirdly, who are you, and what do you mean my life is in danger?"

The woman sat down beside Patience on the piano stool, gently taking her hand in her own despite the slight resistance in her body language. "Time will tell all; trust your mind to tell the truth. The meaning of your name is the key. You may believe, or you may not believe; however, it is I who will bring the truth and light to your life, and it is I who will save you from a fate far worse than death itself. Through my guidance, you will learn a piece of music that transcends all others. It has never been played by your kind."

Patience pulled her hands free and placed them solidly in her lap. "My kind...what is my kind to you?"

Patience felt frustrated with her language of riddles. "Who are you, really? Are you a figment of my imagination? I must be going crazy. I believe it is in the family. We have a cursed family line, you know. Most of the Belluccis' end up in grave trouble or a grave in death—so I have been told."

"Do not despair, my child. That is precisely why I am here. You are not mad at all. I know this is hard to understand, but I am no figment of your imagination."

The woman grabbed hold of Patience once more. "Feel for yourself. I am as real as you are, though my form is a little different."

Patience stared beyond the woman as she apprehensively ran her small, long fingers down her face. She could not help herself. "Beautiful," she declared, feeling the soft, velvet skin and thick, silky hair. She seemed to be wrapped in soft feathers.

"Now will you take heed?" The woman almost pleaded with her.

Patience dropped her hands swiftly, feeling a little embarrassed. "I would like to trust you. Believe me, I could do with a friend...but I need to know who you are and where you are from."

"I cannot give you the answers you so desire at this moment. You will just have to have faith in all that I tell you. I know it is not easy to trust a complete stranger in an uncertain world, but it is impossible to go through life without trusting someone, for you will be imprisoned in no other than yourself, and that, my little one, is dangerous. The piece of music I offer you will set you free, transcend you into experiencing the true essence of life in another world—a world of supreme beauty where you will find the answers you search for. However, I will not hold back the truth from you. There is danger in this world of beauty...an evil most fierce."

Patience could smell an exquisite aroma unlike any other she had experienced before. Her sense of smell was highly developed as a result of her blindness, but she did not recognize this intoxicating aroma. It left her feeling the same way she had on the few occasions her father had allowed her to have champagne— quite dizzy. It was as though she could see a bright, shining light despite her dark world.

The woman interrupted her thoughts. "You must keep our meeting a secret for now. Can you do that? Otherwise, I will not be able to help you, and your fate will follow you to a place you cannot survive."

Patience sighed deeply. "Yes, I understand. Well, I don't understand any of this, but, I mean, I will tell no one...I promise."

The sound of the woman's voice was as magical to her ears as music. She felt intrigued and wanted to know about her and all that she spoke of. There were so many questions. *What did she mean by set me free? Free from what exactly; and why is my life in danger?* How can music be the answer? Somehow she got the distinct feeling she should wait for the answers. She did not want her to leave and certainly wanted her to return; she felt elated in her presence. A dizzying surge of excitement mixed with apprehension and fear coursed through her veins.

The woman seemed so passionate. "Music speaks! Have you ever listened to an inspirational piece that moves you beyond the language of the spoken word? It can bring forth tears of joy like raindrops in an enchanted forest, fresh and invigorating. It can bring forth tears of sorrow like a torrent of glistening waters. It can make you sing and dance in the moonlight. Music can be passionate and full of love. It is so powerful. Do you really feel the music you play?"

Patience smiled for a fleeting moment. "Yes, of course I do. There would be no point in it otherwise. I often try to explain this to my father, but he does not see it the way I do. I sometimes think he is blind, not me. I feel sort of detached from this world, and my father thinks only of this world. You could say we are worlds apart."

The woman suspected a hint of deep sadness in her voice as she spoke.

"Edwina says—she has been my nanny since I was born—she says that we need to feel all of our emotions to feel fully alive. Well, I just wish I could feel more of the happy ones, whatever they are, I think it's the Bellucci' luck to feel sad emotions far too much. It's not fun in this house; that's for sure."

The woman put her arms around Patience's shoulder. "Well, this Edwina you speak of has great wisdom, and you will do well to listen to her. Instruction is better than silver; and knowledge better than gold. You must be wise and follow my command, for my life is much longer than you could ever imagine, and yours is of tender years. If you learn this music and play it to perfection, your life will change, and you will be instrumental in helping so many others. You will become more alive, renewed and able to meet the challenges that pass your way. Music can be a bridge that allows you to pass over from the world you know into a parallel universe for the lessons of a fleeting life that can change the future of mankind. Your journey will begin."

In the blink of an eye, she was gone.

Patience went to bed that night wondering if she had fallen asleep at the piano or had just been daydreaming. She felt she was going mad, but the following evening, the woman returned, and she knew her life would never be the same again.

∞

Weeks rolled by, and Patience proved to be a willing pupil, closely guarding her secret new friend.

Roberto was in his study on that sultry afternoon, clearing out one of his drawers. He came upon a gold-framed photograph of Marissa. The memory of her washed through his mind, and tears threatened to appear.

He remembered clearly the day he had put away the photograph—he couldn't bear to look at it anymore. The pain of her loss was more than he could handle. Why was he so weak? He sat down heavily in his chair. Placing his head in his hands, he covered his face. Others had lost loved ones and survived; why did he have to fight constantly against his will to die—to be with her once again? Would he be with her? What happened after death? No one had been back to tell their story. He was not even sure what he believed anymore, and, of course, there was Patience to consider.

Picking up the photograph once again, he looked at Marissa's long golden hair and green eyes that had taken all the shades of the sea. He thought back to when they first met. A smile passed his face. She had been timid to begin with and seemed so delicate, like a paper-thin flower in bloom. They would walk together in the university gardens, a wonderful, vivid, colorful canvas. He conjured up the image of the sun shining, her smile so beguiling. She would tease him...tease him about his title and his castle, but he did not mind as long as she was by his side. She was gifted in a creative way that fascinated his academic mind. Her love of life itself excited him, pulling him into a different world beyond the serious nature of scientific matters into a place of hopes and dreams.

If it hadn't been for her strong passion to have his child despite the doctor's warning, she would still be alive today. Roberto placed the picture carefully on his desk, a tortured expression on his face. A sudden feeling of unbearable guilt overcame him....Patience....It had been a double blow that fateful day when he was told that Marissa's delicate heart had given up but that she had given him a precious gift, a beautiful baby daughter. His expression turned from sadness to anger. Why...why had she put her life in danger for this child? The resentment for this little life ate away at his soul, followed by guilt. Yes guilt—such an empty, destructive pattern of negative thought that had no value whatsoever in his futile life.

It wasn't apparent at first. Edwina had noticed it while nursing Patience a few months later. Her eyes never focused on her, and she didn't follow Edwina's hand movement at all. Edwina had it checked out. She was blind. There was no doubt about it—she would probably never see.

Roberto sat despondently in his faded brown leather winged chair at his desk cluttered with documents, journals, and reference books. A full library of literary works surrounded him from floor to ceiling on all sides except the very large golden-and-red-brocade-curtained windows. The large oak door was pushed open at that moment, and Edwina hurried in. She wore tailored black trousers and a royal-blue silk blouse that complimented her eyes. Her cheeks flushed at Roberto's intense gaze as she placed down the silver tray. He seemed to look straight through her and beyond, as though she did not exist, an appendage of the tray itself. Under her arm, she carried a bundle of unopened letters that had been delivered that morning. Roberto took them from her without any acknowledgement and immediately ripped open the largest envelope, cursing under his breath. He cleared his throat. Edwina stood in front of him and realized how tense she felt.

"Can I speak to you?" She took a deep breath. "It's about Patience."

He held up his hand. "Not now. I am busy, as you can see."

Roberto shuffled round some papers on his desk and retrieved an appointment book from underneath. He leafed through the pages, not looking up once. He mumbled a date the following week and a specific time.

Edwina did not further the conversation having come to the conclusion that the date he spoke of was the date he could actually fit her in to talk about his own daughter. She shook her head in despair. No wonder she had her hands full with her, she thought as she quickly left the room.

Everything was quiet in the library except the ticking of the ornate grandfather clock standing majestically by the large oak double doors. Then Roberto heard the music floating hauntingly through the slightly open doors. It seemed to be coming from the west wing. He had never heard Patience play such music before. Perhaps it was a new concerto. He was pretty clued up on classical music, but he could not name this one.

Feeling strangely drawn, almost hypnotized, he made his way to the music room and stood for a moment behind the door, listening. As each note reached his ears, it moved him beyond comprehension. His heart beat rapidly; the lure of the music was literally overpowering, and as much as he did not want to interrupt, he felt compelled to enter the room.

He slowly turned the knob and clicked open the door. Patience did not stop playing. It was as though she were in a trance. A sudden flicker of movement caused his gaze to switch suddenly, moving his eyes from his daughter playing the piano to an astonishing vision beside her.

Roberto stood frozen to the spot, mesmerized. There stood the most exquisite creature he had ever set eyes upon. It was only a fleeting glance; she was gone in the blink of an eye, so swift a departure that Roberto wondered if it was his imagination running wild—maybe because of his great sorrow and the inspiration of the music. He rubbed his eyes, amazed that the image was still clear in his mind's eye. She wasn't human; that was for certain. She looked...like...like an angel.

Those silvery feline eyes had shimmered as they penetrated deep into his soul. Doubting what he had seen, or what he thought he had seen, it occurred to him that if she wasn't real...then what was the unusual perfume that subtly pervaded the room? Where had that come from?

He felt heady and confused when his daughter brought him back to some semblance of reality.

"Papa, is that you?"

"Yes Patience, just checking that you are practicing for the concert next week. I see that you are...umm...good...ah carry on the good work...I...I may see you at dinner."

Before she had a chance to say anything at all, he stumbled out of the room. He dared not mention to her what he thought he had

17

seen; she would think him stark raving mad. He wasn't sure what she thought of him really at all, come to think of it.

For the first time in his entire life, he lay on his bed in daylight hours. He felt utterly exhausted.

A deep, deep sleep overcame him.

Chapter 3

The Woman

Venus...

Roberto watched her from a distance in the sun-dappled clearing, crouched behind a tree. She was truly a vision of unprecedented beauty. Her hair shone like pure white strands of silk, softly swaying as she gracefully moved.

Everything about her appearance was perfectly formed. Her face once seen was never forgotten; he remembered her eyes; a dazzling silver. Certainly she was young, for no lines or flaws spoiled her milky white skin, which had the appearance of alabaster, though somehow lit up from within.

Her vibrant aura had an unworldly energy that infused the atmosphere with a wondrously mystical air. He gazed in awe, at the sight before him. She spread her angelic wings, pure, white as snow, yet with shimmering colors of the rainbow, sparkling in the sunlight as though covered in minute crystals or diamonds.

Suddenly, tiny oscillations surrounded her, intensely bright, so bright that Roberto had to avert his eyes somewhat. An unusual high-pitched sound emanated from them, like the sound of the tiniest tubular bells ringing sweetly in his ears. They weaved in and out of the leaves in arcs and loops, their movements exquisitely synchronized. Roberto blinked again, hoping to get a better glimpse of the astonishing tiny creatures. He could just about make out the translucency of their diminutive wings.

The vision was spectacular, breathtaking, the surroundings a paradise. A babbling brook flowed gently beyond her, and blossoms fell softly from the trees like snowdrops, the palest pink imaginable, leaving a fragrant carpet on the ground.

Gracefully she danced, catching the blossoms in her delicate hands, singing a melodious tune, a tune that sounded oh...so familiar.

He did not mean to disturb the tranquil scene. It was the branch that he was holding onto that snapped. The tiny creatures immediately disappeared, and her wings folded just as quickly. She snapped her neck round swiftly and looked directly at his position. He shrank back behind the tree.

"I know you are there, Lord Bellucci." Her voice sounded like a sweetly sung melody; he could hear it as clearly as if she were standing right beside him.

Roberto reluctantly came out from behind the tree. *How did she know my name?*

Within an instant of that thought, she stood before him, yet he had not seen her move at all. Her shimmering eyes once again mesmerized him. He felt almost delirious in her presence, a sensation he had not been acquainted with for a long time.

At last he spoke hesitantly. "How...how do you know my name?" It was so out of character to find himself stuttering, "Who...who are you? What do you want from me...where the hell is this place? If I have died and come to Heaven...I...I am in the wrong place, believe me when I say I don't deserve this...I have been very selfish..."

Before he could finish, the woman smiled warmly. "Rest assured, Lord Bellucci, you are not in Heaven and you probably never will be, but it will be a long time before death will befall you. I have a plan that will free you, your family, and generations to come."

"What do you mean? We don't need freeing; thank you all the same. Anyway, freeing from what? What are you talking about? This is not making any sense at all."

Roberto was feeling irritated by her insinuations. What could she know about his family? He crossed his arms in indignation.

"Look, could you please just tell me where I am and how to get back home? I would be much obliged, thank you."

"So many questions, Roberto; but, you see, this is your destiny. Time will reveal all. I have been expecting you. You have something that you are not yet aware of."

"This is absurd. I am a scientist; I don't relate to this mumbo jumbo...this fantasy stuff. It's just not my world. My world is facts and facts alone. You have chosen the wrong person."

The woman smiled again, which infuriated Roberto even more. "I know how you must feel, but you will get over it."

"You don't know anything about how I feel. You don't even exist! I don't know why I am wasting my breath talking to some imaginary person...a...a beautiful vision, yes, but I have better things to do." Roberto looked again at the surroundings. "I must be dreaming," he mumbled quietly to himself.

The woman moved closer. "Let us give ourselves to the essence of time, when all will be revealed. Now you must eat and rest. There is much to do and little time to do it in. And if I know anything about humankind, they cannot do much on an empty stomach. Come. Follow me."

With a deep sigh, Roberto gave up to the dream. They walked in silence through the cherry blossoms. He was feeling quite heady with the utter beauty of the woman and her surroundings. He felt like a boy again in a magical fairy tale...a time before life ate away his soul until there was nothing left to give and therefore nothing to receive. He did not want to awaken too soon—all his senses were wonderfully heightened.

Before he had much time to think about it, he had been swept off his feet by none other than a giant, muscular, bronzed angel. His huge, snow-white, golden-tipped wings of impressive proportions flew from thermal to thermal, lifted by the rising currents of warm air like an eagle in flight.

Roberto looked down at the dramatic terrain below and the awesome Blue Mountains ahead, his heart beating rapidly, his adrenaline running high. He felt alive...for the first time in years...so alive. He took a sharp intake of breath; the air was pure and invigorating. The flapping of wings in unison sounded similar to that of a rushing torrent of water falling sharply over the precipice of a very high cliff face. He felt exhilarated.

The woman flew ahead. She seemed very much in command despite her petite stature. "Make haste...to the palace, Mikael!"

She had ordered him authoritatively, and he obeyed her without question. Who is she? Roberto asked himself yet again.

The Crystal Palace was magnificent, made out of silver, extravagantly embellished with high-clarity diamonds. It glittered and sparkled in the sunlight, its luminosity a rare spectacle. The palace, the surroundings, the angelic guards—had he died and gone to heavenly places? She had said not. He pondered the thought. Everything seemed too perfect. He did not trust perfect; it was probably a façade, danger lurking through some doors or out there in the forest.

For a moment, a feeling of utter panic overcame him. What if this was Heaven? A life so perfect would suffocate him; boredom would pervade his soul. He had not been prepared for such an existence. He wiped the sweat from his fevered brow.

They entered the palace through large, heavy silver doors. Inside, the walls were covered in mother-of-pearl and all its pastel hues, the floors constructed of fine white marble with a hint of grayish silver running through it. Enormous silver-and-crystal chandeliers shaped like spiders' cobwebs hung from the very high, embellished ceilings, and hundreds of pure white candles flickered all around.

The angelic guards stood to attention. Tiny oscillating creatures, the size of Roberto's hands, fluttered around the vast space, producing a tinkling noise like that of tiny tubular bells ringing harmoniously. Every part of their anatomy was perfectly formed despite their diminutive size, their transparent delicate wings. Myriads of white, iridescent flowers covered in a fine coating of sparkling silver, the green of their leaves bright emerald, adorned the windows and tables, the sweet fragrance filling the air.

Other beautiful young women of human proportions played

soft, relaxing music on silver crystal harps, their transparent wings throwing the light in rainbow sparkles against the walls like prisms. Roberto felt their curious eyes boring into his soul.

He was dumb-struck and very apprehensive. His appetite was waning, and he suddenly felt worn out. The woman looked into his appealing eyes, immediately read his mind, and guided him slowly up some steep, luminous, winding steps that seemed to go on forever. Roberto began to stagger, seeing double. Torches of naked flame lit up one by one as they passed by until they reached an enormous bedroom chamber. Once in the chamber, all that Roberto could focus on was the bed, the focal point of the room—a huge, solid-silver bed heavily decorated in mother-of-pearl and crystal awaited him. The sumptuous feathery softness of the coverlet, pure white, like that of angel's wings, enveloped him.

Roberto drifted into an unusual, peaceful sleep.

∞

The following day, or what seemed like the following day, Roberto opened his eyes to the morning light—emotions that words cannot express encompassed his soul.

"A DREAM...it was nothing more than a dream!" He spoke out louder than he intended. Disappointment flooded him. Another day had dawned—another day with thoughts of death to end his misery and the hollow feeling that consistently pervaded him. *Why would I even imagine it was anything more than a dream...merely an aberration brought about by my overwrought imagination?*

Having performed his perfunctory ablutions, he slowly walked down the grand main staircase, holding on tightly to its ornate black-and-gold wrought-iron balustrade. Large, gilt-framed portraits of his ancestors hung austerely on the thick stone walls, generations of a family held close by the legacy of land ownership. He looked up at the ceiling, which was covered with beautifully executed designs painted in jewel colors of emeralds, purples, and ruby reds interrupted with gold and bronze. Bronze chandeliers of immense proportions hung from the high ceiling, covered in draping jewels casting subdued light across the intricately detailed tiled floor at the foot of the steps. How he wished he could appreciate such opulent beauty, but it meant nothing to him anymore.

Then he heard it...the same haunting melody...the very same as the one in his dream the night before. Again it was coming from the music room in the west wing. The music grew louder as he made his way along the winding corridors, pulled magnetically toward the source of the melody.

His heart began to beat rapidly as he struggled to get a grip of himself. Opening the doors slowly and quietly, he was taken aback by the spectacle before his eyes. A maelstrom of bright, iridescent-colored light mingled with the sweet, unworldly melody swirling around the room. Patience was not at the piano; the piano was playing itself.

The lure of the soft yet potent music compelled Roberto to step into the midst of the swirling matter. Immediately he was swept off his feet, spiraling upward...up and up...intense colored light of every description, like that of an artist's palette, passed through him, the music touching his innermost being. Visions of space and time unfolded in his mind's eye beyond his comprehension...then sudden blackness...

∞

Chapter 4

The Crystal Palace and the Garden's Of Sukra

Venus...

Patience was the first to awaken. Her head nestled upon a soft cushion of feathers; she felt the disorientation of unfamiliar surroundings. A different smell filtered through her nostrils, and the soft feathers that enveloped her instead of her starched cotton sheets told her she was not in her own bed in the Castillo.

Roberto stirred slowly, bemused to find himself back in the bedchamber of his dream the night before, this time with Patience and Wishbone next to him. Can this be real? He was surely cracking up under the strain of his work and grief. He was going to have to take some time out, have a rest, go away somewhere for a while. He remembered the maelstrom of light and color accompanied by the haunting melody but understood none of it. He had never thought of himself as a fanciful man; only facts and figures were his take on life. He scratched his head.

Patience spoke first. "Who's there?" Her heart beat mercilessly. Nothing seemed familiar except Wishbone by her side, quietly whimpering.

"It's me, Patience. Your father; remember me? Don't ask me where we are, though, because I haven't got the faintest idea. I don't know what is happening to us except that I have finally lost it. I had a dream last night, and we seem to be in the same dream

25

having a conversation in a strange place. It's all rather bizarre."

He got up from the bed and walked around to where Patience sat on the other side, her legs dangling off the edge. Grabbing hold of her shoulders, he looked into her frightened green eyes and for the first time noticed how like her mother's they were. It was like a sharp stab in his gut. His paternal instincts came alive, and all he wanted to do was to protect her...but from what?

She froze under his touch, and he stepped back, horrified at her reaction to him.

"Don't worry, Patience. I will get to the bottom of all this. I will protect you if we are in any danger. I am sure we are not," he said, not believing his words at all. He did feel an imminent danger around them.

Patience did not know what to think of her father's sudden interest in her and could not understand what he was talking about. He clearly did not seem himself.

"Well, one minute I was playing the piano, and the next, I felt like I was sucked up into the air. I feel as though have slept for a very long time. I remember only darkness and falling and then...nothing else." She did not mention the woman or how she had learned to play the melody, feeling the softness of feathers all around her. At the same time, she clutched at the crucifix hanging from her slender neck, a small golden cross with arms of equal length, wrought of gold and encrusted with emeralds and sapphires. It had been her mother's, and she always wore it faithfully as the only connection to a mother she had never known. Reassured it was still there, she let go and climbed precariously off the high bed and ran her hands over her dress. "My clothes feel different. I am sure I didn't put this on this morning; it feels so...soft and silky."

Roberto looked at her dress, a charming turquoise gown almost medieval in style, not unlike the attire of some of the ancestors in the portraits hanging in the gallery of the Castillo de Duomo. "It rather suits you. It's like a prom dress. It brings out the color of your eyes."

26

Patience felt suddenly uncomfortable, not used to her father's acknowledgement. "I wouldn't know what a prom dress looks like, anyway," she said, slowly running her fingers down the silky material.

Now it was Roberto's turn to feel slightly uncomfortable. Everyone was silent, even Wishbone. Then, at that moment, the tall, large silver doors opened. Wishbone barked. A young girl with long, red, luscious hair and translucent wings came toward them holding a silver tray with food enough for two and a dish for Wishbone. She cast the huge dog a wary glance and placed the dish on the floor.

Wishbone could not get to his food fast enough, almost knocking the girl over, much to her annoyance.

"What is it, boy?" Patience felt her way from the bed.

Roberto pinched himself. Then he pinched Patience.

"Ouch, who's that? Someone just pinched me, Papa." Patience rubbed her arm.

"Sorry. But that was a fairy I just saw. Are you in my dream, or am I in yours?"

"What? You are in mine; you must be. You see, there is something I have not told anyone about. I met someone from my dream, and..."

Her father didn't seem to be listening and Wishbone continued to bark.

"Sh...sh, Wishbone." Patience grabbed hold of him. The fairy quickly left the room, closing the door with a bang.

Breakfast consisted of many exotic fruits that tasted divine, wonderful eggs encased in a dark green marble-effect shell that had the unusual combination of tasting salty yet sweet, yellow tomatoes off the vine, nice and crispy on the outside and soft and juicy on the inside. All of this was followed by a sweet, unknown drink that gave them an instant rush of adrenaline.

Roberto and Patience tucked in hungrily, forgetting for a moment their unusual predicament—not a word spoken; Wishbone too lapped his unusual contents up voraciously. Patience was in rapture at the magical sounds in the bedchamber, especially the tiny fairies flying around the room making little tinkling noises.

"Papa, I feel sort of funny, giddy. It doesn't taste like champagne, but it has the same effect."

"I think it's some sort of stimulant." Roberto licked his lips and peered into the elaborately embellished silver goblet, trying to work out the flavor of its contents. "I know everything seems so magical here, but we must be wary; we do not know where we are or what they want from us yet. We are obviously in another world; who knows what lurks beneath all this mystical beauty?" Roberto surveyed his surroundings. He felt suspicious of anything that seemed perfect, especially in a world he did not understand.

"You always think the worst, Papa!" Patience declared.

Roberto looked intently at her for the first time in years; she had become a young woman, no longer his delicate little child. He just wished she could see what he was seeing. He tried to explain a little about their surroundings.

Wishbone could not keep still. He was sniffing in every corner, and when he saw the tiny fairies, he jumped up, barking at them, which sent them shooting up to the ceiling sprinkling fairy dust all over him. Wishbone glittered like an adorned Christmas tree as the sun filtered through the many-arched windows.

"Phew, it's warm in here. Should I open a window?" Patience said, fanning herself with her hand. Before Roberto could answer, she had found a chair and proceeded to drag it across the room, holding onto Wishbone's harness as she told him to lead her to the nearest window.

"Where is the window?"

"Wait." Roberto panicked. "The windows are very high. Let me do it."

"I am capable, father. You don't even know what I am capable of," she said indignantly.

Roberto was taken aback by her tone of voice. "Yes, I am sure you are very capable. You play the piano beautifully, but I don't want you to fall. We have other things to think about. We need to be practical, not foolhardy."

28

Patience sighed, and allowed her father to take over. He was actually right for once; she did not know this place enough.

The room was like a chapel in shape, with very high ceilings and windows. The stained glass was embellished with rainbow-crystal fairies, Cherubs, and flowers in a kaleidoscope of many colors. As Roberto opened one of the windows, lo and behold!

Something flew past him at great speed. He almost fell off the chair in immense surprise. It flew around the room a few times before settling next to Patience on the bed.

Meanwhile, the fairies went into hiding, and Wishbone followed suit, cowardly hiding under the bed. Roberto was dumbfounded to find a small, rather chubby little Cherub with glistening red curly hair and large, deep, sapphire-blue eyes sitting beside Patience on the bed.

"By the way, Patience, you have a Cherub sitting beside you, a little fellow with small, pearly gray wings."

Patience frowned. What was her father talking about?

Roberto thought he could not be more astounded. "Hi there, little fellow; what can we do for you?" he asked as though he were talking to a mere mortal.

"More like what I can do for you, I would say, as you are newcomers to our planet, Venus, and I have been here for centuries. The queen has given me orders to take care of you, and she will meet with you later. She has many important things to attend to...umm...not that you are not important, of course, but needs must there is always something or someone to see in our busy kingdom, much like your own, I suppose...am I waffling? Theoretically, I'm cute, as Cherubs are, but I always seem to miss the mark, unlike the other Cherubs here; probably comes from being adopted by the pixie folk, who have passed on an impish character rather than a cute, Cherub-like character. Nevertheless, I am at your command," the Cherub said with a tiny bow and a quick flutter of his small, pearly gray wings.

"That is very kind of you," said Roberto, feeling rather idiotic talking to a Cherub.

"Oh think nothing of it. I like to be useful to our queen. It's a great honor; it means she trusts me and even likes me just the way I am," the Cherub said with a pleased smile upon his face. "In actual fact," he continued smugly, "I would go as far as to say that I am probably her favorite Cherub, and you don't know what that means to me."Ilk leaned forward. "You see, not everyone has patience with me because I tend to waffle, or so I have been told. I personally don't know what they are talking about. It's just that they don't have much to say, or they would be like me, don't you think?"

"Yes..." Roberto wanted to know more about this queen of Venus but could not get a word in edgeways.

"But, of course," the Cherub droned on very rapidly, "not everyone can be like me. It would not do for us to be the same. Life would be boring, and we would have nothing to learn from each other, would we now?"

"No, I—" Roberto tried to speak again.

"Anyways," the Cherub interrupted. Even Wishbone had gone quiet and lain down with his head between his legs under the bed. "My name is Ilk. Don't ask me why—it isn't a Cherub-like name, but as I told you, my guardians are mushroom pixies, and I can't complain because they have been very good to me and taught me all about the Sacred Scrolls. Without such wisdom, there eventually would be no life see. So I have a lot to be thankful for because I can see they wanted the best for me. It is quite unusual for pixie folk, especially the mushroom pixies, to be interested in such things. Now, where was I? Oh yes, I'm Ilk, pleased to meet you!"

"Hi," said Patience, shyly trying to take in everything that Ilk had said. "This is my father...and my dog, Wishbone—who is under the bed as we speak."

On hearing Patience speak of him, Wishbone popped his head forward from under the bed cautiously.

"Oh, hello Wishbone, nice of you to join us at last," said Patience sarcastically. She turned the opposite way to Ilk, who kept changing positions all around the room. "My name is

Patience, and could you be so kind as to tell us where we are and what are we doing here?"

Roberto smiled at his daughter's confidence despite the unknown place they had found themselves in. Ilk surveyed her with avid interest. "Mm...charmed, I'm sure. You have a very interesting name. I hope you are as patient as your name implies. That would be nice for me, but tell me, who are you talking to? There is no one in front of you. I don't know if you have noticed, but I am over here...see." Patience swung round to the direction of his voice.

"Anyways, I would like to show you the Gardens of the Silver Crystal Palace, one of the Seven Wonders of Venus. They are spectacular! And you would probably get lost if you went without me. We could go right now if you like," said Ilk excitedly. "I have plenty of time at present; the queen has given me time off to take care of your needs while you settle in. She is so thoughtful, our queen. You will just love her...you will see."

"I would love to see the gardens, but I cannot. I am blind, and you still have not answered my question."

"What is this 'blind' word?" Ilk looked puzzled.

Roberto jumped in. "Patience was born without sight. Her eyes do not function."

"Oh, that is awful...I am so...sorry for you. There is so much beauty to see; you are really missing out...."

"Yes, she already knows that."

"Oh...hmm...yes, of course. I am always stating the obvious. Quite known for it, I do apologize. Just tell me when to shut up. You are about to see some of the most awe-inspiring places you will ever see...."

The three of them set off, with Ilk chatting away without so much as a breath taken.

They had not walked far when Ilk stopped abruptly and without explanation pulled the little silver trumpet he carried wrapped around his torso and blew into it three little hoots followed by one long note.

Patience stopped, suddenly listening to the sound of powerful

31

flapping wings above. Roberto covered his eyes to shield them from the brightest of light coming from above. With a slower flapping of wings, two imposing male angels of great stature slowly descended from the skies and landed gracefully before them. Roberto stood there awestruck.

"What is it, Papa? What is happening?" Patience felt the presence of something very tangible and powerful.

"To the gardens of the Crystal Palace, please!" Ilk instructed the bronzed, mighty, handsome creatures.

Roberto explained to Patience what was happening as he helped her mount one of the angel's backs, placing her arms tightly around his rather large, honed-to-perfection torso. Then he mounted the second angel himself before he had time to think about it, and the cold, pure air stung his cheeks and burned into his lungs, taking his breath away momentarily.

They rose higher and higher until they were so high the land had shrunken into a patterned carpet of jewel-like colors below. Patience's sensation of weightlessness exhilarated her. In the excitement of the moment, she had forgotten poor Wishbone, left behind to fend for himself in unknown territory. Her ears popped as she adjusted to the new heights. She gripped even tighter for fear of falling; the sound of a rushing torrent of air mixed with the flapping of mighty wings deafened her.

In the distance, Roberto caught a glimpse of the sparkling palace, situated at the summit of the Mountain of Hope, a mountain of majestic proportions glimmering in the sunlight, surrounded by five concentric rings of alternating water and land, connected by bridges and tunnels. The two land rings were made up of unsurpassed gardens, and the three water rings led to the sea by a wide canal, which enabled ships to sail into the heart of the City of Queens. The gardens were astonishingly beautiful, stretching for miles, with sweeping lawns and myriads of trees. The palest blue mountains rose over the distant, hilly forests, and the pure, cloudless azure sky governed the land. All around the well-organized grassy areas stood marble pillars, tall yet unobtrusive, a climbing array of flowering plants creeping prolifically up and across the ornate arches displaying the most unusual flowers never seen by the human eye.

"Hold on tight," the angel shouted to Roberto as he swooped down, ready to land. Patience felt all giddy and could not stop laughing when she finally found her feet. She gathered her senses and instinctively stretched out her arms for Wishbone.

It suddenly dawned on her while her father was deep in conversation with Ilk that Wishbone was missing. She began to panic. "Papa...Papa, where is Wishbone? Have you got him, Papa?"

She turned this way and that way, hands outstretched like someone demented. She had never lost him before. Her heart beat wildly.

Roberto turned back to Ilk. "We have left our dog behind. We need to go back and get him immediately."

Amusement gleamed in Ilk 'sink blue eyes. "Oh no need to worry, he will be all right." Ilk was quite pleased to leave him behind, not quite sure of him at all.

Roberto looked at Ilk with suspicion. "No, we must go back now."

A tear slipped down Patience's cheek. "You don't understand, you silly Cherub. Wishbone is my eyes and my closest friend. I can't do without him. Take me to him at once, or else...or else...or else I will scratch your eyes out. See if you like that!"

Roberto looked shocked at Patience's sudden outburst, and he felt her despair. "Sorry, little fellow, but she means it!"

"OK...OK, I get the picture. I do apologize...I...I did not know he was of such importance to you. I will send one of the angel carriers to go back and fetch him immediately. Do not despair, Patience. I am your friend, not your enemy, as some would be on this planet—especially of late. Everything is becoming so unpredictable. Anyways, he will join us later. But in the meantime, we may as well take a look at the gardens."

"How will the angel know where to find us, if we move away from this spot?" Patience's voice was filled with anxiety.

"Do not worry; he will find us."

Patience interrupted him before he could speak another word. "He just better had, or you are in trouble."

Ilk saw the fear in her—her eyes wide, forehead knitted, her lips pressed tightly shut. She shifted uneasily. He thought how pretty she looked with her silky blond hair now worn loose, waves cascading just past her shoulders, and a certain pity for her overcame him.

"Please do not worry, Patience. I promise you he will be all right. I kind of like your fighting spirit. You will need that. Oh yes...you will need that if you come across the Devatas. Never let them into your thoughts...black pervading creatures of hell...ugly, horrible beings that torture the—"

Robert furrowed his brow. "So...I take it you don't like these creatures!"

Patience covered her mouth with her hand, laughing discreetly. She did not know her father could be so sarcastically humorous.

"No one likes them. You'd have to be insane to allow them anywhere near you. They are out to destroy whoever they can, and they will if you let them. I will not let them near me. No, they won't get near me...I will make sure of that."

"Yes...well, who are they, then?" Roberto was intrigued.

"Oh, I don't like talking about them. Can we change the subject?"

Patience pointed at Ilk in the wrong direction yet again. "Well, as long as they don't touch Wishbone, you need never mention them again."

"OK, OK, I get the picture, but I am here...over here, not there where you are pointing. Anyways, let us think of something much nicer, like these gardens. Could we?"

The kaleidoscope of a bright sunny morning lit up a land full of luscious fruits that grew like colorful jewels from the immense emerald-green trees. Roberto noticed that all the flowers were of a pastel hue; no really bright or dark colors. The green shrubs were silvery colors of jade, turquoise, and aqua. The fragrance was wonderful—top notes of sunny lemongrass, sweet orange blossom, and heavenly rose held aloft by the green woody scents of rosemary and pine. Patience just wanted to bottle the aroma and take it home. She wanted to share the experience with Edwina. She thought of Edwina for a moment. Poor Edwina—she would be out of her mind with worry wondering where they had gone. She suddenly wished she had been nicer to her.

There were many trees in the garden—different types, unusual shapes with exotic fruits and flowers hanging temptingly in easy reach, and spectacular fountains with tiny water fairies dancing around them amid the flora. The water spilled over the edges, sparkling in the sun's rays all the colors of the rainbow. Patience could feel the warmth of the sun on her face.

After walking for quite some time, they came upon some white marble terraces rising high, each above the next, connected by marble stairways. Every tier was planted with a profusion of fabulous trees, shrubs, and hanging flowers cascading down the alabaster pillars.

Ilk fluttered his wings. "This was constructed for Queen Nebula, during her reign, by her husband, Carthage—a Draconian, you know. He came to Venus because of the peace and tranquility he had heard of here and fell in love with our queen. A strange match, everyone thought. Never before had a Draconian married a Venusian, but somehow, they worked successfully together. It was very unfortunate that things went so very wrong for them when the queen disobeyed Elyon, creator of all life forms—but, as you can see, Carthage loved her very much and built many things in honor of her, these gardens being one of the most spectacular of his constructions." Ilk sat on one of the marble steps with his chubby legs and arms crossed, smiling to himself.

Roberto was entranced with the beautiful young maidens wandering about and wanted to know why they did not speak as they passed by.

"They are the naiads—water nymphs. They preside here to protect the freshwater, keeping it crystal clear and free from impurities. This duty is of great importance to them, for if their

35

body of water dries up or becomes contaminated, they wither away and die. I don't really know why they don't speak. Many nymphs do not have the power of speech, but they have a language among themselves. Some speak the same as we do; for instance, the Alpseid nymphs. Why some do and some don't I cannot say. Some are tall, some are tiny...it's just the way it is. I have not really questioned it before, but I see what you—"

Tiny transparent beings fluttered past—the fairies. Ilk pointed at them. "Note their tiny, membranous wings, filmy, transparent and veined. They are found in many places in our world. They have supernatural abilities such as the ability to fly, and most of all, the ability to influence the character of their host, making up their aura. The water fairies are the helpers of the naiads and the auras of the nymphs."

"They are so beautiful and delicate." Roberto leaned forward to take a closer look.

"I wish I could see them. May I touch one?" Patience moved closer to her father.

"Yes," said Ilk, "but be aware that they are not all good fey. Some are malevolently inclined; they are the sprites who take over the tiny fairy auras, influencing the host in a negative way, producing nasty characteristics. You would notice them because they are ugly in comparison to the fairy auras. Oh, sorry. I forgot, you would not notice them, my dear. Maybe it is best if you keep away from them altogether. After all, they are not the easiest to catch hold of. On the whole, though, they are benevolent, representing regeneration and growth. But if their host has been contaminated by the sprites, they have a real battle on their hands to get rid of them and their influence. Believe me you don't want to know the sprites. A tiny type of Devata, but nevertheless not good for the fairy fruits of the spirit!" said Ilk, not wishing to discuss the Devatas yet again—it always sent a shiver up his spine.

Ilk quickly turned his attention elsewhere. "The gardens are watered by fountains fed through underground pipes from cisterns in the topmost terrace. Very clever, don't you think? I think so, anyways."

"Yes very..." Roberto tried to speak feeling left out of the conversation and thinking how much Ilk liked the sound of his own voice.

Patience clung closely to her father, following Ilk to the southeast of the gardens, where a river of pure water ran through the grounds, clear as crystal and surrounded by trees bearing seven fruits, each tree yielding its fruits each month. The leaves of the trees were used for the medicinal purposes. Patience could not believe the sensational feel of the place as a symphony of intoxicating scents ran through her nostrils.

At the entrance to one of the marble terraces, a pair of lions lay majestically by the side of two nymphs of human size, the lions feeding docilely from their delicate hands.

Ilk settled with his legs crossed on the back of one of the lions and continued his education. "You cannot see it from here because the gardens are too vast, but all around the perimeter hover's the Light of Hope, which shines brightly day and night but can be appreciated more in the night sky as a beautiful vision of all that our planet Venus stands for. I love it! I visit every day to see it; it gives me hope of saving our planet from its impending destruction...yes. It's a sad state of affairs...but best not to dwell on it. The other name for the gardens is the Gardens of Sukra— meaning white or bright. Quite apt, don't you think?" Ilk was enjoying his captive audience.

"What impending destruction?" Roberto suddenly felt anxious.

Ilk did not seem to hear him. As they breathlessly approached the uppermost terrace, he showed them a golden plaque built in the floor, dedicated to Queen Nebula and encrusted with gemstones, and sadly lamented that it was a reminder of the reign of Nebula in the good old ancient of days before her fall from grace, which had left them in a predicament.

"I know you must have lots of questions to ask me, but our queen will no doubt fill you in on the details. She must have a plan for you, or she would not have brought you here. You must not be alarmed. She is nothing but goodness itself and will have your interest at heart, but don't be fooled. Her powers are great if you do not follow her path."

"There are many questions I would like to ask; this is all very strange to us humans," Roberto said while he had the chance.

"Yes," groaned Ilk with a deep sigh. "Is it true that you grow old, shrivel up, and die...that must be awful? Our whole planet was a paradise once and our souls immortal, but now, in the northern region of Venus, believe me, it is being destroyed rapidly—all because Queen Nebula many centuries ago disobeyed our maker. She was a good queen who ruled with justice and wisdom. Like the light of the morning her countenance shone. It was a time of peaceful reflection and spiritual growth...until that fateful day when Elyon's footsteps could be heard thundering around in the high heavenly places. Oh, how the mighty do fall...she fell from grace and brought shame and imperfection to our realm. She had everything possible for contentment and happiness; she lacked nothing. She was given the power of the Mantra of Immortality to raise the dead, but she was told never to use it on the unwise as a test of her faith and loyalty."

Ilk put his arms around them to draw them closer, taking a surreptitious look around before he spoke. "You can never be too careful. You can be certain our foes have eyes and ears everywhere, observing our every movement. Spies...sent by Dracon to listen to our spoken word. Anyways," Ilk whispered, "It came about that her heart fell for a Draconian, as I told you before; his name was Carthage, the one who built the monuments for her. He had left Mars because he could not stand the tyranny of Dracon, you see, and the evil he encountered on Mars. They gave birth to a son named Kafa, who became obsessed with his father's origins and male dominium. One day, Kafa went to visit his father's homeland to see for himself the dangerous terrain his father had spoken of. Alas, he did not return. Carthage consulted Astoria, our prophetess, to find out what had befallen Kafa."

Roberto and Patience and even Wishbone listened intently to Ilk's incredible story. Ilk continued enthusiastically, knowing he had their full attention. "When Nebula found out the truth, she was wild with grief. Any Venusian can only have one child, see, so he was her only and last son. Can you imagine how she felt? She sent Carthage to fetch back his body and disobeyed the forbidden law to raise the dead, bringing Kafa back to life. Kafa had been murdered by the Devatas on his travels, having no guardian angel to protect him from his fate—a rather foolish mistake, don't you think? Kafa was beside himself when he found out what he had caused for his mother by his foolish actions. Nebula was banished, cast adrift for her disobedience, and no one knew her fate. Kafa and Carthage went in search of Nebula, only to be killed by the Devatas, a second and final death for Kafa."

Patience felt angry. "It doesn't seem fair to me. Where is forgiveness? Why should Nebula be punished so harshly?"

Ilk threw his little chubby arms in the air. "Why are we all punished? It's not our fault half of the time, and, I might add, it is not our place to question such matters. It will get you in trouble."

Roberto placed his arm around her shoulders, squeezing her slightly. He felt guilt for Patience's newly exposed emotions, which he had been too selfish to consider—too immersed in his own feelings. But what had all this got to do with them, in any case?

Ilk seemed disgruntled. "It may seem unfair to you, but what do we know of such decisions beyond our comprehension as lower living beings? To this day, there have been many speculations as to Nebula's fate. Some say she is in the Chambers of Everlasting Torment at the Castle of Syrtis on Mars; others speak of her death at the mercy of the manticore, who left no trace of her body behind. No one really knows, but I suspect our Queen Celestial has an idea, for she is not a true Venusian, you know. She is one of the first creation, sent by Elyon from the High Heavens to redeem us from our situation. She is an angel of the highest order in the High Heavens, known as the Seraphim. And not only that, but she is an archangel. That's why she is perfect, see, and very special indeed. Anyways, I can see that's enough for you folks to take in for one day. Gosh, you look tired."

39

"No, I..." Roberto tried to disagree, wanting to know more, but it fell upon deaf ears.

"You will be here for a while, but you needn't worry. Time stands still back on Earth while you are here. A day on Earth cannot be quantified here on Venus—so when you return, it will be just as you left."

Patience felt very relieved knowing that Edwina would not be worrying about them, which meant that she could relax for now. She thought about Edwina and how she had been tough on her. She actually wished she were with them.

"I must say, though, no one ever wants to leave here anyways. It's so wonderful to all the senses, and there has always been a peace that no other planet as yet mastered. You could learn a lot from us. Where did you say you were from?"

"Planet Ear—" Roberto tried to answer again.

"Oh, yes, of course, I forgot for the moment. Not that it is any of my business, but I like to know what is going on, and then I can be of assistance—any friend of the queen's is a friend of mine," said Ilk, marching forward, swinging his short, little, stubby arms backward and forward, in control of his situation.

As Ilk chattered on, Patience fell into a world of her own. Pink petals covered the ground, interspersed with sparkling fairy dust. She felt the different textures surrounding her and the movement of tiny flying creatures flittering past. There were beautiful flower fairies and pixies of different sizes. They didn't seem afraid and even flew in front of her face to have a closer look. She felt the presence of a small creature that landed briefly on her hand. It had the delicate electric blue wings of a butterfly; the body of a small pixie with very long, thin, elf-like ears; and long, thin, pointed hands and feet. Patience was intrigued with its unusual structure and the fearless way it allowed her to touch it.

The sound of a new voice brought her out of her daydream. "Why, hello there!"

A large creature that seemed like half person, half butterfly with black-and-red wings settled beside them. The intensity of color in his wings stood out in contrast to the pale background hues.

"Hello, Admiral. How is the clan?" Ilk fluttered around him.

"Good. Good. Yes, everything is in order, as it should be. They all know which side their grubs are buttered on, so to speak. Perhaps you would do me the honor of introducing me to your new friends!" said Admiral.

"Oh yes, of course. This is hmm...hmm...what did you say your names are? Or did you not tell me? Did I not ask? How rude of me; please forgive me! I get carried away when I'm excited, and I haven't been this excited since Cupid set his bow, and that was centuries ago. Anyways, this is my friend Admiral. He is the leader of the Nymphalidaea butterfly clan, and, like me, has great respect for our queen and all that she is trying to do for us. She has done a lot to preserve his kind when they have been under threat in the northern regions from the swarms—"

"What swarms?" Roberto said, only half wanting to know the answer. After all, this was all ridiculous and very boring.

Admiral looked uncomfortable. "The carbonants, of course, Dracon sent them to ruin our planet's atmosphere. And they are doing a fine job up to now."

Ilk cut in. "Yes, the evil maggot sent the swarms that breathe out carbon dioxide, which over time is changing our atmosphere and thus changing our surface planet, making it eventually uninhabitable; and they are coming this way as we speak. Celestial brought the butterfly clans to the southern parts of the planet to save them from sure extinction. How long it will take the swarms to affect this region we can only speculate. But one thing is for sure: our time is running out."

Roberto wanted to know more, but Admiral changed the subject. "You are waffling again, Ilk!"

"Oh, yes. I'm sorry. Anyways, were where we, then?"

Patience held out her hand to shake hands with Admiral. "My name is Patience, and this is my papa, Roberto."

Ilk grabbed hold of Patience and directed her toward Admiral. "She can't see, you know. Isn't it awful for one so young? And pretty, too."

41

Admiral was not so sure what to do with her hand, and he didn't like the look of Wishbone, whatever it was supposed to be. For one thing, he was far too large. But he continued. "Yes…yes…it must be awful. Which planet do you come from? I've never seen your kind before!" He took a sidelong glance at Wishbone. "Has he been fed recently?" He pointed at the dog nervously.

"To answer your first question, we are humans from planet Earth. Patience is used to not seeing. She has other attributes that make her special. And Wishbone is harmless. He only wants to be your friend." Roberto couldn't believe he had managed to say it without Ilk interrupting him.

Patience noticed how protective her father had become, and she thought how much she liked it.

"Yes, I am sure. I've heard much about your planet from Astoria, our prophetess. Aren't you on self-destruct?" said Admiral curiously.

Ilk snapped sharply, "ADMIRAL, you don't just come out with questions like that. It's not very polite!"

Admiral felt suddenly ashamed. His cheeks flushed, and he looked down embarrassed. "Yes, hmm…you are right, of course. I'm sorry. I didn't mean to offend you in any way. I'm just interested in your plight."

Roberto speedily placated him as best he could. "No offence taken; we quite understand. We have been neglectful of our planet, and we are going to suffer the consequences in the future unless we do something about it now."

Ilk, feeling a little uncomfortable, cut short the conversation. "Anyways, must be getting back to the palace, Admiral. Nice seeing you; will see you around, if not, will see you at the annual meeting of all subjects. Will you be there? Of course you will be there," Ilk answered for him. "No one wants to miss that, do they? There are some very important issues to discuss about our future. See you there, then!"

"Well good-bye, nice to meet you—hope to see you again shortly. Ilk is right. I think you will find some of our issues akin to your own—maybe we could help each other," Admiral said in his

42

deep, gruff voice.

"Yes, I hope so, Admiral," Roberto said, secretly thinking, What on earth was he doing discussing important matters such as saving the planet from destruction with a Cherub and some sort of hybrid butterfly creature? Surely he had lost the plot, but then, of course, that would mean that Patience had also. This could not be happening to him! Maybe his mind, exhausted with so much pain, was finally losing its grip on the real world. He felt a surge of unease and reached out to touch Patience's arm to make sure she was really there.

Ilk summoned the angels to take them back to the palace with the little trumpet, which made its familiar, unusual sound. They heard the flapping of wings as the angels arrived. On the return journey, Roberto had many questions running through his head; he found it difficult to be as patient with Ilk as Patience and undoubtedly the queen seemed to be. He could not get a word in edgeways!

At the Crystal Palace, they were immediately led to the Throne Room, a huge, ornate hall of intricate craftsmanship. White marble columns edged in gold formed elaborate arches leading to the throne, which was set back in a vast latticework arch of mother-of-pearl and silver in the middle of the wall. The throne itself was made of silver and mother-of-pearl lined in cream silk. Two large lions lay at either side of the throne, carved in silver and gold. On the vast, high ceilings, murals of heavenly hosts in all their glory reflected the light from the floor-to-ceiling glass windows on either side. The floor mirrored the fresco ceiling, making the hall seem to be two-dimensional.

Wishbone had been reunited with them in the outer hall, much to Patience's obvious relief. They walked precariously toward the throne step by step, Ilk whispering in Roberto's ear, "This is where I bid you good-bye for now, but I will no doubt see you again shortly—at least I hope so. I have grown fond of you in the short time I have spent with you, and I would like to introduce you to my folks and show you the other wonders of Venus, such as the statue of Queen Nebula—it cries, you know! And—"

"That will be all for this present moment, Ilk," the queen said with a half-smile on her face, quite used to Ilk's chatter. "You may take the canis lupus creature with you and entertain him for the duration of our meeting."

Roberto gazed appraisingly at the queen—the very same angel he had first met in the music room of his ancestral home and again in the clearing.

Patience felt unsure about letting Wishbone go. She held onto his harness tightly, but Roberto reassured her, certain that the queen was the same angel he had encountered before and was no threat to them.

"Oh yes, Your Majesty. It's a pleasure to serve you always," said Ilk as he bowed before Celestial with a flutter of his wings.

One of the Aegle fairies ushered him out as nicely as she could before he could start speaking again. Patience sensed Wishbone's fear. "Everything will be OK; I will see you shortly. Go on, Good boy."

Wishbone licked her hand and turned round with his tail between his legs, knowing he was about to have his ears chewed off by a Cherub.

Two male angels stood to either side of Celestial. One was dark haired, with sharp features and an unchallengeable air of authority; the other was golden blond, with a benevolent look about him; both were bronzed and of imposing stature, scantily dressed in white robes with golden belts, swords by their side.

"Rest assured. These are my bodyguards, Gabriel and Mikael. Please sit down and make yourself comfortable; I am sure you have had quite a tiresome day. Nastacia will bring you refreshments."

Roberto noticed that Nastacia was the girl who had brought them breakfast that morning. Her fairy wings were a distinctive color and had the same transparency as other fairy wings but possessed a deep-red streak edged with black through her membranous veins. Her hair was a striking auburn color, falling in voluminous waves down to her feet, her eyes were a pale-blue topaz, and her pouting pink lips were perfectly formed. He felt there was something different about her than her other likenesses, other than the obvious physical differences, but he couldn't quite put his finger on it.

Celestial's magical voice brought him back from his thoughts. "The need for bodyguards has not always been mine. However, times have changed, and this planet and its inhabitants are changing slowly but without question—and not for the good of our planet, I discern." Celestial arose from her throne and seemed to float slowly toward Roberto, her intense silver eyes probing his mind.

"Hear now, my Lord Bellucci, you and yours please turn in to my dwelling place this night and wash your feet." Celestial's intense silvery gaze captured Roberto. "You will be allowed the essence of time to search the heart of man and beast alike during your stay here on Venus. I of the Seraphim entered the spheres of this world; the third creation, after the fall of Queen Nebula. My quest is to protect and redeem this planet from deterioration since the infiltration of a creature most undesirable. The Age of Sorrows has begun!"

Roberto felt tongue tied in her presence, and he had much to take in. He listened intently.

Celestial continued. "After the fall of Queen Nebula, the ancient one, the conflict of the sons of the first creation in the High Heavens waged a most terrible war. Elyon's fury leaped up in flames against his archenemy and his grotesque legions, casting them out from his mighty realm. That day was the beginning of the end—the first day of the Age of Sorrows—and it has had a most reaching effect on both our planets and no doubt many others of the already-formed InterWorlds and those yet to come. All of the inhabitants of Venus are paying the price of Nebula's disobedience, just as you and yours are paying the price for mankind's disobedience. The actions of each individual can have a lasting effect on others; that is why we must take heed of our behavior and think carefully before we act or make a decision. However, our maker has made it possible for us to make amends and find our way back to the perfect state we so enjoyed once. It is imperative that we keep safe the Sacred Scrolls, from the hands of those who would take them away like a thief in the night and destroy them. For they do not believe that the secret of immortality lies not within the scrolls alone but can only be revealed to the chosen ones of the morning star. There is no other path for them—only the path of destruction."

"If I may speak Your Majesty...where are these sacred scrolls now?"

"They are in the Inner Chamber of the Temple of Immortality in the Valley of the Queens, heavily guarded by the Seraphim and the Cherubim, and only I hold the Key of Dreams to enter the chamber.

I will try to speak plainly, for the words of angels can be the speech of riddles to man. I have been in the presence of Elyon for many centuries as an angel of the Seraphim. We call Him Elyon, meaning Almighty One, but He has many names. I am his messenger. He has sent me to save Venus and whoever I can in the battle against Leviathan, the leader of legions of fallen angels—the Serophoth, enemies of the Lord of Hosts. Leviathan was once a mighty angel of the Seraphim who succumbed to pride. He had intelligence, beauty, radiance, and power in Heaven, but he became ambitious and surrendered to his vanity—rejecting universal allegiance, disregarding his heavenly obligations, and embracing sin. Self-contemplation is most disastrous, even to the exalted personalities of the celestial world."

Celestial walked back to her throne, each step taken as though she were floating on air. She beckoned them closer. "During the rebellion, Leviathan's forces—all the angels that rebelled with him—were defeated by the Heavenly Hosts, led by Archangel Michael. They were cast out of Heaven and became enemies of Elyon and all others who have allegiance to the Almighty Maker of all Creations. The devil is a human term for the same angel of darkness, and his works are evident on both our planets and probably many others. Leviathan, as we know him, began to build his own empire in the depths of the Abyss. Legions of fallen

46

angels became his army against all that is good and true."

"His army is known in our world as the Devatas, or Devas, demon entities who reside in the three Lokas—worlds, dimensions of existence—in the underworld of the Abyss. The Devas are ugly creatures now they have fallen from grace. Their appearance matching their characters, they are the epitome of evil. They have certain supernatural powers, changing form being one of them. Their powers are not as formidable as they would like, but they are malevolent spirits and need to be dealt with. They are also known as the Serophoth and work under Leviathan's rule, trying to confuse the inhabited worlds. Power of all the universal kingdoms is his quest. He has been roaming the InterWorlds for centuries, wreaking havoc on the inhabitants and tempting them away from Elyon.

Celestial hovered before them, a stream of light shone forth from her being. Transfixed Roberto remained silent as the weight of her words hit him.

"Leviathan is a liar, and he has the ability to influence the mind. He begins by bombarding the mind with cleverly devised patterns of thought, suspicions, doubts, fears, reasoning, and theories. He moves slowly and cautiously—after all, well-laid plans take time. He has a strategy for his warfare. He knows your insecurities, your weaknesses, and your fears, and he is willing to invest any amount of time it takes to defeat you or anyone else. He holds everyone in bondage by manipulating their thoughts— but only if we allow it. I am warning you so that you can be aware to keep your own thought patterns strong so that he cannot conquer you."

Patience felt soothed despite the serious subject of Celestial's words, the sound of her voice like that of a soft musical instrument.

"Life and death is in our own hands—right thinking is vital for life—as a heartbeat is vital. As you think, so are you! For as a tree is known by its fruit; the same is true in our lives. Thoughts bear fruit."

"Those are very profound and heavy words Your Highness,"

said Roberto, mesmerized by Celestial. He knelt before her, soaking up her essence.

"Surrender yourself to a higher power. You will encounter things you do not understand, for Earthling man is nothing more than a slight exhalation of a greater being. The errors of your forefathers must be wiped out once and for all—the fate of mankind depends upon it. At this moment, Dracon of Mars is my most immediate concern," continued Celestial. "He is a great example of evil thoughts; he dwelt upon ambition and pride, the beginning of all other sins. Without really knowing it, he came into alliance with the prince of destruction Leviathan and is consumed with the desire to hold in his hands the sacred scrolls."

As Celestial spoke, Patience hung onto every word that came forth from her mouth. She couldn't believe a real angel was talking to them; the very same woman who had visited her in her ancestral home had brought her to this new world just as she had promised. She was totally awe inspired and felt a warm tingling sensation through her body. Her only wish was to see her through her own eyes, not through the eyes of her father.

"The Venusians' imperfect state is affecting their auras. No doubt you have seen the tiny, fairylike creatures that surround all of us," said Celestial as she spread her wings to display her array of oscillating creatures.

The tiny fairies hovered around the head and wings of Celestial, delicate and innocuous creatures of fascinating proportions for so diminutive a size. Their transparent wings fluttered in a display of beautiful pastel colors, their perfectly formed tiny bodies swathed in gossamer garments.

"They are intriguing," Roberto said, completely drawn to Celestial's aura oscillating around her.

"Far beyond their apparent beauty, there lies a much more significant role. They are the Fairy Spirits that make up the auras of each individual on Venus. Each spirit depicts a characteristic of the fruits of the spirit—love, joy, peace, long-suffering, kindness, goodness, faithfulness, gentleness, and self-control. They are in constant battle with the Devatas auras, the sprites who want to destroy the good characteristics and bring evil to the Venusians," said Celestial with great sorrow in her voice.

"The ugly, tiny creatures I have had the misfortune to stumble upon are these whom you speak of Your Majesty?" Roberto felt uncomfortable speaking in the presence of an angel.

"Yes...they are the Sprites, the auras of the Devatas that battle with the fruits of the Spirit Fairies. It is since this imperfection has infiltrated my people that Dracon, the cruel leader of the Draconians on Mars, our enemy, heard of our weakness and is trying to destroy our planet, taking us all into captivity as slaves. He has already destroyed a large part of our habitat by sending in the swarms, small, lethal creatures that not only give a nasty sting but breathe out carbon dioxide. Over the centuries, this has caused our planet to change. It is something you are well aware of, Roberto—it has had a catastrophic effect, drying up the waters and changing the landscape in the north, rendering it uninhabitable. And the swarms are heading this way. He must be stopped!" Celestial said passionately.

Roberto rose from his kneeling position. "Yes, indeed. I understand what you are saying and I can see your plight, but we are mere humans Your Majesty. I don't see how we can actually help you. We can't even help ourselves, it seems!"

"You would be amazed at the actions a mere human can be capable of, Lord Bellucci. You are the chosen one for a special reason, and that reason will be revealed to you when time cannot deny it any longer. Has not your life caused you concern? Why does your soul feel so destroyed? Have you ever contemplated why your family history over the centuries has been blighted with death and destruction? Did you not yourself suffer at the hands of your aunt, Cavelli Bellucci, after the tragic accident of your beloved parents and then, the loss of your beautiful wife? Now your daughter is without eyes. How much longer can you allow this to go on? The power to stop it is in your hands."

Patience was taken aback. "Papa, why did you not tell me? I did not know you lost your parents...my grandparents. All this time, Edwina led me to believe that you were estranged from them, that they had left the country!"

Roberto had never forgotten his losses and cruel neglect at the hands of his aunt. The very mention of her name spawned dark, brooding thoughts, which kindled a rage inside so intense that it scared him. His hidden emotions bubbling under the surface, kept at bay by his cool, distant demeanor, felt as if they were about to explode. His gaze grew steadily colder.

Patience pleaded with him to tell her everything about his past.

Roberto was not sure he wanted to hear any of this. *What does Celestial know that I do not?*

"We are a cursed family—that may be true, but I will not allow it to affect Patience anymore. I will live my life to protect her!"

Celestial looked at Patience standing there quietly. "I do not wish to frighten your daughter, but she is as much a part of this as you, and her fate affects all of mankind. Know this, my child: if you are to survive the evil that is hunting you and your generations to come, look deep within yourself and find the truth of whom you really are; embrace it and conquer. You cannot run—there is nowhere to hide. You must stand and fight with all that you have."

Roberto found all of this too much to take onboard, but he could see an element of how a cursed family line could be true. *But how can this be connected with a spiritual realm?*

"I am sorry to say Your Majesty, but you put too much on so young and vulnerable a person. What exactly do you want from us?"

Celestial sensed the apprehension in his stance as he spoke. "It is not so much what I want from you or your daughter. Someone far more important than I desire's your allegiance."

"And who, may I ask, is it? I give my allegiance to no one."

Celestial smiled assuredly. "Oh, I think you will change your mind. Say this to me when you have learned who you really are."

Roberto shook off a mild foreboding as his eyes fixed intently upon her. "Tell me now. I am willing to listen."

"Are you willing to take heed? I think not. Now is not the time;

you are too eaten up with rage and pain, which destroys the most powerful of creatures. Little by little, all will be revealed, and then you will be more prepared for what your future holds for you and your precious daughter. She is more special than you realize."

Celestial held up her hand before Roberto could speak again. "Stop!" Speak no more. I want you to think about your decision to stay and confront your heart and mind very carefully. I will give you some space and time to become acquainted with our planet and ask any questions you like. We have nothing to hide here. We are a planet of truth and light; however, the InterWorlds are woven together like braids of angel's hair, and the darkness spreads like a contagious disease from one world to another with the subtle corruption of the pure hearts of creatures great and small.

"If you decide to stay, you will witness the very forces that have shaped our exotic landscape. You will see vast canyons and their ever-changing colors gouged out of the land, thundering crystal waterfalls, towering rock formations, exotic reef systems filled with myriads of life forms, placid, mysterious lakes, spouting geysers, extraordinary mountain ranges, glacial rivers bluer than blue, and the bringers of fire from the earth itself. You will see monuments, mausoleums, fortifications. And yes, you may say, I have seen all of these on my own planet. However, here, all is not what it seems in its natural form. Its beauty is not skin deep. Do be prepared to fill your senses and experience a fantastical journey to some of the most awe-inspiring places that you will ever see. I am holding a meeting of all subjects in two eons of time. I hope we meet again"

In the blink of an eye, she was gone!

Patience turned to her father. "Papa, I am afraid! What can we do? Why did you not tell me of these things? You should have told me."

"It has been more difficult for me than you could ever know, Patience. In my way, I was trying to protect you. I feel rather guilty that I have let you down. I have not been there for you at all," said Roberto sincerely.

51

"I felt so angry with you, Papa. I did, but now I'm too scared to be angry. Do you think Celestial is speaking the truth? You know...I have had many dreams of this very world we are in now; and some awful nightmares as well. I have seen vividly in my mind's eye the things you describe to me here and other things that I dare not even mention."

"I am not sure of anything right now." Roberto placed his arms around her. "I am sure that I will protect you, though. We are in this together...whatever the truth may be. You must tell me more of these dreams you have had. Maybe together we can make some sense of all this. She does make it sound rather appealing, though I am not sure I trust her."

Patience shuddered, afraid for her father, afraid for herself.

"Right now, I need some time to think alone. I'm going to take a walk in the gardens. Better that you rest in the bedchamber. You have had more than enough excitement for one day, Patience."

"How will you get to the bottom of the mountain? It will take you ages, Papa!"

"I am sure Mikael will be glad to take me; he seems an amiable young man. I will go and ask him." As he turned to walk away, Patience quickly grabbed his arm. "Take me with you." Roberto looked down at her small delicate hand and placed his hand hesitantly over hers. He was proud of her—she had survived quite alone, apart from Edwina, and he had not been there for her, thinking more of himself than the adversity she had been born with and the lack of parental love.

He may have lost Marissa, he thought, but he could count his blessings that his daughter had not been tainted by worldly demands. And now he had been chosen for something he did not fully understand in an unknown world. *What does it all mean?*

He had never felt so vulnerable. Celestial certainly seemed plausible and her beauty—mesmerizing. He felt lacking in many ways; maybe this experience was meant to humble him. Celestial's aura was powerful, and he felt the desire to help her too in her quest to save her own planet from destruction. *How? Is the burning question; and what is so special about Patience and my*

52

cursed ancestry? I need to know the answers.

Patience was feeling restless; her mixed feelings of excitement and apprehension rendered her incapable of resting. She quietly tiptoed toward the large doors with Wishbone by her side.

Closing the doors slowly behind her, she decided to explore the palace. She took a left turn down a long corridor and down some small winding steps that led to a broad ornamented vaulted vestibule.

Through the portal, she came to an inner courtyard with turquoise and gilt-tiled facades. An octagonal pool with a fountain surrounded by alabaster pillars and cascading foliage and flowers symbolically brought nature inside the building. She felt her way slowly along the walls and found herself holding on to a large pillar. She could hear girlie laughter and the splash of water. The atmosphere was misty and humid. She felt tiny drops of water form on her forehead and trickle down her face. She wiped it off with her sleeve. "Phew. It's warm in here, Wishbone."

Wishbone just wagged his tail exuberantly and barked at the sound of the laughter.

"Sh...sh, boy; we don't want to be seen."

No one seemed to notice her as she sidled along toward two open doors and down another winding corridor, Wishbone leading the way, obediently quiet. She could not see the many pictures hung gloriously on the wall depicting vapid youths and maidens fair, lazily dallying in a landscape of eternal spring. The lion and the lamb basked side by side in peace and harmony. As she passed some closed doors on the left-hand side, she heard raised voices coming from inside. Everything and everyone she had met so far spoke softly—so to hear raised voices made her curious. Her fingers of one hand slid against the wall; the tips of her fingers rippled over the textured surface. A little farther along, she felt for the handle of the door, fear mixed with fascination. She embraced the handle; the metal's coldness crept up her arm. She placed her ear close to the door. She could not hear very well, but it was the voice of a woman saying something about Queen Celestial, and she mentioned the name Dracon. She only caught fragmented bits of the conversation, but it didn't seem to be the words of someone who revered Celestial; she could tell by the tone of her voice. There was a man's voice too, but he didn't seem as angry. She heard movement down the corridor—slowly, each footstep cautiously measured, she retraced her steps back in the direction she had come, afraid that someone may have seen her.

As she approached the bathing pool, Wishbone began to bark.

"Here, boy-come here."

He glanced at her pulling on his harness, snuffling and whimpering at the same time. No one said a word; a rhythmic cadence invaded the silence as the nymphs stared in horror at the dog. Patience began to feel uncomfortable. Fear flared in her eyes. "Who's there?"

She was just about to make a run for it when someone or something rose up out of the water and up the steps at the side of the pool; Patience froze on the spot. The nymph pulled her hair loose and tugged at her arm. Patience pulled back slightly hesitant. Yet she felt sort of intrigued; she did not feel overtly threatened. Others came forward to touch her and smell her— something that was not alien to Patience. They played with her fingers and hands gently. They did not speak!

"Who are you? I can't see you...what do you want?" Patience allowed herself to be pulled along.

Drawing her closer to them, they led her into the water, giggling and splashing around like children. Her clothes soaked up the surrounding water as the nymphs slowly led her into the warm, shallow pool. She felt a sudden peace encompass her as one of them played with her hair while another massaged her hands with a sweet-smelling ointment. One of the nymphs did not pull away when Patience slowly ran her sensitive fingers over her face and hair.

It was blissful. She was entranced by the mystical feeling of pure serenity she was experiencing until she remembered that her father might shortly return and would be anxious at her disappearance. She hastily plunged through the water, feeling for

54

the sides of the pool. Wishbone barked, showing her the direction to follow. The nymphs pulled at her outstretched arms in an attempt to make her stay.

She tried to make them understand but was not sure they could hear her. It became apparent that they were not listening to a word she said as they pulled her under the water, giggling and laughing. Taking a gulp of water into her lungs, she coughed and spluttered as she emerged. Wishbone was barking loudly by this time, walking backward and forward at the edge of the steamy baths. The nymphs kept on dragging Patience down with them; they did not understand why she struggled. Panic-stricken, she fought madly. She was not sure if they meant her harm. She managed to break free and swam furiously until her lungs couldn't hold anymore. Surfacing, she gulped a deep breath and pulled herself up the stone steps, breathing heavily. She grabbed hold of Wishbone's reigns, and he pulled her out of the water.

She was not sure what they wanted from her. They had seemed so nice at first. She felt suddenly very vulnerable and afraid. Breathlessly, she allowed Wishbone to direct her steps swiftly back to the safety of the bedchamber.

She grabbed hold of Wishbone's head and covered him in kisses, much to his sheer delight. "Good boy. I can always rely on you, my knight in shining armor."

Wagging his tail from side to side, he began to lick the dripping water from her skin with relish. "I know you are glad you saved me, Wishbone, but you must calm down. I don't want father to know that we have been on a mystery tour. He will be angry with me, just when he has realized that he does actually have a daughter. Don't want to spoil that, now, do we?"

She opened the door slowly and entered the chamber precariously, not knowing if her father had returned before her. Phew! It seemed she had gotten away with it. Wishbone appeared from the bathroom with a toweling cloth in his mouth.

"Thank you boy, just what I needed," she said, rubbing at her clothes and skin vigorously. "I just hope whoever they are, they don't follow us."

Patience felt her way into the bed and wrapped herself in the luxurious, feather-like coverlet. She waited apprehensively for the return of her father.

Chapter 5

Nastacia Meets With Dracon

Mars...

Now it came about that the red-haired Venusian with the distinguished red streak through her wings was extremely jealous of Celestial. As a distant relative of the royal lineage, she wished to be a mighty queen; she craved the power to rule the kingdom.

Nastacia felt that it was her birthright. After all, she was of direct lineage following Queen Nebula, whereas Celestial had been sent following the fall of Nebula from the High Heavens to rule and redeem its inhabitants. Nastacia was eaten up with jealousy and tormented by her hate and unfulfilled ambition.

Her aura had become unbalanced. She missed the most important fairy spirit of love. As each good fairy of the spirit was lost from a fairy's or angel's aura, this left room for nasty sprites to enter into it, much like atoms and electrons when they are incomplete. These negative spirits produced bad characteristics, which would wage war with the good fairy spirits to dominate the character. Nastacia's aura had become unbalanced on the negative side; her sprites of jealousy, hate, torment, and unkindness had taken over many of her good characteristics, creating an unpleasant aura and negative thought patterns, which was what Roberto had sensed earlier.

Celestial was aware of Nastacia's character; however, because of her grace and kindness, she still met all of Nastacia's needs, even allowing her to live in the palace as part of the royal family. She never lost hope that Nastacia's fairy spirits would win the battle against the sprites.

Unknown to Celestial, Nastacia had formed a small group of followers whose negative spirits were also more dominant to their auras—to get rid of Celestial, make Nastacia queen, and change all that Celestial had lovingly achieved during her reign.

Nastacia had already made her acquaintance with Dracon on Mars—Leviathan, ruler of darkness, had made sure of that. Dracon had promised her that he would capture Celestial and take all of the Venusians as slaves. Then he would make her queen to rule at his side after the impending death of his father, Perilous the Great.

She was happy with this promise for now, knowing that Dracon desperately wanted to capture Celestial. She did not trust him or like him; she had every intention of disposing of him after she had used him for her purpose. When she had gotten hold of the sacred scrolls and the power of immortality had become hers, there would be no stopping her. At this point, she needed him to destroy Celestial—nothing more.

Nastacia looked for an opportunity to escape for a while from her duties within the palace. She would excuse herself to Celestial with a need for a vacation, as she was feeling oh so worn out with the constant battle of her mind, and she wanted to take some time to learn from the Order of the Sukras, the manuscripts of life and wisdom. Maybe she would be able to redeem her spiritual gifts of the spirit. Yes, Celestial would like that and would give her the time willingly, she thought, pleased with herself.

One of the things that bothered her was that she hated the journey; it was arduous terrain, and the atmospheric conditions were extreme. Not to mention its inhabitants on Mars—frighteningly unpredictable at the best of times.

Although Nastacia was not of good character; she was a saint compared to the Draconians and other terrifying creatures on

58

Mars. She felt very exposed and vulnerable. Dracon had warned them not to harm a hair on her head, but they treated her with suspicion. If it had not been for her passionate desire, growing rapidly stronger inside of her, to be queen above anything else—she would never have put foot on Mars again.

Not feeling completely sure of her own safety, she decided not to travel alone. The angel Orion accompanied her. Orion had once been in favor with Celestial as one of her many guards of the Temple of the Secret of Immortality, built during Celestial's reign as a sacred place to protect the Chamber of Secrets from those who would like to reveal and capture its consecrated contents. His beauty was great, his eyes an intense gold like that of a burning fire. He had been a mighty warrior before he became blinded by the spirit of lust and fell for the female manipulations of Nastacia, hoping that one day he would become her constant companion and bodyguard.

The next day, Nastacia and Orion set forth on their journey to the portal on the east coast of Cushara, north of Castra. It was a long journey to the Castle Syrtis, and Nastacia noticed Orion's thin smile of doubt as they reached Tharsis, west of the portal on the border of Tharsis and Hillarion.

Orion had warned Nastacia of the beasts of the forest of Asan, willing her to choose the much longer route that passed the edge of the forest leading to the north of the Valles Marineris region central to Mars. They flew onward, oppressed by the dark gloom and stillness of the land, steering as straight a course as possible.

Under the first shadow of night, they stopped to rest. They found some kind of inn, a chamber carved out of gray stone. There were no windows, and the entrance was open to the elements. The opening gave way to a dark, winding, rocky corridor lit by burning torches leading to the chamber of the Draconians' merriment. Inside, it was musty, filthy with dust. Large silvery cobwebs hung from every crevice, and curious artifacts adorned the walls. Various shaped stone surfaced tables were scattered around the chamber in no distinct order, serviced by large gray iron chairs. A collection of oversized candles mounted on black metal posts provided a subdued glow, and the smell of burning wax mingled with dust overpowered any other odor.

Orion's attention turned to a large opening in the distant, uneven walls—something threatening stood in the shadows. A shape he could not discern. Something watching...waiting. He felt uneasy. Orion beckoned Nastacia to stay behind him while he tested the reaction of the Xanthurus guards, the corners of his eyes constantly aware of the shadowy figure's movement.

The noisy banter ceased, and silence prevailed as Orion walked bravely forward. "Good eve to you, sirs. Could we possibly—"

Before Orion had a chance to get his words out, Nastacia's small frame jumped in front of him. "What he means to say is that your King Dracon awaits me. I will one day be his queen. His own words, I might add. So you better treat us well and give us a bed for the night and some food."

The tall guard, robed in black, stood up from the shadows. His snarl was apparent to all, but his face was hidden in the darkness of his hooded robe. "Well...Venusian, we don't have to give you anything. Dracon only commanded us to keep you safe. In our view, that does not mean we need treat you as one of us. Go find your own food and drink. Or would you prefer that we hunger for your soft flesh?" The Draconians joined in with the Xanthurus guard, causing an uproar that made Nastacia back off willingly.

The shadow in the distance wavered in the unsteady glow of the flickering torchlight. Orion was curious as to who it might be but not enough to find out. Immediately he grabbed hold of Nastacia's hand and pulled her in retreat through the corridor back to the path of their journey north. He said nothing of his suspicions that they might be followed.

The arduous journey through the volcanic plains was exhausting. The stifling heat wearied Nastacia to the point of collapse. If it had not been for Orion, she would not have been able to go on. He carried her through to the North Syrtis Major region of Mars and to the Castle of Syrtis.

60

Nastacia felt a shiver run down her spine; the ugliness of the place had chilled her to the bone. The castle stood before them, a dark, brooding monolith, gray like a huge tombstone. Above the gray stone walls, like a warden watching the dungeons, stood the tall tower gleaming in the bleak wind that was blowing from the depths of the polar region.

They entered the merciless walls tarnished by unnatural forces. It was dark and dingy, and the heat was stifling. On the outside, they had been freezing with the high winds as they walked through the ice caps surrounding the castle, but inside, it was as though it were on fire—the change of temperature was dramatic. Beads of sweat appeared on their foreheads.

The walls were of gray stone and resembled a cave more than a castle. There was a faint pungent smell of burning flesh and the distant sound of muffled screams. The dead lay in silent mounds—the smell of defeat in the air. Nastacia shuddered, swallowing her rising terror. She had heard rumors of Dracon's cruelty, and after meeting him, she had suspected them to be true. Now she could see the evidence all around her. *But I will be OK,* she thought. He wanted her, did he not? Of course, she reassured herself as a seed of doubt became planted firmly within.

The walls were full of dark recesses, which unnerved her; she wondered what was lurking there. She felt eyes watching her every step and heard strange, curious noises that made her want to watch her back constantly. Orion sensed his own fate approaching with each step deeper inside the cursed domain. Nastacia mocked him and refused to listen to his pleas.

"Follow me!" said a deep, rasping voice that seemed to come from nowhere out of the darkness. As footsteps approached, a black-cloaked figure appeared, hardly distinguishable in the gloom. Despite the heat, a large hood covered his face. In his hands he carried a burning torch.

Nastacia and Orion were startled when the creature turned around to face them, for although he had the semblance of a Draconian, he had the face of a rat, with gleaming red eyes, and a

61

long tail that protruded out from under his cloak. He loomed over them. His size was intimidating—even to Orion, who was no small creature by any means, standing a full seven feet tall. Nastacia was a typical petite, four-foot Aegle Venusian female. She suddenly felt insignificant.

As they walked through the bleak maze of stone, they had to stoop low amid a mad frenzy of shrieks and flapping wings. Bat-like creatures surrounded them, hanging from the ceilings, eyes shining pure white in the darkness with no pupils in sight—scary-looking things!

The sharpness of their sound startled Nastacia. She sprang away from Orion, screaming, hands flailing desperately in the air among the mass of suspended gargoyles. Bats squealed and flapped thin wings at her. Orion ripped out one that had become entangled in her long red hair. He beat the others from her body, struggling to rid her of the creatures, which began to attack from behind. Nastacia felt tiny claws digging in to her flesh. Gripping her elbow, he pulled her swiftly onward, violently thrusting his unsheathed sword in all directions. The creature watched with certain glee and no intention of helping them.

They finally listened to the retreating sound of the wings. Nastacia was breathing hard when Orion slipped his arm around her waist to support her. They moved on slowly. Her eyes were blazing, her face screwed up in anger as she spat out her words, "I should not have to go through this torture. Surely there is another way through to Dracon's throne room. I am to be his queen. He will not like what you have caused me to suffer. I will make sure you are punished."

The creature laughed wickedly. "For one so small, you think much of yourself. Come, follow me. Dracon awaits you."

Tiny buzzing creatures hardly discernible by the naked eye stung their flesh. Nastacia rubbed her skin protectively to alleviate the stinging sensation. They entered a small cave, where a raft awaited them. Rat Face had to go on all fours to fit through the opening. Following him, Orion did the same. Nastacia was small enough to walk through, though she did not fancy touching anything. As she looked at the dark, murky waters tinged with red, she slipped and steadied herself on a rock formation. The cold, green-and-red jellylike substance that covered her hands turned her delicate stomach.

"Are you hurt?" Orion looked down.

"Of course I am not hurt," she said indignantly as she wiped her hands on her garments. What else could she do? She felt contaminated. She hoped this was all going to be worth it. Perhaps she could have thought of an easier way of getting rid of Celestial herself. The Venusians would never have accepted her as their queen under those circumstances. No, the blame had to be laid on someone else; Dracon was the only answer. She would have to be brave. It was too late to turn back now, and at least she had Orion by her side this time.

In the distance could be heard a monotonous chanting, which became louder and louder as they approached some vast iron doors. The last time she had met Dracon, he had come to meet her on the outskirts of the planet. She did not realize the ugliness of the place he resided in; maybe the fortress of Deimos was much better than the hellhole of Syrtis.

Orion had kept silent following Nastacia's reprimand, but he could not hold back any longer. He whispered quietly to her, hoping that the rat creature would not hear him. "Are you sure about what you are doing, Nastacia? Are we not in any danger in this godforsaken place? You know your wish is my command. I am your loyal servant, but I hope you know what you are getting yourself into with these degenerates. They are renowned in the InterWorlds to be the cruelest and evil worshipers of Leviathan— opposite to anything you have ever known."

"I know," Nastacia replied, impatiently gritting, her teeth. "Just trust me, Orion; this is not the place or the time to discuss it, when we have gotten to the point of no return!"

As they slowly approached, the enormous iron doors opened with an electric device, and they followed the rat creature through. The chanting continued from hundreds of creatures in long black cloaks. The glow of the red eyes and the long protruding tails made them unmistakably the same race as Rat Face. His real name they did not know, nor did they wish to find out.

Rat Face beckoned them forward toward the throne of Dracon. His throne was huge, as one might expect of someone egocentric, made of iron and standing out in contrast to the bright-red garments Dracon wore.

Dracon himself was by no means handsome. He was a formidable figure of human form, standing a towering nine feet tall, his frame long and lean. His green-gray-tinged skin shone with a glossy shine, and his hair, very long and white, was slicked back off his forehead. His appearance was half man, half lizard. He had some redeeming features; his teeth were a dazzling white, but his lips, the same continuous color as his skin tone, belied his cruel disposition. It was his eyes that Nastacia found disconcerting—white, bulbous protrusions consisting of black, elongated pupils not unlike those of reptile. Nastacia looked away as she felt his eyes upon her. She felt vulnerable again in his presence, but she would not be deterred from achieving her goal. She would just have to get rid of him somehow. No Martian was going to get the better of her—no, never! She must be strong, she thought as her legs betrayed her turning to jelly.

"Who is this creature who dares to come before me?" Dracon said with a deep, commanding voice reaching decibels that would hurt a human ear. The chanting stopped, and there was an uncomfortable silence.

Nastacia bravely broke the silence. "This is Orion, My Lord; he is my trusted and faithful servant. I need his help to fulfill our quest. He knows more about the sacred contents held within the secret chamber than I do; he guarded them at one time—but only Celestial has the Key of Dreams to enter the secret chamber of the Temple of Immortality. The temple itself is heavily guarded by many angels, and the secret chamber has two golden angel statues ten cubits high, standing wing-tip-to-wing-tip, guarding the door. It is said that when the door is unlocked, they come to life wielding fiery revolving swords in a passionate endeavor to protect the Secret of Immortality and Wisdom."

"I am not interested in wisdom," said Dracon as he clasped his hands together.

Nastacia noticed his very long hands with long, white, curved nails that looked more like claws. She shuddered at the thought of him touching her. "I just want the Secret of Immortality that Celestial has. You must get this for me, and I will reward you greatly. You and I will rule the universe together. No one will dare come against us, for we alone will keep this secret to ourselves."

"Are you male or female?" Dracon directed the question at Orion mockingly, pointing his long bony finger at him. "For you have the beauty of a Venusian woman and the stature of a man. It must be confusing for you; you must not have a sense of your own gender! Surely you don't want to tarnish your impeccable appearance by getting involved with the Draconians. They will eat you alive after they have played with you. You are everything they are not, and they won't forgive you for that. How do I know that you are not a spy sent by Celestial?"

"I am here on behalf of Nastacia only, as her bodyguard and loyal servant, and I am at her command. I do not need to like you or for you to like me. But if you are a friend and ally of hers, then you will have my allegiance. If, on the other hand, she becomes your enemy, then you will be my enemy also. Do not underestimate my loyalty to Nastacia; I would die for her. I, on the other hand, can take care of myself; my strength is known on Venus as second to no other," Orion stated not feeling as confident as his anger made him sound.

"Mm...I see," said Dracon, more than amused, his eyes darting from side to side. "Hit a sore spot, did we? I get the feeling there is more than friendship going on here for you. You would do well to remember that she is mine and mine alone. Whatever I request, she will follow through, if she knows what is best for her."

"Oh, no, My Lord," Nastacia quickly intervened. "He knows I am to be yours and yours alone. Make no mistake, he is just trying to make the point that he will do anything for me—and therefore, ultimately for you."

Orion knew she had no intention of being with this degenerate; nevertheless, he felt a surge of anger toward Nastacia for making him feel small in front of Dracon. He hoped Dracon could not see through her, or they would be doomed there and then—he didn't possess the powers he used to.

"Good," said Dracon as he walked toward Nastacia and stroked her long, silky, red hair. "I am sure that you have not come all this way to talk of love, Nastacia. What other news have you got for me?"

Nastacia tried not to flinch, though revolted by his touch. "No, My Lord, you know me well! Venus has visitors; Earthlings. It seems they are plotting against you as we speak." She dared not move, frozen solid to the spot.

"Interesting," he said thoughtfully, turning away from Nastacia as he scratched his long, pointed ears. "How many are there?"

"It is not so much the numbers, if I may say so, My Lord, for there are only two and a strange-looking creature they call a dog. However, with Celestial's powers and Hosts of Elyon combined with mankind, their strategies need to be carefully monitored, and it may be better to destroy Celestial sooner rather than later, My Lord. There is an annual meeting of all subjects coming up shortly, and they will be making plans as to their next course of action. I will be there, of course, to glean any information. Celestial does not suspect me, for I have been pleasing in her eyes this past time and have worked hard to be in favor," Nastacia said, hoping to appease Dracon.

"Excellent! Then you must return immediately and do all that you say. I am much pleased with your efforts, Nastacia. I can see you will make me a good queen when the time comes. My father's days are numbered; his death is imminent. Soon I will rule and have no one to answer to. Go now! Ego will escort you out of the castle," said Dracon, satisfied.

"As for you"—Dracon pointed at Orion—"one step out of line and your beauty will be a thing of the past. Is that understood? I will feed you to the manticore and lick my lips with satisfaction."

The ultimate punishment for Orion's type of fallen angel was to lose his aesthetic appearance. He had already fallen from grace, and his beauty was all he had left to offer. "Yes," he mumbled reluctantly.

"You mean, 'Yes, My Lord!'" demanded Dracon angrily. His voice had risen, and Nastacia could not help place her hands over her delicate ears.

"Yes, My Lord," Orion spat out furiously. Nastacia gave Orion a sidelong glance of disapproval.

"Return when you have more information." Dracon waved them on dismissively.

When they had departed and Egor had returned, Dracon ordered more carbonant swarms to be sent upon Venus.

"We need to send more swarms and quicken the destruction of Venus before these Earthlings become more involved. As for Planet Earth—well...they are already doing a good job themselves without the swarms. Human pollution is breaking down the ozone layer beautifully. I cannot see how such foolish creatures with no foresight can be of any threat to us, or any assistance to Venus, for that matter. Nevertheless, we will be prepared for all eventualities. Act now, Egor!" Dracon commanded.

"Yes, My Lord. Consider it done!" Egor replied, eager to please Dracon.

Egor was the leader of the Xanthurus—the Rat Race—a position he relished due to his egotistical character. The Xanthurus had been looked down upon through the ages, not normally liked or respected by others, as they were known to be unclean creatures that spread disease and battled to the death when cornered.

It was only their acquired position as Dracon's Mighty Vermin Army that gained them any respect and power. Perilous the Great did not approve of his son's choice of army but was too frail to wield power anymore.

The appearance of the Xanthurus was scary. Having the face of a rat and the semblance in shape to the body of a lithe, slim human, they possessed blood-red eyes that shone like rubies with

67

no evident pupil to be seen. Both male and female were formidable creatures, serving in the army side by side. Their fangs were sharp and snakelike, capable of ripping one's head off. The flesh-tone skin of the Xanthurus was tattooed with the sign of their forefathers, said to be more serpentine in form many centuries earlier—which would explain the snakelike features still apparent. Spikes ran down their long lean torsos, and their fingernails, the same flesh tone as the skin, were long, talon-like protrusions.

Egor was Dracon's bodyguard, and as such usually accompanied Dracon most places. Their main place of residence on Mars was more central to its core, with a different terrain than the North Major Region of Syrtis. The Fortress of Deimos, named after the second moon formed in orbit around Mars, was a huge fortress built out of molten rock with high towers that reached up into the shifting clouds.

The atmosphere there was not quite as dense as other areas on Mars and had the movement of clouds. It was an area of changing colors due to blowing sands and was named the Valles Marineris region, mostly drab with a pinkish-red hue created by the dust storms. Many meteor craters and volcanic plains could be seen on the surface of Mars, the largest volcanic plain being Hellas, 2000 km across. In the Valles Region could be found vast gorges, some larger than the Grand Canyon on Earth.

The terrain was difficult to travel across; vast sedimentary deposits lay everywhere, making the surface very uneven. In general, water did not exist as a free liquid on the surface except in the polar region, where immense oceans of salt water was present. However, the odd body of freshwater still remained in remote parts of Mars.

There was evidence that it did exist freely at one time. Channels as much as 1500 km long and 200 km wide appeared to have been cut by running water, probably freshwater. The inhabitants who needed free liquid to survive devised a way of collecting the dry ice and turning it into water. Others adapted over time by means of evolution.

The high winds correlated with solar heating that produced dust storms were not as acute as the high velocity winds of the polar region, making life much more bearable for the humanoids and creatures that lived there. But, like everywhere in the InterWorlds, the weather patterns were becoming more extreme and unpredictable. The ruler of the universe, Leviathan, was roaming around like a roaring lion, knowing his time to destroy all that belonged to Elyon was limited. The Kingdom Age was about to begin!

Chapter 6

Celestial's Abduction

Venus...

Time passed—time that Roberto was unable to quantify; it was a wonderful experience becoming accustomed to their new surroundings on Venus. Ilk had become a good companion and guide, providing a great tour of the spectacular wonders of a planet far different from what Roberto and other scientists had ever imagined. It became quickly apparent to Roberto that Ilk loved to show off his knowledge of his great planet, which, to Roberto's grateful amusement, helped his tolerance of Ilk's incessant chatter.

The magnificent statue of Queen Nebula constructed by Carthage was situated in the gardens surrounding the Fortress of Solitude—in the Asuras Region—meaning place of meditation. The statue was made of silver (the precious metal of Venus). The drapery of her gown was delicately sculpted, encrusted with myriads of tiny semi-precious tanzanite stone flowers, each flower shenanigan array of colors through each individual facet. The palest of pink flowers were regularly hung on the statue by the garden nymphs and cascaded over the gown. Her crown was adorned with glittering yellow diamonds, and she had blue sapphires for her eyes.

"Some say the statue cries real tears. Others say they are tears of blood and wonder if it knows the fate of Queen Nebula or if her soul lies trapped within," lamented Ilk, looking wistful. Roberto was sure he saw the sapphire eyes move, watching them as they turned to walk toward the fortress.

The fortress was a skyscraper standing a staggering six hundred feet high, the summit an open place surrounded by silver columns with a dome-shaped roof encrusted with emeralds all around the perimeter. Multiple facets effortlessly blended into one another, intercepted with azure blue and gold. Dreamily exquisite visuals of heavenly hosts prevailed. The silver stars lit up the high ceiling with a serene glow.

Roberto was in awe of the spectacular views. Ilk rambled on. "Before now, Celestial could see the beautiful land—as far as her superhuman eyes could see, a wondrous sight to behold—but the queen now tells us that the landscape is changing, and the thick, dark clouds looming in the far distance are a warning sign of the destruction of our planet."

Ilk looked sad again, then, quickly switched moods. "One must enjoy and count each blessing every day of one's life in order to be happy. If we were to dwell upon the negative things and worry endlessly, we would be miserable all the time and miss out on what could be happy times. So we are told, solutions—solutions, not problems. Wise words, don't you think?" said Ilk cheerfully.

"It is rumored that Celestial speaks directly to Elyon in this holy place. In conversation with Elyon, she withdraws herself from all external things and immerses herself in the ocean of spiritual light. Hey, I don't think Celestial could have put it better herself." Ilk giggled. "I only wish I could have this privilege; some Cherubs live in the upper realm, you know. Her Majesty plans her strategies for Venus in the Hall of Many Mirrors; things unseen are made clear to her."

"The Elves who make up the Order of the Sukras also have the honor to meditate in the holy place. They inhabit the Great Forest of Alvor—another one of the Seven Wonders of Venus that I will take you to sometime soon, I hope. They are the Order of the Sukras, a wise and angelic people of youthful-seeming men and women of great beauty—fair, slender, and tall. They possess unearthly speed and agility. They live by the code of Elyon—the

71

seven heavenly virtues—and their wisdom and benevolence transcend that of mere mortals with keener senses, and they have a closer empathy with nature. Like many species on Venus, they are long lived or immortal, with certain magical powers attributed to them. They can be killed in the same manner as a man, but then they return to Heaven as an angel of the spirit realm," said Ilk speedily—for he was beginning to feel hungry.

"Enough of that for now, I want to take you to meet my folks. They live near here, and I am sure you are feeling hungry," said Ilk.

"Oh yes!" cried Patience. "I had forgotten all about food. Everything is so interesting, but my stomach thinks my throat has been cut."

Wishbone barked as though he agreed; he had been very subdued of late, probably worried as to what creatures they might meet next after he had been turned into a tiny creature resembling a worm that the sprites fed upon. It was only because a fairy had changed him back quickly that he was not eaten alive! It was an Aseal Elvin, also known as the Dark Elvin, that was responsible for his demise, and he sure did not want to meet another of the ugly beings.

"Patience, why would your stomach think that your throat has been cut? I don't understand!" said Ilk, looking a little puzzled.

Patience laughed. "It's only a saying of ours, meaning that we are so hungry that our tummies wonder where the food is. And if your throat has been cut, then you could not eat—you know you are hungry when your tummy starts to make strange rumbling noises, saying, 'Feed me!'"

"I think you are making it more complicated for Ilk to understand, Patience," said Roberto, laughing loudly at the look on Ilk's face.

"Well, I have to say that my tummy never makes rumbling noises," said Ilk, looking puzzled.

"It just goes to show we are different, doesn't it, Ilk?" Patience chuckled to herself.

Ilk sat beside Wishbone to reassure him. He had grown quite

fond of him recently, especially when he realized that Wishbone was Patience's eyes. He was glad that Celestial had helped them.

"Come on, then, homeward bound. Home is where the heart is. I love my home. It is situated in the mountainside of the Asuras region, west of the Caves of Cau-Cas; you will love it, I'm sure; at least I hope you do. Most people do. I am sure you will." Ilk chattered away as they were flown across the vast gardens toward the stunning hillside region.

Set in the Asuras region stood a landscape of "fairy chimney" rock formations—tall spires of rock formed from volcanic ash and lava that had resulted from the eruption of Mount Evian about two thousand years ago. The setting was spectacular, entirely sculpted by erosion. The valley and its surroundings contained a multitude of rock-hewn dwellings, the home of various pixies and faery folk.

Pretty flowers grew prolifically around the rocky openings, with star-shaped petals that had a divine aroma subtly perfuming the atmosphere, producing an intricate and elevating enchantment. Small fairies flew around with fluttering, tiny, iridescent, delicate wings—their wings the colors of the rainbow, almost transparent. The sun was shining, and the scene was splendid.

Ilk beckoned them to follow him through one of the rock entrances.

"Hello there. Is anybody in? I've brought my friends from the palace. They would like to meet you," said Ilk, wondering where they were hiding.

A head popped up over the top of a wooden seat with a hat that looked more like a mushroom than a pixie hat. "Oh, they are here somewhere," said Elks rather shyly.

"Alto, Hicks, and Trix...where are you?" Ilk shouted.

"Roberto, Patience, and Wishbone, this is Elks," chirped Ilk. He put his arm around Elks. "He is the best. I am not sure he thinks the same about me, but there you go. He's stuck with me now; I like it too much here. Celestial offered me a position living in the palace, but no—I refused. Why would I refuse? You are probably wondering. Well, it's like this, you see. I would not leave my folks for all the treasures of Venus, so to speak. It's my home, my roots, and where I want to be. Celestial was pleased with my loyalty to my folks and gave me a good position anyways as her messenger."

"Yous knows we love yous, silly," said Elks, patting him on the head. "Wes wouldny swap yous for one of ours own kinds, Ilk.Yous are one of us nows, for betters or for worser."

Ilk smiled smugly. "Anyways, this is Roberto, Patience, and Wishbone, whom I have been telling you about."

"Nice to meet yous, Ilk speaks very highly of yous—you knows," said Elks.

"He also speaks very well of you." Roberto was sure Elks looked somewhat taller all of a sudden.

Ilk raised his chin. "One should speak highly of one's family out of respect. It is written—"

Before Ilk could say another word Elks almost sang the words, "In the Great Manuscripts of Life."

They all laughed. Ilk looked irritated for a moment and turned on his heels. "Come on. Let's find Alto, Hicks, and Tricks. They won't be laughing at me. At least I don't think they will. They better not do..." Ilk continued muttering to himself as he led the way.

The pixies' inner dwelling was a series of interconnecting, winding tunnels excavated into the rocky hills, richly decorated with colorful frescoes and myriads of monuments expertly carved out of the rock face. Roberto had to bend over to accommodate the inadequate height of the ceilings in certain places as they descended down some steps leading into the bowels of the earth. They passed through torch lit tunnels and over walkways that stretched across sheer drops until at last they entered a large, cave-like dwelling filled with furniture made of iron and silver and unique objects of art. Three more pixies with mushroom-shaped hats popped up from a small hole in the ground.

"There you are." Ilk began to introduce them one by one.

They knelt down on the soft earth. It was covered in a carpet of green grass, which seemed a very odd thing to have deep down where no natural light filtered through. Trix brought them a special sweet tea that tasted of cinnamon, and they ate little flower-shaped chocolates that Jinx devoured heartily. Patience thought she would still feel hungry on account of eating so little but was pleasantly surprised at how full she felt.

It was unfortunate that their happy moment was interrupted by a knock on the door. It sounded urgent. Much to Ilk's surprise, it turned out to be Mikael, one of Celestial's bodyguards. "This is an unexpected visit," said Ilk. "What can we do for you, Mikael?"

Mikael looked distraught. "It's our queen. She has been taken by the Draconians."

Everyone present gathered round in shock. "Hows did this happen?" said Elks.

Ilk was beside himself. He began to pace backward and forward.

Mikael fell to his knees. "Gabriel was guarding her chambers. I was off duty. When I returned, I found him on the floor, dazed. He caught a glimpse as he was attacked by a Xanthurus. He remembers the unmistakable red glowing eyes and the great looming size of the creature. He was so taken by surprise that he was not prepared—as you know, it is a rare thing for a Xanthurus to set foot on Venus. We have searched the palace and its grounds, but, alas, we cannot find our beloved queen and can only come to the conclusion that Dracon has captured her," said Mikael anxiously.

"How can this be?" Ilk could not comprehend how the Xanthurus could capture Celestial. Her powers were so much greater than theirs.

"I do not know! Gabriel is out of his mind; he feels responsible and berates himself for not being prepared for such an attack," said Mikael, wishing he had been there with Gabriel to defend the queen.

Ilk panicked. "Whatever shall we do? This is the most awful news, our beloved queen in the hands of Dracon. I hate to think what he may do to her. Oh, dear, what shall we do? We must go straight away and bring her back to safety without delay. Come, we must go," said Ilk with a flutter of his wings in preparation for his departure.

Roberto held on to Ilk's wings. "Calm down, Ilk. It's not that simple. We must plan her rescue carefully, or we will all lose our lives. And then we would be of no use to her, would we?" Roberto tried to think logically. "We must gather everyone who can help together and formulate a plan of action. When is the annual meeting of all subjects you told me about?" asked Roberto thoughtfully.

"One aeon of time, but we's cannot hold it without our queen," said Hicks.

"I know," said Mikael. "The Venusians will panic when they learn that their queen has disappeared. It will cause mayhem."

Roberto paced up and down the small room, deep in thought. The clock on the wall ticked loudly in unison with his steps. At last he spoke, everyone's eyes intently upon him. "We need to form a team to rescue Celestial. I need to know everything you can possibly tell me about Dracon, his people, and what we are up against on Mars. Who do you propose will be able to help?"

"We need to consult Astoria. She is our prophetess. She may have some insight as to where Celestial actually is and what we are up against," said Mikael.

"Yes, and we must go immediately to the forest of Alvor to see Rusalka. She will be able to guide us with the wisdom of the Order of the Sukra," Ilk added, at last able to think more clearly.

"I cannot imagine for one minute, Ilk, that they would harm our queen. Dracon has always been in awe of her beauty, and he would want her to succumb to him. It is true he would probably want to render her powerless, and he may try to deplete her aura by taking away her most powerful fairy spirit, Shimm-rae. How, I do not know!" said Mikael thoughtfully.

"It may bees the Key of Dreams he's after. Then he's may let her go," said Elks.

"I doubt very much he will let her go that easy, for lust and power will prevail enough for him to want to possess and win

76

over such a precious one of the Lord of Hosts. We know she will never succumb to his temptations—but that in itself is a problem, for he may lose his temper and punish her." Mikael paced the ground fretfully.

Panic overcame Ilk. "Oh dear, oh dear, I will never sleep again until we find her!" He began to cry in desperation. Patience put her arm around him, and Wishbone licked his face, drool dropping into Ilk's lap.

"Yuk...that was wet Wishbone," Ilk said as he wiped his face with the back of his hand.

For that moment everyone forgot their plight and laughed.

"Come on, then. Let's not get carried away with speculation. Where do we find Astoria? We have not got time to waste!" Roberto opened the door. The sunset had dwindled into twilight, streaking the landscape with orange and pink.

"She may be at the palace; she usually is at this time of night," said Ilk.

They flew hastily back to the palace in silence, pondering their queen's abduction.

At the Crystal Palace, Nastacia felt uneasy after her encounter with Dracon. Since her return, she had noticed a change in atmosphere. She wondered what was going on. Had Celestial found out where she had been? Why were Ilk's folks at the palace, and why had they consulted Astoria?

They were all in the Throne Room, but where was Celestial? Every time she entered the room, everyone became quiet, and as soon as she departed, the whispering commenced. She tried to listen through the doors, but it was no use; the doors were too thick, and they were too far away in the huge hall.

She looked for Orion to see if he knew what the commotion was all about. He was in the dark also; he knew nothing.

"Useless," she muttered to herself as she walked away from him. Annoyed, she stomped around the palace looking for clues.

Meanwhile, Astoria had a vision of Celestial as she looked into her glass globe. The clear glass clouded over, and then a picture of Celestial down in the dungeons of the Castle of Syrtis became clear.

"She is safe for now. She is in the dungeons of the Castle Syrtis in the North Syrtis Major region. He will not kill her—not yet, anyway. She is worth more alive to him." She paused for a moment. "Wait. I can see Shimm-rae. She has been captured by Dracon·and separated from Celestial."

"He must have had Leviathan's help to accomplish that," said Gabriel.

"Yes," agreed Astoria, "More than likely. I can see Shimm-rae is being held captive in a small box of some sort with a lock on it. He probably knows she is rendered powerless if she cannot see."

Ilk was concerned. "Poor Shimm-rae, it must be awful, confined in such a small space, not being able to see in the darkness."

Patience could sympathize with that feeling. "Yes, it is awful... poor Shimm-rae."

"Oh yes of course...It must be awful for you as well, Patience." Ilk fluttered around Patience so she could feel his presence close to her.

"Well, I have never had my sight, so it is nothing unusual to me, Ilk." Patience shrugged.

Astoria could not see a greater vision at that time, but she knew that more would be revealed later. "I will come with you to see Rusalka and the king and queen of Alvor. They must be informed, and we must use their wisdom in these matters." Astoria spoke with a soft, gentle voice.

Astoria was the prophetess of the Aegle Venusian race. She used the Silver Vessel of Truth to see into the past, present, or future, depending upon the vision provided by Elyon. The Lord of Hosts only allowed her to see certain things, always for the benefit of the universe and with just enough information to be able to work things out and learn from experience and past mistakes.

Astoria was a faithful servant of Elyon. She was a fairy of pure light, lighting up the way on a dark night. Her hair was golden, falling down her back in beautiful waves of silk. Her eyes were an unusual pale lilac and her lips a soft pink. She was very petite, true to her Aegle Venusian nature, with a perfectly formed hourglass figure and flawless skin, silky to touch. She adorned herself with pale-pink flowers to complement her garments of lilac and silver.

Her aura was almost perfect. Only one of her fairy Fruits of the Spirit was missing; the spirit of long suffering. And up to that point, a sprite had not managed to take her place, so Astoria was working hard to restore and perfect her character to its former glory.

Mikael and Gabriel escorted them all, with the exception of the pixie folk, to the Great Forest of Alvor. The Great Forest of Alvor was one of the Seven Wonders of Venus—a mystical place where the Elvor or Light Elvin dwelt. Situated in the far Northeast Vedic Region; the forest was full of magical enchantment and was the dwelling place of the mystical Zentaur, a sacred creature of peace and tranquility. It was said that the Zentaur could only be captured by a virgin—symbolizing the power of love over fierceness. However, the Zentaur was fleet of foot and difficult to catch. As an endangered species, it was protected by the Elvor, with whom they lived side by side in peace. It was said that to chop off its golden antlers would surely unleash great power— but to violate such a creature with a violent act could only lead to destruction and death when the power was used.

Patience was moved closer to hear more about the mystical creatures.

"Yes, they are wonderful to behold, but it is forbidden to touch them unless one is pure in mind and spirit," Astoria warned her.

"What would happen if someone who wasn't pure in mind and spirit did touch one, Astoria?" Patience asked, wide eyed.

"No one knows for sure. Such a thing has not occurred thus far, and I hope it never will—for the Zentaur's sake above all else," said Astoria.

"Anyway, it is time that you met Rusalka. She is the high priestess of the Elvor. Her realm is a special order from the High Heavens—the Order of the Sukras; she is the appointed master of the Sukras. She is very wise, following all her Lord of Hosts directs her to do. Her reward for such loyalty is true inner contentment that surpasses all our understanding, and it guards her heart and mind from all that is evil. After her maker, Rusalka takes orders from one other—the angel and our Queen Celestial, whom she loves as a sister as well as her queen. She works side by side with Celestial in her spiritual quest."

Roberto seemed to remember Celestial telling him something about the Order of the Sukras. He wanted to know more. "What is the Order of the Sukras responsible for?"

"They are collectively responsible for the writing of the Sacred Scrolls, but they have several tasks to perform. The Sukra is made up of the Elvor, forty Elves under the leadership of Rusalka. Rusalka is the appointed teacher sent to reprove and set things straight according to the wisdom of the Sacred Scrolls, in order to return to the perfect state they once enjoyed."

"They sound cool...people who could help us?" said Patience as they approached the mystical forest.

"Yes, they are. They can penetrate into the Councils of the Seventh Heaven, where they are given instruction. Some have the position of instructor of youth in the kingdom. They are responsible for teaching the wisdom of the ages and military accomplishments, especially the often-unsung song of the bow, and yet others are responsible for the powers of healing. However, I must warn you of the Dark Elvin. You will be able to distinguish them, for they are evil, destructive, and unattractive. Their main abode is in the mountainous region of Syrtis on Mars. It has been noticed on occasion that they have ventured over through the portal of Venus into these forests of Alvor disguised as Light Elvin, taking on the physical form of the Elvor. But they cannot hide their true nature for long. Look into their eyes, and you will know."

Astoria led the way through the depths of the amazing forest. It was truly magical.

Golden fruits hung from lush evergreen trees, and sweet, fragrant flowers grew in abundance among the rich groves of woodland. A place of profound mystery, enduring power, and deep enchantment, the forest of Alvor was filled with wonder and the pure essence of eternal love. The atmosphere was humid, akin to tropical forest—misty and quiet with the exception of the distant sound of a waterfall, the call of some exotic creature, and the soothing, soft melody of the Elvish song.

Roberto bent down to catch a falling leaf as it fell slowly from a nearby tree; it glittered like gold in his hand yet felt like velvet to touch. Tiny droplets that had the appearance of stars at night filled the air, lighting the way as dusk approached. Patience held on tightly to Wishbone, uncertain of where they were being taken, and Wishbone stayed close to Patience, fearful of being changed into some other form that would render him vulnerable.

"Do not be alarmed, Wishbone. You are safe here, boy," said Patience, stroking his shiny brown-and-white coat. "I will take care of you—I won't let any harm come to you."

"Yes you are safe here," Astoria reassured them. "The code of practice for the Sukra involves the Seven Heavenly Virtues, which can only produce a peaceful existence."

"What are they?" asked Patience.

Ilk was quick to answer. "Love, humility, kindness, chastity, faith, fortitude—and I've left your namesake till last, which, of course, is patience."

"Well done, Ilk, "said Astoria. "Now tell Patience the Seven Deadly Sins—the code of the Dark Elvin. Can you remember?"

"Oh yes, wait a minute. I know what they are...mm...pride, gluttony, lust, anger, greed and, hmm...I always forget at least one of them; I can't remember...oh, yes, sloth," said Ilk with a smile on his face.

"There is one more. Think carefully," said Astoria.

Ilk could not remember. "Don't tell me—it will come." He rubbed his chin thoughtfully. Astoria smiled patiently, knowing how important it was to Ilk to get everything right.

They soon came to a clearing where Rusalka stood engaged in deep conversation with a female Elvin in a gorgeous jade-green gown trimmed with gold. Her transparent wings shimmered with a golden glow, and her dark-brown hair fell softly around her shoulders with streaks of gold twinkling in the moonlight. Patience noted her pointed ears and vivid green eyes surrounded by a halo of gold.

Rusalka turned to face them. Her dark tresses and steely-blue, catlike eyes exuding warmth and kindness contrasted beautifully with her lily-white skin. Roberto thought she was an exquisite creature, her blood red lips inviting. Her tall, lithe body and small, pointed ears gave away her Elvin nature. Her every move was graceful. She wore a regal garment of the deepest blue sapphire trimmed with gold, combined with a wreath of crimson flowers in her hair.

Astoria walked up to her and kissed her hand. Rusalka held out her hands. "Hello, Astoria. What a pleasant surprise! What brings you here at this unheavenly hour? You must be tired after so long a journey. Come, follow me and introduce me to your friends. Celestial told me about your acquaintance with Roberto, Patience, and Wishbone, if my memory serves me correctly!"

She held her hand out in friendship to Roberto. He grasped the delicately outstretched hand and gently kissed it. "It is a great honor for us to meet you."

Rusalka withdrew her hand in surprise at such a gesture and placed her arm around Patience. "Celestial told me of your great talent and the faith that brought you here, Patience. You will be rewarded for such qualities, for they are priceless. I would love you to become my pupil, for you are receptive of all that is good. Elyon will have great things in store for you in your lifetime; you will see."

Patience beamed with satisfaction, although she was not so sure she deserved such words of praise. *Didn't I behave so horribly to Edwina? And I feel so angry that I cannot see more now than ever before.*

Rusalka turned her attention to the others. Elvin stood in their midst as the light began to fade swiftly, bringing the forest into a magical haven of soft, twinkling lights and the sweet aroma of jasmine surrounding them in the black velvet beauty of evening.

"This is Kisseiai, my most recent pupil. She learns quickly and willingly the wisdom imparted to her day and night until she holds it within like a shining torch, showing her the way in the darkness." Kisseiai acknowledged them humbly with the shy demeanor common to the students of the Sukra.

"Come, let us not tarry, for you must have some message of great importance to discuss, or you would not have come all this way at this lunar hour. We must go to the castle of Alvor and meet with the elf king and queen, Kinway and Kinshasar." Rusalka beckoned them to follow her deeper into the forest.

The moon hovered over the darkened woodland, and there, in the distance below, a swath of stars stood over the great stone castle. A glorious fairy-tale castle, with magnificent, huge, gleaming towers; and round turrets with pointed roofs and golden spires glimmering underneath a canopy of starlight. The wondrous trees surrounding the castle grew golden apples; every time a breeze went by, it tossed the branches, and a shower of golden apples fell, rich and mellow fruit. A climbing plant with subtle white flowers covered the exterior walls, filling the air with an entrancing fragrance.

They crossed the threshold of the castle through two very large, heavily embossed oak doors, Astoria lighting up the way down the long hall.

As they entered a round room, Roberto noticed the delicate silver filigree masking the ceiling, and the pink-and-pale-gray marble below his feet. Large intricate stained-glass panes filled the gracefully arched windows on one side of the room. Opposite, he could see the full moon through a plain-glass round window, drifting dreamily in the sky. As he stared at it, a strange shadow of some sort passed through it; the shadow of something sinister. He shivered and hoped he had imagined it.

They were invited to sit at a large spherical mirrored table in the Elvor study. Roberto was amazed as he gazed at the table. He put his hand on the surface, for it seemed that tiny versions of themselves, everyone present, were actually inside the table moving around, looking for a way out. It was a scene of utter confusion—everyone tumbling over one another in exasperation. He looked at the table again, and then looked at Rusalka, puzzled.

Rusalka smiled. "Do not be alarmed! The table has the power to read the state of your heart. As water reflects face, so a man's heart reveals the man. The vision of yourself is not real, of course—it merely shows that your heart and soul are under observation; the minute he is happy, your vision will fade and the table will become clear again. It is necessary so that treachery is not brought before this table when important matters are discussed."

"Awesome," exclaimed Patience, a little nervous of what the table would reveal about her innermost thoughts.

Manuscripts surrounded them on every inch of the walls in the great round room; each assigned to its own little pigeonhole, with written titles they could not discern—written in the language of Elvor.

They had only just sat down when the king and queen entered the round chamber. Roberto followed the others, standing up to bow out of courtesy.

The elf king and queen of Alvor could have been brother and sister, they looked so much alike. Rusalka had mentioned their grand old age, but their faces were little marked by the passage of time. The queen wore a stupendous white dress of glittering diamonds and pearls, with a crown to match, which was very high and had the delicate intricacy of a woven bejeweled spider's web. Her ice-blue eyes and long platinum-blond hair gave her the appearance of an ice queen.

The king had the same ice-blue eyes and a slightly shorter version of white-blond hair than the queen, adorned with a much heavier crown of regal sapphires and rubies. He made his way to the round table, his dark-blue robes gently rustling as he moved. The queen followed daintily, picking up her many layers of organza with her long, delicate fingers and a shimmering allure.

Rusalka was the first to speak after the formal introductions. "Now, Astoria, you must tell all."

Astoria swallowed hard. "It is not good, I am afraid. Celestial

84

has been abducted by Dracon—"

A gasp of horror escaped the king's and queen's lips. "Pray please continue." Rusalka tried to stay calm for the sake of everyone.

"She is being held at the Castle Syrtis in the North Syrtis Major Region. Dracon has managed to render her less powerful by capturing Shimm-rae, who is locked in a small box in darkness, and you know what that means!" lamented Astoria, feeling more than a little desperate.

Roberto's eyes met Rusalka's across the table. He was captivated by her serene beauty as he watched her in his own silent world for just a moment. He was brought back to reality with the sound of Patience's voice. "I am sorry to interrupt, but who is Shimm-rae?"

Rusalka looked gravely at Patience. "Shimm-rae is the most powerful fairy of the auras on this planet, and she is an integral part of Celestial's aura. Without her, Celestial has little heavenly power against Dracon. We must find her and return her to her rightful place; she will not survive for long without Celestial. They are reliant upon each other, as your soul is to you. It is without doubt that Dracon needs them alive, at least for now. We must, of course, rescue them without delay. Does anyone have any thoughts on the subject of their rescue?" said Rusalka thoughtfully. She hated to think of her beloved Celestial in such an awful place as the Castle Syrtis, but she knew she had to be the one who showed strength and faith in adversity as an example to others.

"May I offer my services to go to this place? Maybe Mikael and Gabriel could guide me." Roberto surprised himself with his gallant offer.

Rusalka considered his proposition carefully. "I do not see any reason why you should not go Sire. You will also take along two of our best Paristan warriors, their horses, and flaming swords."

Roberto liked the sound of the flaming swords and wanted to know more about the Paristan, but before he could ask, Patience interrupted. "Can I come too, Papa? I want to help Celestial."

85

"Not possible Patience. This is too perilous a journey. I have lost your mother, and I will not take the chance of losing you," said Roberto passionately.

Rusalka got up out of her chair and walked slowly toward Patience. She placed her soothing hands upon her shoulder. "No, little one...your father is right. You can stay here with Astoria."

"And Wishbone—he must stay too?" added Patience, not wanting to be split from him, for his sake as well as her own.

"Of course, my child," Rusalka reassured her.

"Please be careful, Papa. I will not forgive you if anything happens to you," said Patience anxiously.

Her father hugged her. "Don't worry; I will return before you know it, with Celestial by my side."

Ilk was getting all tearful as he listened to their premature, tender good-byes.

"I am coming with you, of course, Lord Bellucci. Being much smaller than you, I can get into places none of you can, and I can fly quite high anyways."

Rusalka decided that it was a good idea for Ilk to accompany them and bid them a good night's sleep in preparation for their impending journey. Everyone found a bed for the night in the rambling castle. Ilk followed Patience, mumbling to himself. "Did I really say I wanted to go with them? Oh no, I can't...I mean, I should not have said that at all...what is wrong with me? I will have to decline in the morning, but what will that make me look like? Oh my..."

"Are you coming to spend the night with us, Ilk?" Patience turned to him smiling; she had heard everything he had said.

"What? Oh, yes...yes, of course. I would like that." Ilk wanted the comfort of friends and quite envied the attention Wishbone always got from Patience.

"Come along then, Ilk. You can kip in our room tonight if you like."

"What is this 'kip 'word?" Ilk followed with a little flutter of delight, and Wishbone proceeded to lick Ilk once again, much to Ilk's distaste. "I've told you before about that, Wishbone. Don't drown me again!"

That night, Roberto was unable to sleep, thinking of his journey to Mars, the land of the evil Draconians. For the first time since his wife had died, he sought prayer.

Rusalka had told Astoria to stay with Patience and Wishbone in the Castle of Alvor, where they would be safe from harm. The king and queen of Alvor were more than happy to have them stay, and Astoria could report to them from time to time what she could see through the Vessel of Truth. Roberto knew she was in safe hands, much safer than with him on the perilous journey he was about to make.

THE CAU-CAS MOUNTAINS

The next break of dawn, they traveled north by flight, transferring Roberto to the Caves of the Paristan in the Cau-Cas mountains. As they arrived at the caves in the northern hemisphere, the scenery was rugged and breathtaking, very different from that of the Asuras region.

"The Paristan are the warriors of our planet," explained Rusalka. "They are all female, but do not let that put you under any predetermined illusion, for they are worthy opponents in war. They are of a different nature and appearance to the Aegle race; though beautiful with a human form common to Venusians, they have dark skin, jet-black hair, and pale-topaz eyes. They are taller than average, about the same height as you, Sire. Like other Venusians, they possess certain supernatural abilities but are able to change form unique to their own breed. They ride their warrior white horses with golden hooves and long, flowing, golden-tipped manes. They only fight, however, against evil and tyranny under the command of our queen to rid the kingdom of any evil that may try to infiltrate our peaceful existence. The reign of peace has been a long time, but now, I feel it is about to end."

The Caves of Cau-Cas were indeed a vast range of caves—a maze of connecting caverns that looked as if they would go on forever. The Paristan had made their home there, enjoying the outdoor life, living close to nature on the verdant land surrounding the mountains. To the northeast lay the region of Samosata. There the Underworld of Semiramis was situated. The deep, curious ocean of Semiramis was inhabited by the merfolk, the Oceanids, and other aquatic creatures who had built a golden kingdom deep, deep down in the bowels of the ocean.

The kingdom of Samosata was one of the Seven Wonders of Venus. There all the treasures of the deep were guarded by the Oceanids. The treasure there was the most beautiful in the universe, a collection of gold and silver and precious stones. Diamonds of all types were more numerous than the stars. The underworld itself was built of solid gold—really something to behold.

As Rusalka told Roberto all about the wonders of the deep, he was puzzled as to how Rusalka knew of such a place. "Surely you have not seen for yourself the depths of this ocean you speak of. Have you got the equipment to survive underwater?"

Rusalka smiled warmly. "I possess the power to change form and become an aquatic creature. So yes, I have seen it, in all its hidden splendor. I love to listen to the beautiful, harmonious voices of the merfolk. It is very pleasurable—a chorus of sweet harmony." Rusalka recalled her last visit many moons ago and smiled.

"I would love to see it sometime. It is a great pity we don't have diving gear here like we do back on our planet," said Roberto regretfully. They landed a short walk away from the entrance to the caves.

"It is not always necessary to have man-made material, Roberto; it is surprising where true belief can take you. If it can shift mountains, it can do almost anything you truly believe in. Faith is so much more powerful than most humans have experienced yet on planet Earth. Maybe you will learn this lesson during your stay on Venus. Elyon has a plan for all of us," said Rusalka.

"Yes, I hope so," said Roberto a little skeptically. He found it difficult not to stare at Rusalka and get lost in her beauty—her beauty was so much more than skin deep. In many ways, she reminded him of Marissa except for her hair, which was dark, in contrast to Marissa's blond locks. Her steel-blue eyes exuded warmth even though they were such a cool color, and the contrast with the color of her hair was stunning. His heart missed a beat as he listened to her soft, gentle voice. He could not fall for her—she was not human and way beyond his grasp. He had not had feelings that had stirred his soul since he lost Marissa sixteen years ago. *What a fool I am,* he thought.

"Are you OK Lord Bellucci? You look so...far away?" said Rusalka softly.

"Yes...yes, of course, but please call me Roberto," he said, clearing his throat nervously. He felt like a schoolboy.

They flew over smaller and smaller tributaries until they got nearer the caves and then approached them on foot, the trail ascending a flash-flood gulley, abruptly ending at a vertical cliff face. Many of the caves lay out of reach to all but a few. The Paristan were known to be the finest climbers of their world; their spiderlike agility helped them to reach all but the most inaccessible cliffs.

It was without hesitation that Roberto followed Rusalka and the others, climbing up the rough limestone rocks, his feet cautiously searching out the little ledges in the stone. They crawled through tree limbs hanging perpendicular from the rocks. Roberto looked down to see how far he had climbed, gripping root, rock, and the constant web of falling vines, only to see the swirling mist below his estimated two-thousand-foot climb. As he perched on a misty ridge, his own madness perturbed him slightly. If the angels had not had wings, he would certainly have been a fool to attempt such a climb without training.

This new world opened up so much more to him than his

small, little life back on Earth, where once he thought he was someone important. Now he did not know who he was any more or what his reason for being in such a place of extreme beauty with a whispering of danger could be.

Finally they reached a rock overhang about fifty feet high. Roberto noticed the quiver of arrows against the wall. The featherless arrows were about four feet long. Each had a point designed for a different prey, one with a carved hardwood point and a foot of sharp, backward-angling notches. Roberto followed Rusalka, hunched beneath a low overhang, and then stumbled into a gauntlet of unusually shaped skulls, some of great enormity, lined up as spoils of military action. The craniums had stood the test of time but looked as though they would disintegrate at once if barely touched. Their dark, haunting eye sockets no more.

He cautiously slipped past the skulls, trying not to touch them, conspicuously silent. Rusalka seemed to be lost in her own world, and Ilk stayed close to Gabriel and Mikael. They wandered through the connecting caves until they came upon a wide-open arch that shimmered with a warm, flickering light against the terracotta walls. Sprawling inscriptions and imposing carvings adorned the magnificent, shadowy portal, starting with depictions of battles most fierce of the Paristan and angels at war against mighty beasts and human-like forms, and then representations of a life of peace and tranquility when life was beautiful and their stomachs full, pictures of faery folk, angels, and Venusians living in harmony in verdant lands of plenty. The scripts he could not make out were written in an inscription unknown to man.

He could smell the welcoming aroma of stewed beef coming from a large, black cauldron as the juices bubbled gently, releasing its steam. Colorful fruits and vegetables lay in a tempting display upon a wooden table nearby.

A warrior named Elga came forward to meet them, placing her arm across her chest in the usual Paristan greeting. She glanced in Roberto's direction and then looked puzzled as she turned to

Rusalka.

"It is good to see you, Rusalka. What brings you here at this hour?"

Rusalka explained what had happened and why Roberto accompanied her on her quest to save Celestial. Again Elga turned to Roberto, placing her arm across her chest. "You are most welcome, Sire. It is a pleasure to meet you."

Roberto mimicked her actions, placing his arm across his chest. "I am so pleased to meet you too." She was slightly taller than his six-foot frame.

At one side of the cave was a large bronze wheel with various symbols engraved upon it. Elga made a loud noise as she struck the bronze gong with some sort of implement. Many female warriors marched into the cave in a single line and stood to attention as though awaiting orders. It was a sight to behold for Roberto—women warriors.

Their leader was slightly taller than the rest and introduced herself as Brabantia. Her athletic body was completely encased in light armor, and she certainly looked capable of handling the long, jewel-hilted sword at her side. Her warrior garments gleamed like silver yet fit like a glove, almost liquid like in texture and cutting a striking image on her tall, lithe body; her skin, the color of golden honey, was flawless except for a scar above her strongly defined right eyebrow and a long arched scar on her forearm that had faded with time. Her eyes, honey brown, complemented her long black hair, which was held to one side in a thick leather braided plait.

She listened carefully to everything Rusalka had to say.

"I will come with you, and Serepha will come too." Brabantia called her second-in-command forward. "Lilith, you will take care of everything while I am away. We will bring our queen back. I do not fear Dracon, and neither will Celestial. We are at your command in her absence, Rusalka." She did not seem to notice Roberto at first.

Brabantia had been leader of the Paristan for many centuries and had fought many a battle in the ancient days. She beckoned

91

Roberto to follow her through a labyrinth of smaller caves that opened up into a cavernous space.

"Here, with much toil and equal pleasure, our armor is forged."

Roberto steadied himself as he walked a rugged path. A huge fire roared in a hearth, beside which stood an anvil. Roberto watched the woman handle the sword with a nimble motion, placing it first in the fire and covering it well until it had attained a sufficient degree of heat. She then drew it out and laid it upon the anvil, moving it skillfully about while her assistant hammered one part of it to a consenting shape. Having finished, they laid it carefully back in the fire, and when it was very hot, they plunged the glowing steel into a vessel of liquid.

In another corner of the cave, two other women had drawn freshly made swords and, with a ready response of hand and a certainty of eye, began to test the strength of their defense with great precision and agility. Roberto was sufficiently impressed with their dexterous display and felt assured that he was in good hands.

In the corner of the cave stood a warrior named by all, Standing Rock. Brabantia explained that the name derived from former days of battle when she would stand and watch for days on end with no sleep, keeping her eyes on the approach of the enemy. Roberto noticed that she was gently stroking a braided strand of sweet-grass.

Brabantia picked up another braided strand and began to do the same, looking up at Roberto. "To stroke the strand gives power to strengthen the mind's resolve. It is our way at this time when we celebrate the Springtime Restoration Feast."

Brabantia offered Rusalka and Roberto a strand. Roberto began to feel the blades of braided grasses between his fingers. "What do you do to celebrate?"

"We are preparing as we speak. We planted taro, pumpkins, cucumbers, bananas, and tobacco. They are now ready, and our new weapons are forged. We meet at Standing Rock Reservation, which we named after Standing Rock. We eat and sing songs of thunder to welcome the rebirth of nature and conjure up the big cumulus clouds to bring forth the rain and the hail, thunder, and lightning, all the things that renew life after the winter."

Standing Rock smiled at Roberto. "You must join us. Your mission is important, yes. But we cannot deny our need for the Springtime Feast, or the order of the seasons may be changed."

Brabantia spoke out. "It is true we will go with you, Rusalka, but only after the feast; therefore, you must join us in the celebration. And then we will go together, prepared for anything we may encounter. We need the elements to be on our side."

"Of course," Rusalka agreed.

Roberto could not say one way or another. He was merely human; what did he know of such things as the elements anymore? Science as he knew it had been forgotten—for now, at least.

Brabantia pulled Rusalka to one side. "Are you sure this human should come with us? He will be of no use to us. Infact, he will be more of a hindrance. You must realize this, Rusalka!"

Rusalka placed her hand on Brabantia arm. "I hope you deign to trust me on this one, Brabantia. You know not the ways of man or why this man is so far away from his place of dwelling. But all will be revealed in time."

"Well, for all our sakes, I hope you are right and he will not be the downfall of all of us. Humans are weak and have no true value."

Rusalka glanced coolly into Brabantia's blazing eyes. "They have their weaknesses. That much is true. But do not underestimate the strength and integrity of some of their kind."

Roberto noticed that Rusalka was deep in conversation with Brabantia and got the distinct feeling that he was the topic of conversation. He felt suddenly uncomfortable but was thankful to Standing Rock, who was more than happy to educate him about her people.

She told him of how they lived, men and women in separate caves, the men largely having the responsibility of rearing the children and hunting for food. During the reign of peace, the women had shared these responsibilities. But now the time had come for them to take up their weapons once again.

The prophecies told old and new for them to take heed, and thus be eternally ready for battle when the time came, for they knew not the time or the hour.

She told of how they had located their place of safety high up in the cliffs. Even though at times it required treacherous climbs for some, it provided a natural fortress that once protected them from the enemy before peace reigned. Now their enemies, no less dangerous, posed a threat once more. Before, headhunters and cannibals threatened their land and their lives. But now, the forces of nature and the supernatural threatened their very existence, and their fortresses would be of no comfort.

Standing Rock shook her head in dismay. "Now our men will gather to make sago for the feast, and we will prepare everything else at the cave of Standing Rock Reservation for the feast at full moon."

The men did not have the feathery wings of an angel or the distinct features of anyone Roberto had seen on Venus. They had the dark skin of a native Indian with long black hair half braided, like their women, their stature the same but their musculature so much bigger. He could not get over the fact that they were such docile creatures when they looked as though they had been pumped up with testosterone.

Roberto accompanied the men, descending from the top and approaching from the plateau on its far side. They backed slowly down the steepening slab. Roberto's pulse quickened; reaching the first crevice, he watched Amerilo pull the climbing vine inward, edge his way twenty feet to the left on a small ledge, and stop at another crevice where another vine rope had been strategically placed. Roberto followed cautiously, watching Amerilo's every move as they shinnied down, swaying like a pendulum above the deep-shadowed gorge, until they reached the bottom, followed by the rest of the group of cave dwellers, rippled with muscles thickened by frequent climbing. They followed a trail to the nearest cluster of palm trees, where they began to cut down and hack out the pulp from the heart of it, transferred it into a trough filled with water, and squeezed it against a coconut filter, pressing out an orangish-white paste.

They worked like this for six long hours in the blazing sun, glistening with sweat. Roberto could not take the heat of the day and chose to watch from the canopy of a tree. Now he understood. By the time the sun had begun to set, they had collected forty pounds of gummy sago.

They made their way back to the reservation, where the Paristan and their children waited with the others, ready to start the feast. The women made fire-fried sago pancakes to eat with the rest of the fare they had prepared earlier and smeared themselves with sap and clay in order to become as white as specters and as the moonlight. They danced until they could dance no more, scantily clothed, as was their tradition, reserved exclusively for the women of the tribe.

Sitting on their haunches by the campfire, some told tales of battles most fear, and others sang songs of thunder. Roberto was mesmerized with the beauty of Rusalka sitting by the golden flame of the fire. He drank of the wine of the Cau-Cas grape and felt more chilled than he had for years, almost forgetting where he was and why he was there. Standing Rock told of how each cave had an owner and a name, and ownership was passed down from mother to daughter. Only each cave holder could pass down the secrets of that particular cave.

Many had laid down their swords and daggers and their bows and arrows after the games, when the children had been sent to lay down their heads. One by one they squatted by campfires, rolling tobacco leaves to smoke. The clarity of the moon and the brightness of its light told a story of an especially clear sky to follow at dawn.

Brabantia offered Roberto some of the leaves.

"Oh...no thanks...I ga...ve that up a long time a...go...this Cau-Cas vintage serves me well." He slurred his words slightly.

Rusalka held her hand over her mouth, smiling at Roberto's state. "Don't give him any more, Brabantia. Remember where we must go at sunrise. We need to be prepared."

95

"No…I am quite o…kay…bel…believe me…it's rather…bit…ter swest, but very, very go…od." He looked at the milky liquid, swirling it around his cup.

Brabantia laughed this time with everyone, enjoying the effect it was having on him.

"It is Soma—a fermented liquid found near here. In order to be purified, the sap of the plant must be extracted and passed through a sieve made of animal wool. The soma is then poured into wooden containers and mixed with water and milk. Beware; it can untie the tongues of men and rapidly become your nectar."

Brabantia left the party and returned with another drink, which tasted horrid after the sweet taste of the vine.

Roberto spat it out. "What the hell is that? Are you trying to poison me?" He felt his throat burning. "My throat's on fire," he croaked.

Brabantia gave him a vessel containing the purest of mountain water. "Drink this. It will soothe you. You will be thanking me at first dawn when you feel fit to travel."

Roberto drank the water cautiously at first, then gulped down the rest. He was not sure of Brabantia at all; she was a little intimidating. *Women warriors—who do they think they are? They could never beat this Dracon and his armies. I will have to kill him,* he thought bravely, feeling less confident by the second.

He managed to pull himself up off his feet with great effort. But for the glow of the campfire, it was impenetrably dark, and he could hear water pouring over the edge of a nearby precipice relentlessly beyond a rock overhang, slapping the giant rocks beneath, which sort of reminded him how high up he had been earlier in the day. Rusalka came to his rescue, holding him up as he walked farther into the encampment. She guided him to a makeshift bed and laid him down to sleep.

"Sleep well, Roberto. You are going to need it. Yes…you are going to need all the strength and fortitude you can muster." She covered him up with a gray woolen blanket and watched him sleep in the flickering light of the fire torches strategically placed on the cave walls.

As the sun set on the horizon, Roberto awoke to the banter of females as they drew bags of water from the fresh water well. The two angels, the two warriors, Rusalka, Roberto, and, of course, Ilk bathed in the warm spring waters and dressed in clean garments in preparation for the journey to the unpredictable planet of Mars. Roberto did not remember much of the night before and was amazed how refreshed he felt after what could not have been a long sleep. Ilk was quite happy to explain the reason why he did not nurse a huge hangover.

The portal crossing from Venus was situated at the border of Castra and the Asuras region, not far from the forest of Alvor, and they hoped to be there by nightfall.

Brabantia and Serepha said their good-byes to their families and the remaining unit of the Paristan warriors. Mounting her magnificent white steed, Brabantia instructed Roberto to join Serepha upon her horse. Roberto was delighted to share a ride on such a beautiful, splendid creature. He thought of how much its golden hooves alone would be worth back on Earth. It would soon be an endangered species with the treachery of man.

Rusalka led the way, and they arrived by nightfall, as planned. "Now, Roberto, you must follow everything that we do, and we will be transported to the border of Tharsis, the other side of the portal on Mars."

Roberto thought how disorienting it was to wake in this new world he had abruptly found himself in. Through the essence of time—time he could quantify no longer—he had gotten used to his new surroundings. His life before had easily become a distant memory, and now he was bound for new territory yet again.

The sun disappeared behind the hills as night washed over the landscape. The magnificent, vast golden gates stood before them, visible yet not tangible, rippling in and out of vision. They gave the appearance of easy access, as though one could walk through the mirage, but it soon became evident to Roberto that it was not as easy as it seemed.

Rusalka gave out instructions. "We must form an enchanted circle, purified by calling on the element of light."

97

Everyone gathered round to form a circle holding hands. "Do not let go, Roberto...for there must be no break...there must be no beginning and no end, no way out and no way in. From its sacred center, a place of protection, it must be equidistant, representing unity and perfection. We recall the power of the dome of the sky, the sun and the moon, the wheel of seasons, and so time everlasting. We create a place of confined sacred energy that stands outside of time and space, connecting our realm with others. Then and only then can we pass through. Close your eyes."

Suddenly, a strange low sound emanated from their mouths. At that point, Roberto had to fight to keep his eyes closed.

"Concentrate hard, Roberto, and keep your eyes closed," said Rusalka, quickly returning to the unusual chant. It seemed like a long period of time before the sound came from Roberto's mouth, and when it did, he had no control over it. He found himself battling against the heat and the winds in an unknown place surrounded by frightening creatures of the dark—it was only a second in time, but it seemed like forever, and he felt death for a fleeting moment, a stranglehold of pain and anguish in a forgotten world. His body dropped abruptly, and the vision faded; he drifted into the nothingness he had previously encountered.

Serenity ensued!

$$\infty$$

Chapter 7

Celestial's Rescue

Mars...

Roberto opened his eyes. He felt the sudden extreme change of temperature and struggled to stay on his feet as the high winds encircled him.

"Are you with us, Roberto?" said Rusalka, her voice raised so that he could hear despite the sound of the high-velocity winds. She steadied him as she spoke.

"Yes, I think so." Roberto found it difficult to speak. "Are you sure we are not in the Antarctic on my own planet?" Shivering, he blew into his hands and rubbed them together in an endeavor to warm himself.

"We do not feel the change in temperature as you do. We have the ability to adapt to such a change in climate. These are the polar regions of Syrtis, and the terrain and atmosphere here is not conducive to human beings."

Rusalka shouted as she placed her delicate, warm hands upon his shoulders and instructed Roberto to look in to the depths of her eyes. Roberto would normally be ecstatic at such a command—looking into her beautiful, soulful eyes—but he could not concentrate because of the blistering cold pervading him and the biting gusts of wind threatening to blow him off his feet at any moment.

No sooner had he managed to set eyes upon her when his burning brown eyes looked out into another dimension...into another world...a world of peace and utter tranquility. He floated out of his fragile body. His spirit soared high into nothingness, feeling the warmth and security surrounding him. There was no vision of anything, just him and his utter peace. Then, out of the void, Rusalka appeared, floating toward him in pure white garments with angel's wings and a halo of golden light surrounding her.

He lay there immobilized as she wrapped her soft wings around him. He melted into her arms and howled like a madman, letting go of all the pain he had held on to since the loss of Marissa, until his eyes felt dry. "You will cry no more now, Roberto. Your pain has gone—you are healed of your sorrow and will now find the inner peace you so lacked and so long desired."

He opened his eyes once more. He could not feel the cold. The weather had not changed—HE HAD CHANGED! Ilk fluttered past him, giving him a wink. Roberto laughed at the cheeky little chappy.

He looked at Rusalka, and she smiled a warm, knowing smile. He smiled in return, searching out her lovely eyes, which conveyed a beautiful soul and gave him the feeling he had the power to conquer the world. A rush of ecstatic excitement filled his being. He felt renewed; his faith had been transformed. He knew in his heart that life would never be the same. He felt alive. He felt reborn! The numb feeling he had been living with for years had passed away.

Rusalka felt the passion in his soul as she gazed in to his deep brown eyes, and she felt something stir within her heart. She turned away briskly. "Come. We must find the Castle Syrtis; it is in the northerly direction."

The surrounding mountain ranges were covered in polar ice. It was easier to fly some distance than walk the difficult terrain. They did not know what difficulties they would encounter on their journey through the forests of Asan in the Phebus region, for it was home to the Aseal, Dark Elvin, and the much-talked-about ferocious beasts seeking to devour flesh. Their only way of surviving was to trust in the almighty protection of Elyon as they battled not just flesh and blood but the supernatural forces of the Prince of Darkness Leviathan and his evil followers.

There was another way from the portal to reach the Castle of Syrtis, but it would have involved a journey twice as long, and time was imperative. Ilk would have avoided the journey altogether if he had been able to do so, but he knew he could not let Celestial down; he would never have forgiven himself. He knew he had to be brave. He shuddered.

No one could be seen from the portal for miles ahead. They drove forward resolutely in the direction of the forest, reaching the outskirts as the sun sank low on the horizon. Forming a circle, they held hands in order to strengthen their unity and trust in one another when entering the forest, the very thing that would destroy the opposing forces they would encounter ahead.

The forest was dark and foreboding, and moonlight filtered through the dense trees. Weeds flourished everywhere, a tangled web of leaves and flora past its prime wearing into decline, petals curled and brown. They hacked their way through to a clearer area trampled down by huge beasts over time, aware that the forest would soon be a very dark place.

Brabantia and Serepha surveyed their surroundings apprehensively. They traveled deep into the forest, following a very indistinct path. In the bleak stillness of the silvery night, a haunting cry filled the skies. Roberto woke himself up from his state of daydreaming, not really realizing the dangers that could befall them. Instantly, he placed his hands on his chest defensively, and a powerful, pungent odor filled his nostrils. He had little time to think, only to react. He fell to the ground suddenly. Rusalka ran to his side, unsure of what ailed him. Ilk began to panic.

"Oh dear, what is wrong Lord Bellucci?" He looked in all directions to see if he could see anything coming. They heard an almighty roar in the distance.

"It's is a dart from the manticore," said Brabantia. "It will only paralyze him in readiness for the manticore's kill. We must be alert, for it will be stalking us at this moment and will know our every move."

"I really don't like the sound of this manticore," said Ilk his face contorted with fear. He hid under Celestial's wing trembling.

The manticore was also known as the man tiger—with the face of a man with horns, gray eyes, three rows of iron teeth, and a loud trumpet pipe roar. It had the body of a lion and the tail of a dragon scorpion, which was capable of shooting out paralyzing spines or hairs to incapacitate its prey. The meaning of its name manticore was enough to describe its nature, and its very existence depended upon it.

"I have the power to disguise our scent, at least for some time while we get away from here," said Rusalka. "But we will have to carry Roberto until he recovers from his slumber."

"Come. We must move quickly and quietly." Gabriel swept Roberto up into his arms effortlessly.

"Dracon may not be in the castle, "said Brabantia. "His main domain is the Fortress of Deimos."

"Where is this fortress?" Gabriel asked.

"It is more central to the core of Mars, in the Valles Marineris region, where the atmosphere is not quite as dense, at least, as there is the movement of clouds there."

The fortress was huge, made of molten rock with a high tower that reached up into the shifting clouds. It was surrounded at all times by the Vermin Army, the Xanthurus.

Brabantia knew many things about Mars and their enemies. She had made it her responsibility to find out, knowing the time would come when her knowledge would be of immeasurable value, and she had done her research well.

"The Castle Syrtis contains many chambers—including the Eternal Inferno Chamber of Torture, which the Xanthurus are responsible for, under the command of Dracon."

"What can you tell us about the Xanthurus?" said Mikael.

Mikael had been very quiet since the disappearance of Celestial. He stood there, arms folded, his long gleaming sword by his side.

"I am sure you already know of their appearance—not a pretty sight! Every sense of the Xanthurus is highly developed except the eyes. Their vision is blurry, especially more than a few feet away, and depth perception is poor. Unfortunately, their other senses are far more sensitive than the human fingertips. They can detect sounds at higher frequencies, into the range of ultrasound. The tail of the Xanthurus is another weak spot. It has a thermoregulatory function; it serves as a heat loss organ when necessary to cool them down," said Brabantia.

Roberto chuckled. "They are probably glad of that when stoking the furnace."

Brabantia continued, oblivious to Roberto's comment.

"It is good that we know their weaknesses. The tail is used for balance."

"So cut off their tails, and they will fall over," laughed Roberto nervously.

"Well, I don't like the sound of this Xanthurus army," Ilk cut in. "They are evil and very huge. Maybe I should stay outside the castle and wait for you. I could look out for anyone entering the castle and let you know, couldn't I?"

"We are better off staying close together at this point, Ilk," said Rusalka, feeling for Ilk, knowing that bravery was not on his list of good qualities.

Roberto sidled alongside Brabantia. "What are Dracon's weaknesses?"

Brabantia showed her obvious contempt. The thought of her bare skin passing within lunging distance of that great fanged lizard made her want to scream. "He is a cold-blooded murderer who would murder his own. To cut off his tail would do no good, for he can move more swiftly, leaving his tail behind wriggling. It is of no consequence to him, as he will just grow another one, even if it is a little shorter and a different color. To catch him at the time he sheds his skin is probably the most vulnerable time for him. To cut off his tongue would be of more use, but care must be taken in doing so, as the tongue is venomous in more ways than one. One bite, and his toxic saliva will weaken your immune system, followed by a slow death. He has highly acute vision and a voneronasal organ, which he uses to taste the air, much like a snake."

Roberto almost wished he hadn't asked.

Castle Syrtis - The Dungeons

Meanwhile, far beneath the level of the ground, under the Castle of Syrtis, Celestial had been placed in the gloomy dungeons and without Shimm-rae was powerless to escape.

There were many others in the dark, dank dungeon waiting execution or torture. The clanking of the weapons of the Xanthurus, who kept guard, fell mournfully upon the prisoners' ears. Every moment reminded them of their impending fate at the hands of Dracon. They felt despondent in the knowledge of the impossibility of their escape. The light of the heavens could not penetrate the horrible subterranean cell. Celestial stood out in contrast as a shining light in the darkness. Some seemed afraid of her, others curious. She felt a compassion for them—lost souls in the hands of Leviathan—and she could see the madness that they had been driven to, the battle of the mind against evil forces. She wanted so much to save their souls.

In the corner of the large, cave-like dungeon was a petite woman with the wings of an Aegle fairy—though they had lost their brightness and were covered in dust, ripped open by the ravages of time and bad treatment. Her clothes had once been grand but were now torn and dirty, revealing a thin torso. She was slumped over, weeping quietly to herself. Celestial felt great pity at the sight of her and walked over to see if she could help.

The woman looked up. Could it be? Celestial gazed into her soul. Recognition struck her. She placed her hand carefully on her shoulder. The woman shrank back in fear.

"Do not be afraid anymore, Nebula. I am here to help you."

Celestial fixed her eyes compassionately upon Nebula. "I know who you are, and I know of your pain and suffering. All of that ends now it is time to move on and return to your previous life."

Nebula did not realize that the woman had used her name. She could not look at her as she spoke.

"Who are you? Why do you speak so kindly to me? I am a fallen one, kept here to be punished by Dracon for my disobedience to Elyon. The enemy has pursued and persecuted my soul. He has crushed my life down to the ground. He has made me dwell in dark places like those who have been long dead. You do not understand. No one can help me. My spirit is overwhelmed and faints within me; my heart within my bosom grows numb. I am beyond help, and I am tired, so tired I just want it all to end. But I know it is a sin to end my life myself, so I must endure the torture. I try to remember the days of old, but, alas, they fade further into the distance with each passing day. I am so very tired. Please leave me alone. I don't need empty promises."

Celestial turned Nebula's face toward her with her soft hands; she could not help but notice the deep haunted look in her eyes.

"Listen carefully. I cannot leave you alone. I am here for a purpose; I know that now! I am Celestial. I was sent to Venus to save the condemned after your fall from grace." She spoke with divine authority. "I am of the Seraphim in the heavenly realm, and I am in battle against Leviathan. I can save you and restore you back to the perfect state you once enjoyed. You must have faith and work hard in repentance of your wrong actions, and the grace of Elyon will prevail against Leviathan. It is your choice. We all have free will, as you know."

Celestial felt great sympathy for the hard lesson Nebula had endured.

Nebula looked up to Celestial with hope in her heart. She could not believe, after all the passing eons of time, that she was going to be given another chance. She fell at the feet of Celestial and wept. "I have dreamed of this day. Please help me, for I am weak and broken, but I want to return and bask in the grace of Elyon. I do not expect to be queen again. I just want to be a faithful servant and feel the happiness I once felt so long ago."

105

"You will, Nebula, you will. For I see your heart is good, and I will be your strength and protector, your guardian angel. But for now, you must sleep and refresh yourself, and we will think of an escape plan for the next dawn." Celestial caressed her hair consolingly as Nebula drifted in to a restful sleep she had not experienced for such a long time.

Celestial stood up to stretch her limbs while Nebula slept.

"Are you an angel?" said a deep voice in a dark corner of the dungeon.

"Yes, I am. Who speaks there in the shadows? Come out and reveal yourself," said Celestial in a commanding voice.

A Draconian stepped out of the shadows. She had a deep, empty voice. "I usually do not take orders from anyone except Dracon, but I am intrigued—I have heard about you. What is it like to live on Venus? I have heard good things, things I am not to speak of. It is punishable to talk of such things here," she whispered, looking around suspiciously.

"Is that why you have been imprisoned?" Celestial could not believe that the punishment would fit the crime, if one could call it a crime!

"Yes, but I don't know the punishment yet. I do know it won't be pleasant," said the woman.

"What is your name?" said Celestial.

"Cava," whispered the woman as she slid out of the shadows cautiously.

Celestial took a closer look at her. She was dressed in a one-piece suit of deep purple, which looked striking with her dark skin and pure white hair. Her hair was scraped back severely, falling down her back in one heavy plait, and her eyes, shaped like those of a Siamese cat, were a stunning pale, iridescent violet. Celestial had never seen a Draconian before; she stared in silence at her unusual lunar beauty and then moved closer to whisper in her ear.

"Well, Cava, listen well. You can either accept your punishment—which I believe to be unjust—or you can escape with me, and I will show you a better world, where you will not

106

only feel free but will have happiness and contentment and everything your heart desires."

Cava had shown the first step to change by questioning the life and existence that she had been born into, and Celestial wanted to help her; however, Cava was not too sure if she could trust Celestial.

"I am not sure of what you speak. What I am sure of is that I hate my life on Mars under Dracon's tyrannical rule. I would like to see something different; then I can decide for myself. I will come with you, but you are not my master. Is that understood? I am master of my own destiny," said Cava, anxious not to be taken over by Celestial as a slave of her kingdom.

Celestial understood her fear. "You have free will, but I know that you will not regret your decision to come with me. For is it not better to have a choice, a choice that is of your own making? For what free will do you have now, but none?"

"We will see. First, how do we get out of here? It is heavily guarded by the Xanthurus, and they are not easy to get past. I have been here two moons waiting for my verdict, so it could be any time now that I am called for trial. How about you? Why are you here? I suppose that is a silly question, really. It's obvious that Dracon would want your power and your planet. Can you not use your supernatural powers to get us out of here?" said Cava, more than a little puzzled.

Celestial sighed. "No, I am afraid not. Dracon has taken away such power, and I must get her back!"

Cava was confused. "Did you say HER? Don't you mean IT?"

Celestial smiled. "No. My supernatural abilities are in the form of the fairy Shimm-rae, whom Dracon has captured, rendering me almost powerless. Without me, she is powerless herself. She is an important member of my aura."

At that point, she spread her wings, and the remaining fairies of the spirit fluttered around her. Others in the dungeon gasped in surprise at the tiny creatures that made such a sweet sound, sparkling in the darkness. Celestial closed her wings, and immediately they were gone, as though they did not exist. She

107

told Cava all about her aura and how it worked for her.

"Now we need to get some sleep before dawn breaks, and the next dawn, we will plan a strategy together with Nebula, who sleeps quietly right now. I will introduce her to you when she wakes." Celestial told the story of Nebula's downfall as an example of the importance of obedience to the Mighty Elyon.

The only light that could be seen in the dungeon was Celestial's shining light of hope. Others tried to touch her, amazed at her purity and soft-spoken voice. Cava felt excited at the prospect of learning about a new world full of new and interesting things, but the question nagged at the back of her mind: *Will there be a place for me? Will they want me?* She looked so different, but others of her kind had done it before. Carthage had even become king of Venus in the ancient days—surely this bedraggled fairy was not the Queen Nebula of that time? She stared at Celestial with a great intensity that would have made a human uncomfortable.

She could not stop looking at Celestial. She wondered if this was what real beauty was. She was considered one of the most attractive beings on Mars. Her hair was pure white, scraped off her face, revealing her harsh, pointed features and large, pointed ears. Her white, bushy eyebrows sloped upward, standing out in contrast against her sallow, shiny skin. Her garments were those of a warrior, made of metal and rubber—the harsh color of purple mixed with gunmetal gray.

Yes, she was sick of her life on Mars. She wanted to see the universe and its diversity. This was her chance. But she must be cautious; this could be a trap to imprison her on Venus, and it would be difficult to get back to her own planet, as Draconians did not have the independent ability to travel to another planet without the help of other planet wanderers. She would see what the next dawn would bring along.

EVIL STRIKES

The forest of Asan was vast. If it hadn't have been for

Brabantia and her great knowledge of the place, they would most assuredly have gotten lost. The manticore seemed to have lost their trail, at least for the present, and they reached the open land by mid-sun.

The day passed slowly as they trudged through the treeless tundra. Suddenly, darkness descended upon them. An unsettling sound came down, the wind ominous and threatening. Brabantia glanced skyward, sniffing in the atmosphere.

"A powerful force has broached our parameters. It will soon descend upon us."

"There is no shelter...what can we do? There is nowhere to hide...oh no, no what are we going to do?" Ilk put his hands to his face, fluttering backward and forward.

Everyone ignored him, intent on how fast the wind was rising from the north. They were struggling just to keep on their feet; the gale-force wind stripped earth savagely from the ground as it swept toward them.

"Elyon, preserve us!" shouted Rusalka, holding on to Nebula tightly. The swirling wind whipped her voice from her lips, so Roberto could barely hear her. The others tried to steady themselves. Ilk tucked himself safely under Gabriel's right wing as he struggled to keep his balance.

Brabantia pulled at Rusalka's arm pointing upward to the darkened sky. They seemed so far away, their form hardly detectable at first sight. The force of the wind sent Cava reeling into Mikael's arms. She glanced at him for a brief moment. She thought she detected a look of fear in his face. She thrust her words past the wind as she tried to shrug him off. "I can manage myself."

He nodded, smiling, holding on to her anyway as the dark creatures encircled them overhead.

Roberto had never seen such appalling creatures. Although they weren't particularly big and had the semblance of faerie or sprites, they had a nefariousness about them, vile and evil. Their skeletal bodies were devoid of flesh and blood, and their long gray hair fell over their faces; their gray-black-veined wings, jagged round the edges, projected out from bone. As they flew, they called to one another with a deafening shrill cry showing their sharp, hooked teeth.

A rotten stench filled Roberto's nostrils. He struggled to move; trepidation filled his soul. Ilk hid behind Gabriel's wings in his usual fashion. As she continued battling against the power of the wind, Cava picked up a rock with all her given strength and aimed it at one of the pursuing creatures.

"No, Cava, don't throw it! You must stay still. Do nothing. Just close your eyes and tell yourself that they do not exist," shouted Celestial. Mikael grabbed hold of Cava once again as he battled against the high winds. This time, she did not try to escape his large frame.

Rusalka and the angels knew what was necessary for their survival, drifting beyond the present world to a different plane, one of sweet serenity and silence, in the stillness of the light. Brabantia too realized that she must not fear closing her senses to all that surrounded her.

Serepha could not stop herself from feeling the fear, allowing it to pervade her mind. She quickly changed form. The Paristan were capable of transition into either a wolf on land or a swan on water, the former being more appropriate for the circumstances she had found herself in. She took one last look around her. She could see Mikael nearby, holding on to Cava through the tearing dust. Overhead, the creatures all seemed to be intent on her and her alone as they prepared to pounce at any moment.

Serepha, struck dumb with fear, began to run and reached at least forty miles per hour, as fast as her short legs would take her against the force of the winds in the unsheltered expanse. She glanced behind her for one second as she continued running desperately. The sound was deafening to her wolf like ears.

Terror possessed her as she saw one of the creatures of darkness glide effortlessly toward her. She howled in desperation at the sight of its dispassionate features, hollow eyes illuminated with a harsh, shining light striking her soul. With a choked cry, she fell to the ground.

The creature was then joined by others of its kind, clawing at her flesh. In her endeavor to tear away from the pain, she screamed, "Elyon, help me please!"

The cry of the dark creatures consumed her mind. The stench filled her throat. She lost consciousness.

After what seemed like a long lapse of time, a great silence and calm filled the vast, open land. Rusalka was the first to move. They lay on the ground among the earth and the debris that had been blown about during the gale. The winds and the creatures of hell had disappeared. Mikael, coughing and gasping, pushed himself to his feet. Cava still held on to him tightly, just in case the creatures returned. Ilk trembled under Gabriel's wing, not wishing to venture out. Roberto shook himself free of the dust. What the hell were they?

Rusalka held out her hand for Roberto to help her to her feet. "They, my dear Roberto, were only a figment of our imagination, put there by Leviathan to test our fear of him and our lack of faith in Elyon. They are called Villa, evil sprites of Leviathan. They could harm us only if we allow the fear to consume our minds. Then they become as real as you and I. Always remember that Elyon is more powerful than anyone in the universe. The problem lies within us and what we truly believe in our hearts. Have faith in Elyon and conquer all."

The wind had piled dust over Serepha. Her movement disturbed it. It filled her throat and mouth as she coughed and spluttered. She had returned to her humanlike form; her head throbbed painfully. But she was alive. Her first reaction was to remain where she was; she felt so weary. She pushed herself up from the ground and stood unsteadily in the open. She tried to clear her mind of the creatures, scared of their return. She searched all around her, catching sight of the others in the distance.

Grasping her sense of direction, she started walking straight toward them with an unsteady gait. Her eyes looked feverish, wild, and a little dazed. She hoped they had all survived. Her progress was slow. The uncertainty of her steps made her stagger repeatedly, but she kept on going.

"Look," said Gabriel. "It's Serepha walking toward us!"

Mikael speedily flew to Serepha's side. She fell heavily to the ground, sobbing uncontrollably. He picked her up and laid her gently by the side of Brabantia.

"What happened?" Gabriel asked.

Brabantia held her hand tightly. "Fetch some water! She can hardly talk, the poor thing."

Mikael went in search of water. When Serepha finally calmed down, she drank of the water, rubbing the heel of her palm against her head. She told of all that she had experienced before she lost consciousness.

Everyone listened intently, thankful that Serepha was still alive.

"It is because you allowed the fear to become larger than your faith, Serepha. Let this be a lesson to us all. It is a challenge you all face, and in an imperfect state, all will fall short. It is the grace of Elyon that preserved your life—proof that he loves you, for he knows that your heart is good but you will fall short at times. It is inevitable."

There was a pause; Serepha shook her head, looking down ashamedly. "I don't deserve it. My faith is but the size of a mustard seed compared to yours, Rusalka."

"You must never think that way. Elyon has granted me with perfection; it is easier for me than it is for you. Yet I can still fall; remember, your perfection is yet to be redeemed. Come, we must move on!"

The journey to the castle proved to be long and arduous. When they finally arrived at the Castle Syrtis, they were amazed at its sheer size. The entrance had the appearance of a monstrous face carved out of the drab, gray stone above the large opening below. As they entered the opening, the change of temperature and the fact that there were no guards present surprised them. Rusalka closed her eyes for a moment so as to adjust to the darkness. Brabantia instructed Serepha to stretch out her sword, which immediately burst into flames to light the way.

112

"They are amazing swords," said Roberto, astonished at the sudden outburst of fire.

Brabantia lifted her sword up to show Roberto the intricate detail of the weapon.

"These are the Flaming Swords of the Paristan, given to us many years ago by the Light Elvin in honor of our victories in the past against intruders from other realms who wished to destroy us and our planet. They have proved to be a blessing and great protection to us, with the power to scorch man and beast with fire. They cannot be used by any other. In the hands of anyone who is not of the Paristan, the sword becomes blunt and the flame of victory disappears."

The Flaming Swords were first forged by the great Carlita of the Paristan back in the ancient days during the reign of Queen Nebula. It was thought that Carlita had the power of foresight—for no such weapon was necessary during that period of tranquility.

Its blade was tapered, and its shaft was long, with the inscription Eulalia, meaning Victory. It was made of solid silver, with its handle heavily embellished with precious stones in strategic positioning for a comfortable grip, essential in battle.

"This way," Rusalka opened her eyes as she felt a connection with Celestial. The way became clear, but before they could go any farther, they saw in the distance two guards at a second entrance to the castle, tall and menacing.

"Prepare your sword, Serepha. They have not seen us yet, but they will if we move forward. It is better to attack from the side, where their vision is poor," cautioned Brabantia, directing them close to the cave walls in a single line.

With a swift movement of their swords, both Brabantia and Serepha leaped forward and ran out of the shadows toward the Xanthurus guards. Brabantia swiftly plunged her flaming sword directly in to the heart of her opponent before he had time to fight back. Clutching his chest, he fell with an almighty thud across the rocky floor beneath him. Blue blood seeped from his wound. Serepha struggled with the enormity of the other

Xanthurus and thrust her sword aimlessly. The guard struck her hard with his weapon, sending her reeling backward and falling to the ground. Brabantia immediately attacked from behind, chopping off the Xanthurus's tail in one fell swoop, leaving him unsteady as he turned toward her. Gabriel and Mikael jumped on the guard's back and held him still while Brabantia thrust her sword into his beating heart.

Their attention turned to Serepha, who was just gaining consciousness in the arms of Rusalka.

"Are you OK?" said Brabantia anxiously.

Serepha spoke quietly, a little dazed. "I am so sorry, Brabantia. I feel like I have let you down yet again."

Brabantia would have no such talk.

"Nonsense. You did your best. That is all that matters. We have each other so that when one is weak, the other is strong, and that is why two are always better than one."

Serepha was relieved at her words and stood up, ready to move on. "I am all right. Let us go on."

Deeper in the dungeons, Celestial had sensed Rusalka's presence and was waiting at the prison gates with Nebula and Cava by her side. She turned to the others in the dungeons, feeling responsible for their lost souls.

"You all have a chance of freedom this very day. When my savior comes to rescue me, you will have the opportunity to escape. To escape may seem a wonderful prospect to you, or it may seem hopeless because your lives are empty and full of despair. I say to you: call on the name of Elyon and repent of your treachery and ask for forgiveness. Pursue him, and you will be free. Tell this to all your people!"

Everyone cheered, some at the prospect of freedom, and others for the hope Celestial spoke of. Some fell at her feet, bowing down as though she were a god.

Celestial helped them to their feet. "You must not bow to me. I am only Elyon's messenger. Bow to Elyon, the Almighty One."

A voice rose from the shadow. "Traitor! You speak blasphemous words punishable by death. Do not listen to this little vixen. She speaks lies."

"Who are you to speak against the word of Elyon?" said Celestial. "Show yourself!"

The Xanthurus had been lying low in the darkness so that no one would recognize him—he was in fear of his life among the Draconians and others who despised his type.

"I am Rastus, once a guard of Dracon's at the Fortress of Deimos."

Everyone turned to look at the large stature of Rastus as he stepped out of the shadows. Celestial took a step toward him, unafraid.

"No! Celestial, he is dangerous. Do not speak to him," whispered Cava urgently.

"Why is it you are here if your allegiance is with Dracon? Forgive me if I do not understand." Celestial moved closer slowly as she spoke.

"I did not say my loyalty is with Dracon. My allegiance lies with someone much more powerful than he," said Rastus calmly.

"And who might that be, and why are you here if that is so?" Celestial knew the answer but wanted to hear it from his own lips.

"Leviathan, the ruler of our world...and finally the ruler of all worlds. Dracon is a mere pawn in his battle to rule the universe," said Rastus with conviction.

Celestial moved closer fearlessly. "I tell you now, Rastus, you have got it all wrong. You have been misled by the master of lies and deceit. It is Elyon who will take back what has always belonged to him, and he will put an end to all the wickedness and evil that exists through Leviathan."

Celestial stood firm as Rastus pointed his large clawed finger in her face.

"You had better be careful of what you speak. Leviathan will find you and destroy you. He will persecute and taunt you till you succumb to his will. Out of my way...insignificant one."

Celestial continued bravely. "My lord is stronger than your lord. You do not frighten me. Where is your so mighty lord when

115

you need him? I will be set free today. Will your god set you free, or will he let you burn in the inferno as befits your sin? Think about it, Rastus! Today you are being given a chance, but you choose death."

Rastus uttered words under his breath and walked back into the shadows. The others had kept silent, wondering if he would attack and kill Celestial, as his nature would imply. They were taken aback when he retreated, defeated, back into the shadows.

Rusalka ran up to the gates and placed her hand through the bars to hold Celestial's hand.

"Rusalka!" shouted Celestial joyfully. "It is so good to see you. I know the dangers you must have faced to come all this way. I do love you, my sister. I knew you would come."

"You know I would do anything for my queen, for why would I not love my sister more than myself?" said Rusalka, pleased to see that Celestial had been unharmed.

"Here! I have the keys to your freedom; we must get out of here before we are seen by the rest of the Xanthurus army."

Cava could not understand their unnecessary words of devotion at such a time of urgent action. She sighed in exasperation. Rusalka unlocked the gates. Everyone filtered out one by one.

Then a bright voice said, "What are we to do now? We don't know where to go!"

Celestial thought for a moment, knowing she couldn't take everyone with her. "What is your name, young man?"

"Marsala."

Celestial looked at him. His face was bright, young, and fearless; his eyes fervent and keen; and his voice full of hope. "Well, Marsala, you must lead these people to safety and tell others of your experience and how you escaped the tyranny of Dracon. Brabantia will point you in the right direction, and you must ask Elyon to guide your every step. Do you think you can do that? If you are sincere, you will lead these people to a better world. Elyon be with you."

"Thank you. I am honored to be such a vessel," he said, bowing down before her. To him, she was a source of solace amid the gloom of affliction.

"We will be back. Gather as many people as you can, and we will take the throne of Dracon. Your people must not suffer anymore. Go, my friend."

Brabantia gathered them together to show them which way to escape safely.

Rastus had fled the moment the gates were opened. Celestial believed he would not tell of their escape, for he feared for his own life—she knew he was a coward underneath.

Celestial turned to Rusalka and the others. "'Greetings' we meet again, Lord Bellucci. I see that you decided to stay. I am pleased you did."

"Yes, I thought it was the right thing, and now I am sure," said Roberto sincerely.

"I cannot leave without Shimm-rae." Celestial felt as though her right hand were missing.

"Come. We will find her," said Rusalka urgently as she closed her eyes once again to search out where Shimm-rae was being held captive.

Celestial introduced them to Cava and Nebula. Rusalka was ecstatic by the grace of Elyon to find that Nebula was still alive.

They crept quietly in the dark recesses of the castle as they followed Rusalka in single file. She led them to a small cavern. As they entered the dark hole, a Xanthurus creature leaped out of the darkness and in one fluid motion drew his weapon from underneath his cloak and raised his arm as he moved toward Roberto.

Roberto reacted instinctively. He lurched forward to attack the Xanthurus head on, not aware of the rough stone beneath his feet. Tripping over the stone, he dropped his club. Before the weapon could reach him, Gabriel snatched up the club and struck the Xanthurus's arm with it. In a shower of white sparks, the weapon lit up as though lightning had struck. The Xanthurus was flung as if blasted away by an explosion. The force of the hit vibrated through Gabriel's hand to his elbow, rendering his arm

117

temporarily paralyzed. The club slid from his hands to the ground. Roberto gazed in wonder, thinking, how?

How was that possible?

He looked at the Xanthurus's large, crumpled form. Raising himself off the ground, he picked up the club suspiciously. Pins and needles rushed through his fingers as he slowly surveyed the club. There did not seem to be anything out of the ordinary about it, but Brabantia reassured him that things are not always what they seem, and an ordinary thing can be adequate protection in the right hands. Wow! He could see what she meant.

As he gripped it hard, he glared around to see if any other menacing creature was approaching, wondering if the weapon would have such tremendous power for him too. All seemed clear for the moment, thankfully.

Roberto tried to lift the weapon the Xanthurus had dropped. "This may come in handy."

Brabantia helped him as he was struggling to hoist it. "It will be useful with those lethal spikes," she said as she surveyed the iron sphere hanging on a large, heavy chain. "Although I think Mikael should carry it. It is far too heavy for you to carry, Bellucci."

Mikael grasped the weapon from Roberto's laden arms as though it were a light weight.

"Yes, somehow I think it is a good thing that you are carrying it, Mikael. Jolly decent of you," Roberto said laughing.

Rusalka noticed a box made of calcite on top of a large rock formation in the middle of the cavern. "That is where Shimm-rae has been kept captive."

Celestial quickly opened the box. She was heavily disappointed to find Shimm-rae was no longer there. "We must find her, I cannot leave without her. There is only one consolation so far. Leviathan would not touch her, for he knows that the minute he touches someone so pure, his very hands of evil would melt before his eyes. So it is more likely that Dracon has her under the control of Leviathan. I need to speak directly to Elyon, but I'm sure it is not possible in this godforsaken place. Oh, Lord of Hosts,

118

King of Kings, please help me find Shimm-rae," pleaded Celestial heartily.

At that moment, a loud rumbling noise descended upon them as an orb of white light shone from the calcite box, blinding them for a split second. Everyone shielded their eyes except Celestial, who was drawn to open the box once again.

This time the box was not empty. She retrieved a piece of parchment that was inscribed with a map of the Syrtis Region of Mars. They all looked closely at the map. Rusalka pointed out that the shining star at the far left of the parchment could be the place where Shimm-rae was imprisoned.

Celestial agreed. "Yes. More than likely, for it is Elyon who has given us this papyrus of hope. Brabantia, do you know where this place is?"

Brabantia studied the parchment closely. "That is the Forgotten Caves of Syrtis. It is at least in this region—but it is inhabited by the Naga, known to squeeze the life out of their prey. The Peryton once lived there, but it is said their ravenous taste for flesh led them to pastures new, leaving room for the Naga to dwell."

The Naga were a race of supernatural beings with both snake and human attributes. In the distant past, the Naga was a very vast army that conquered numerous realms in the InterWorlds. They served a ruler now extinct, named Viperasp—a powerful snake-man. They dwelt in the southeast region of Gaspra, named after the first moon of Mars, a desolate geological region.

When the Draconians finally conquered them, their empire collapsed, and only a small number of the Naga remained. They were cast adrift by Sartorious of the Xanthurus and settled in the polar regions of Syrtis, where they found the Draconian treasures collected through the ages.

It was known that they did not desire to destroy the pure in heart, for the effects of such an undeserved death resulted in their transformation into the lowly position of fully serpentine under the dominium of the superior hybrid Naga.

Brabantia had heard things about these caves, and she wasn't so sure she should tell of such tales.

"No one dares venture into these caves, for there is talk of a most unusual ecosystem populated with invertebrates that have adapted to their underground prison over many moons."

Roberto suddenly became excited. "I have seen written reviews of such a process called troglomorphy." He was impressed with Brabantia's knowledge of scientific things.

"I do not know its correct term, but they have lost pigmentation, learned to navigate blind, and survive on bacteria and fungi that derive energy from the sulfide hot springs beneath the surface. The vast majority are anthropods belonging to the classes of arachnida, crustacea, myriapoda, and insect," said Brabantia.

Ilk was becoming quite concerned as he listened intently. "Are they a threat to us in any way, Brabantia?"

Brabantia realized she had probably said too much and tried to reassure him. "I doubt it, Ilk. Some say they are, but I look at it this way: they seem to live in harmony with the Naga."

Ilk was not convinced. "That's not saying much, though, is it? After all, they may be in league with the Naga, and they aren't exactly going to like us, are they now? We will be intruding upon their territory, and they aren't going to like that, are they? Anyways, I don't feel sure we should go right now. Maybe we should go back to Venus and return with more help." He fluttered his wings in readiness to take off home.

"Calm down, Ilk," said Celestial, patting his red curls. "We must go now to the Forgotten Caves. You know I cannot leave Shimm-rae. Think if it were you who had been captured. You wouldn't want us to leave you in such a place, would you? What is one of the great lessons you have learned from the Sacred Scrolls, Ilk?"

"Yes, I know, I know, Your Majesty. We must do to others as we would like them to do to us, and then we can't go wrong," said Ilk rapidly. "But it is difficult at times like these, don't you think? I don't mean to sound selfish. It's just that I am afraid. Look at me! I can't stop trembling; I am afraid of my own shadow. Oh dear, I am sorry, I'm sorry, I am not much use, am I?" he said as he began to sob.

Cava spoke harshly to him. "For crying out loud, don't be such a wimp. You are wasting our time. I just want to get this Shimm-rae and get out of here before Dracon catches up with us. So shut up!"

Celestial put her arm around him to comfort him. "Do not be anxious for anything, Ilk. Trust in Elyon."

And thus Brabantia led the way to the Forgotten Caves of Syrtis.

Chapter 8

The Kingdom Of Semiramis

Venus...

Meanwhile, back on the planet Venus, Astoria gazed into the Silver Vessel of Truth in the castle of Alvor. Patience grasped her arm. "Can you see anything, Astoria? Can you see Papa?"

"Look into the vessel yourself, Patience." Astoria grabbed hold of Patience's hands and placed them around the silver vessel. "What do you see, my child?"

"What? I can't see. You know that, Astoria."

"Then look with your mind's eye. You already have the gift of sight, moments of...synchronicity...connections with others...messages of increased awareness that very few humans possess."

"No, I can't see anything...no...wait...yes...yes, I can see a tiny fairy....she seems to be...in some sort of cave. Yes...she is being held prisoner in a huge shell there. Would that...could that be Shimm-rae? I think it is...that means that they have not yet rescued her, doesn't it? I wonder if they have rescued Celestial. I can see everything so vividly...she is so tiny and perfect...wait...I can see something else approaching...oh my God...I am not sure how to describe it...some sort of ugly-looking creature. Poor Shimm-rae...do...do you think they will harm her?"

Astoria was quick to reassure her. "I doubt very much that they would harm her. She will be of use to Dracon. He will want her alive in the hope of finding the Key of Dreams or taking over

Celestial's powers through her. No, for certain, she is too precious to destroy."

Patience bent down to stroke Wishbone. Licking her hand, he could feel her anxiety as she spoke. "I hope they are all right. I am so worried about my father, Astoria. I feel like I have got him as part of my life for the first time. I don't want to lose him again. I have already lost my mother. I never knew her, you know."

Astoria looked at Patience with new eyes, feeling her vulnerability acutely. "He is in good hands, little one. Try not to worry; it is a waste of energy. It is much better to hope and bring positivism into your life. Many things become self-fulfilling prophecies if we allow them to. Come; let us do something to divert your mind. I have to deliver a message to the Underworld of the Semiramis." Astoria grabbed hold of Patience's hand. "I will take you with me. It will keep your mind occupied."

"Where is that?" Patience suddenly felt her spirit lifted.

"It's in the northeast region at the coast of Samosata, east of the forest of Alvor. It is a deep and curious ocean inhabited by the merfolk the Oceanids and other aquatic creatures who have built a kingdom deep, deep in the bowels of the ocean."

"Oh, yes. Rusalka spoke of such a place."

"Yes, you listen well, little one. It's just farther north past Castra and beyond the Cau-Cas mountains. I think you will be mesmerized by the Semiramis Choir—it is the most beautiful sound ever to be heard. I know you like music, Patience. The mermen and the mermaids both have beautiful voices that complement one another in a chorus of sweet harmony, and the mermaids have long, flowing hair and iridescent fish tails that glitter in the aqua-green salt water. The merfolk have built a gleaming golden palace with many chambers to swim through and many delights to feast the senses upon. It is a place where imagination has no foothold. Come, let us prepare for the journey."

"It sounds too good to be true. I would love to go, but of what use is it to me when I can't see these wonders? I'm sorry, Astoria, but you would not understand. Life sucks for us humans sometimes—well, actually, most of the time, unless I am playing my piano," said Patience glumly.

"You are wrong, my dear child. I do understand more than you know; however, I think the sounds and the feeling you will get will far surpass the sense you're devoid of. You will see."

Astoria left Wishbone with the king and queen at the palace after giving the man explanation of her intentions regarding Patience. Off they went in earnest to experience the delights of the Semiramis' deep-blue ocean with a secret she did not want to reveal to Patience at this time. They made their way to the wild and untamed shoreline, where nature knows no boundaries and beauty knows no limits. Majestic mountains surrounded the shore, where rugged ramparts and spires of jagged rocks had endured the extreme elements throughout time, the cliffs rising to the heavens. The great ocean stretched for miles before them, mysterious and inviting. Imbued with serenity, they stood balancing precariously on the edge of a cliff.

Patience could feel the expanse of the drop. "Is it a long drop, Astoria? I could not possibly dive from here, and I cannot go down deep under the water for very long. We humans cannot breathe underwater. You do know that, don't you?" said Patience with a touch of hysteria in her voice.

"Trust me, Patience. This is where you need to practice great faith. Hold my hand, and we will jump together. Listen carefully. At first, when you enter the water, you will struggle against it; you will think you are drowning. Try not to struggle—if you do not fear, you will adapt quicker to your new surroundings. Are you ready?" Astoria grabbed hold of Patience's hand firmly, not giving her time to think about the leap she was about to take.

Patience braced herself as Astoria pulled her over the cliff edge. She fell through the air as though she could fly...down, down...it seemed forever. Then she entered the water and instinctively let go of Astoria's hand to struggle to the surface. Astoria grabbed hold of her hand once again, pulling her down, farther and farther. Her eyes bulged till she thought they were going to come out of their sockets. She kicked and struggled as

Astoria held on to her tightly. Her terror-stricken features were vivid, the horror clear in her eyes. She suddenly remembered what Astoria had told her to do and tried not to struggle. At the point when she thought she may have even died, she looked at the lower half of Astoria's body and saw that she had acquired a beautiful tail like that of a mermaid. She pointed at Astoria's tail excitedly.

"You can speak now that you have adapted, Patience. Yes, the tail is beautiful. Take a look at your own tail. It is shining all the colors of the rainbow." Astoria pointed in the direction of what should have been her legs.

Patience was ecstatic to see such a transformation for herself. She soon forgot her fear. She could not believe her eyes. Yes, her eyes...why...she could see...see everything. She was not exactly sure if it was her mind's eye, a dream...or what it was...but she liked it. She was a mermaid and wanted to explore the treasures of the deep. Am I dead or dreaming?

"Did I not tell you that you would see?" Astoria smiled.

Patience could hardly speak; she was so filled with great emotion and excitement. The colors of the ocean and its creatures were something to behold—the greens, the blues, aqua and turquoise, indigo, and all shades of red. They swam deeper and deeper into the depths of the ocean. She did not know what to feast her eyes upon first. Everything was so beautiful to behold; her eyes were pools of wonder and delight. She moved in to a shoal of tiny fish, electric blue with a dash of green and yellow, their impact soft as snowflakes. Patience loved the feeling of weightlessness in the infinite, liquid space all around her. She drifted into a seascape of ultimate beauty, a steeply sloping seafloor in an orchard of white, soft coral trees. A peculiar-looking creature with bright-emerald-green eyes slowly swam toward her through the sea-weed, then disappeared down the shelf below. She could hear the most melodious sound she had ever heard gliding through the water, streams of harmonized overtures singing to the movement of the sea. She slipped down into the cooler depths at the sight of an oversized pearl shell.

Buffeted from all directions by a mass of sea creatures swimming in one direction, she turned in the water, flapping her arms, trying to stabilize herself amid the rising currents caused by the swift movement. A slight panic ran through her until the waters became still once again and she could see Astoria swimming slowly ahead.

There were so many things to see. Her eyes were wide open with wonder, and she twisted and turned in every direction, afraid of missing something she would most likely never get another chance to see. They swam even deeper into the ocean, and she saw mermaids lazily relaxing on the surface of some rocks, swishing their magnificent tails back and forth, surrounded by the countless colors of the corals and sea urchins while green-and-blue sea grasses swayed backward and forward in the undulating waters of the deep.

Patience thought of the tales she had heard of mermaids back on Earth, and she felt a little apprehensive of the creatures around her. Astoria read her mind. "The Venusian mermaids of Semiramis are different in nature from others of their species. I know that in other realms, they are capable of luring sailors to their death or squeezing life out of drowning men while giving the illusion of trying to rescue them. Here they have typical Venusian natures and are called Aycayia, pronounced Aye-cay-eea, meaning she of the beautiful voice. As you can see, they live in these deep waters in a beautiful underworld of a rainbow of colors and unusual shapes. They share this world with many other underwater creatures and are ruled by their princess, Shakira, meaning woman of grace."

They swam past two mermaids, one embracing the tail of the other, leaving their tails entwined below; their hair silken strands of fire swirling around their shoulders, their skin white and gleaming. They looked at Patience with curiosity and smiled shyly at her, gesturing with lovely, graceful hands.

The mermaids all had long, flowing hair of various colors and tails that complemented the color of their jewel-like eyes. Patience noticed her own hair had escaped, floating in the water as she swam through the golden algae and silver sea grasses. She felt a surge of joy at the experience and felt free of constraints and boundaries.

Some of the mermaids looked a little different from the majority and seemed more intent on the pursuits of the ocean than the leisure activities of the others. They passed by swiftly, without so much as a glance, transported on some sort of golden transport surrounded by dolphins, all set for some destination of purpose.

"Where are they going, Astoria?"

"They are the Oceanid nymphs; their essence is with the saltwater and its purification. Unlike other mermaids, they have the ability to change into human form and walk on dry land. Their preference is to be here in the deep ocean keeping everything in order and taking care of the environment, which is getting increasingly difficult as the pollution from the north vicinity creeps ever nearer. The deeper recesses have already been infiltrated with some unknown creatures that have adapted to the eerie world where no sunlight can penetrate—the abyss of the ocean."Astoria shivered at the prospect of ever going any deeper than this world she knew of.

She continued to educate Patience of the strangeness and beauty of this new world. "It is said that those who eat of the flesh of a mermaid will become immortal. In truth, this never happens. When eaten they either die or become horrible monsters of the sea. Like nymphs, the merfolk expect their world to be respected as they would respect other worlds."

"Papa has always taught me the same. He has always cared for the Earth, even as a boy, and always wanted to be a scientist. I was jealous of his work because he had no time for me, but I can see now why it was so important to him." Patience felt she had matured so much in a short space of time.

"That is good, Patience. I am sure you will follow in your father's footsteps and teach other humans about the need to care for their planet much more than they are doing now. You know, the merfolk respect the realm of Celestial and would do anything in their power to support it, knowing she serves Elyon, but they can be very jealous of their sea. Legally, the sea belongs to no one, but the merpeople take claim to it and have fought for it for centuries. Celestial does not interfere in their quest of ownership as long as the balance of nature is kept there, and that is what the merfolk do—they take care of the ocean. They are aware of the coming destruction because of the effects of the swarms sent by Dracon and can only hope that Celestial will find a way of saving them and the planet Venus from the hands of the evil ones. The mermen are the consorts of the mermaids; usually having fishtails from the waist down while underwater. But they have the ability to transform on dry land. The actions of mermen in different worlds have always been known to vary wildly, depending on their source and period of existence. The Venusian mermen are ruled by the princess Shakira and are well known for their wise teachings and benevolent nature unless they are crossed in any way. Venus has always been predominantly female ruled, in contrast to Mars."

Patience noticed the mermen. They were not as colorful, possessing green, seaweed-like hair and beards. They blended in with the aqua-blue-green shades of the sea and had the full form of a very large male human being with a tail instead of legs. They passed one holding a conch shell in his mighty hands. He blew into the shell, which emitted a smooth trumpeting sound.

"The mermen are the trumpeters of the sea and use different sounds to suit the purpose of their call," explained Astoria. "I don't know the meaning of them all. I do know the call of the gathering of the Semiramis choir; it's definitely not that. Everyone seems to be swimming toward the Golden Palace. Come; we will follow. I have a message to deliver to the palace."

Just has she had spoken, an iridescent, octopus-like creature passed by, curling its many tentacles. Its numerous beady eyes looked at them and then ballooned away. Patience was mesmerized by its colors and delicate movements. Astoria grabbed her hand once again and pulled her along with the rest of the aquatic creatures. The sight of the merfolk all swimming in one direction created a spectrum of shimmering iridescent color.

The Golden Palace was impressive. The Oceanids passed in golden chariots, the nymphs all shades of autumn—browns, bronzes, and gold's, with golden globes of light surrounding them like photophores as the dolphins swam obediently by their side.

They passed through many chambers filled with beautiful swirls of fish of the sea—many colors and shapes never seen by the human eye. Some surrounded Patience inquisitively and swam alongside her. The corals and the reefs also were all shapes and colors, a diver's paradise.

They entered a great chamber teeming with merfolk and other aquatic creatures. Clumps of colors gleamed like jewels. The prince and princess sat on huge, ornate thrones made of solid gold. Astoria whispered into Patience's ear, "There is Princess Shakira, and Prince Ovid, who rules by her side, helping to keep peace and harmony in their underwater world of the curious deep."

Princess Shakira spoke first. "Salu sankrat salu Astoria." (Welcome to our kingdom.)

"Salen kar salsoor sinsay?" (What brings you to visit us this day?)

Astoria replied in the Ramis language, the language of the merfolk. "Satu si cara sin cavor sa kin orvo—Celestial cor sinta calvora ee sun Draconians ka say songa cor sinta kinka salow ee so sanson kara Leviathan. Rusalka ka sansons su kantara kar saltana songa suk see spake."

She leaned toward Patience. "They speak the language of the merfolk—they know no other. They have welcomed us, and I have explained our situation on land."

Shakira gasped in horror. "Kanga si sukha cava! See seer Rusalka saltanas dey cray sun sara ko kanga questo krast. Kis satu si carona see khan sok systeme kit ken co." (That is not good. We hope Rusalka rescues her from the hands of that despicable creature of darkness. If there is anything we can do, please let us know.)

Astoria reassured them that she would not hesitate to ask for

129

their help if necessary and would let them know as soon as possible of Celestial's rescue. "Tris si Patience cray Planta Earth ka say saska si seco Rusalka." (This is Patience from Earth; her father is on a quest to find Celestial with Rusalka.)

Shakira told them about their meeting of the turning of the tide, held at regular intervals to discuss up-and-coming venues for the kingdom. "Kola kay cray kis kola sway soar Astoria sans sealy kola sun cestras ko sun sinka sa Samasaris." (We will discuss this matter with my council. You may stay if you wish, or you can show the Earth girl the treasures of the deep in the Golden Chamber of Samota.)

Astoria brought Patience quietly back to reality, touching her on her shoulder gently. She interpreted the words of Shakira. Patience's mind had wandered while they were in conversation. She was mesmerized by Shakira and her velvety royal-blue tail. Her bustier was a matching blue too—identical to her large sapphire eyes, which complemented her flaming auburn hair. She had a delicate lacework tattoo across her forehead and dark-blue ribbons hanging from her luscious locks, interspersed with tiny freshwater pearls. A tiara of pearls rested on her head. Patience thought how striking she looked against the backdrop of the aqua blues and greens.

"Oh, yes...yes, I would love to see the treasures of the deep, if it's all right with you...umm...Your Majesty!"

The princess began her speech as Astoria and Patience swam out toward the nearest exit of the vast chamber. The merfolk smiled at them as they passed by.

A golden-haired mermaid swam over to Patience and greeted her in Ramis, holding out her arms to embrace her. It felt quite strange to Patience to be hugging a complete stranger, not to mention a mermaid. She had not believed such creatures existed before her amazing journey on the planet Venus.

They swam through many more chambers before they arrived at a cave as large as the grand one they had just left. There were many compartments, and a fountain of cascading gold liquid stood in the center of the cavern. Patience rushed forward to touch the golden liquid.

Astoria shouted, panic stricken, "Do not touch, Patience!" She pulled Patience away from the fountain. "I forgot about the fountain. It will turn your hand to gold if you touch the liquid. It was put there as a reminder that you have to be careful about the unknown—all that glitters is not gold, at least not the gold everyone seems to yearn for. What good is gold if you are a statue?"

Astoria felt relieved that she had remembered in time to save Patience, for she herself did not have the power to free her from such a curse.

"I must warn you that all the treasures of the deep are carefully guarded by the Oceanids—but most of them will be at the meeting this day."

No sooner had she spoken than two Oceanids swam toward them at great speed.

Astoria reassured them that Shakira knew of their presence and informed them of her relationship with Celestial from above. They had heard all about the prophetess, so they smiled and swam away as fast as they had come without saying a word.

"Can the Oceanids speak?" asked Patience.

"No, they do not have the power of the spoken word, but they do have other powers that we do not possess, so you don't need to pity them. They wouldn't want you to feel sorry for them; they feel very privileged to be the sustainers of their environment."

Patience could understand them; after all, she felt the same way when she could not see. She appreciated the gift for music she had been given, but it was lonely being blind, and now she could see she wanted to see forever. "Do you think I will see back on land now? Or is this my mind's eye, as you said?"

Astoria genuinely did not know. "I am sorry, my child. That much has not been revealed to me. I do hope so."

They looked at some of the treasures they encountered as they swam farther through the cavern. It was the most beautiful in the universe, a collection of gold and silver and precious stones, diamonds of all types, more numerous than the stars. She was stunned at the treasures but did not dare touch anything in case she was turned into gold or silver—or anything inanimate, for that matter.

They left at the back exit to the Golden Kingdom and began the journey toward the surface of the ocean. They hadn't gotten far when a troop of mermen stopped them in their tracks. They looked positively angry, and Astoria could not understand why they had followed them.

"Kar si Astoria, si kar sorel?" The leader of the mermen said.

(It is Astoria, is it not?)

"Sa," said Astoria with a puzzled expression. (Yes.)

"See solay corlo kola sul kar sun solder sarray." (We will escort you back to the Golden Palace.)

"Soroy? Si tris sertray? See sora kar saga senta, sun Kinka ka Sinsa ko Alvor surretti oor," said Astoria anxiously.

(Why? Is this necessary? We need to go home. The king and queen of Alvor await our return.)

Patience could not understand what was being said, but she could detect the anxiety in Astoria's voice and body language. She felt scared. "What is it, Astoria? Are you all right? You look worried. What do they want from us?"

Astoria continued to question the mermen insistently. "Salen si kar? Soroy sok see sora kar colar, sesta selt oor?" (What is it? Why do we need to return? Please tell us!)

"KOLA SOLAYSE!" said the merman impatiently as he clasped them in thick golden chains. (You will see!)

As they dragged them back toward the palace, Astoria pleaded with the mermen, telling them that there must be some sort of mistake and the palace would verify it and let them leave peacefully.

The mermen were not concerned with their pleas and took no notice, leading them back to the palace—this time to the dungeons.

Patience was afraid...very afraid!

∞

Chapter 9

The Manticore's Feed

Among the leonine race was a creature so terrible on the one hand yet piteous on the other. A great appetite characterized this beast. No hunter was safe from the poisoned barbs of its tail or its triple row of iron teeth.

The Forest of Asan...

The full moon was clear-edged and pure against the deep, dark sky. Blood! The scent of it hung heavily in the air. The manticore's nostrils flared, and a jumble of scents fluttered through his brain leading to the smell of bleeding flesh. His belly groaned with a painful, gnawing hunger. The kill was recent and the meat was still warm—the deep crimson blood had not yet dried. Surging forward, the manticore plunged into the thick, twisted branches. He wove in and out of the dark undergrowth, moving silently and freely in the blue light of dusk. It was as if the plants and trees made way for him, the king of the forest.

The manticore burst into the clearing and came to a sliding halt. His thick black claws made deep tracks in the soft earth. He cautiously approached his feed, which bathed in the pale moonlight as he checked the many scents in the air to make sure no one else had been there and then moved toward his feed, licking his lips with anticipation.

The massive head lowered, and a black-as-coal tongue flicked out and lapped up the crimson liquid. The iron taste was welcomed by the manticore's hunger, which consumed his very being. With less caution, the great jaws opened wide, revealing his iron teeth; he began to tear open the flesh. The life of the kill still clung to the meat. Hungrily, the manticore devoured his meal until the excruciating pain of hunger left his living being. The dark beast loomed above with a shadow of despair attached to his long-lost soul. He hated himself and his very existence! His angry sorrows howled across the thick dark forest.

When he had finished, he found a stream and drank heartily—washing the innocent blood from his jaws. The powerful head jerked suddenly up, and nostrils flared wide to catch the prevailing scent. A different scent than any he had experienced before pervaded the air—a youthful, light composition that was enchanting. The thought of an unknown creature excited him. He lifted his head, sniffing the air once again, and then bristled, pulling his lips back in a drawn-out, menacing growl. It echoed through the forest and soared to the raven sky.

Unsure of what to do, he was not ready for another kill; he made sure he kept out of sight from the creatures while he stalked them, stiffed legged and tall, his ears erect, hackles bristled slightly. Taking advantage of the trees and the bushes, he moved swiftly yet silently.

Within minutes, he was in visual range of them. His eyes came into sharp focus and saw the aura surrounding Celestial—shining a bright, illuminating light. Her intense perfume exuded a haunting, exotic scent that wove an intoxicating spell over him. At that moment, the others paled into insignificance. Intrigued, he continued to watch.

Rusalka felt his presence. "Sh…sh…someone or something is nearby, watching our every move." She closed her eyes as the others stared at her, waiting for her to enlighten them. "I sense a great beast of the forest watching…waiting…hungering for blood." Her voice betrayed her fear.

"The last encounter with one of the beasts of this forest was

134

enough for me. I still have pain in my chest where the dart entered, and I hadn't even seen the damned thing." Roberto rubbed his chest frantically as he spoke.

Rusalka caught the manticore's scent—inky, musky, with a hint of death. "He is very near," she said, listening carefully, her Elvin ears stood upright.

Ilk blanched, hiding under Celestial's wings and trembling yet again.

"What are we to do? Do we stand a chance in combat with such a ferocious creature?" Roberto's words fell swiftly out in panic.

"Oh, that I had wings of an eagle instead of these useless little wings. I could fly away as fast as possible. Fearfulness and the terrors of death have come upon us," moaned Ilk.

"We must always believe in the power that we have been given," whispered Celestial. "Cast your fears away; you will be sustained. Take heart, for it is written: courage can be sought by all creatures, great and small."

"Let us not antagonize it," cut in Brabantia. "As Roberto said, we have already experienced the spikes on its tail, which can be hurled like an archer's arrow at more distant enemies, and he can kill instantly with one bite, eating the victim entirely, bones and all."

Ilk moaned again. "Spare us the details, Brabantia. Let us get some distance without him knowing our whereabouts. That seems a good idea to me. After all, he may be looking for someone else, not us. We don't know what he is thinking."

"Rusalka...disguise our scent?" Celestial requested as Brabantia showed them the way.

"I will do my utmost. There is one consolation. At least he has just satisfied his hunger, for I can smell the scent of blood and open flesh," said Rusalka, closing her eyes in silence.

Meanwhile, the manticore continued observing them as Rusalka's eyes were closed. The woman in white gave an aura of supreme serenity. She spread her angelic wings and wrapped them around her companions, engulfing them, their auras drowned in the sheer perfection of hers.

135

He stayed crouched down; his muscles tensed apprehensively. His chest tightened in loneliness so deep and so complete he could not breathe. The thrum of energy suffused by Celestial confused him. His instinct was to attack and devour, but he felt immobilized. He was filled with rage as the creatures disappeared into the darkness; he had not taken his chance to experience the flesh of something so rare. He would have to hunt them down. His nostrils flared one more time, but try as he must, he could only pick up the scents of his usual feed.

The manticore was enraged. He could not understand the mixed emotions stirring his soul. He pounded his large, claw-like feet on the ground and walked in circles, wondering which way they had gone.

It took hours to find them. They were sitting by a creek, deliberating about something.

Celestial was the first to recognize his presence this time. "Do not be afraid by what I am about to do. Have total trust, and your eyes will be opened. I have seen into the soul of the manticore that follows our trail...trust me!" She knelt down, facing the thick grove of tall trees and bushes that the manticore was stationed behind.

"We don't stand a chance against the manticore. I don't know of anyone who has escaped its attack before. Our only chance is for you to do your stuff and allow it to lose our scent and scarper, if you ask me, but I've a feeling you won't listen to me anyway." Cava sighed heavily.

Ilk backed up Cava. "Of course we will listen to you. You know this creature better than we do. Isn't that so, Your Majesty?" said Ilk speedily, trying to be brave but feeling very unsure.

Celestial moved closer in silence to the dark, dense bushes. The others watched nervously. Ilk felt as though his little heart was going to jump out of his chest.

Then she did a strange thing: she spoke words to the beast. "Come...come, you need not be afraid. You will not harm me...I know you are afraid of your own instincts, but you can control them. It is a lonely, desolate life you live. I can help you...come to me," said Celestial as she raised her eyes to the heavens in supplication. *"Great maker and spirit of my life, a great warrior stands before you seeking your place of refuge and peace."*

Shocked not only by her words but the sincerity of them and the kindness and the warmth she exuded, the manticore moved out from behind the nearby bushes slowly and gracefully. *Everyone is afraid of my barbaric nature, but she is not,* he thought, puzzled.

He approached her hesitantly, his large, clawed feet heavily hitting the ground one step at a time. A soft growling noise escaped his lips. His nostrils flared once more, taking in the exotic scent of the creature before him, his huge shape looming terrifyingly near. The others drew back in fear as the beast bared its teeth and snarled, tendrils of saliva dripping from its mouth and soaking into its huge paws, with sharp nails digging into the dirt as it took an aggressive stance. Suddenly, the manticore was engulfed in the pure light of her power. His eyes scanned Celestial's face, moving from her unique silver eyes to her mouth, over her hair, and back to her eyes again.

There was a pause, and then, to the utter amazement of the others, who watched in awe, the manticore's form dissolved, no longer solid. For a split second, he was scattered particles contained in the atmosphere. A thrill of panic went through him as he suspected he had ceased to exist. Then he realized he was solid again, a cloud of white-hot light surrounding him. He stood almost naked. A spreading canopy of white-feathered wings—silken, shimmering—began to unfurl from his back and shoulders, rising to meet above his head.

The others looked at him, bewildered and shocked by what they saw. He stared back at them in the same fashion. He had changed form, no longer the vile creature he so hated.

"Welcome to our world," said Mikael, breaking the silence. "You have been favored by Elyon and have become an angel, the same as us my brother."

He fell down on his knees before Celestial. "I am your servant. Where you go, I go. I will follow you and protect you all the days of your life. You have set me free—I hated who I was, and death was my very existence, my essence, and I was in bondage to it. Leviathan had me in his grip, and I choose to be in yours so that you can lead me in to a new way of being. You showed pity on my treachery and my abhorrent nature and gave me kindness and understanding. I am forever in your debt."He fell to his knees in adoration of such a beautiful creature.

"It is not I you are indebted to, as you will learn. I too am indebted to a higher power that works with you, and He could see deep into your soul and know the state of your heart that your actions belied. It is Elyon who has saved your soul and showed you His great mercy." Celestial spoke as she rose from her knees, humbly. Gabriel helped her to her feet. She continued, "you will be in his presence one day. It is He you must learn about and walk with for eternity."

Ilk flew by the angel's side, fluttering his wings in front of him. "Wow...wee...I am so glad to have you on our side. For a moment there, I thought we were meat—good meat, mind, but phew, you gave us quite a fright. Anyways, my name's Ilk, by the way. Everyone thinks I waffle, but, you see, they don't understand." Ilk fluttered up and down and around him, ready to give his life story, when Celestial fell to the ground with exhaustion, for her power was weak. Nebula came to her side immediately, gently laying her down to sleep in her arms while they rested for the night moon. Even Ilk fell asleep with exhaustion, cuddled up closely to Celestial and Nebula.

The evening air was crisp with dew as the yellow sun, now tinged with orange, was setting in the west behind the snow-capped mountains. In the east, storm clouds were gathering rapidly. Flashes of lightning could be seen off in the distance as low rumbles of thunder gently rolled across the sky.

"I have never heard this rumbling sound before. What is it?" Ilk didn't like the sound of it anymore than he liked the unfriendliness of the forest of Asan.

"It is called thunder," said Brabantia. "It is unusual for Mars to experience such weather at this eon of time; the weather patterns are changing everywhere of late."

"We must give you a name," said Rusalka to the angel as the rumbling sound moved closer.

"Corsivo—yes, Corsivo...meaning mighty warrior. You will be a warrior for Elyon, Lord of Hosts now. Your thirst for blood has been replaced by your thirst for knowledge and wisdom, and your mighty strength will be used to protect all that is good against the forces of evil."

"I am honored to hold such a name and intend to live my life as a great warrior of Elyon. I owe Him much." Corsivo turned to face Celestial. "Do not worry. I know your power is in a weakened state at present, but I am here to protect you alongside my fellow angels."

Gabriel felt a hint of jealousy at the words Corsivo spoke. He thought of how he had let Celestial down and felt very disappointed with himself. Anger flared in his eyes for the first time in his existence. He did not like the emotion, and no sooner had it arose in his chest than he whipped it into submission.

Ilk was considerably relieved of his apprehensions about reaching the edge of the Forest of Asan, but dread began to fill him as the hour of meeting the Naga drew nearer. They crossed the desolate plains at great speed. A loud crack of thunder filled the sky, followed by heavy rain. In a blinding sheet, it drove against them, bitter cold. They reached the cliff bottom and stood among many boulders and rough stones, wet and slippery with the heavy rains.

Finally the hour had arrived. Brabantia pointed at the Forgotten Caves of Syrtis. The entrance was an impressive sinkhole 1165 meters deep with a diameter of 60 kilometers, descending 48 meters, on the bottom of a great abyss. Brabantia surveyed the sinkhole.

"The caves are a great labyrinth of many passages, many of which have not been surveyed by any species other than the Naga. They consist of a complex multilevel system—one main active passage and three main fossil floors with hundreds of interconnecting caves. In its lower part, there is a small lake, which connects the adjacent cave with the water table. The passages continue underwater and form three air bells, the atmosphere very rich in carbon dioxide and poor in oxygen. It is very deep, consisting of lava caverns with opal-volcanic formations, salt lakes, and thermal mineral karst," shouted Brabantia, wrestling against the sound of the unrelenting rain.

Roberto was impressed yet again with her knowledge. He climbed onto Corsivo's back for the descent in to the underground world apprehensive about what they would find.

They flew down into the depths of the open cave entrance, the flaming swords lighting the way before them. The Paristan warriors left their steeds in the large chamber as they moved into another gallery. Thick layer of bat guano covered the surfaces.

The farther they moved into the numerous caverns, the darker it became, and the eyes of the large, bat-like creatures, devoid of any pupil, stared back at them as they descended. They stood tentatively on the fossil floor, taking in the surroundings. It looked like a tropical oasis in a temperate region. A warm air current charged with vapors passed by. The cave was supplied by thermal waters of 20°C—rich in sulfide hydrogen, as Roberto expected. He bent down to take a closer look. "This chemical compound enables the chemosynthetical processes. Thermophile and thiophile invertebrates colonize the underground environment during climatic periods." He did not think it was a good idea to elaborate on the subject too much but wondered what sort of creatures may have evolved in this environment over the centuries.

They walked through a lava cave about a mile long and came upon a small entrance. It was difficult for Gabriel, Mikael, and Corsivo to physically get through. A momentary shape shift to a smaller form made it possible to crawl into the next cave.

The surroundings could not be so different on the other side. The rock formations had been replaced by gold formations, and a small, liquid-gold lake ran through the cave, flowing in tubular conduits beneath the surface much like a lava flow. The molten gold had formed aprons as it meandered backward and forward, creating sinusoidal passages and opaque fire opal was abundant.

Roberto was enthralled with the beauty of the caves. Formations resembling aragnite—crystallized forms with a crystal structure that had resulted in sparkling, treelike formations of vast proportions—filled the cave, and crystal droplets hung from the branches in the shape of teardrops.

It looked so magical yet mysterious, with the mist floating in the air, that Roberto did not see the creature descend upon him from above. It knocked him face down into the ground. It was just about to consume him when Corsivo swept down and picked him up, removing Roberto from the clutches of some sort of depigmented arachnida, very large with white, furry legs and huge white eyes devoid of any pupils.

Brabantia and Serepha fought with the spider, seizing the advantage of the flaming swords. Serepha and Brabantia attacked until their hands were weary, and then Serepha struck the spider's chest in one fell swoop while Brabantia battled from the rear. The giant spider staggered backward, then moved forward again, ready to strike. Its mouth seemed far too large, spread open wide, revealing its top and bottom canine teeth—two rows of long slender fangs, almost translucent. Mikael struck its skull with the Xanthurus weapon; the spikes ripped into the head of the arachnida, shattering its skull to pieces. A clear substance gushed from the gash in its forehead, and it began to sway backward.

Finally it fell with a great thud to the ground, its translucent liquid spreading fast on the rocky surface. Brabantia paused, and then withdrew.

"Well done, Serepha. You fought well," she said, putting her sword back into its sheath and searching for her breath. Roberto examined the carcass thoughtfully.

"There may be more like it; I feared that this might be the case. There will probably be other species that have evolved over the centuries, and we don't really know what they are capable of. I am amazed at its sheer size."

"Nothing we cannot handle," said Brabantia, knowing that Ilk was becoming more and more afraid.

"Do you think I should go back to the surface and keep watch for anyone who may pass by?" Ilk shuddered, not wanting to go any farther.

"No, Ilk, you will be safer with us than on your own. Just keep close to me." Corsivo winked at him playfully.

As they moved through another gallery of fine structures, Roberto noticed that the atmosphere was gradually changing. He felt that he could breathe much easier. "Have you noticed as we descend that there is more oxygen and less carbon dioxide? Surely that is not possible, although I should know by now that anything is possible in your world." He pondered how it could be.

Then Brabantia gave him the answer. "Yes," she said. "The oxygen is produced by one of the thermophiles named semillions. They are like albino millipedes, twelve inches long with a forked tail and many legs. They are essentially harmless and will bite only when threatened."

Roberto suddenly became excited. "That's it!" he said, grabbing hold of Rusalka without thinking about what she would think of such an action—and to make matters worse, he planted a kiss on her cheek. Everyone seemed bemused, waiting for his explanation and wondering why he was so excited. "What if we transported these creatures back to Venus and bred them until they are a source of extra oxygen to combat the damage that the carbonants have caused already?" Roberto said enthusiastically.

"You may have a point." Brabantia looked hopeful. "Hmm...Yes, but, of course, we will have to stop Dracon and his swarms from doing any further damage to our planet. Then we can use these creatures—if it is at all possible to breed them in a different environment than their own ecosystem."

"It is worth giving it some serious thought when we have rescued Shimm-rae," said Rusalka.

At that point, Rusalka closed her eyes to concentrate on the whereabouts of Shimm-rae.

"Can you see her, Rusalka? I can feel her presence is close," said Celestial, feeling a little drained without Shimm-rae as part of her aura. Shimm-rae provided her with unsurpassed energy, and she was definitely feeling the effects of her absence. Rusalka sensed her despair and reassured her that they would soon return Shimm-rae to her rightful place.

The air became purer and purer as they descended into the heart of the vast caves. Other species of troglobionts seemed oblivious to them. In fact, they were beginning to feel quite safe again when they came face to face across the ravine with the largest serpent they had ever seen. It seemed to be guarding the entrance to one of the caves.

"Maybe that is where Shimm-rae is being held," said Gabriel, "beyond that cave entrance."

"How on earth will we get past that thing?" Ilk whispered, hiding behind Corsivo. They crouched down behind the rocks to survey their position.

The serpent was about thirty feet in length and four feet in girth. Its scales were an iridescent purple-green color. Its head was extremely large, especially its jaw.

"We must be careful that it does not see us. Its vision is very good, but it cannot hear airborne sound waves. But it can perceive low-frequency vibrations transmitted from the ground to the skull," Brabantia informed them.

A loud hissing noise filled the cavern, and the serpent seemed to look in their direction. Its jaw opened wide, and a long, forked tongue protruded out of it.

"Ilk, this is your time to show us what you are made of!" said Gabriel, knowing that Ilk would find it difficult to be brave. "We need you to fly halfway across the ravine on the left-hand side to distract the serpent toward that area. Then we can get past on the other side, and, if we need to, we can attack from behind."

Ilk stuttered turning pale. "Yes, yes…b…but what if the serpent grabs me? It will surely devour me, yes…yes, it will eat me alive, and I am not ready to die just yet…in fact, I never want to die…no…no, I never want to die."

"Just stay out of its reach and tantalize its senses so that you distract it, and we can attack the serpent from behind. Do you

143

think you can do that for us, Ilk? We do need you to do this. You cannot fight the serpent directly, so this is your way of contributing to our quest," said Rusalka softly.

Ilk reticently agreed, knowing he wanted to help. But fear made him tremble. He knew he had to feel the fear and do it anyway; he would never be able to forgive himself otherwise. He was so ashamed of his cowardice.

No sooner had Ilk flapped his little wings to keep airborne over the large chasm than the serpent turned its huge head in his direction, its long, black tongue lashing out at him. Ilk looked down into the depths of the cave and looked up at the serpent's movement toward him. Terror immobilized him, and he began to fall swiftly, down...and down the immense ravine. He was sure it was the end for him. Then, suddenly, Corsivo swept him up in his arms just in time to save him.

"You did well, little fellow! We don't want to lose you, now, do we?" Corsivo flew back to the battleground with Ilk on his back and dropped him to the rear of the serpent's head, then joined the others in battle. They had managed to attack from behind while the serpent was preoccupied with Ilk. But the serpent had proved not to be an easy target, and the battle still ensued. Ilk was beside himself with fear, standing rigid like a frozen statue.

Gabriel and Mikael had managed to encircle the serpent's neck with a stranglehold while Brabantia and Serepha thrust their flaming swords in to its pelvic girdle. The snake writhed and struggled out of its stranglehold, throwing Gabriel and Mikael off the edge of the cliff. It immediately turned its head toward Celestial, Nebula, and Rusalka, who stood without weapons, and thrust itself around them in order to squeeze the life out of them.

Corsivo flew up to the level of the serpent's great jaw and wrenched it apart with his mighty bare hands. Gabriel and Mikael saw what he was trying to achieve and joined him. They struggled against the utter strength of it; the serpent's tail swished back and forth, releasing the others and knocking Nebula over the edge of the cliff. She hung on tightly with all her might, fingers clinging to the rough edge of the slippery stone face. The rock was crumbling beneath her fingers, and her wings were too damaged to fly to safety. "Help me...please, help me. I can't hold on."

Brabantia grabbed hold of her arms. She tried with all her strength to pull Nebula up, but Nebula was slipping, little by little. Celestial and Rusalka ran cautiously past the writhing tail, staying close to the rocky incline in an endeavor to save Nebula.

The serpent's tail caught hold of Rusalka once more and threw her from side to side as it battled with Corsivo and the angels until the whole of its body finally fell limp, releasing Rusalka. She sat panting, her heart thundering in her chest.

Brabantia shouted for help. Nebula had let go and was falling down the deep chasm to what seemed like a certain death, her poor torn wings of little use. Corsivo flew down the rugged face of the mountain at rapid speed, swept her up in his arms, and returned to the summit. He carefully placed Nebula on her feet and turned to Celestial. "Are you hurt?" He helped her to her feet.

"No. Thank you, Corsivo. Now you can use your instincts and great strength for the good of others. How does it feel?"

"Great." He smiled. "Wonderful...now I am happy to be me. Before, I hated my very soul."

Ilk looked at the dead serpent and its gigantic size. "Are you sure it is truly dead?" he said nervously.

"Yes, he is most certainly dead," said Gabriel, sitting on its thick torso. "We are pleased with you, Ilk; you took a courageous step."

"Yes, I...um...feel good about it now. In fact, yes, I feel great. I don't feel like a coward anymore. I did it; I did it, didn't I?" Ilk stepped forward with a little flutter of his wings and a little bow. "Always glad to be of service. You can count on me."

Everyone laughed. "Let us still be guarded for we must go on and face whatever lies before us in this unknown place," reminded Celestial on a more serious note.

They had to wade through a lake of thick molten gold to get to the next cave. Gold liquid clung to their skin and their clothes, slowing down their pace of descent. The caves below were filled with mineral and rock formations of tanzanite, lapis lazuli, jade, opal, and sapphire—in other circumstances, a sight of breathtaking beauty.

Roberto picked up a small piece of corundum and noticed its beautiful asterism—a twelve-star-shaped pattern radiated from the royal blue of the stone. He rubbed it against his clothes to clean it and placed it carefully in his pocket, looking around him to see if anyone had seen him. He had a special reason for wanting a stone of such rare beauty.

They eventually came upon a small ink-black lake where the passages continued underwater, containing the three air bells that Brabantia had spoken of.

"Fear not, Roberto. I know you cannot adapt to swimming under the water long enough to reach the first air bell. However, neither have any of the others performed this feat before, with the exception of Rusalka. You will struggle to breathe. There will be no way of getting to the surface on time, so you will have to keep as calm as you can until you adapt to breathing underwater. You will adapt, but first you will think you are going to soak your soul in the waters of death. Prepare yourself!"

"Oh, not again," said Ilk. "How many times do we have to endure such difficult tasks? Not that I don't want to prove my courage, of course. It's just that these tests are a little bit on the difficult side, don't you think? I mean, feeling like i'm going to die is not at all pleasant, and what happens if I doubt at all? Will I surely soak the waters of death like many before us anyways?"

"No, not at all, Ilk," Celestial reassured him. "For the very fact that you will be feeling like you are going to do so will mean you have already proved courageous and obedient. You will not die. Have I ever let you down before?"

"No," replied Ilk, studying the warm, misty, aqua-green water hesitantly.

"I think I can speak for all of us," said Roberto firmly. "We can do it. We will follow you. Lead the way, Your Majesty."

"Speak for yourself," Cava said sarcastically, knowing she had no choice now but to follow the others, however reluctant she felt.

Rusalka held Roberto's hand and led him to the water's edge.

Ilk jumped on Corsivo's back. Everyone else followed, diving in to the depths of the ink-black waters, not knowing what would greet them on the other side.

Roberto thrashed around under the water, and his life flashed before him. He needed to get to the air bell quickly. He felt that it was the end. His head throbbed, and his eyes bulged out of their sockets. He had let go of Rusalka's hand in an instinctive attempt to swim to the surface.

Rusalka swam beside him and wrapped her wings around him once more, the same way she had done in the mountainous polar region, until the peaceful calm he had encountered before in her sweet embrace befell him. She let go. He was still alive and had adapted to his new world, breathing underwater. He looked around and smiled at Rusalka, giving her the thumbs up. She waved back at him and pointed to Ilk, who was producing bubbles as he tried to speak.

Cava swam a little way, feeling her heart pounding heavily against her chest. No one else was in sight. Panic overtook her. Her legs kicked wildly, her hands pushing down the water in swift, sweeping movements in an attempt to reach the surface. In her desperation, she swallowed a gulp of water just as she pushed her head out of it. She gasped for air, but she was choking. She tried to breathe through her nose and thrashed around in the water, trying to reach the edge.

For a moment, she could not breathe at all; her face changed to a purple color—this was it! She was going to choke to death before she had a chance to see a new world. Just in time, she managed to take that vital breath of air, and when her breathing became more regular, she swam to the side and dragged herself onto the rocks. A chill scurried up her body; she was alone...she had not made it to the other side; she was alone in this forsaken place. They would surely leave her there, and she would have to trace her steps back to the entrance of the cave, with its many dangers. She shuddered at the prospect.

Meanwhile, Celestial noticed that Cava had not made it. "I will return from where we departed to see what has become of her."

Celestial found her way back. When she finally reached the rocky edge they had leaped from, she saw Cava lying on the ground recovering her breath.

"Could you not face the belief in yourself, Cava? I know it is difficult to even consider something so against the belief of your learned nature, but you can do this. It is a process of change before our belief in our own capabilities grows to such levels; however, our time is limited here. Have I let any of you down yet?"

Cava was silent for a moment, still recovering her breath. "You are right, of course. I don't believe I can swim underwater without breathing; I have just proved that to myself. I can't do it again. I would rather die a different way. I can't believe you have even come back for me, yet you stand there in front of me. I didn't expect that. But as you can see, there is no hope for the likes of me, a Draconian. I cannot think or be the same way as you."

Celestial helped her to her feet. "Yes, I came back for you. So you can believe in me, and you must learn to believe in yourself. Come, and I will help you through." She held out her hand to Cava. "Come...you can do it; I will help you."

Cava slipped her hand into Celestial's hesitantly, and they both jumped into the black, swirling water. A few minutes elapsed before Cava began to struggle to the surface. Celestial held her under the water firmly. She fought desperately against Celestial's strong grip, her face contorted, eyes wide open, as she swam furiously until her lungs could hold no more. It seemed an age in time. She thought she would never make it...arms and legs flailing, bubbles of water surrounding her. Then, suddenly, calm. The transition had taken place. Celestial let go of Cava and swam ahead. Cava followed; amazed that she had survived with so little of this so-called faith that Celestial always talked of. She felt so angry with herself for not believing, always doubting. She wanted to believe. This was awesome. A surge of excitement filled her being.

The others awaited them at the first air bell. "Glad you made it, Cava," said Corsivo sincerely. Cava nodded without smiling.

Corsivo winked at her. Cava just turned on her heels, embarrassed, and faced Celestial.

They all safely managed to get through to the second and third air bells, Cava ever more certain of her survival each time. The third opened up into a large cavern with spring water in its center, a pool of warm, sulfurous water—a milky pale-green color. A huge stone serpent statue stood at the head of the large pool, its great jaws open wide, revealing long, threatening fangs. The water glistened and rippled as small bubbles emerged on the surface. It appeared very inviting.

"Wow, I could do with a swim in there, now that I have powers I never thought I possessed..." Before Celestial could stop her, Cava dived into the depths of the warm spring water. Everyone watched in amazement at Cava's reckless move.

She surfaced rapidly. "Come; you must experience this. It's lovely and warm, and the colors of the corals are something else. Come on, Corsivo, you will love this!" She splashed around carelessly.

"Watch out," Roberto pleaded. "We don't know what creatures live down there."

Cava laughed. "Don't be a cynic; there is nothing here, only..." As her words trailed off, she felt something slippery wrap itself around her legs and pull her under the surface. A split second, and she was gone from sight.

Ilk clung to Corsivo's leg. "Well, I hate to say it, but she deserved that, although I don't want her to die, Your Majesty."

Celestial said nothing. She suddenly spread her wings and hovered over the waters. Her aura surrounded her, tiny oscillating orbs of light. A blinding, bright light emanated from her being. The glare compelled them to cover their eyes, for they could not see for its brilliance. She chanted words in a language they did not understand, the sound of her voice like a multitude of voices as the glow intensified.

Myriads of long, thin, slimy, white, wormlike creatures surfaced and swam around in confusion. There was an almighty sound like that of water being sucked forcefully down a

149

drainpipe. Cava was miraculously swept up from the pool of water and landed safely on the rocky ground, with no more than a few bruises to remind her of her ordeal. Rusalka comforted her. She had compassion for Cava's previous hard life.

Celestial returned to the ground, her wings tucked in, head down. The creatures had disappeared, and the waters slowly returned to their original calm, inviting state. Cava was eternally grateful. "Thank you, yet again, Your Majesty. I was sure that was the end of me. How could I be so stupid? I just did not think. I told you I am a lost cause. I don't know why you bother about me!"

Celestial raised her head and looked straight into Cava's eyes. "Take heed. It is not good for a soul to take action without knowledge. He who falters hastens with his feet."

"Yes, of course. I...I...will try to think first, Your Majesty."

"You may call me Celestial, Cava."

"Thank you, Your Majesty." Cava looked down, ashamed at her rash behavior.

"We all need wise council," said Corsivo, smiling at Cava.

Cava smiled back; she decided she liked this caring business. It felt sort of...good.

Ilk tapped Cava on her shoulder. "Wowsa, that was close, wasn't it? I am so glad I didn't dive in. Not to say that I am glad that you dived in, of course. You gave us all a fright, although I have to admit I did think you deserved it—not to die, of course, just to learn a lesson. Anyways, what I am trying to say is that I am glad you are OK."

"Don't worry about it, little fellow. I know what you are trying to say, and you ain't bothering me. I am quite happy to learn this new way of living. It's good," said Cava, looking in Corsivo's direction with a smile on her face as they climbed the rocky surface. She did feel good! These people seemed to really care about her.

Could this be happiness? She thought.

∞

Chapter 10

Patience' Demise

Semiramis...

Astoria and Patience sat together in the dungeons of the deep, low down in the unknown abyss. They had been there for an unrecognizable amount of time. There was no change of light to distinguish day from night, only the unremitting cold and darkness, followed by the sound of some distant creature of the deep recesses of the sea.

Patience shivered, not knowing what to make of their unusual plight. Astoria attempted to reassure her. "Do not worry, little one. When Shakira finds out that we are here, I am sure she will set things straight and we will be back in Alvor in no time at all." She embraced Patience tenderly.

Back at the Castle of Elvor, the king and queen were vexed. Knowing that Astoria would not stay away for such a long period of time when important matters were at hand, they had begun to imagine all sorts of happenings that could have transpired.

The king ordered the Elvin Calendula, accompanied by Kisseiai, to seek out their whereabouts in the Kingdom of Semiramis. Calendula was very knowledgeable about the world of Semiramis, having lived there for some time among the merfolk. He had fallen in love with Oceana, a nymph of the salt water, many moons ago. He had spent time in her world in the understanding that if she left her duty to the preservation of the ocean, she would die a certain death. Then, one day, she disappeared, never to be seen again. No one knew the reason for her departure, Calendula was heartbroken. He was advised by Shakira to leave the kingdom of Semiramis to return to his own people for healing and solace. Shakira felt moved to compassion for his loss and blessed his return to the forest of Alvor.

Calendula had never returned to the place of his loss, but his time had been spent well since his return and he had found an inner peace that kept him in good health. Kisseiai, as a new member of the Order of the Sukras, was more than willing to accompany Calendula on his quest to find Astoria and Patience. She had initially felt drawn to his emptiness, feeling a desire to fill the great chasm in his heart, and had watched him flourish under the tutelage of the Sukra. It was also an honor to be chosen by the king and queen for such an important mission at such an early time in her training. They set off before dusk to the Samosata region in the northeast territory.

Meanwhile, Nastacia was going frantic in the walls of the Crystal Palace. Where was Celestial? No one had seen her for some time. She sent Orion to the Silver Fortress and to the Temple of Immortality in search of her. She thought it even more peculiar that Ilk, Mikael, and Gabriel were missing too, not to mention the earthlings.

In desperation, she decided to visit Ilk's folks in the hillside region of Asuras. She found the pixies having afternoon tea outside, giggling and frolicking in the sun. They certainly did not seem perturbed in anyway. The mushroom pixies denied any knowledge of Ilk's or Celestial's whereabouts.

"We's ourselves are worried abouts our Ilk's. You sees, we aven't seen or heard from him for some time nows."

"You do not seem worried at all to me," said Nastacia with a hint of sarcasm.

"Well, we's doesn't see the point in wallowing in sadness when there's nothing to be sad about. We's never crossed our bridges before we's comes to them. We's sure Ilk's will be all right, and we's will carry on believing that unless we's are shown any different, you sees," Hicks replied with his legs crossed and a smug smile, smoking his clay pipe, the smoke forming his words as he spoke them. He didn't particularly like Nastacia, and Ilk had told them not to trust her at all.

"Perhaps yous would like some refreshments?" Tricks said, amused by the look on her face.

She spun on her heels and walked away in exasperation, not looking back once. She could feel their eyes, full of mockery, following her. She quickened her step; she knew they were not telling her the truth.

There was only one way she could find out. She would journey to Alvor and ask the prophetess Astoria. After all, she was so worried about her queen, was she not? Astoria would be fooled. She made her way back to the palace to prepare for the journey and tell Orion he must accompany her.

∞

Meanwhile, in the depths of the Semiramis Ocean, the guards came to release Astoria from her cell.

"You only!" the guard commanded, pointing at Astoria. "The young one must stay for now."

Astoria turned to Patience. "You must stay for now, and I will go to plead our cause." Patience hung on to her, afraid of being left alone. "I promise I will come back for you," said Astoria, shaking free of Patience's grip.

Patience's world spun out of control, but she had no choice but to be brave. For once in her life, she did not want to see. The water surrounding her, no longer warm, made her feel cold and clammy. Shivering, wrapping her arms around herself, she surveyed the rocky walls of the dungeon. They had no distinct eyes, no features, yet she felt the benign gaze upon her. How long will I be safe here? In the still silence, she shuddered.

Astoria, meanwhile, was brought before Shakira in the Golden Chamber of Semiramis. "As a follower and friend of Celestial, ruler of Venus, and a friend of mine, I must warn you of your little Earth girl's treachery toward our kingdom. It has been brought to my attention that she has stolen the Great Pearl of Wisdom from our treasures of the deep. An act that is punishable by death. My guards are searching her at this moment—then we will know the truth."

Shakira looked shocked to the core. "You are my trusted friend. I am hoping for your sake that this has just been a huge inaccuracy."

"I am sure it is, Your Majesty. Patience would never do such a thing; that much I know. She would probably not even know what a pearl is or its value, as she is used to a dark world of no sight."

They sat in silent anticipation until the guard appeared holding the Great Pearl of Wisdom in his mighty hands. Passing it to the princess, the guard affirmed that he had found it tucked into the girl's tail.

Astoria gasped. "There must be some mistake. I know Patience well—she would never do such a thing; of this I am certain."

Shakira felt compassion for Astoria. "I cannot let her go; you know that, Astoria. I know you to be honorable, Prophetess of the Most High, and for that reason, I will give you the chance to prove her innocence. I cannot see how there can be any other truth of the matter at hand, but I will give you the gift of time to find out if another truth exists. My punishment will be lenient under the circumstances, but it must suffice as a lesson to others of my kingdom. Do you understand, Astoria?"

"Of course I do, Shakira. I am grateful for your thoughtfulness on this matter. Please, may I solicit one more favor, Your Majesty? May I speak with the Earth girl before I search for answers?" Shakira spoke with her council, and they were happy to allow Astoria this one last visit to the dungeons before she ascended to the lands above.

Thus, Astoria returned to the abyssal dungeons accompanied by one of the guards, a merman of gigantic proportions carrying a trident in his hands. They swam down into a seascape of ultimate simplicity, algae-covered boulders rising from below, forming a mountainside in the darkness. At first sight, the seabed seemed empty and devoid of any movement. Only the sound of a softly breaking wave broke the silence. Below them was a deep, brooding bay, a territory of uncharted waters. Down they descended, deeper and deeper, until they were surrounded by coral-faced rocks.

At the edge of her vision, she saw movement. A small head emerged, peered around, and then ducked out of sight, rippling the sand beneath them. Astoria gasped—it was chinless and toothless, with shifty eyes. It gave her a cynical stare, flexed its gummy jaws, and then disappeared in the sand. Another of its type popped up nearby—and then another, and soon she were surrounded by the snake-like creatures. As they swam closer to the dark, coral-encrusted rocks, Astoria caught a glimpse of movement, creatures camouflaged so perfectly that they literally materialized before her eyes. And then, suddenly, the still waters became agitated in the distance behind them, and, to her horror, a ferocious-looking creature with long, sharp incisors lining its enormous mouth was swiftly swimming in their direction. The fangs were so large that they did not fit inside its mouth. Instead they curved back very close to its eyes. Astoria froze, hoping the guard would prove his prowess with the trident. But the guard just grabbed hold of her and pushed her through the opening in the rocks leading to the cell. She let out a sigh of relief when she realized that the menacing creature could not gain access to the cave opening due to its sheer enormity.

Astoria trembled in fear. She had never experienced the like before and wondered what other creatures lurked below in the dark, extreme depths of the ocean. Venus was changing, both on land and in waters, and not for the better!

The guard allowed her but a moment of time to speak to Patience.

"You have to believe me, Astoria! I have not laid hands on the pearl. After the golden fountain thing, do you think I would have dared touch anything else? I don't know how it got there; I swear on my father's life. What will they do with me? Please help me, Astoria. Please don't leave me here with these damn fish people. Oh, how I wish I were dreaming. I would even give up my sight

155

again to be home and with Edwina. I've learned my lesson. Let this be a dream. I am going to close my eyes and go to sleep and wake up in my own bedroom in my own bed—in my own life." Patience was hysterical.

Astoria felt responsible for Patience's predicament. After all, had she not brought her here to Semiramis? This would never have happened, and how was she to explain this to her father and Celestial? "Do not worry. I will do my best to get you out of here. I am so sorry to leave you alone for a while, Patience, but I must go in order to find the truth of the matter. Try to sleep. You may be dreaming." Astoria thought it better for her to think she was in a dream. It was the only way she could calm her down.

"I know. I will try to be brave. I hope I'm dreaming, but just in case, please be as quick as you can. If my father returns, he will be out of his mind with worry."

Astoria planted a kiss on Patience's head. She felt so awful and hated leaving her in the dark, dank place that even she had never experienced before.

Astoria's best way of finding the answer was to consult the Silver Vessel of prophetic waters back in the palace of Alvor. She informed Shakira of her return to land and asked her to take care of Patience's needs in the meantime. She had never swum so fast in her life. The merfolk questioned her earnest retreat to the surface, but she divulged nothing, swiftly passing by without a word until she reached the surface of the watery deep, climbed the jagged rocks to dry land, and dried out her wings, ready for flight.

King Kinway and Queen Kinshasar awaited her return with nervous apprehension. "Why did you delay your return, Astoria? We were so worried. And where is Patience? Sit down and tell all."

Astoria told of Patience's plight and her need to find out the truth. "Oh. This is an unbelievable tale you tell. Yes, of course, you must consult the vessel. But we have sent Calendula and Kisseiai to find you. You must return as soon as possible to bring back all three."

156

The silver Vessel of Truth was clear. Astoria prayed to Elyon to shed light upon the truth.

"Almighty One, you are the Spirit of Truth. Please save Patience from the treachery of those who conspire against her." Almost immediately, a wavy vision transpired before her eyes within the clear waters. It revealed the departure of Astoria and Patience from the Golden Chamber after speaking to Shakira. Astoria remembered the golden-haired mermaid who had embraced Patience as they left. She saw the mermaid place the pearl in a fish scale at the back of Patience's tail. So that was how it had gotten there! 'Praise you, Mighty One. You reveal the truth once more.' Astoria bid the king and queen farewell yet again.

"Take care, Astoria. We hope you can prove the truth to Shakira. We will wait two dawns. If you and the others have not returned, we will send the Paristan to rescue you."

Astoria reached the cliff edge by sundown. Her thoughts of Patience were her only company as she surveyed the small, crashing waves from the cliff edge. Without hesitancy, she dived deep down under the calm, blue-green waters. At first, the undulating waters revealed the golden shafts of sunlight that filtered through the glistening surface. She speedily plunged into the deeper realms, where the sunlight disappeared as she swam toward the Golden Palace of Semiramis. The inhabitants of the gleaming palace waited patiently with bated breath.

Shakira was apprehensive. She yearned for Astoria's return, for the truth to be told. "I am so glad you have returned so swiftly. Calendula and Kisseiai are here; I will call them to the Golden Chamber, and we will discuss this matter that has vexed my soul."

Calendula and Kisseiai embraced Astoria, happy to see her safe. Shakira and Ovid sat at their golden thrones in anticipation, and the wise mermen council present was called upon to listen to what Astoria had to say.

"I am so sorry to inform you that it was one of your subjects, a golden-haired mermaid who attended the meeting when we first came to see you, who took the pearl. I have consulted the Vessel of Truth, and Elyon has revealed to me the truth of the matter.

157

She placed the pearl upon Patience for some unknown reason, a reason we must find out to clear Patience's name." explained Astoria.

Ovid spoke first. "If this is what Elyon has revealed, then there is no doubt that you are telling the truth, Astoria. I think it would be helpful to call a meeting of all mermaids with golden hair so that Patience and Astoria can pick out the mermaid responsible for such a grave act."

Shakira asked the council their thoughts about such an action. After conferring among themselves, the wise mermen pointed out that it would be better to gather all mermaids rather than just golden-haired mermaids, so as not to give whoever she may be the opportunity to hide. So it was decided to call a meeting of all mermaids in the kingdom—thus allowing no room for suspicion.

The conch shell trumpet was sounded, and it did not take long for all the mermaids to gather in the Golden Chamber before the throne of Shakira. The mermen council was still present, which caused a whispering among the mermaids. Patience was brought before the throne with two guards, one either side of her. The mermaids gasped at the sight of Patience held by the guards of the palace. What could she have possibly done to be arrested, and why had they been called upon so urgently? Many questions filled their minds.

Shakira had already decided that they would not mention the pearl until Patience identified the mermaid. The mermen ordered the mermaids in rows so that Patience and Astoria could take a close look at each one of them. They walked slowly, carefully taking in each feature of the golden-haired mermaids one by one. When they finally reached the last one, Patience was dismayed to find that the golden-haired mermaids looked more or less the same to her. She couldn't identify anyone, for she was not at all sure and didn't want to cause trouble for some innocent mermaid. Astoria was not sure either, feeling very frustrated with their plight.

Shakira spoke. "I am afraid, Patience, as you cannot identify any of these my mermaids, that I can do nothing else but presume

158

you are guilty, and therefore give you the most severe punishment as a lesson for my subjects."

Astoria gasped. "Please, Shakira, you must believe me. I wouldn't lie to you! Patience did not do it. She would not steal the pearl!" Astoria fell at the feet of Shakira in desperation.

Everyone gasped in horror when they realized what the meeting was about. How dare she do such a corrupt thing in their kingdom? Shakira looked horrified. "Take her away—I will confer with the council as to her punishment, which will take place the day after the next dawn."

Astoria continued pleading with Shakira as the guards led her away, and she was astounded that Patience appeared to accept the decision without a fight. The mermaids departed in a frenzy of gossip, for no one had dared to steal the treasures of the kingdom before, especially the Pearl of Wisdom—the most treasured possession of the underworld.

Astoria, Kisseiai, and Calendula were taken to the dungeons to see Patience. Meanwhile, the mermaid named Mercy, responsible for Patience's demise, became fretful. It had been her plan to place the pearl in the possession of Patience and then to take it back when Patience was near the surface of the waters, but it had gone horribly wrong when the missing pearl had been discovered so quickly. She had never intended to get Patience into such trouble.

A strange creature never seen before in these regions had blackmailed her into stealing the pearl. She was afraid of the unknown mermaid creature. Unlike her own kind, she was ugly and cruel-looking in appearance. Her tail was a cold gray, smooth, and shiny like that of an eel, and her torso was thin and scaly, the same color as her tail. Her face was that of a catfish, with the fangs of a shark.

She had held Mercy by the throat with her long, talon-like fingers, threatening the life of her daughter, Aurora, if Mercy did not deliver the pearl. She felt sick to her stomach knowing that the creature would soon return for the pearl. Not only had she not gotten it, but this young Earth girl was going to be punished for something she had not done. What a mess, she thought, and wondered what she could do to save the girl without getting into trouble herself.

After much deliberation, Mercy decided what action to take. She requested an audience with the princess. Shakira was willing to see her immediately; it had been her strategy all along to lure the mermaid into giving herself up under the pretense that she was about to punish an innocent girl, in order to make the mermaid feel guilty.

Mercy told of the creature she had encountered and all that had transpired between them. Shakira felt pity for the mermaid. "In view of your honesty under such a fearful situation, you will go unpunished. This creature you speak of sounds very much like a selkie of the deep recesses of the ocean. They are desperate creatures who have the power to transform into human form and lure unsuspecting males and females into the underworld, never to be seen again. You were fortunate she did not take you to satisfy the needs of her male species. I do have one request, however. I would like you to meet the selkie as planned, with the pearl as requested. The guards will be on watch for the appropriate time to seize her."

Although apprehensive of meeting the selkie one more time, Mercy was more than happy to aid Shakira in the capture of such an evil creature. Unknown to Astoria, Patience had been forewarned of Shakira's plan to entice the mermaid to confess her crime and was delighted at the outcome.

Shakira gave Patience one of the pearls of the ocean as an offering of peace and goodwill. "I am so regretful of your awful experience in our usual, peaceful world. Of late, we have had a number of infiltrations of these selkies and other unknown aquatic creatures, and they have wreaked havoc in our kingdom; we need to prepare for more vigilance to protect our world. I hope to see you again, Patience. You are, of course, welcome at any time. Please do not be put off by this encounter. Semiramis is full of beautiful places, and it's a peaceful retreat from the sometimes frenetic world above."

160

Patience embraced Shakira before she departed, relieved to be free to return to Alvor. Thoughts of her father filled her with fear. Would she ever see him again? How could she face life alone in this unpredictable world? She dared not think about it.

CORSIVO AND CAVA

Corsivo found himself smiling at Cava. He could not understand his interest in her; she was not exactly beautiful like Celestial and Rusalka—she was bony, sharp featured even. In fact, he hadn't considered any female form before—only the scent of a meal. Her long, pure, white hair was scraped harshly off her face. Her violet eyes had a certain allure, he supposed. She was looking at him with a degree of speculative interest he found embarrassing. Her eyes, very piercing, were constantly on his face.

At last she spoke. "I know it's probably rude to pry into one's past—but you must be overwhelmed. In the blink of an eye, you have been transformed into a mighty angel of beauty from a mighty creature of horror. What made you want to change from such a powerful position as the great warrior of the forest to a servant of Elyon, whoever He is?"

Corsivo felt a little uncomfortable. "I was in bondage, living for the kill and nothing else. The destiny of the cursed was mine. Now I feel free," he said, more curtly than he intended.

"I would like you as a friend. You could teach me about the meaning of life. 'Cause I sure don't understand why we are here." Cava smiled.

A sudden possibility struck Corsivo. It could be that this strange, uninviting female had found her way to reach his heart despite her superficial unattractiveness. The offer of friendship, something he was only just becoming aware of, might well appeal to those like him, who hungered for solid companionship. There was something about her that resonated with his previous existence. He almost voiced the thought, but he thought better of it. Instead, with reluctance, he thanked her. "I will take that as a compliment, but right now, I am thinking of the future more than the past. As I said, I did not relish my last position too much and was very lonely. What about you?"

Cava sighed, her eyes downcast. For a split second, Corsivo was quite certain he glimpsed a sorrow so profound that it threatened to swallow her whole. Her voice trembled slightly. "Oh, I was lonely; I didn't seem to fit in anywhere. I lost my warrior family in my youth, and I've battled alone for survival ever since. I began to question my life and was incarcerated because of my curiosity on such matters as other planets and ways to exist. Celestial came along, and the rest is history."

Corsivo saw her in a different light. Her vulnerability was appealing. "Ah, you don't have to know the answer to everything. You just have to trust the right people and believe in yourself."

Cava looked up at him. "Like you, you mean?" Her enthusiasm was infectious; her face was bright, and her eyes sparkled. She looked as though some other planet might have judged her beautiful.

Without realizing it, they had fallen behind the others. They were quickening their pace to catch up when suddenly; Corsivo grabbed hold of his head with both hands. An increasingly tight band had invisibly clamped around his head. Pain made him feel giddy. He felt dizzy and could see two of Cava as he staggered in front of her...her face was eloquent with sympathy.

"What the...!" Cava quickly laid her hands upon him and slowly laid him down with his head upon her lap. As though he were viewing these events through the eyes of someone else, he saw himself being half led, half carried to a soft spot. In this dreamlike state, he began to feel warm and peaceful; the heavy beating of his heart lessened. The sweat from his pores turned from hot to cool.

Cava bent over his large frame, clasping her arms around his shoulders and rocking him back and forth in a continuous, soothing motion. His hands clamped around her small frame, and he felt his eyelids miraculously falling into a deep, healing sleep.

Time passed.

When he awoke, he felt curiously relaxed. He felt purged. How long had he been asleep? In the time he had slept, something calm and peaceful had occupied his mind. Where had he been?

He formed a word silently and liked its colossal meaning... "Heaven."

He sat up with a jerk.

"What is it?" Cava whispered in his ear.

"I...I have seen Elyon in the High Heaven. I have seen the High Heaven. Can you believe it?"

Cava smiled, sure he had been hallucinating. "You were sleeping—you were probably dreaming; you had a high fever."

"NO," he shouted, louder than intended. "No, believe me...I felt the utter peace, joy, and tranquility—beauty beyond explanation. I could not look at Elyon directly, for His illumination is like no other, but I felt His presence. There was a sea of silver—like crystal between me and Elyon—and I could not see beyond that, as I had to cover my eyes from the blinding light. The joy was so...so indescribable."

Cava grabbed hold of Corsivo's hand. "I hope it is true what you saw. Do you think there is a place for me in these heavens?" she said with a hint of sarcasm.

Corsivo really did seem excited; he didn't seem to notice her skepticism "Yes, I do. I feel there is a place for anyone who believes." He rose to his feet with a new vigor. "Come, Cava. We must find the others."

She followed him. A new friendship had begun.

Chapter 11

The Abyss

Mars...

In the majestic forest of Alvor on the planet of Venus, Nastacia had questioned the king and queen as to the whereabouts of Astoria, but, alas, their answers were evasive. An oppressive sensation came over her. What was the meaning of all this? Wildly she searched the castle for evidence of Astoria and Patience, but to no avail. She felt as if her brain were reeling, as if she were going mad, struggling with the energy of desperation. Orion made an effort to comfort her, but she would not allow it. "I must see Dracon. I will be driven insane if I do not find out what is happening."

"I will go with you, Nastacia. We will leave the morrow at the first sight of dawn," said Orion.

"No, no. We will go right now, for I know that sleep will elude me. But we must first return to the palace; I noticed that Celestial left behind the Crystal Sword of the Seraphim, and it will be my weapon, as it should rightly be."

"Nastacia, you do not know the powers of this sword. It is of the Seraphim. You could be inviting trouble and even destruction. It is the sword of an archangel. Let us leave it in its place," Orion begged her.

"You are negative, Orion. You anger me so. No, I will possess that sword. If Celestial can have it, so can I. Anyway, she told me herself that when the handle of the sword shines brightly—all seven facets give a pulsing glow—it is a warning sign that danger is imminent. It will be very useful to us on Mars."

So with no thought for Orion's words or right to rest, they began their journey once again to the place that Orion had previously cursed, promising himself to never return to under any circumstance. He felt so weak of character around Nastacia, cast adrift by the whims of a female.

The journey through the portal was easy enough; however, their long and tedious voyage to the Castle of Syrtis was a wasted journey. They arrived only to find that Dracon was presently staying at the Fortress of Deimos. They were forced by fatigue and darkness to stop for the night. The thought of meeting with Dracon gave Nastacia a chill, and she lay sleepless for half the night under the cold mockery of the stars.

The next morning, they changed their course, veering somewhat southwest—climbing more and more to the heart of Mars. The Vallas Marineris region was more temperate than they had so far encountered, much to their relief. They had managed to stay unseen and free from attack, but unease weighed heavily upon their every movement.

Suddenly, without warning, an almighty gust of wind swept them violently off their feet. The clouds shifted abruptly above. Dust flew heavily in the air, covering everything that passed its way. Nastacia coughed and spluttered, trying to stand up despite the fitful gusts of wind. Orion grabbed hold of her. He swept her into his arms and sought shelter. For once, she followed Orion's lead, thankful for his protection.

The storm did not last long, leaving its mark in their path. The sunset traced shadows across the great canyon. A pinkish-red hue ensued, and the atmosphere had changed in density. Nastacia's breathing became labored, and she coughed and choked as she lay in the arms of Orion. Orion struggled himself against the arid atmosphere.

Nastacia fell into a slumber for a short period, only to awaken to a sound nearby—the anguished howl of some unknown creature. All was still. She could hear the beating of Orion's heart close to her head. Horror took possession of her soul as she searched out Orion's eyes fearfully. She unsheathed the crystal sword and held it upward to examine its facets carefully. Her hand began to tingle. She felt a surge of excitement course through her veins. "See, Orion? The sword is warning us of the danger that pursues us. It will protect us; we need not fear."

Orion silenced her, holding his large hand over her mouth. He was prepared for battle if the beast appeared.

The howling continued, but there was no sign as yet of any creature. The tingling intensified in Nastacia's hand until it became unbearable. Suddenly the sword felt like burning coals. Nastacia quickly let go, and the sword fell to the ground, glowing fiercely. Orion attempted to pick it up, but the sword was too hot to touch. "We are clearly in great danger," said Nastacia. "We must flee to safety."

"I think you are missing the point here, Nastacia. The reason the sword is burning is because we are not its true owners. It will not protect us, and I worry of the consequences of leaving it here."

"Oh...just leave it. We don't need the silly sword anyway. At least it is not in the possession of Celestial. That is good enough for me."

So, leaving the sword glowing on the floor, they traveled swiftly from the source of imminent danger hoping to outrun the creature they had heard but not yet seen. The howling had been replaced with a low, continuous growling noise and seemed uncomfortably near to them despite the distance they had covered. Still, there was no visible sign of the pursuing creature.

They finally settled, exhausted by the necessity of so rapid a departure. The deep growling sound continued, and still they could not see its source. Puzzled, they stood guard, catching their breath, in fear of what they could not see.

Time elapsed rapidly. Orion pleaded with Nastacia to move on despite their fear of the unidentifiable creature. "We cannot stay here forever; we must try to ignore it. Maybe it is just a ploy to slow us down or lead us into captivity."

166

Nastacia agreed, and they cautiously continued their journey to the Fortress of Deimos, accompanied by the fearsome growling sound. The terrain was tedious for a long distance, and they came to a grinding halt at the edge of a vast gorge. Blinking away the blur of weariness, Orion asked Nastacia which direction they should take.

"How do I know? Perhaps we should fly over the gorge and carry on south."Nastacia felt tired and angry.

"Perhaps YOU should have studied the area before we came," retorted Orion, feeling frustrated with Nastacia's lack of foresight.

"Well, perhaps if YOU had sought out the creature in pursuit of us and ended its life instead of cowardly running away, we wouldn't have been forced in this direction in the first place. And anyway, who is to say that this is not the right way?" said Nastacia defensively.

At that point, Orion noticed they had lost the sound of the prevailing creature and with satisfaction persuaded Nastacia to journey south as planned. They traveled in silence for some time, until a disturbing scream departed from the back of Nastacia's throat.

Terror shone from her eyes. Orion was startled, for he could see nothing that would elicit such a reaction. He moved closer to her; she seemed not to notice him.

"What is it, Nastacia? There is nothing to be afraid of. The beast has left our trail!" he said, shaking her.

Immediately she fell to the floor, conscious no more.

∞

THE ABYSS

There was a great quake, and the sun became black and the moon became like blood. The stars fell from Heaven one by one. Nastacia found herself in a bottomless pit—a reservoir of evil. The

167

fallen stars became fallen angels, and malevolent demonic beings encircled her, the sound of their wings like chariots pulled by many horses as they charged for battle.

Fire and smoke filled the abyss like a great furnace. Out of the smoke, myriads of locusts burst forth, a symbol of deception. The smell of death permeated the atmosphere so badly, Nastacia felt about to suffocate. She wanted to flee, gagging on the stench, but she could not move. All around withered in the scorching heat, consigned to everlasting flames, their cries filling the void. She heard the same growling noise she had experienced earlier; she turned her head slowly toward the source of the noise, and there stood a majestic leopard of vast proportions.

Fear pervaded her every thought. She trembled uncontrollably in his presence. Nastacia did not want to accept where she had found herself. How had she passed through the doors into this cauldron of evil in the bowels of the earth? She could not comprehend it. A grotesque gallery of unknown faces surrounded her, their shifty eyes darting to and fro, faces twisted with fear, watching...waiting.

One dark angel stood out above many, a mighty angel of the Serophoth of imposing stature. His torso had great muscles of a man, his arms the likeness of a wild beast. His face was the face of a human, but his eyes were devoid of pupils, like illuminated fiery orbs. Two horns adorned his head and formed part of his eyebrows, covered by his voluminous dark hair. A spreading canopy of six huge black wings unfurled from his back and shoulders, the largest Nastacia had ever seen. He stared into her soul.

Leviathan, ruler of the three Lokas of the abyss and its legions of fallen angels, conveyed his thoughts to Nastacia without opening his mouth. She could hear his words loud and clear in the recesses of her mind.

"I think you know who I am. I am the greatest enemy of your Elyon, and no one mightier than I have ever lived apart from your creator. However, behold—I am going to take everything that belongs to Him and rule all Kingdoms to come. I will be master of *all worlds, and they will quake with terror under the very mention of my name. Who is YOUR master?"*

Horror and dismay appeared to have taken possession of her soul, Leviathan frightened her so. She could only give one answer in fear of her life. "You are, of course...My Lord. Have I not tried to help Dracon capture Celestial?" she said with terror in her heart, willing him to believe her.

"Be aware, I will be watching your every move. You belong to me now!"

Leviathan's words weighed heavily upon her. The leopard stood by his side, sure of his master. A constant quiet growling sound emanated from his mighty jaws, red vapor poured from his nostrils, his talons were bared...poised for attack at the slightest provocation.

∞

Orion shook her furiously. "Nastacia, Nastacia, wake up...are you all right?"

The night was dark and tempestuous; lightning flashed at short intervals. Orion had carried her to shelter in a rocky cave. Nastacia awoke with a contorted look of pure terror across her otherwise beautiful face, her green eyes wide with fear. Covering her face with her hands, so as to close her eyes from anything external, she endeavored to look inward to scrutinize her own soul. What had she done?

She had pledged allegiance to the worst creature that ever existed! For a moment, she labored on the possibility of being under the influence of a dream, but deep down, she knew that was just denial.

Her limbs were feeble and trembling. Much to Orion's surprise, she embraced him with a fondness and warmth she was not in the habit of displaying. "You must have been having an awful dream, Nastacia. Your body was writhing as though you had a great fever. I was worried for you."

"I am well...just hot and exhausted, that's all."

She told him nothing of her encounter with Leviathan, for she knew he would be angry that she had sold her soul to evil. She kept quiet...in her own sphere of silent torment.

Chapter 12

Shimm-rae

The Caves of Syrtis...

Finally, Corsivo and Cava stumbled upon the others some distance ahead.

"We thought we had lost you forever." Rusalka embraced them heartily. She sensed a familiarity between them that had not been present before.

Happy to have a full party once again, Celestial led the way forward through the intricate convolutions of stone and dark passages of mystery until they happened upon an opening in the golden rock. At first glance, it seemed an insignificant entrance.

Mikael was the first to examine the hole. "Wow. Look through here! It's a treasure trove." He entered slowly, climbing over the rocky formations, followed by Rusalka and the others.

"This is amazing," said Roberto appraisingly.

The cave was vast through the small entrance. Gold, silver, and many varied jewels gleamed in the darkness. A pale haze loomed like a silvery net of faint, swirling cobwebs. Brabantia and Serepha thrust out the flaming swords to shed some much-needed light.

Rusalka closed her eyes. "I can sense Shimm-rae's presence. We must all search for her here; she is among this treasure somewhere. Her presence is strong—the greatest treasure of Celestial's aura hidden among the superficial treasures of this cave."

Celestial began to dig frantically, concerned for Shimm-rae's safety. The others followed.

Ilk glanced at a large oyster shell, much larger than he. It was set upon the ground between two rock formations at the far end of the cavern. His swirling wings passed by in a pearl-gray blur as he flew toward Celestial and tugged unyieldingly at her arm.

"Your Majesty, come. Look at that large shell over there. Can we open it? Maybe Shimm-rae is inside there. It's just a thought...but she just might be. It would be a good place to hide her, don't you think? I may be wrong, but we won't know if we don't look, will we? I mean..."

Everyone moved closer to the shell as Celestial asked Gabriel and Corsivo to open it. They attempted to lever it open. Mikael joined them, eventually prying it apart.

There, to the delight of Celestial, was Shimm-rae, sitting in the middle, legs crossed, arms folded, looking very glum until she realized who had come to rescue her from the darkness she hated so much. Celestial opened her wings to the sound of her oscillating fairies, their consummation of great joy apparent as they flew around Celestial. She wept with tears of happiness as Shimm-rae regained her rightful place as part of Celestial's aura.

Rusalka felt a surge of relief. "You may be tiny, Shimm-rae, but you are a giant in my eyes. We are so glad to see that you are safe."

Celestial commended Ilk on his intuitive find, and Ilk stood tall with a look of pure satisfaction, arms folded, feeling very pleased with himself.

Brabantia was aware of the danger they could still encounter. "We must get out of here quickly...before the Naga find us."

They exchanged terrified glances as their attention was drawn to a strange noise.

Mikael quietly, swiftly made his way back to the entrance. The constant uneasiness grew worse as the curious noise drew closer.

"I presume it is the presence of the Naga," Nebula said quietly. "We must look for another escape route, for they will most assuredly not thank us for our interference."

Ilk paralyzed with fear, gazed with vacant despair upon the opening before them. Gabriel grabbed hold of him while he searched for an alternative opening in the cavern.

Rusalka felt incredibly calm, as if somehow she had always known they would meet the Naga, had always seen it coming. A great dread fell upon Roberto, as if he were about to meet his end, long foreseen and vainly hoped never to be spoken of.

There was no escape. Many of the Naga slithered into the vast cavern, led by a female snake-like being with six human heads and one that spoke for the whole. They possessed a human upper torso and head with both snakelike and human attributes. Their expressions were blank; their eyes were cold, and there were fewer than twenty of them. No one moved toward them, and no one spoke.

Hydra, their leader, spoke first. "We will make no mistake in trust or in doubt. Will you accompany me?"

All eyes narrowed, and all faces stared at her suspiciously. Rusalka whispered to Celestial, "I sense no great evil."

Celestial came forth and stood face to face with Hydra.

"We come in friendship and need—seeking safety and help. If you mean us no harm, we will gladly follow you. We would surely be in battle now otherwise."

Hydra beckoned them to follow her to a nearby chamber, the main plaza of the Naga community. When they were satisfied that the Naga meant them no harm, they relaxed. They found themselves in a spacious cavern lined with marble, hung with rich tapestries, lighted by silver-and-crystal lanterns, brilliant by means of reflection from the crystal pillars supporting the ceiling. Suits of armor and martial weaponry encrusted with gold and set with precious stones produced an effect both dazzling and beautiful. A rich curtain heavily fringed in gold trimming hung as a backdrop to the gleaming golden throne.

Hydra encouraged Celestial and the others to be seated upon red silken cushions. A female Naga offered them heavy goblets of plated gold filled with the sparkling, refreshing waters of the caves, said to be of unrivaled nutritional value and invigorating to the mind and body. Corsivo tasted the water first before he would deem it acceptable for his queen. After that, they all gratefully swallowed the contents, benefiting from each potent drop, rejuvenating their weary souls.

The Naga stood peacefully in order to listen to their leader. Hydra began, "As you have already gathered, we have no wish to harm you. In fact, we have been expecting you—on account of Dracon hiding Shimm-rae here. I am just sorry you had the unfortunate battle against Serpees, the guardian of our chambers. We can never leave the caves unguarded, as you can imagine, on such a planet as this. We do not wish to fight, unlike Serpees; his destiny is to kill at random since he became fully serpentine. Serpees fought to the death an innocent; therefore, his fate was to become lower than us, a mere serpent kept to protect us all. He will now be replaced by Boidae, who was unfortunate to follow in his footsteps. We, on the other hand, only attack evil—our discernment making us superior."

Brabantia dared to speak. "Yes, Hydra, we have heard something of the Nagas' story and understand your enmity toward Dracon and the Xanthurus. I am sure we can be of service to each other. Our code of practice regarding life and death is similar to your own."

Hydra smiled. "We will help you to return to Venus unscathed, and in turn, we ask you to return with an army to join forces in battle against Dracon the Destroyer and his vermin army. Our ancestors once fought alongside Dracon's father, Perilous the Great, until he turned against us and conquered us in the days of Viperasp. It was revealed to Dracon from one of his prophets that a son of Viperasp would slay the lizard man. Dracon therefore commanded that Viperasp's and Vasu's children and their sons and daughters should be slain at birth and took the rest of the Naga race as slaves. However, it came about that one of the daughters was hidden in a far-off place, the caves of Syrtis, protected by the inhabitants of that time, the Peryton. The Peryton were enemies of the lizard race, and the Xanthurus and were more than happy to teach her all they knew about survival

174

and the love of the kill. But unbeknown to Perilous the Great and his son, this daughter grew more powerful than her predecessors.

"She stayed with them for a long time until she could see the vanity of the Perytons' existence, futile and incomprehensible. For although she had lived with them, ate with them, shared their company, and, yes, killed with them so many living things without escape, she could not live that way forever. You see, she was a higher being, able to contemplate her existence, and she desired more than the hunt of flesh, eating and drinking and merriment. She desired meaning to her continuation of life.

"Thankfully, an opportunity arose for her to speak of her desire to stay and look for her own kind without causing any ill feeling among them when the Peryton expressed their intent to move to new pastures in search of virgin flesh. The Peryton did not care and agreed to leave her to her own destiny now that she was strong enough to fend for herself.

"She found the remainder of her people who had not been slain by Perilous and his son Dracon. She brought them back to the caves of Syrtis, where they have prospered ever since. She was reared in secret, kept apart from her kin, but when the time came for her awakening, she was greatly saddened by the fate of her brothers and sisters. It became her purpose to get revenge, and she has bided her time respectful of her saviors, the Peryton. She was given to the Peryton as fragile as a lotus flower, but now she is as mighty as her ancient predecessor, Viperasp."

Everyone had fallen silent. Brabantia got up from her kneeling position and placed her hands upon the shoulder of Hydra. "You are this daughter, Hydra?"

Hydra folded her arms. "Yes, I am the daughter of Rashti, and I am compelled to seek revenge. Dracon cherishes boundless desires, but what good are they limited by death? So he will go to Venus and search out the secret of immortality, and he must be stopped before it is too late, for he is enveloped in the meshes of delusion. He will sink into the depths of hell and join ranks with the dark angel himself, Leviathan. Together they will be ruinous to all souls. These ones are born for the destruction of the universe."

Hydra wore a rich red costume, a bra-shaped top fringed with gold, complementing her deep black, shiny lower serpent half with red markings. All twelve of her oriental eyes conveyed ruby-red pupils, and her auburn hair fell in voluminous waves adorning each of her heads. Two identical males of the Naga sat on either side of her throne, their torsos strong and well-formed, bejeweled with gleaming accessories; their long, burnished black hair falling down to black, shiny, snakelike lower bodies.

Celestial stood up. "I give you my word, Hydra, we will return with a mighty army; fear not. It is our vision to stop Dracon from reaching his own thirst for power under the control of the dark angel Leviathan. There is, however, one small request that could be the answer to our prayers in order to save our planet from destruction." Celestial explained to Hydra's willing ears the demise of Venus due to climatic changes and the possibility of breeding the Semillion creatures that inhabited their caves in order to help Venus counteract the damage the swarms had achieved so far.

Hydra was more than happy to exchange favors. "We can only hope that these creatures can survive your climate to fulfill your intentions. You can but try."

The Naga provided them with nourishment for their return journey to Venus and bade them farewell for the present. "The semillions will be yours on your return."

The two males accompanied their exit to the caves, knowing a short, safe way out without facing Boidae. Hydra pointed out to them a shorter, safer route back to the portal. "We wish you a safe return and await your troops to join us in battle against our most evil oppressor."

∞

Chapter 13

Oze

Mars...

"Did you hear that?" Nastacia turned to face Orion. A cold tremor came over her.

Orion looked puzzled. "I cannot hear anything." He listened intently in the dark stillness. Nastacia could hear the low, continuous growling they had encountered before her dream. *Is it just a hideous dream? Or have I really visited the depths of the abyss?* It was unmistakably the sound of the huge leopard she had seen at the right hand of Leviathan, but there was no vision of the animal.

"Listen carefully, Orion. You must be able to hear the growling sound again. ARE YOU DEAF?" she shouted. "It seems to be coming from below the surface of where we are standing." Nastacia bent down rapidly to lend an ear to the ground.

Orion felt uncomfortable. He didn't like to upset Nastacia; she always snapped his head off. "I am sure I cannot hear anything. Maybe I am a little deaf."

Nastacia felt frustrated. "Of course you are not deaf. You just want to be awkward," she snarled.

Orion sighed, and Nastacia quickly moved on, hoping to rid herself of the persistent growl.

Orion followed her. They had covered some distance, but the growl continued. She covered her ears protectively, her face blanched with fear. Orion could not understand her. He could hear nothing; however, he made an effort to comfort her.

At the gates of the Fortress of Deimos, Egor the Xanthurus was called forth to identify them before they were allowed to enter. They were led to a huge iron door with massive bolts and chains. It stood open, allowing a glimpse inside. The glare of the fire torches cast shadows on the surroundings. The interior looked like a sepulcher. Orion felt stressed by the evidence of Nastacia's anguish. He stepped forward and placed his hand upon her shoulder.

Egor pushed them through the large entrance, where he left them without a word, barring the door behind him. They could hear the clanking of the chains and the turning of the large iron key. Scarcely had he locked the door when the growling noise returned.

Orion sat down on a seat to reflect on their position. This time, he could hear the sound, loud and clear, as though the animal were standing beside him. Nastacia's limbs were feeble and trembling. Thud...thud...thud, her heart beat faster with each passing second. Furious, giddy, she steadied herself. She caught a glimpse of herself in the looking glass hanging on the wall. She gasped in horror at the sight before her—haggard, aged by decades in an instant. Taking a few paces back, unable to take her gaze away from her reflection, she dug her nails into Orion's flesh, tearing away at his skin.

Orion whimpered in pain. "Nastacia, what the hell is wrong with you?"

She released his wrist at last. Her brilliant green eyes flashed. "Look in the mirror at my reflection. What do you see?"

Orion turned to the mirror. "I see you and myself standing by your side. What do you expect me to see?"

A flush of anger filled her. "ARE YOU BLIND AS WELL AS DEAF?" She could contain herself no more. She rambled on like some madwoman about all that she had seen in a vision or a dream, she knew not what. Nastacia's world was spinning out of control, and she blindly sat down, blinking.

Orion sat down beside her. "Listen to me! I know of this place

178

you describe. It is surely the eternal abyss of Leviathan. I now think I know the source of the growling noise. The leopard you talk of at the right side of Leviathan is a demonic force named Oze. He is the leader of ten legions of fallen angels, the Devatas. His supernatural force is that he is the master of illusion that gives cause for madness."

Nastacia searched Orion's eyes. "You mean I am imagining things because I am under his spell."

Orion walked over to her, "Something like that, yes. You must be strong of mind to destroy the hallucinations he conjures for you, or he will over power you and you will lose your senses, if not your soul. You must pray to Elyon, asking him to give you strength in adversity."

Nastacia did not tell him of her pledge to the dark angel of the abyss. She shifted uncomfortably. "You can plead my cause for me, Orion. You always know the right words to say."

Orion looked at her suspiciously. "It isn't about the right words, Nastacia. You know that. It's about the right heart condition, and I must say I don't think Elyon will be best pleased with us right now, do you?"

Nastacia ignored Orion's words, turning away from him, not wanting to own up to anything. At that moment, the key turned in the lock, and the door was flung open. Dracon's large frame filled the doorway. "Ah...nice to see you so soon, my dear. What news brings you to Mars this time?"

Dracon moved closer to Nastacia and placed his hand upon her shoulder. Nastacia tried not to flinch, although her nerves were already frazzled. "Celestial is missing, it would seem. No one has seen her for some time. I was wondering if you know where she is, My Lord."

"I have not the faintest idea. I do hope you intend staying here for some time, though. I could do with some amusement. My poor, wretched father passed away the night, so I have much to celebrate. You must join my party this twilight."

Suddenly four guards of the Xanthurus entered the room and seized Orion. "Transport him to Syrtis and throw him in the dungeons. I will delight in his torture when I am ready."

Nastacia blanched a pale color but dared not speak or show her fear or concern. Orion spat at the foot of Dracon. Dracon's laughter boomed forth, filling the room with a deafening sound. Turning his back on him, he grabbed hold of Nastacia's arm forcefully and dragged her out of the room, up a long, narrow corridor, and up two flights of steep, winding steps. A female Xanthurus opened the door of a dark, dismal chamber and received Nastacia, obviously aware of her duty to perform.

"Prepare her," said Dracon, leaving Nastacia to her fate.

DEATH VALLEY

As Celestial and the others approached the valley of Syrtis, the ground was covered in a very thin layer of minerals, once a lake. The heat and constant winds had caused the water to evaporate, leaving behind minerals and salts.

Roberto crunched through to lukewarm water and mud, sinking up to his calves, then his knees. It was as though he were walking on crusted snow. With each step, he thought the crust would hold, but as he put his weight upon it, he crashed through. His mind became occupied with tall tales told by the whisperings of the faerie. It was said that many a wanderer had been swallowed up by the bog, never to be seen again, gone forever in the world of the bogwaders, doomed to a dark and dismal world.

The bog seemed endless. Roberto turned to Rusalka. "Are you sure you want to go on ahead? We should have gone back the way we came from the portal."

"I could not be more certain, Roberto. It would have taken far too much time to return that way. We need to get back to Venus as soon as possible. Any journey with purpose is arduous and sometimes dangerous, but the end result or destination will be worth it. We must carry on regardless. I will give you strength in

180

your weakness."

No sooner had Rusalka spoken than the crusted surface beneath their feet began to ripple gently. Ilk turned to Celestial. "W...What's happening? L...look, there's something moving under us!" He flew onto Corsivo's back, covering his eyes.

The crusty surface began to break up at an alarming rate as long hands and arms broke through without flesh. "Take flight!" Celestial called out.

Mikael picked Roberto up in an instant as he flew upward, away from the eerie cackling sound of the bogwaders.

As they looked on from above, the bogwaders emerged— round, small bodies with long, gangly legs, their hair long and scraggy down to their feet, and void of any facial features. A low, mournful cry came forth in unison. Celestial felt pity for the sorrowful creatures, advancing armies of darkness.

Rusalka swiftly led her party by flight to the summit of the mountainous region of Phebus, as far away as possible from the bogwaders' domain. They stopped to look down into the pit of Death Valley. A wind came upon them with a tremendous force. They struggled against the unleashed power with difficulty. The horizon to the east was ablaze; rays of purple and red light shot out of the sky, destroying anything they touched in fiery explosions.

"The end is here!" screeched Ilk from beneath Corsivo's wings.

Rusalka beckoned them down the mountainside into a crevice. "These cosmic reactions are a sign marking the progress of our age. Do not despair, for we have protection from the wrath of Elyon. We must press on regardless. Follow my every step as I follow Celestial; let her be our guide."

Mikael held on to Roberto as Celestial cautiously climbed down, following Rusalka. "This is only the beginning of the cosmic cataclysm that will produce a kingdom that cannot be shaken. For us, it is a good sign, a sign that it is near Elyon's time to interfere in the affairs of the InterWorlds. Woe to those on the side of darkness. They will not only see the wrath of Elyon, they will feel it and wish they were no more."

The noise from the cosmic explosions surrounded them as they carefully descended the mountain. The sky was alight with fiery red, purple, and orange rays. Brabantia had warned Roberto of the extreme temperatures that they would encounter as they approached Death Valley, but no way did he expect to ever feel such intense heat. The air was stiflingly hot. Death Valley was the hottest location on the planet.

No other life form existed there, with the exception of the Mesquite. The extreme changes in temperature that occurred from time to time made it very difficult for other life forms to cohabit with the Mesquite.

Roberto began to sweat profusely. His breathing labored, he looked questioningly at Rusalka.

"I know what you are thinking, Roberto, but if you relax and do not think about the heat, you will not be affected by the extreme temperature. Did you not make it possible to adapt to freezing temperatures and to swim underwater? Why would you not think that you can conquer anything that this world throws at you from the power within you?"

Roberto wiped the sweat off his brow, earnestly searching for the power within that the beautiful Rusalka spoke of. He did not want to let her down—he needed to be in control. *I will be in control,* he thought, battling ahead.

The valley was naked. The sun shone relentlessly for miles ahead. From where they stood on the quest of the dunes, they looked out over the oasis. The dusk crept in from the desert, shading the dunes with a purple hue. They flew low for endless hours, the sky now calm from the previous cosmic display. The landscape was eerie in its quiet desolation. All that could be seen for miles were sandy hummocks anchored by the stubborn roots, the homes of the Mesquite.

They traveled until dawn, eventually arriving at labyrinthine canyons that gave way to a maze of strange, spooky rocks. On the upper slopes, there were green trees with bayonet-like leaves. With little water to share, the trees became sparse. Roberto estimated the distance from the valley floor to their current position, approximately six hundred feet above where the air was much cooler.

They came upon a much-welcomed stream, a rare commodity on Mars. The water gently rippled in the light—the stones steamed with the warmth of the sun. It was the most silent, eerie place Roberto had ever seen. They sat by the stream for a little while, drinking of the clear, crisp, cool water, shaded by the tree close by.

It began to snow lightly on the trees. Serepha and Brabantia waded through the stream, giggling at the beauty of their surroundings. They had never seen snow before; the whole experience reminded them of a time so long forgotten. The last rays of light danced through the leaves, and the air was refreshingly cool.

Nebula lay close to Rusalka, feeling the weariness of their journey. Celestial searched for time alone to meditate in tranquil solitude. Corsivo, Ilk, and Cava joined the girls and playfully relaxed with a water fight, releasing some of the tension they had been holding on to for too long.

Roberto sat close to Rusalka, drinking in her presence, the adrenaline in his veins enhancing his senses. He watched her stroke Nebula's silky brown hair compassionately. Rusalka shone like a midnight star glittering in a swath of indigo velvet. Nebula fell into a deep, healing sleep.

Silvery moonlight shrouded Rusalka like a glistening veil, and Roberto felt himself succumb to a dreamlike state. Suddenly, Celestial broke his daydreams. "It is time to move on! I do not know if the bogwaders are following us, so we should not stay too long. Make no mistake, they may be small; nevertheless, they are vile, malicious creatures wanting revenge for their sorrowful existence brought on by themselves for their bad deeds toward others."

As they made their way north toward the sliding dunes, Roberto was staggered by the sinuous shady walls, where rocks lay in light and dark layers. The geology of Death Valley was astounding, eerie but beautiful in its quiet, desert-like state, but

183

he reminded himself that he was in Draconian domain and needed to stay alert at all times.

Just as they were beginning to relax into the idea that they had left the bogwaders far behind, two leaped out from the nearby rocks attacking Nebula, clawing at her with their bony protrusions. Their nails sank into Nebula's flesh, ripping her delicate skin like a wild animal. Nebula screamed, beating furiously with one hand while she steadied herself on the ground with the other hand. Her writhing body was covered in the creatures in no time at all.

Brabantia rushed to Nebula's side, followed by Serepha, the swords of the Paristan thrust into action. Meanwhile, more and more of the creatures ascended upon them. A strong wind had picked up, growing stronger by the minute. Their screeching cries filled the land. A battle ensued, and out of the darkness, a horde of gigantic insects, like giant gray moths accented by glowing eyes, seemed to appear from nowhere.

"The Mesquite," screeched Cava.

Brabantia and Serepha quit their swords, turning instantly into their wolf-like state in order to fight the bogwaders on land. Their jaws in unison slowly parted to reveal sharp, pointed teeth. Then, a low growl rose to a full-throated roar as they pounced on their prey, viciously ripping them apart one by one, leaving the Mesquite to the angels in the sky.

Meanwhile, the three male angels attacked the Mesquite from above, the angels' sheer size and agility in their favor.

Seizing the advantage of the Paristan sword Brabantia had thrown to him, Roberto struck the bogwaders, their little round bodies shattering to pieces. Roberto remembered that the sword was blunt in his hands, but it made a good truncheon. Rusalka picked up the other sword and followed Roberto, striking each one of them with great force, although speed and surprise was her main weapon.

Ilk stayed by Nebula's side, shrieking and beating himself in frenzied terror while the battle raged on. Cava used the warrior skills and stealthy movements in combat that she had learned so

184

well in her youth against the aggressive prey.

Blood dripped from a jagged gash in Roberto's forehead. He paused and withdrew, looking a little dazed by the blow. Celestial could see the battle getting out of hand as more and more of the enemy appeared. Roberto was encircled by the bogwaders, who were waiting to devour him as he staggered from side to side, dropping his sword to the ground.

The Mesquites' large, red, glowing eyes filled the sky. Celestial opened her angel's wings swiftly. Orbs of blinding light zig-zagged from them, connecting with many of the flesh-eating Mesquite. A high-pitched wail came from the oversized moths as they were enveloped in the light. They dropped to the ground like flies in an instant.

Afraid of this unyielding power before them, the bogwaders began to flee. No one except Rusalka could look into the holy brightness. The others had covered their eyes. The fairies of the spirit had been unleashed in the power of love to protect Celestial's loved ones.

Celestial hung in midair for an eternal instant. Her wings slowly changed, losing their brilliant white glow as she stepped onto the ground below. The winds had abated, and silence filled the region once again. She turned toward her people, the setting sun creating a golden halo around her shoulders, a calm serene look upon her face.

Rusalka licked Nebula's wounds, miraculously healing them before their eyes. Rusalka looked at Roberto's surprised expression once again. "You too can have this power to heal if you surrender your life, your soul, and spirit to the Almighty Master of the Universe. The power is within us all through intimacy with Him. Just believe and reach out, Roberto."

Roberto looked at her with exasperation in his eyes. "Of course I desire such intimacy, believe me."

Rusalka stepped toward him as he stepped back. "Hold still. I only want to heal you," she said, smiling. She licked his wound. Roberto felt uncomfortable and stepped away as soon as he could. He was afraid of his feelings for Rusalka because he did not want them to deter him from keeping Patience safe, and he did not understand her world—it was beyond him. It made him feel out of control. How he hated to be out of control; he barely recognized himself. He had tasted the glory she spoke of, and it left him wanting more, like a holy addiction. He could not have one without the other; would he ever feel peace in this situation? His confusion continued to persecute his soul.

Ilk cuddled up to Nebula, happy that she was healed. "Isn't our master wonderful? Lord Bellucci, he is our savior. Anyways, I trust in him. I think I do...well, most of the time, anyways."

Celestial smiled. "Your trouble, Ilk, is that you fear too much. Let go of your fear, and you will see the difference. Fear restrains our growth and accomplishes little."

Ilk looked down, feeling ashamed. "Yes, Your Majesty. I will remember that." He looked beyond Celestial to see that Brabantia and Serepha had returned to their normal state, positioning their swords back in their hilts, ready to journey forth.

Chapter 14

The North east-Region of Venus

The Cau-cas Mountains...

A sudden tremor filled the Cau-Cas Caves in the northeast region of Venus. Vallia was cooking food with two others of the Paristan tribe when she felt it.

"Wow." Vallia was looking at her friend, eyes wide, when they felt a second stronger tremor. It grew dramatically into a series of vibrations, shaking the foundations of their dwelling place. Cracks appeared in the ground at an alarming rate.

Lilith shouted the command to flee, sounding the great brass gong that rang as a warning sound throughout the caves.

"We will be buried alive if we do not get out of here at lightning speed!"

With no time to lose, the Paristan moved quickly as rocks fell around them. Showers of choking dust rained down from above. Lilith led the way through the debris, coughing and spluttering, climbing carefully over the uneven stones in search of the entrance to the caves; the darkness gave way to the fact that the large opening was blocked by heavy rocks.

Rocks fell from all directions. Lilith stumbled, falling down in the dirt and debris and gashing her leg. She ignored it, pushing herself up steadily. Vallia ran to help her.

"I'm OK!" Lilith assured her, her stealthy movements showing no sign of pain as she swiftly ripped the sleeve from her garment and wrapped it tightly around the bleeding wound. She pulled herself to her feet determinedly and strode forth toward the blocked entrance. Bracing herself, she began to push against the rocks with all her might, others joining her. There was no movement at all. Lilith turned to face them all. "We know what we must do. Our only chance is to unite our will."

The Paristan began to chant in a language unknown, louder and louder, holding hands in strong unity of mind and power. The warrior horses reared in fear as they encountered the death of some of their breed. All seemed hopeless. Surely they will not die this futile death, Lilith thought. All she desired was to die in battle for Elyon as a mighty warrior for Him. She switched off her thoughts, closing her eyes, choosing to search for the presence of Elyon. Suddenly, the rocks blocking the entrance tumbled forward with a mighty thundering noise. A great shaft of light shone through the opening to the caves, revealing their means of escape. They climbed carefully over the fallen stones out into the open, coughing and spitting in the dust-consumed atmosphere.

Lightning filled the sky. The tremors beneath became less, but the mighty fall of the landslide was evident. Everyone looked on in shock. Never in their existence had they encountered such destruction on Venus. Lilith checked the safety of her tribe and their warrior horses. "At least we are alive; we must be grateful for that. It is sad that we have lost some of our valiant steeds." The remaining horses paced the ground outside, eyes wide with fear.

Looking to the north in the distance, Lilith noticed the summit of a distant mountain glow with a bright red light; then, soon after, loud detonations followed. Great, red-hot stones, glowing in the darkness, were projected into the air and then rolled down the slopes. A prolonged rumbling noise could be heard, and, in an instant, it was followed by a red-hot avalanche of dust a thousand feet high. A cloud of dusty debris girdled the northern region, blotting out the life-giving rays of the sun, plunging part of the planet into darkness, and causing temperatures to fall sharply.

The heavy rains that then fell caused enormous explosions, producing clouds of steam and dust that shot up to a great height, filling the rivers with black, boiling mud.

"The time of sorrows has begun! It is only a matter of time before our region will follow the same fate as in the north. We must go to Alvor and warn them, although I am sure the aftermath will be evident on the planet as a whole. Those without horses, double up."

The Paristan horses departed at great speed toward Alvor. Their mighty, golden-tipped wings struck the air with a great force, relieved to leave the destruction behind. Lilith did not look back, afraid of what she might see.

THE SILVER FORTRESS OF SOLITUDE

The elf queen lay soaking in the Spirit of Miracles at the Silver Fortress of Solitude in the Valley of Aloha, west of the Forest of Alvor, fervently praying for the safe return of Celestial. In her absence, she had made a commitment to visit the fortress at the rising of the sun each morning. She embraced the serenity of the Hall of Prayers and Sanctification with great gratitude.

Kisseiai entered the fortress grounds through the east gate, which was framed by silver statues of the Cherubim dripping in the palest of pink blossoms. The surrounding trees spilled a silver shower upon the blossoms, changing their color at random intervals—silvery pink, lilac, and white.

Kisseiai had never before entered the holy place and was in awe of the secret peace of the surroundings, which few had experienced. The garden was dressed in magnificence! As the sun spilled all her glory on all who sat below, the songs of angels filled her heart with joy. And although outside among the peaks and the crags the storms may pass in wild fury, inside no tempest ever blew. Against Heaven's backdrop of crystal-blue sky, the waving leaves of the trees shimmered silver and gold as the breeze gently shook them with playfulness. Flowers bloomed, and springs of living water gurgled along the wayside as trees cast their grateful shadow and birdsong filled the air.

Such is Elyon's way of peace.

As she walked in the garden under the sun's embrace, she praised Elyon for preparing a place of true intimacy that was beautiful and blessed. It cost him so much sacrifice to build this road of redemption. She thought of what toil and tears and blood had been shed—to redeem the lost and the broken.

Her spirit left her body for one moment of bliss and roamed the realms of heavenly glory. She entered the Great Hall as though she were floating, the flame above the altar a symbol of life cleansed. Fountains and vast, silvery-white marble columns filled the great hall, creating a type of illumination that dominated the atmosphere, displaying tones of majesty and enchantment. The purity and vitality of the waters cascading down into each pool provided a source of inspiration, producing an aesthetic balance in which beauty and harmony prevailed and creating a relaxing sensation of unique well-being.

She saw the elf queen lying face down on the marble floor before the altar, oblivious of Kisseiai's presence. She leaned over the prostrate body and gently touched her arm.

"Sorry to interrupt, Your Majesty," whispered Kisseiai, half afraid to awaken her from her trance. She could see the queen was in a higher realm and did not want to alarm her. Shaking her gently again, she spoke a little louder. "Your Majesty...Your Majesty, your king has sent me to fetch you."

The elf queen tried not to be annoyed at this sudden intrusion of her peace and tranquility. Dazed from her meditation, she rose from her prostrate position and turned to face Kisseiai. "Oh, how I love to soak in the spirit of joy. It is only a matter of time during the process of your training for the order of the Sukras that you will understand what this means. I do hope that day is soon for you, my child."

The queen looked ageless, yet she held much wisdom in her soul. She held out her hands for Kisseiai to help her to her feet. "Now, what is it that the king wants me so urgently for that he sends you to this sacred of places? Has Celestial returned?"

Kisseiai noticed the serene glow of the queen's face; a look of pure joy. She felt awful bringing such bad news to one so at peace. "No, I am afraid not. It is a message we have received from the Paristan. A quake in the northern region has caused landslides at the caves of the Cau-Cas Mountains. Some say that a large section of the caves has been destroyed. Lilith says it is a miracle that none have died except one or two of their faithful steed. The king is frantic, Your Majesty. He is afraid for the rest of the planet."

Surprise flared in the elf queen's eyes as her joy turned to fear. "And so he should be. This is tragic news, especially without Celestial to protect and guide us. We must make haste. Return to the castle and call a meeting of the Order of the Sukras."

Without a moment's delay, they left the Silver Fortress, galloping at great speed on their fine steed. An easterly wind blew through the forest. The sky was ablaze of red and black in the distant north.

When they arrived back at the castle, the king was waiting anxiously, having given orders to feed and water the Paristan warriors. The Paristan were resting from their weary travels, uncertain of their future, having been rendered homeless and hoping for the safe return of Brabantia.

The elf queen returned in anticipation. The king looked unusually drawn, his face ashen with anxiety. The elf queen embraced him and then gestured him to sit down beside her.

"We must call a meeting of the Sukras immediately, Sire, before we make any plans. Without Celestial and Rusalka, it is difficult to know if we are making the right decisions for the people. We need Astoria."

The king gradually brought his panic under control. "Do you realize what bearing these weather changes will have on our planet? It is something I fear to contemplate!" At that moment, a loud crack of thunder crashed above the castle turrets; the great chandeliers swung to and fro.

The elf king's whole demeanor—his countenance, speech, and body language—seemed that of a defeated man. There was a slight tremble in his voice.

"My love, I don't know what more there is to be done. I have sought counsel, but we cannot change the forces of nature. It is beyond my control, and I fear for our people and all beings of our once-beautiful and sheltered planet. I have seen the anger of nature itself thrust upon our shores by the hand of the evil one...I dare not speak out his name. To hold his name upon my lips would be an abomination."

The king held his face in his hands.

The elf queen sidled alongside him and placed her hand upon his bowed head. "The matter is now out of our hands, My Lord. You have done all that you can by protecting the Paristan and our immediate elf community. Now we must wait for Celestial's return."

The king looked searchingly into her eyes. "But it is not enough...is it? Many will lose their lives, and I feel helpless."

"I have never seen you like this, My Lord! Have faith...all will be taken care of by the Illustrious One. He will have a plan for us, and although it is beyond our understanding, we must believe, My Lord."

The silence was heavy and uncomfortable. Neither of them spoke. Then, suddenly, the doors flung open.

Lilith entered, followed by some of the Paristan warriors and the order of the Sukras. "May I speak, My Lord? It is of some urgency."

The king stood up wearily. "Speak."

Lilith looked a little nervous. "I speak on behalf of everyone involved. If we are to have any hope of survival, we must leave Alvor at once and make our way to the Temple of Immortality. There we will meet up with the Seraphim and await Celestial's return. Where else would Celestial return to but the temple to consult the divine inspiration of the spheres contained in the Sacred Inner Chamber? She will guide us to victory over our enemies."

The elf queen looked at her husband in anticipation of his answer. She was sure Lilith was right in her assumption.

"What if Celestial is no more?"

The queen stopped briefly to catch her breath. She looked at the king, absolutely stunned.

Shaking her head she protested, "No, that could never be. Elyon would not allow that. We may not be masters of our own fate, but I am certain that Celestial, archangel of the Seraphim, is master of her own. She is like no other angel I have ever known, My Lord. She is from a much higher place than any other angel that has traversed this planet. It is not for us to understand why she was allowed to be taken. There will be a plan. None of this is by chance, and all will be revealed in the passing of time."

By this time, the king had reined in his emotions.

"At least we have no evidence of her death. You are right; we will leave soon, but first, we will gather together with Astoria and the Order of the Sukras and form a plan of action."

Nastacia's Fate - The Fortress of Deimos, Mars

Nastacia lay soaking in the sensuously perfumed, soapy warm water of the large gray marble bath that dominated the center of the austere chamber. Candles burned, filling the room with subdued light. She had been forced to drink the elixir of pleasure administered at Dracon's command.

The Xanthurus loomed over her menacingly, placing the tall, jade-green iron goblet in her small hands and ordering her to drink of its dark viscous contents. Nastacia swallowed it nervously, the hot liquid burning her throat as she caught sight of the wry curve of the Xanthurus's mouth.

A fire smoldered as incandescent embers. The gray of the walls gave the chamber a dark bleakness that Nastacia had become less aware of as the warm, tingling sensation flowed through her veins, making her feel good...oh so good!

She almost forgot where she was. She felt the innocence of a child overcome her spirit, yet the appearance of a woman belied her feelings. She stepped out of the bath, swaying slightly as she approached the soft, absorbent cloth held out for her to dry herself. Exotic perfume filled her nostrils; she felt giddy and out of control.

The Xanthurus passed her a black silk gown. "Is this my wedding dress?" She giggled as the Xanthurus zipped her into it. "It's an odd color to choose, don't you think? It is customary to marry in silver on my planet. I must speak with Dracon; this will not do."

The Xanthurus snarled, her lips curling into a cruel smile. "I personally think black becomes you, my dear—the color of death set against your fiery red hair. I believe Dracon knows exactly what looks right for his pleasure."

Nastacia was oblivious to the Xanthurus's intentions.

"You think so?" she said, swirling around in the slinky silk dress, her auburn hair falling to her ankles. "I am about to become a queen. You must dress my hair with great patience, for it is very long, as you can see." She brushed it slowly. "I think a diamond tiara would suffice." Her vanity and the effect of the elixir overcame her senses. She was oblivious of Dracon's intentions. Nastacia crowed with eyes wide in anticipation of meeting her groom. She smiled at her own beauty, admiring her slender figure, noting how her silky, flowing hair, all the way down to her feet, enhanced her slimness. Her green eyes glowed with satisfaction, her tapered fingers running down the silk gown that hugged her curves superbly. She laughed. Who would have thought such beauty held within a vengeance so violent and terrible? Then, suddenly, she felt a stab of guilt, which she quickly whipped into submission. She could not afford such useless feelings that could stop her in her tracks from fulfilling her quest. "Oh...he will not be able to resist me this night. I will be in control; you will see." She laughed, certain of herself.

The Xanthurus laughed with her. "Yes, you are beautiful beyond compare. He will not resist you; that much is true, for you will give him freely all that he desires."

The Xanthurus whispered to herself, "Yes, you will see, deluded one…and death will become your only friend."

Nastacia looked puzzled. "What did you just say?"

The Xanthurus turned to look straight at her. "I said you will see more than you can ever imagine, my dear."

Nastacia felt a little uneasy. The Xanthurus's stance was erect and hostile. Her intensity silenced her for a moment. After some deliberation, Nastacia hiccupped and dared to speak. "The greatest ruler of all is on my side. No one would dare harm me!" She looked down, stroking the silk of her gown nervously.

The Xanthurus leaned forward, threateningly looking into Nastacia's small, delicate face, baring her long, yellowed canine fangs as she spoke. "Do not deceive yourself. I hope you know who your master is. You cannot serve two masters and please them both; they will spit you out, and only death will be your savior." Her viscous saliva dripped into Nastacia's lap, leaving the fetid smell of the Xanthurus as a reminder that all was not well.

Nastacia moved quickly away from the creature with disgust and grabbed a cloth to wipe down her dress. She began to question herself. Was she really happy to become queen alongside Dracon? Was he not an evil follower of Leviathan? She felt utterly confused and unsure. She shuddered as she pondered the subject. Would Leviathan protect her the way Elyon protected His own children? Her thoughts fell upon Orion. *Oh, what has happened to him? I wish he were here by my side, to guide me and to comfort me when I feel unsure.* She felt guilty for her actions toward him. How could she have not seen what a true friend he was?

She turned to look at the Xanthurus once more. "Where is Orion?"

The Xanthurus had become irritated with her questions. "Where do you think he is? Eating at Dracon's table? His fate will be far worse than yours; I can assure you of that much."

The notion that Orion was in real danger filled her with terror. *What will he have in store for me?* She thought of Elyon. Her shame damned her. She shuddered at the thought of what was in

195

store for her future. The Xanthurus was happy to leave her in her torment. The door closed heavily, leaving Nastacia alone. She heard the key turn in the lock. She had never felt so alone before in her life. Her mind twisted and turned, no more her own thoughts but the thoughts of another. Yes, she knew who was responsible...she was! *How could I have opened the door to Leviathan, the father of lies?* Fear passed through her fragile body, fear of death, fear of life even. If only she could turn back the clock. She felt cold; a tormented laugh escaped her, and she spoke out loud. "Evil is at work, and I am part of it. I must put an end to its destructive power if it is the last thing I do. I must kill Dracon!"

The Order of The Sukras—Venus

The senior members of the order of the Sukras gathered together with the elf king and queen in the round chamber of the Castle of Alvor, as was the custom.

They sat once again at the large spherical mirrored table. There was a glow to the Alvor study due to the sun's unhindered rays reflecting a rainbow of colors through the arched stained-glass windows around the walls.

It wasn't long before they recognized that one of the senior members was missing. Calvor had been a little odd in his behavior of late. Everyone had noticed his unusually serious, almost stern demeanor. Shula, a member of the order, had even asked him what ailed him, but he just dismissed her coolly. No one dared broach the subject that he may not have been in attendance due to the certainty that if any treachery had entered his existence, the table would reveal all.

The king spoke first. "We must continue in his absence and search him out later. We have more important matters at hand right now. I am sure you are all aware of the latest disaster in the north, also affecting the northeast regions. It is certain that these are critical times."

Shula stood up suddenly. "May I speak, Your Majesty?"

The king nodded. "Speak, Shula."

"We need not despair. Astoria prophesied about this age, pointing to the great changes the whole universe would encounter leading to the biggest battle of all times. It is a battle when all of Elyon's people will become warriors, and it is a time we must not fear if we are walking in the Light of the Divine Spheres. We can only help one another through these hard times leading up to the great battle that will bring about great changes when perfection will be ours once again, as in the days of Queen Nebula. Astoria herself spoke of such a day when a queen will rule in righteousness once more. Therefore, we must take cover from the tempest under the shadow of a great rock in a weary land until the time comes for action. All I have spoken of today is true and is told of in the sacred manuscripts of old."

The king was not sure he liked what he heard. "You speak words of wisdom, Shula. We will take heed and be a strong force against all evil. In the meantime, we have practicalities to discuss."

Shula had taken the place of Rusalka as leader of the Order of the Sukras in her absence. "We must all pray for the safe return of our loved ones, especially Celestial. Let us sing our prayers to the Master."

A symphony of heartfelt song filled the air, a symphony of notes that transcended the music of men. After the last sound had reached the heights, the elf king noticed a change in the face of the mirrored table. Everyone's attention turned to the table. "It looks like Calvor Sire," said the elf queen, "but who is the young maiden with him?" The vision was not clear.

Shula leaned closer, and a strange feeling overcame her. She began to sweat profusely, unable to breathe.

"Go fetch some water!" commanded the elf king, patting her back gently.

"What is it, Shula? Who is this maiden? I don't recognize her as one of us."

197

Shula tried to calm down, aware that she needed to speak. She coughed lightly, clearing her throat. "I am almost sure she is not what she seems and that our brother is in danger."

The elf king looked into the mirrored table once more, but the vision had gone.

"We must find him. Send out a search party immediately," the elf queen interjected. "Yes, we must send groups out in different directions to cover more ground."

Shula arose to join them in the search for Calvor. Where was he, and what danger could have befallen him? She knew they had to find him and soon.

The Tale of The Zentaur

In the walls of the Castle of Alvor, everything was quiet. Then a voice spoke out of the silence.

"Where is everybody?"

Astoria was not quite sure how much to tell Patience; she did not want to worry her. She had noticed her looking sad of late, missing her father and her homeland. "There is a meeting as we speak in aid of the Paristan, who have come for our help following a major landslide in the Cau-Cas mountain region. They will be taken care of here."

Patience looked concerned. She thought of her father so far away. Anything could happen to him. Astoria hoped to lift Patience's spirits a little by taking her thoughts away from her anxieties. "Do not worry. I have a good plan for this day. Let us go for a walk in the forest; I have something very special to show you."

Patience looked through the mullioned windows at the translucent beams of sunlight filtering through, casting rainbow-colored shapes across the high-ceilinged bedchamber. She suddenly felt excited about the prospect of a walk in the enchanted forest, which always made her gasp in awe with its

198

mystical beauty.

Outside the castle, the fresh air seemed pure and invigorating. Astoria and Patience covered some ground before they came upon a sparse grove of elms leading to a stream of sparkling water. Patience was still a little sensitive to the light and shaded her eyes from the sunlight filtering through the trees.

Astoria beckoned Patience behind a huge oak tree. "Come sit here. I have a surprise for you, a feast for your eyes."

Patience wondered what it could possibly be; she had seen so many beautiful and wondrous things since her sight had been restored.

Astoria placed her fingers to her lips. "Sh...sh...We must be quiet. Keep watching down by the stream."

Patience watched and waited. "What am I looking for?" she asked, a little puzzled.

"You will see," Astoria assured her.

Patience drank in the beauty of the forest. Small fairies fluttered past with their translucent wings shimmering in the afternoon sun. Flowers bloomed abundantly, and the greenery of the plants in their different shades swayed gently in the soft breeze. Birds sang their sweetest song amid the canopy of the verdant trees.

"That is the star song," whispered Astoria. "It is a sign of the gentle sacred Zentaur."

Patience was intrigued. Her heartbeat speeded up.

"We must sit still and stay quiet. They are easily frightened."

The sun filtered through to the glistening water. It shone as if a shower of diamonds had fallen from the heavens above. Petals fluttered from the trees, gathering in drifts of fragrant blossoms some heavy with fruit.

A trailing mist wove like ribbons in and out of the tops of the highest trees. Then, out of the thinning mist, from under the canopy of trees, appeared the wondrous creatures. Patience felt something stir deep in her heart. Her entire spirit sparkled with pure delight at the sight of the enchanted Zentaur. Colors flickered. The shapes, the elements, winds, and feathered wings—

199

all flickered momentarily in unison to the rhythm of the star song. Such beauty could not be found on Earth.

First, the mother appeared. Her golden crystalline antlers lit up with luminous globes of soft golden light, her green torso the shape of a stallion but the enchanting color of forest green, dappled gold, her twofold tail swaying backward and forward in unison. Filling the forest with her wild, untamed power, she raised her head, her gold liquid eyes aware of her surroundings.

A young Zentaur followed, with the same iridescent green coat as its mother. The mother shook her golden mane and looked back to see her other companions follow her trail.

There were six altogether; they took Patience's breath away. Astoria glanced at Patience's wide-eyed expression. "They are beautiful creatures, are they not, Patience?"

Patience took in a deep breath. "They are gorgeous. I only wish I could take one back to Earth with me. I would be the envy of everyone. No one is even going to believe they exist, never mind that I have actually seen one. They will just think I am off my head."

Astoria laughed. "What is this off your head? You have a way of lifting my heart, Patience. You know only the pure in mind and spirit can touch such creatures, and even then, they are so fleet of foot they are difficult to catch."

Patience wanted to touch such beauty. "Has anyone ever touched them that you know of? Have you ever been so close to them?"

Astoria smiled. "No not I, but they will come willingly to Celestial and Rusalka because of their purity of soul, spirit, and flesh."

Patience thought about this for a moment. "Could I become pure at all, or do I have to be born pure?"

Astoria put her arm endearingly around Patience. "You could, my child, but not in this world. You will surely be perfected in the new world if you seek truth and walk a different path than that of your fallen ancestors."

Patience gasped with delight when the young Zentaur trotted

200

gracefully toward where she sat and looked softly, knowingly, into Patience's eyes. Her golden eyes remained fastened upon the mortal intruder until Patience felt uncomfortable. She froze in fear of touching something so pure. She felt relief when the Zentaur shook its golden mane and trotted back to its mother once again, its hooves making no noise in the quietness of the glade.

Astoria looked surprised. "I think Melaina could see the goodness in your heart, Patience. They can detect good and evil in one glance, and they never normally come so close to us. The young, especially, usually stay very close to their mothers, aware that there are those who would harm them to access the power that the Zentaur possess."

Patience whispered softly, "What powers do they have?" She felt the sudden shift from darkness to light in her soul for just a fleeting moment. It felt amazing.

"They are the rarest of creatures that have the power of natural forces—the wind, rain, and fire. Only they have been given the power to rule such dramatic forces because they have been created pure and peaceful and thus keep order. Anyone cutting off their antlers receives this gift...but only for a short period of time...then, most certainly, death will follow like a thief in the night."

Patience shocked herself by hugging Astoria. She was not used to outward displays of affection. "Thank you for showing them to me. They are special, especially Melaina. She is so beautiful. It is an experience I will treasure in my heart forever, Astoria."

They dragged themselves away from the spirit of the Zentaur and walked back to the castle through the maze of majestic trees, exhilarated by their experience. They had not walked far when they heard the stamping of the herd of Zentaur and a wild call of distress. The forest suddenly turned dark as the air thickened. Birds set off in flight, flapping their mighty wings. Small animals and the faerie scurried into hiding.

Quickly Astoria and Patience retraced their steps downstream and across the bridge to the far bank, hoping to see the Zentaurs once more. The stream had turned silver as the first shadows of evening fell. The trees looked black in the shadows. Patience shivered. The air had cooled, the atmosphere now disenchanted.

Astoria felt afraid for the Zentaurs' safety. "We must return to the castle and see what has happened here. I must consult the Silver Vessel of Truth."

They followed the quickest route back to the castle, and the shadows of the forest crept silently, hiding the mysteries within its grip. The tall trees denied the clear light of the full moon from reaching the ground, and the forest was strangely silent.

Astoria turned in time to see undergrowth swaying in the distance. Panic-stricken, she quickened her pace periodically, looking back to see if anything was following them. The sound of something crashing through the forest reached her sensitive ears. The tenseness in Astoria's chest stretched to the rest of her body as she caught sight of something...something, no definite shape, lumbering after them.

Before Patience realized what was happening, Astoria swept her up off her feet, taking flight...up past the soaring treetops...up into the indigo-and-purple sky. Astoria looked down at the swirling sprites beneath her, circling the treetops. The spiritual climate had changed for sure...she could feel it...taste it. A voice spoke inside her head, not in words but in impressions and images of a lifetime. She understood the meaning: "Once more, dark hierarchies shall roam Venus—disorder will reign." A shudder ran through her body in a warm, stifling wave.

Patience's weight became too much for Astoria to bear, for although she was of similar size, her bones were much heavier. Her wings seemed useless, flight impossible. Astoria fell through the air at an alarming rate. The sprites gathered around, gleefully waiting for an opportunity to taunt the fairies of her aura. She fell through a tall tree, hitting the branches one by one until she grabbed the bough with all her might, Patience hanging onto her feet desperately.

Slowly...slowly, Patience's hands slipped until she could hold on no more, and she fell as if in slow motion, hitting everything in

202

her way. In the same split second, the bough that Astoria was holding onto broke. She leaped away into the air, fluttering her wings in an attempt to save herself. Then, quicker than the human eye could see, she broke Patience's fall as they landed on the forest floor's yielding carpet. A flash of relief washed away her fear temporarily. She pulled Patience to her feet.

Patience brushed the soil and grass from her pants. "Phew. That was close."

Astoria pressed her palms against the earth and slowly lifted herself up to a sitting position under the boughs. All was not quiet for long.

They heard a shuffle, feet dragging across stone and the drawing in of a rasping, labored breath. Their eyes met questioningly.

Astoria quickly pulled herself to her feet, grabbed hold of Patience's hand, and pulled her through the undergrowth. Every fiber of her being was on full alert.

Patience's eyes kept playing tricks on her. Was she really seeing sinuous shapes in the darkness?

They finally crouched down behind a huge old tree trunk and hid there...listening...waiting...wondering. Astoria held her breath and bit her lip as she crouched downs low as she possibly could, pulling Patience down beside her in frozen silence.

In the bleak stillness of the silvery night, a haunting cry filled the skies.

Patience looked up to the dark sky, her horror-stricken features vivid. Astoria followed Patience's eyes, and there she beheld the spectral figure, white and gleaming, fast approaching.

The large, wraith-like creature hovered above them, his face terrible to behold. His skin was crisscrossed with a great many paper-thin wrinkles. It looked so delicate, like the finest parchment. His face was hairless—no trace of eyebrows or eyelashes—and no nose, no mouth, only one large eye governed the whole. The eye was black as the night itself and told of great torment and a soul long gone from the joy of life.

Astoria pushed Patience slowly behind her, searching the eye of the beholder at large. The spectral held out his long, bony hands, withered and worn and charred by everlasting fire.

Astoria spoke first. "What do you want from us, spirit of great sorrow?"

His voice came forth from the eye in streams of vibrations that only Astoria could understand. "I am the prophet of Asan from Mars. But wait…do not fear me. I will do you no harm. That is not my intention. On the contrary, I have come to warn you, Prophetess Astoria. Yes, I know who you are. I was once a man of true evil in life, but I have paid my penance over and over again. Oh, I wish that I could die in peace, but that is not the way for us."

Astoria felt compassion for his abominable existence.

The vibrations became more intense. "All there is left for me is to at least try to help others not to end up like me and warn those who are not safe in the face of the evil one. I have been cast adrift to wander aimlessly in nothingness, for I have no master. No master wants me anymore. The pain is excruciating. But there is no alternative, so I must bear my load. If I could have my time again, I would repent and change, but it is too late for that now."

Patience felt something sting her leg. She looked down to find hundreds of brown horny toads flashing their red, long, flicking tongues like those of snakes. She let out a stifled scream, jumping up and down to avoid them

The vibrations from the wraith continued. "Do not take heed of the toads. They are just a reminder of what is to come. They will do you no permanent harm. The truth is that the spiritual climate on Venus is now changing. Your planet will be infiltrated with evil if you do not fight back. Leviathan is here. Go to your people and prepare them for battle. Tell the Seraphim it is almost the day and the hour. They must be armed for the greatest spiritual war of all time since the InterWorlds time began."

Before Astoria could ask any more questions, the spectral had disappeared along with the toads. An eerie quietness transcended the forest once more. Patience looked at Astoria for answers.

"There is no time to explain now, but the spectral was trying to help us. So do not worry. But we must get back quickly. The forest is not safe this night."

Astoria and Patience hurried back to the castle, aware of the sounds of the night...aware that something was following them—but who?

∞

Chapter 15

Calvor

Now ye may well deem that such a youngling as this was looked upon by all as a lucky elf without a lack, but there was this flaw in his lot, whereas he had fallen into the toils of love of a woman exceeding fair...
William Morris

The Forest of Alvor...

Calvor was a good elf in every way. His only weakness was his spirit of adventure and love of the unknown. One beautiful sunny morning, he was feeling a little frivolous. That was when he first saw her drifting through the forest.

Her hair, long and luxuriant, shone a gleaming blue-black in the glory of the sun as it filtered through the majestic trees. Her movements were fluid and graceful. She was certainly not Elvin. Calvor found her utterly mysterious. *Who is she? Where did she come from? What is her purpose in the forest of Alvor?* He thought.

She disappeared from sight as he tried to follow her.

Disappointed, he returned home in the cool of the evening. That night, he found he could not sleep; his mind was full of thoughts of the beautiful maiden who had so mysteriously wandered about the forest.

The next day, he awoke from his fitful sleep. The forest around was overcast in a gray hue as the first rays of a new day burst forth. An ill sense came over him, which he shook off, bouncing out of his place of slumber. Calvor did not let much get to him; he was a jolly, amiable elf. He was typical of Elvin physically—tall, lithe, and slim, with fair hair and light eyes. He had no intention of straying from the path of Elyon. He knew he must forget the girl, put her out of his mind; there was something not right about her, but he couldn't put his finger on it.

He carried out his daily tasks, but by midday, he found his mind wandering unwittingly back to the young woman who had captured his interest. He wondered if she would be in the same place this day. Surely it would not do any harm to have just one more look.

After much deliberation, he meandered down the previous track of the day before, and, sure enough, she was there.

Her stance shifted slightly at his approaching footsteps. It was as if she had just appeared out of thin air. He watched her closely as she gathered the pretty, white, star-shaped flowers, making them into a circle wreath to adorn her hair. A beautiful, exotic fragrance wafted past him as he crept closer. She turned toward him and beckoned him to her as though she had been awaiting him.

Calvor felt a sudden thrill of anticipation mixed with apprehension. Somehow he knew there was danger in this liaison, but he felt compelled to meet her.

Her eyes were darkest black, rimmed with emerald green.

"Hello," he said, lost for words.

"Good day," she replied in a seductive tone that could ensnare any unwitting man.

Her aura pulled him into her sensual presence. He felt alive and beyond control of his senses.

"I...I must go!" Calvor repeated again and again, yet he lingered behind. The pull was too strong.

"Come follow me." She beckoned.

"No. I must leave!" Calvor replied, almost certain of his departure. He reminded himself to repel the desires and enticements of temptation, remembering that even the most hallowed are tempted by evil, and he was not certain of her virtue. Those dedicated to goodwill have a lifelong battle to be rid of the constant calling of evil.

Alas, the pull was too strong for him to bear in his moment of weakness.

She grabbed and pulled him toward her, her dark eyes flashing. The day had turned into night much faster than it should, or so he thought. The moon hung like an evil eye peeping through the dense, dark treetops moving to and fro in the breeze, casting menacing shadows on the ground.

He failed to take any precautionary check to see if anyone was watching. He followed her slim form through the deep forest. All that he passed seemed lit up a golden hue although engulfed in the surrounding darkness of dusk. Each leaf had a glow from within that enchanted his soul.

Then he heard a voice in his head. "Do not allow her to be the agent of your destruction."

The certainty that some unknown entity pursued him overwhelmed him. Suddenly, the maiden had disappeared from view and the golden light had all but gone, replaced by a pervading darkness throughout the forest. He hastily darted into the nearest hiding place. Holding his breath, he stood perfectly still, waiting for the entity to pass by. After a short while, he gathered the courage to move. He felt queasy, his heart crumbling to dust inside his chest. Where was the girl?

A melancholy passed through his very being as he traced his steps back home. He staggered across a wide path that bordered a small pond and plunged into the water. Its coldness seeped through his clothes to his bones. His adrenaline rushed with full force as he swiftly moved on. The mask of evil had stared him in the face, and he had nearly succumbed to its charms.

His endeavors to thrust her away from his awareness failed miserably. He covered the miles at great speed, not wanting to speak to anyone. Thick, leafy branches loomed above, throwing menacing shadows across the ground. Soft, whispery sounds, ghostlike, mingled together, floating around him from all directions. The whispering increased as he approached his home. He quickly opened the door and slammed it closed behind him, his heart beating wildly in his chest, sweat pouring down his brow. Then the whisperings ceased.

Calvor fearfully looked through his tiny, curtainless windows, afraid of what he might see. He could see nothing...nothing at all! There was nothing amiss, nothing out of place; everything seemed normal again. He scanned the room once more and retired to his bed, where he lay down thinking of all that he had seen and heard that day. He dared not move. His eyes could not make sense of the shapes in the blue, inky darkness. Dreams can be as real events, he reassured himself...nothing out of place. Yes, he must have been dreaming. Gradually, his weariness won over him, and slumber overtook him.

The Fate of The Zentaur

Beyond and around was the all-encompassing forest of Alvor. Never before had the atmosphere been threatening like the experience of that night. Now cold from the early morning air, Astoria's and Patience's footsteps did not slacken for a moment. They passed by a river; the waters darkened as a storm brewed, the trees swaying heavily in the wind. Loud thunder roared above them.

Something flashed in the corner of Astoria's eye, and fear welled up inside her. Someone was still following them. She could see a slimy black void in the distance, and a strange, unnatural cold filled the air. They had to run...run.

She took no heed of where she was running. She just grabbed hold of Patience's hand and ran and ran until Patience stumbled and fell, her feet slipping in the soft earth. She could hear the sound of the pursuer coming nearer. She picked herself up speedily. "Come...we must run faster...we need to run faster."

Patience began to cry, grabbing hold of Astoria. She carried on, running, stumbling over sticks and stones as she followed her. She could not go any farther. "I can't run any...more...please, Astoria."

They took shelter under a large cedar tree. "We can only rest briefly…our pursuer will catch up with us." Soaked to the skin by the lashing rain, it was difficult for Patience to hear the sound of anyone against the thunder, her thudding heartbeat and heavy breathing.

Astoria saw the figure first. He held an unreadable expression. Another wave of fear flushed through her body. She needed to keep Patience safe, and she felt that she was not doing very well at what should have been a simple task.

The figure in front raised an arm; she saw the gleam of something silver in the darkness—a weapon of some sort. Astoria held Patience close to her. A streak of lightning crossed the sky. Astoria pulled Patience even closer so that she could not see. She closed her eyes tight, waiting for a promise of premature death. Clutching her stomach tight, she heard the clash of iron upon iron. Much to her surprise, she opened her eyes apprehensively to see her pursuer confronting someone else.

He moved incredibly fast, his blade like a flash of silver as he ducked and dived, weighing the weapon in his strong hands. He blocked a blow and sliced upward, cutting deep into his opponent's side. Grasping his sword with both hands, he lunged forward, piercing the heart of his enemy, who disappeared from sight immediately. He wiped the blood from his sword on his side and sheathed it with a look of satisfaction, as though the steel itself had served its master well.

Patience remained huddled up to Astoria, afraid of the warrior. Was it their time to die now?

He reached out a strong hand, but she flinched away and hesitated. Astoria pulled Patience up from the ground; she felt no threat from this young warrior.

"I will not hurt you. You are safe now. You must both return to the castle; these woods are no longer safe."

"You lead the way, and I will follow you safely home."

Astoria showed him the way home, but as they arrived at the castle of Alvor, she turned to find him gone.

The king and queen of Alvor ordered a warm bath and food on their return, and they listened to the events of their experiences in the forest. They could not believe the change that had come about so rapidly from one day to the next.

"Perhaps these changes have been happening for a while in the forest and we have not been observant enough. It was divine intervention that gave you protection, Astoria. You have encountered Asaph, the keeper of the forest, guardian angel of Alvor."

"Oh, I did not realize. I would have liked to thank him, but he was gone in the blink of an eye."

"He will know you are deeply grateful without flowery expressions of speech."

The king sighed. The time had come for all big changes in his world, and he did not feel prepared. It had hit them like a thunderbolt.

Astoria consulted the Vessel of Truth as soon as she recovered from her ordeal. She explained to the king and queen of Alvor all that they had encountered in the forest, with the cry of the Zentaur and the sudden change of atmosphere and darkness, and then the wraith-like creature that had warned them of the invading spirits of darkness upon the once-peaceful Venus.

The queen spoke. "We have all known that it has been merely a matter of time since the fall of Nebula. It has come quicker than we expected, but nevertheless, it is written in the manuscripts of old and cannot be changed," she said with an air of defeat.

The vessel did not reveal much at first. The forest seemed its usual enchanting self once again. They were just about to turn away when darkness revealed itself. The young Zentaur known as Melaina had been caught by the ghul Devata tainting her purity.

Astoria gasped in horror. "I cannot believe our forest has been infiltrated by the evil ghul. How have they crossed the portal? You are right. There is no turning back now. We have to prepare for battle, but first, we must wait for Celestial. We cannot do anything without her command."

The king looked grave. "Now is only the time to prepare. We will know when to fight."

Astoria continued looking into the globe as it revealed

211

Patience's father and the others at the tempestuous Ring of Fire. "It appears that they are close to the forest of Asan. Let us pray that they make it home in safety. There are others with them I do not recognize, but I sense they are all right so far, just tired from the journey." She did not mention the dangerous land they traveled through in front of Patience.

Patience was happy to see Wishbone again, who, in his excitement, managed to knock her to the ground. He drooled all over her face in warm welcome, glad to see her safe. She rolled over, laughing, wiping her face with the back of her hand.

The elf queen was deep in thought about Melaina and the fate of the Zentaur. "Poor Melaina...She will suffer from the inter-ference of her soul until her powers are restored at the death of the ghul."

"Yes, but it will eventually mean a certain death for the ghul!" Astoria reminded her.

"Good," said Patience indignantly. "Evil should not live."

The Elvin queen looked at Patience. "Hmm...but it also means that the ghul will have power over natural forces until its death."

Chapter 16

Calvor's Temptation

The Forest of Alvor...

The next day, Calvor awoke as the last stars were fading. His dreams troubled him. "There are things in this wilderness that are masters of deception." These words echoed in his head.

He could hardly remember the escapades of the day before. He could only see a vision of a beautiful maiden with black raven hair beckoning him forth into the realms of fantasy. He felt dazed, confused, and unreal.

Not feeling in the mood for work, Calvor walked along a narrow, winding path through the enchanting oak wood, eventually merging upon a large clearing. The dark, green, leafy trees stood out against the light-blue sky.

Calvor lay down on the soft, green grass; thousands of dragonflies danced in the sky, a shining spectacle of electric blue and vivid red. The long grasses swayed gently in the cool breeze as shafts of light streamed down through the gaps in the foliage. Ferns and wild flowers abundantly surrounded the majestic oak tree in soft lilac and violet hues. Serenity encompassed him as he closed his eyes.

The pleasantness of his surroundings allayed his fears from the night before, and yet, and yet...there was still that niggling unease at the back of his mind that could not be sensibly clarified.

Gently and silently, the maiden approached him. Startled, he felt her presence. He opened his eyes, and she stood before him, a silhouette of ivory silk, beaded with hundreds of seed pearls, her long, black, flowing curls falling over her delicate shoulders. Exquisitely beautiful, she looked so angelic his soul overrode his resistance with an all-encompassing urge.

Once again, a sense of enchantment permeated the atmosphere. Seething with excitement, he stood up and took her hand in his. They wandered through the forest like two young lovers; the leaves withered as they passed by dancing in the wind, but Calvor did not notice. Her radiance mesmerized him, luring him like a moth to a flame.

To him, the forest came to life. Colors became more intense, flowers were in full bloom, the sky was the clearest, purest blue. She led him to a large tree where the red orbs of fruit hung temptingly low and conveniently reachable. She picked off the fruit and offered Calvor a sweet-tasting bite. They gorged on the fruit heartily before he followed her to a remote hilltop.

She stood at the entrance of a small, enchanting cottage, beckoning him to her. "Come in," she said with the voice of an angel.

When he made no move, she held out her hand. He looked at it for a long moment—the smoothness of her skin, the slim, tapered fingertips.

"Come in," she said again, aware of his hesitation. "Please."

As he looked into her eyes, she looked pleadingly into his. He took a tentative step forward, unable to resist her charms.

Calvor found his voice at last. "What is it you want from me?"

"This is where I used to live," she said. There was a look of sadness to her face as she spoke. "It once was beautiful in its simplicity."

As she opened the old wooden door, a stale, malodorous wave of air swept past him, as though it had not been opened for time long gone. Nevertheless, he reluctantly followed her over the threshold into the muted light. The room was streaked with dusty bright rods of sunlight that came through the holes in the wooden structure, the quaint windows covered with dark cloth. He ventured farther into the room. It was bare—no seat to sit on, notable to eat from. A flickering fire and the warm glow of many candles lit up the gold in her eyes with a tinge of red. The fire had been recently lit with kindling; freshly cut logs lay by its side. His breath caught in his throat as he felt her penetrating gaze upon him. There was a long moment of silence that Calvor found hard to bear. There was something about her eyes; the freshness of her youth was apparent, yet...those eyes...even her face at closer inspection...yes...ages of time looked out from those eyes, and they changed suddenly...this time a fey blue light shone forth, as though she knew what his thoughts were made of. She stood there for a moment, looking so ageless and beautiful he felt a deep inner yearning to hold her close to him. A silence fell over them momentarily. He felt her eyes upon him, searing into his soul, and suddenly he felt afraid again.

He looked away from those penetrating eyes at the flickering flames. After a while, the fire took on shapes of something evil and sinister. He looked back into her eyes and felt trapped under the spell of her enchantment...he could not move...he felt totally immobilized for a brief moment.

She left the room through a small wooden door to the back of the house, saying nothing. Calvor felt suddenly uncomfortable, wondering what to do. He sat down upon a faded red velvet rug next to the fire, endeavoring to reflect upon his position. A dark shadow passed the scantily dressed windows. He felt uneasy, and his stomach felt like a lump of lead, heavy and distended.

A faint suspicion flashed in his mind as she returned and knelt before him. She offered him a goblet filled with red wine, looking appealingly into his eyes. Calvor sniffed its aroma before taking a sip, searching her face for answers. *Who is this girl that has enchanted me?* He placed the cup down and moved closer; softly stroking her velvety, chocolate-brown skin, his fingers faltered...*Was her skin not milky white before she brought me to the cottage?* The thought perturbed him. He reassured himself that it was a trick of the light. Placing her hands in his, he noticed her nails, long and strong, unusually thick and yellow...razor sharp like knives. She caressed his hair, pulling him toward her, moving her face close to his. His heart beat rapidly, and he closed his eyes for a split second, and when he opened them—unexpectedly—a smile bared her sharp slender white fangs.

She moved closer still, dripping saliva, thick and viscous, from her parted lips, slowly bringing her hands to his face. Her gemlike eyes glinted with long-awaited revenge. At first, he seemed almost to relish the unleashing power, mesmerized. She drew back her lips, showing her fangs yet again, sending a primal message of alarm.

Calvor sat motionless, looking at her until gradually he realized the reality of the filthy angel of the Devata that stood before him lusting for his death. His face became dark with fury. How did I succumb to this? What had once been a beautiful maiden was now a grotesque visage moving to attack Calvor as he pushed himself to his feet and staggered backward.

The thing hissed and gnashed its teeth, running toward him. Its long, slimy, sinewy body had grown to new heights, towering above him. The atmosphere became oppressive. Calvor found it difficult to breathe amid the pungent odor of sulfur. A low guttural sound came from its throat; yellow, bulbous eyes darted backward and forward as the abomination moved toward him, its fists of fire held out in pursuit of his soul. Calvor turned, stumbled to the ground, and crawled backward, not taking his eyes off the unnatural creature in front of him. In one swift motion, he picked himself up and turned round, running fast—faster than the human eye could see.

Spurred on by his own terror, he ran desperately toward the darkened forest, clutching his stomach. His body became taut; his teeth gritted as energy surged to propel him forward at great elf-speed. He was shaken and terrified. As he retreated downstream, he heard the mocking laughter singing among the trees and felt the prickly sensation of being followed. His breathing was fast and shallow. He crossed over to the far bank on the stepping-stones of his childhood, moving on at a great speed, ears and eyes alert.

If the creature caught up with him, he must remember the

things he had been taught about the Demons of hell. His mortal soul depended upon the knowledge of their weaknesses. He tried to remember, talking out loud. "The horns made of iron...yes...hack them off to make them vulnerable...but I have no sword, only bow and arrow! Avoid the tip of its tail because of its deadly toxins...slice through at the tip...at speed, but what with? Oh Elyon, help me, please."

The forest became still once more, but the gloom weighed heavier still. It seemed too silent; even a whisper seemed irreverently loud. Calvor felt the dusk was fast becoming threatening, the shadows between the trees foreboding. Branches above were like contorted arms, a complex mass of twigs and branches, some reaching down as if ready to capture him.

He twisted his head to look behind, quickly looking every which way. Something slithered between the foliage. Other eyes were in the forest, watching...waiting. He felt something breathing down his neck. He ran and ran until he had begun to feel somewhat safer, and then the slithering shadow showed its true self.

A cobra reared its head and in one quick strike buried its fangs deep into Calvor's skin. He immediately fell unconscious, into the depths of haunting nightmares. All sounds muted, the evening was tranquil. Calvor lay on the ground motionless. The Alpseid nymphs saw the fate of Calvor and knew him to be of the Order of the Sukras.

The smallest of all nymphs bound to the glens and groves, they were the most introspective of their kind, largely keeping a low profile. They danced among the brightness of the moon's silver reflection at night. Their powers waned with atmospheric change and pollution, so it was an important duty for them to protect their natural surroundings in order to keep their supernatural powers in the realm of the forest.

They took pity on Calvor. It took many of their kind to transport him to a safe haven in the midst of the dense forest, where their magical powers restored his health from the poisonous bite of the cobra.

In his weak state, Calvor stayed among the Alpseid nymphs until his strength returned enough to journey home. One particular nymph named Larina was loath for him to leave when the time came and gave him exclusive care and attention. He was grateful for their strength of character, kindness, and compassion. They may have been small in physical appearance, but they were large in their spirit of goodness.

He had learned a great lesson in the experience of the ghul, a diabolical class of the Devata, capable of changing into any desirable form to entice good people towards the dark side of destruction.

He was sad to say good-bye when the time came and promised to visit them regularly in the future. Larina cried as he departed, wondering if she would see him again as he had promised. Calvor held her in his hands for one brief moment before he left. "I will come back to see you; please don't cry. I want to see you smile before I go. Come on, just one teeny, teeny smile for me."

Larina managed a halfhearted smile as Calvor placed her carefully on a nearby flower, afraid of squashing her delicate wings, and he bid her farewell.

His journey home was not a pleasant one. He feared the chance of meeting other Devatas, whatever form they came in, and felt unsure of anyone or anything he met along the way. He ran home at great speed, praying incessantly and asking for forgiveness and redemption. How long he had been away from his people he did not know; they would be very worried about him. He felt ashamed of his behavior but knew he had to face them once again.

∞

Chapter 17

Leviathan, The Dark Angel

The Forest of Asan...

It was night, the dark sky vaguely alight with the moon and the stars, a thick mist surrounding them. They wearily stumbled over each stone in their path. They had alternated between flying and walking, and the angels' wings, tightly closed, rested from their long journey across the sky.

To have reached the forest of Asan was a relief to Roberto in one way, but the apprehension of all they could encounter along the way through the dark, foreboding forest did nothing to negate his fears. Roberto's thoughts turned to the manticore. He was so pleased that Corsivo was one of their own now; at least they had a fair chance against such a beast—if not by sheer physical power, then by strategy.

Brabantia was the first to see a dark shape in the mist. A low growling noise could be heard close by. Everyone stood still, guarded by Brabantia, Serepha, and the male angels, their swords unsheathed. They moved round in a circle, the growling noise moving ever nearer. The air thinned within a matter of seconds...and suddenly...there he stood tall. The Master of Deceit himself, Leviathan, the dark angel, flashing his glowing orbs of fire that made his eyes.

Ilk ducked under Corsivo's wings. Celestial moved forward. "Do not be afraid," she said confidently, her wings rising slowly. She held everyone back.

There was an echo of the beauty he had once possessed, the rippling muscles of a mighty angel, but his hands and forearms were now covered in the hair of an animal, one hand shaped like the long talons of an eagle. Horns framed his face, continuous from the eyebrows up and protruding from the luxuriant golden hair falling around his large shoulders. His face was sculpted, with high cheekbones, and his lips were as black as coal against pure white, perfectly aligned teeth amid his two sharp, white canine fangs. A serpent adorned his neck with the same fiery eyes that shone forth with evil conspiracy in the darkness of the night.

He moved closer, flapping his expansive, black, hairy wings, six in whole, layered one behind the other. He glared at Celestial defiantly for what seemed like an eternity.

Celestial was the first to speak. 'It has been a very long time. Leviathan, I believe, is your name, now, is it not? I can see great change has befallen you since we were as one brother and sister.'

The leopard standing beside Leviathan growled continually. Leviathan gave a cruel smile. "Yes, it is one name above many that I am known as in the InterWorlds. I am the morning star and the moon at night, and yes, I have changed, as you can see—for the better, I might add. My outward beauty used to be of concern, but it is now replaced by my inner beauty, revered by all. I will become mighty beyond compare. My legions grow day by day, ready for the battle that must be. I will take Elyon's place as God of all worlds. I could wipe you out now, of course, but my time has not yet come. Every beast of this forest belongs to me, so as you travel, you need to be afraid—very afraid. I will leave you to be devoured one by one, and I will wait to consume your souls."

Oze growled louder. "Hold still," Leviathan commanded him. "I wish to play with their lives first. I do not need to soil my hands with such unworthy creatures. I want to see them squirm. Yes, Celestial, your God will not be able to save you now!"

Celestial said calmly, "You give your mouth to evil, and your tongue forms deceit, devising destruction like a sharp razor. Your works are corrupt and abominable in the sight of Elyon. I beg you to seek mercy, for you will certainly be destroyed."

220

Leviathan laughed with a mighty roar. "Mercy! I know of no such thing. I am the mighty destroyer. This day, I will put the fear and the dread among all of you. Go to your destiny."

In an instant he had descended in a flame of fire, which died down as fast as it had come. Roberto was in shock. He had looked upon the face of evil and survived. It was said that anyone looking into the eyes of the Devil would never recover his sanity. He felt concern for all worlds at the hands of this angel of the abyss, as they had no idea of the deception he could and would create in order to consume life.

Gabriel could still remember the darkness in the heavens, the shrieking, the horror, and the fierce attempts to escape the searing pain. He remembered the whole consuming battle that had resulted in the fall of Leviathan as he was finally delivered that last blow, sending him over the Bridge of Heaven to plummet down into the depths of the abyss—the bottomless pit. The darkness had fallen from Heaven, bringing back peace and the brightness of the light of Elyon shining upon them in renewed glory and victory. To set eyes upon such darkness again sent a shiver down his spine.

Celestial threw herself on the ground, followed by Rusalka and all the angels. "My heart is steadfast and true. All glory is Yours, My Lord, in these calamitous times. Let your glory shine upon us as the light of day approaches. In the shadow of your mighty wings, we, your people, will find refuge. Be merciful, O Elyon, for many seek to destroy us."

The Spirit of Elyon passed through the forest, and they lay down in peace to rest.

Sleep came easily to Celestial. A vision appeared of a burning forest—and the words came to her more than once: "See how great a forest a little fire kindles." She felt an intense heat that awoke her from her slumber.

Roberto and Rusalka were already awake, intent in their conversation. The forest had been unusually quiet from its sinister sounds. Celestial kept repeating the words. "See how great a forest a little fire kindles." Nebula joined them to hear the words of Celestial repeated again: "See how great a forest a little fire kindles."

Taken aback, Nebula excitedly told them she had heard the same words in her dream over and over again. Celestial gathered them all together. "Have any of you had the same dream?"

"No" was the reply.

"I still think Elyon is trying to tell us something, it may not be literal, but somehow, I think it is."

Rusalka agreed. "Yes, it would make sense. If we start a fire, it would destroy many of the beasts of the forest."

"If that is so," Gabriel pointed out, "we would need to be on the outside of the forest to keep ourselves safe."

"We could turn north to the forest perimeters, toward the Arcadian coastline in the Polar Region. There we could set the fire as we retreat from the forest and then journey onward through Phebus territory, leading northeast to the border of Tharsis, and finally the portal," said Mikael.

Cava quickly interjected, "Oh yes...just journey near the most dangerous, tempestuous Ring of Fire on the north coast. Why not? We are really going to be safe there! Even the Draconians fear that place."

Corsivo did not like her tone of voice. "Cava, why do you have to look at the negative side of everything? We must follow and trust what Elyon is trying to say to us in order to be safe."

Cava looked ashamed. "Well, I am just warning you of the dangers, that's all."

"I know you are frightened, Cava, but I think it is the lesser of two evils. And the rest we will leave to our protector," Celestial said hopefully.

Ilk flew in front of Celestial. "I have to agree with Cava, but I wish there were another route. Let's look at your map, Brabantia. We may have missed another option; you never know. We often miss things the first time, anyways."

Corsivo laughed. "Nice try, little fellow, but we have looked at all our options. Stay close to me; I will protect you."

Brabantia took out the map she had found in the caves of

Syrtis. "Look, if we follow this trail as Mikael suggested, we can stay as far away from the coastline as possible. It will take longer than the forest route, of course, but I too think it's our safest option considering Leviathan is on the rampage."

They all agreed—Cava reluctantly, but even she could see the sense of it in view of Leviathan's beasts on the prowl. So north they traveled.

∞

Chapter 18

Calvor's Return

Venus...

Calvor's return brought great relief to everyone at the Castle of Alvor. Shula was shocked at his tale regarding the ghul but happy he had come through it in one piece.

"Let this be a lesson to us all, Calvor. We are all susceptible to evil temptation. You must give your testimony to the members of the order so all can see that even the most hallowed can be open to the conniving mind control of Leviathan."

Kisseiai threw her arms around Calvor, happy to see he was safe and sound. Surprised at her reaction, Calvor looked at Kisseiai through fresh eyes. He had never really noticed how beautiful she was before. Her vivid green eyes, encircled by a golden halo, complemented her chestnut-brown hair, and her delicate wings surrounded her in a soft golden glow. She smiled, shyly embarrassed but quietly pleased by his intense stare. She had been his pupil, and he had not even noticed her loveliness. Yet he had seen her love of the study of the manuscripts. She had changed; he could see that. Her face bore witness to the light, her spirit a candle to the One. The Divine Spirit had touched her soul with heavenly fire and set it ablaze.

"Come walk with me and tell all that I have missed while I have been away," said Calvor. Kisseiai walked beside him, delighting in his company.

The elf queen was still concerned about the whereabouts of

Melaina. Her need for protection was greater now, as her purity had been contaminated by evil. She sent a search party out to find her and her mother to guide them to safety. No one was safe anymore with the presence of the ghul, and she would not allow them to hurt her Zentaurs again.

She returned that day to the Silver Fortress of Solitude, where she walked through the Chamber of Many Mirrors seeking truth, but she did not like what she saw in the mirrors. The future did indeed seem a dark place. She looked up to the heavens. "Oh, My Lord, do not forsake us; have we not been true to you? What is this that is happening to our planet? I know you speak of these times, but must your loved ones suffer so? Please help me to trust and understand that your way is always the right way."

The elf queen climbed to the summit of the fortress, an open place surrounded by silver columns with a dome-shaped roof encrusted with emeralds. She looked to the north with her superhuman eyesight at the changing landscape, which was creeping nearer each passing season. A cloud of dusty debris restricted her vision in the distance. Her mind wandered to the plight of Planet Earth. Roberto would soon return, and she must warn him of the sister star to the sun, Nemeses, the death star. The day or the hour she did not know, but when the death star entered a cloud of interstellar debris that existed on the outermost margins of the solar system, the penetration would cause a gravitational disturbance, loosing a spectacular comet shower of maybe a billion comets at one time. Roberto needed to warn the human race of this impending disaster.

Her other concern was the infiltration of the ghul on their otherwise peaceful planet. It was possible that others from Mars could come now that they had access by means of the existing ghul. In the past, it was a rare thing to encounter the Devata on Venus, but it was becoming more commonplace of late. She continued to pray for guidance and wisdom, afraid of what would come next.

Orion's chains weighed heavy. He lay slumped against the wall with an air of defeat, his body worn out with the daily torture of mind and body. The Xanthurus took great delight in his punishment at the direction of Dracon. Dracon was always present at such times to witness Orion's ill fate with great satisfaction.

Orion thought of the nights Nastacia haunted his dreams with images of pulsing light. Her beauty and fiery demeanor filled his soul with an insatiable passion. He could hear her softly spoken voice, low and husky with a rich musical tone and an exotic accent. She would be the death of him, but her power over him was more than he could manage in his weakness.

Orion's wings were ragged and torn, and blood seeped from his wounds. Thorns protruded from his torso, embedded deep within his skin; his long, luxuriant hair now hung lank with perspiration. His eyes were closed when he heard a voice in close proximity. His thoughts turned to the Lord of Hosts in the High Heavens and the torture he had encountered for the sake of redemption of the universe. His own torture was meaningless, a waste of life. He could not even save his true love by means of his own death.

"Why don't you fight back? You are a warrior angel, are you not?" His voice fractured, he spoke in breathless gasps. "I for one know there is no escape for me alone, but you could help me, and we could escape together. Have you no power left? I was told angels possess great powers. What is the matter with you?"

Orion opened his eyes wearily. His vision was slightly bleary, but he could see the small stature of the male with Draconian features dressed in a black robe sitting beside him. His bones stuck out from underneath his robe, his face was gaunt, and his eyes looked demented.

Orion made a reluctant effort to speak. "I was once an angel, but I am a fallen one. I don't deserve any favors or even grace for the path I have taken, and my loved one may be no more."

He thought of Nastacia. She would not survive a life on this planet; she could even be dead already. He could not face life without her. It was too painful; he wanted to die—to exist no more. Then he would not need to feel the intense pain of his tortured mind. The physical stuff he could endure, but the mental torture was too much to bear. He could not ask for help. It was too late; he could not live without her.

The Draconian did not like what he was hearing. "Pathetic! You are pathetic. Look at yourself...listen to yourself. You can't just give up; you must fight back." He took a deep breath. "Fight for your life. Dracon will bring you death; the certainty is undeniable...but...but it will be slow and very painful. Be not entangled with the yoke of bondage. Death is better than the torture of Dracon." He lamely grabbed hold of Orion's shoulders and tried to shake some sense into him but instead fell to the ground weeping in despair.

Orion did not respond. He just lay there, defeated. A flush of anger filled the Draconian. He hissed in exasperation. Orion was dimly aware of the clanking keys that opened the dungeon's gates. The commanding presence of Dracon overwhelmed him. The Draconian sat back in the shadows of the dark dank dungeon watching in despair as two of the Xanthurus guards let loose Orion's chains, his chance of escape fading before his eyes. He knew Orion was on his last legs, and the torture he must face could be the last, fatal blow.

The Xanthurus pulled him from the dungeon, his feet dragging behind him, leaving tracks in the dust. Orion wished for death; he thought that the heavenly court had deemed him fallen. He felt detached from the situation as Dracon gave the command for the whipping of his body. The weapon was riddled with the sphere of merciless spikes. With each blow, Orion screamed out in agony, but he did not resist.

"STOP!" shouted Dracon. The Xanthurus stopped searching out Dracon's eyes, confused by his interruption. Dracon walked up to Orion, who was held up in chains. He looked into his eyes closely.

"Why do you not fight back? I expected more pleasure than this! If this is not enough for you, I will have to put you in combat with Elastus, my most fearsome Xanthurus. Then you will have to fight for your life. Nastacia waits for me at the fortress of Deimos. She is now my queen, and how I enjoy her sweet aroma. But her days are numbered, as are yours. You cannot protect her now."

Orion writhed in his chains. She was still alive! This knowledge changed everything. He needed to fight and escape now in order to save her. He spat at Dracon.

Dracon laughed loud, causing the caves to rumble. "I always know your weak spots, Orion. You are pathetic, and weakness is your downfall. Send him back to the dungeons until the final fight—one that he will not endure."

The Xanthurus dragged Orion back to the dungeon and threw him on the floor, fit for nothing.

The Draconian tried once more to talk him into escape. Orion weakly whispered, "Now that I know my loved one is alive, I must escape. And you will help me, yes?"

The Draconian agreed and with renewed hope dragged himself up from the ground.

The Forest Fire

As far as the eye could see, majestic trees traced a winding course. The forest grew dark and perilous as Celestial and her companions reached the northern tip of the forest of Asan. Spirits of darkness gathered around them. They traveled by foot so as not to be seen as they passed through the dense trees and plants. As the forest thinned out, it became quieter, but the shadows remained.

Celestial came to a sudden stop. "We will rest here for a while, and Gabriel and Mikael will prepare the kindling of fire farther back in the deeper forest. On their return, we shall depart first north and then turn toward the northeast. Is everyone in agreement?"

"Why, yes!" said Cava in a strained, unnatural tone. It was unlike Cava to be so afraid; it made Ilk even more terrified than he had been before. The others were without doubt trusting Celestial's judgment in such matters.

For a moment, there was a frozen silence. Ilk settled on Rusalka's shoulder and whispered urgently in her ear, "Don't you think it would be better if we set off now, and Gabriel and Mikael can catch up? That way, we will not be in danger of the forest fire spreading toward us. What do you think, Rusalka? Do you see the sense in what I am trying to say, anyways? I mean, we must take the necessary precautions. Elks always taught me to be careful, and we must be—"

A faint smile touched Rusalka's lips. "You know, you do have a point, Ilk, but I think the direction of the wind is in our favor. Let us take a short rest and eat the food we have gathered from the forest, and then we will move on with haste."

Ilk sat back down, not at all convinced.

Gabriel and Mikael wandered back in to the thick of the trees in search of the appropriate place to start a fire. A terrible sound that seemed to vibrate to the bone could be heard nearby. Celestial and the others could hear the tremendous roar from the edge of the forest.

Ilk's eyes darted quickly from side to side as he began to tremble. "Ah, see...I told you...we should be moving along now!" He fluttered his wings, ready for flight.

Corsivo knew exactly what the noise was. "The manticore's roar cannot be mistaken! Maybe I should help my brothers," he said, pulling on Ilk's wings to stop him from taking off.

"No," said Celestial. "Your protection is needed here with us right now, and I am sure that the manticore will not end up with the satisfying meal he so desires. Come; we must move quickly north. Mikael and Gabriel will join us later, when they have finished what they must do."

"I hope you are right, Your Majesty," said Ilk, clinging to

229

Corsivo. Ilk was not the only one clinging to Corsivo; Cava did not feel too sure either.

Gabriel and Mikael heard the footsteps of the manticore as it drew nearer. They decided to light the fire there and then before the manticore found their position. The fire was lit in no time; supernatural powers made sure of that.

The manticore leaped out from behind the bushes and came face to face with Gabriel, next to the smoldering flames. Its growl filled the air. The power of its mighty wings beat heavily to its every step. Three rows of sharp teeth were exposed. Gabriel braced himself against the oncoming creature. With one fell swoop, the manticore's large, sharp claws gouged into Gabriel's side, knocking him to the ground. The shock of his landing stole the strength from his legs and his wings, and the pain stole his breath temporarily.

Mikael jumped onto the manticore's back, his arms locked around its strong neck. The manticore reared onto its hind legs, and Mikael's bare hands held on tight. Coughing in the smoke-laden air, Gabriel forced himself up onto one knee. In one last movement, he plunged his dagger into the manticore's heart. Pushing his hands into its chest, he ripped out its treacherous heart and threw it into the emerging flames. The manticore fell to the ground with a mighty thud and lay there, motionless. The mighty screams of its soul could be heard in the heart of the fire.

"That looks painful!" said Mikael, pointing to the blood dripping from the wound in Gabriel's side. He knelt beside Gabriel to take a closer look. "Ah...it is nothing that Celestial or Rusalka cannot fix, my friend!"

The fire had taken hold, the trees alight, ravaged by the flames spreading through the Forest of Asan. Mikael helped Gabriel take flight. Spreading their wings like mighty eagles, they escaped the leaping flames beneath them.

On their return, everyone cheered, relieved that they were safe. They looked back toward the forest. Smoke rose in gray clouds above it, and the flames leaped higher and higher in the distance. The howling sounds of beasts consumed by fire filled the forest. Rusalka miraculously healed Gabriel's wounds. Cava could not believe the power that the Almighty One could bestow on such faithful ones. She dared not say it, but she wished it were possible for her to attain such gifts. Why would Elyon love her as he loved his chosen ones? No, she must accept she would never be like them, but...hey, she was with them, and Corsivo was so appealing she just wanted to be by his side. Never before had she wanted to get close to anyone; never before had she trusted anyone.

Corsivo put his arm around Gabriel, pleased that they had conquered a creature he once was. He of course knew the strength it possessed, and he had really feared for their lives. He needed yet to learn more about being an angel of Elyon. He yearned to ascend to Heaven to be in the presence of Elyon, his salvation.

Cava kept by Corsivo's side, afraid of what may befall them on their journey to the northeast. For once, she listened to Celestial rather than her inner counsel. As a child, she had heard of terrible things that rose from the Arcadian seas. Corsivo felt compassion for her, knowing her misery as a consequence of sin—after all, he had been there too, before his new birth. He just wanted to protect her—and, of course, little Ilk. He reassured them that he would take care of them. Cava glanced into his benevolent eyes and was sure he meant every word he spoke. She smiled happy to be with him, away from her awful existence under the rule of Dracon. The thought passed her mind that she could give allegiance to his God, and then Corsivo may be interested in her despite her uncomely appearance.

The swirling clouds above seemed to be closing in. It was time to move on rapidly toward Phebus. They continued in silence, finding refuge as the sun rose at the base of a group of exotic rock formations.

Roberto struggled for breath. He felt exhausted and was in need of water. He fell to his knees before Celestial. "I cannot go any farther without water," he gasped.

Mikael helped him to his knees with Gabriel's assistance.

"Elyon will provide water in a desolate land. Look behind you in the depressions of these deformed rocks. You will find living waters. Drink, and you will thirst no more."

Roberto climbed two steps up the rock formation and peered over the top to find Celestial's words to be true. He cupped his hands and drank fervently of the fresh, sparkling water and then climbed back down, sated and refreshed.

Cava had watched in anticipation, and she stepped up precariously to take a look at the water. She had not experienced pure, clear water in her life, and she felt compelled to try it. Cupping her hands in imitation of Roberto, she leaned forward to taste the living waters. But alas, it was gone in an instant and was as gray as their natural surroundings. Cava was angry. She shouted, "Why, Celestial? Why can I not drink of these waters like Roberto? What favor belongs to him and not to me?"

Rusalka gently held on to Cava's shoulders. "It is not that you cannot drink of these living waters of life. Anyone can. Corsivo, show Cava; you drink now!"

Corsivo stepped up the rocky formation slowly toward the dip in the surface above, not daring to look back into Cava's desperate eyes. Sure enough, the water was evident for him to partake of. He did not drink but placed his hands into the shallow water.

Rusalka continued. "It is because you have not given yourself to our Mighty Creator. This holds you back from enjoying the fruits of his chosen ones."

Cava's heart was still hard; her soul had no light. Her only light was her feelings for Corsivo, but she did not dare hope to become his.

"I am not ready to give myself to something I do not understand. I don't think I am the type of being that your Elyon is looking for, and anyway, I don't need to drink your precious water," she said, searching the sky desperately for answers.

Corsivo put his arms around her shoulders. "Give it time, Cava. You may change your mind. Just let go of the strongholds in your life from your difficult past, and Elyon will do the rest. I can't push you into it because it has to be your walk with Him, not mine, but I sure wish I could do it for you because I care…we all care about your life."

Cava shrugged her shoulders. "Deep in my mind, I always thought it would be dark." Her eyes shone with tears. "I know of darkness beyond anyone's awareness. Mutters of evil, hints of being dammed, and I can't seem to free myself from it."

Celestial spoke softly to Cava. "You have to want to change from your very core being and show evidence of that change. We are here to help you."

Cava softened slightly, afraid to show her true feelings. Corsivo tried to comfort her with passionate words. "You will rise to a glorious life yet." He said, cradling her in his arms. The sun battled her melancholy, bathing her in its rays and whispering of a new hope.

Chapter 19

Dracon's Bride

The Fortress of Deimos...

The time had come. Nastacia looked up, eyes wide as she sprang up from her sitting position. The Xanthurus had returned to escort Nastacia to her wedding. She had no choice but to follow her fate.

She shuddered at the prospect of meeting Dracon once again. The Xanthurus noticed something about her eyes that belied her submissive image, but her face betrayed nothing. As she walked through the dark corridors of the fortress, her mind raced unwillingly; the dark walls whispered things she did not want to hear. Engraved with the paintings of evil beasts, the walls' crevices were covered in serpents, hissing with threatening pursuit. Several shadows passed her body. She turned round sharply; afraid of what lurked in the darkness.

The Xanthurus reveled in her fear. "There is more going on here than the careless eyes can see. They are the unseen." Her eyes darted from side to side as she spoke.

"Plead for the case of your wretched soul." The Xanthurus laughed mockingly.

Nastacia's scream echoed through the walls. "Leave me alone."

"That, my dear, is not going to get you very far." The Xanthurus's chilling red eyes met hers.

Rage swelled up in Nastacia like none she had ever felt before. She glared resentfully at the Xanthurus. She did her best to stifle unwelcome thoughts. She was ready to sacrifice her soul to pay the cost of what she had done. Thoughts of Celestial entered her mind. *What have I done? And Orion—what has become of him?* She hated herself. Her responsibility for him weighed heavily upon her. Her body became taut. Her teeth gritted as new energy surged through her body. Her eyes blazed, and her face screwed up in anger as she spat out her words. "You will pay! You better believe it. I will soon be queen—remember that!"

The Xanthurus bared her sharp, yellowed fangs as she snarled, looming over Nastacia. "Do not make a mockery of yourself. Who are you but a small fairy? You delude yourself, girl. Your previous master has disowned you, and you think your new master will care about you? Ah, no. You will desire to escape life, day and night." The Xanthurus let loose a high-pitched laugh that echoed through the thick stone walls.

A host of dark visions invaded Nastacia's head. Tears of anger ran down her cheeks. Deep-red snakes with black markings covered the floor, slithering past and in between her tiny feet. She held her breath and tried not to think or feel. She heard a voice inside her head. "Get out...get away while you still can."

But it was too late, as she was approaching the two large iron doors, open and ready for her entrance. Reluctantly she entered the banquet hall of the Fortress of Deimos. The Xanthurus pushed her from behind, willing her forward to the king's throne. She struggled against each step, her eyes filled with terror.

The vast, gray, stone, windowless hall had been prepared for her wedding. Myriads of candles and torches filled the chamber, casting shadows across the low ceiling, and a carpet of black rose petals covered the ground.

The Xanthurus began to chant as she walked to her doom, the sound of their drums more like a death march than a wedding. She looked up into Dracon's leering, bulbous eyes, which darted disturbingly from side to side as he beckoned her forward with his long talons. At that moment, a greater, darker shadow passed over them—some creature seemed to move across the ceiling without legs or feet, hovering over them, more of a slithering of blackness darker than night itself. A strange, unnatural coldness filled the atmosphere. Nastacia shivered uncontrollably.

She stood before Dracon's towering stature. His skin gleamed in the candlelight. She felt sick; nothing seemed quite real.

Dracon smiled sardonically. "You need not be afraid, Nastacia. Now that Orion is dead, you have me to take care of you—until the day I tire of you, that is."

Nastacia's heart stopped in her throat. She thought of kind and caring Orion. She knew she had taken him for granted, had been too headstrong in her dealings with him. She could not believe the extent of her treachery. Sorrow and other fierce emotions welled up inside of her, and she clenched her jaw, quelling the sensation by strength of will power. She would not give Dracon the satisfaction. No, she would leave her grieving until later.

She returned his gaze longer than she should before slowly prostrating herself until her brow touched the floor. Her bearing was proud as she spoke. "Well, I will just have to make myself indispensable to you, of that you can be sure. You will not want to rid yourself of me; you will see." She stepped by his side in readiness for their vows.

Dracon was intrigued. No one had ever challenged him this way. She looked like some tiny, mystical goddess, with her long, wild, berry-red hair. Her emerald-green eyes penetrated his mind. *Perhaps I am going to enjoy this union after all.*

All the time she was repeating her vows, she was filled with thoughts of murder. *My time will come. I will make sure of it.* Her soul was consumed with hatred, and a deep and terrible rage burned within her, beyond compare. *I will have revenge!*

Dracon looked satisfied. "Come, my bride. I have laid out a feast fit for a king and queen." He held out his arm for her to walk by his side into the banquet hall. As she passed the Xanthurus chambermaid, she held her head up high, giving her a haughty sidelong glance. The Xanthurus bared her fangs, seething silently.

The hall was full of musical merriment, the eyes of the entire Xanthurus army watching her every movement. It was such a carnivorous feast, and Nastacia had no appetite for any of it.

"You must eat, my queen. You will need all your strength to satisfy my needs."

"Worry not, My Lord. I hunger not in your presence, for my excitement takes away my appetite. I will eat later."

"Ah…I see. Then you must drink this elixir. Shall we say it will surely make your eyes shine and give you an appetite for later…Ha…ha…ha." Dracon roared with laughter.

Nastacia drank a little of the viscous liquid—but not too much; she needed to stay in control of her senses.

The bedchamber was heavily curtained against the light. Candles burned brightly all around the room, casting shadows in the darkness. The furnishings were unexpectedly grand; an enormous four-poster bed lavishly curtained in red and gold dominated the room, providing color against the dark-gray walls. An open fire raged, flames leaping high in the vast stone fireplace. At first, she sensed his presence, and then caught a movement in the periphery of her vision. The great, macabre shadow of Dracon crossed the walls of the vast chamber. Nastacia twisted and turned, looking for a way out. But there was no way out; she had to face the madness of the lizard king. She would not allow him to fill her with fear. No, she would not. She would be strong until the time came for his death. Yes, his death—not her death; she was not ready to die until she had put right the wrong she had done to her own people, especially Orion. Oh…how could she have been so blind?

Dracon walked up to her slowly, his eyes bright with treachery and his laughter filling the air with impending slaughter. She stood in the dim light, motionless. Fear held her in its grip. She was frantic, unable to draw breath.

"Well, my little muse. I see you did not fulfill your promises regarding Celestial. I do not take to that very kindly."Dracon encircled her deliberately…slowly…taking in her essence, his greenish-gray skin smooth, iridescent in the candlelight. "But…I have decided to be kind to you. After all, you are my queen. I could do with a companion who gives me pleasure for a while, whenever it takes my fancy. We could have some real fun

237

together, you and I."

He lifted her face up with his long, scrawny hands, digging his sharp, claw-like nails mercilessly into her soft flesh. Blood ran down her neck from the puncture wounds, but she held herself in check; she did not wince. She just eyed him with a stubborn, unblinking stare. Her silence infuriated him.

"Oh, yes, you will please me."His long, slim hands gathered around her delicate throat. "Or else...you will know the meaning of true despair and desolation, and I will have no mercy."

He released her, pushing her to the ground in a humiliated heap, reminding himself it was not yet time to take her life.

Nastacia held her hands to her throat gently, coughing and spluttering. There was a look of intense sadness and hopelessness on her beautiful face, which unusually charmed Dracon. His austere features eased into a smile. The pounding of her heart was more than she could bear as Dracon lifted her up into his arms and carried her to his bed. Only a miracle could save her now.

Chapter 20

The Beginning of Destruction

The Forest of Alvor...

Kisseiai and Calvor had taken it upon themselves to meet every morning before temple service, after the song of a new dawn had been sung, to discuss their future intentions as training members of the Sukra—a very sacred position to hold in the natural order of things known to them. High elves of the order, according to custom, had always sung at the first sign of dawn; the light awakening the hauntingly mellow Elvish song heard across the forest and far beyond.

This particular morning, they had wandered far without realizing the passage of time. They found their way to a beautiful glade and sat among the wild flowers, sun dazzled with many colors standing still in the early morning sun. The birds sang their songs of joy cheerily above, and small butterflies, sparkling silver and gold, fluttered past. There was no evidence of the changing atmosphere that morning; Calvor was just thinking how content he felt as they sat in rare silence, soaking in the sun, when all of a sudden, the ground beneath them began to break up violently.

The trees swayed, the birds had flown away, and the small animals begged a retreat in search of safety. Calvor grabbed

Kisseiai's hands as she slipped down into a crevice formed by the tremors. He struggled as he pulled her up, but they managed to take flight as a second tremor caused more damage.

The sky darkened as though night had crept upon them. The tremors had ceased, but an almighty wind ensued, blowing them in all directions as they fought against its force. Huge clouds of dust hindered their visibility and breathing, and the humidity dropped vastly as the temperature increased. Flames swept from treetop to treetop as the oil in the eucalyptus trees broke down into a flammable gas. The air became filled with smoke and ash, and an ominous red glow colored the sky to the north.

Calvor and Kisseiai reached the castle, ragged and torn, black soot covering them like an evil cloak amid a pure spirit. The castle was unbelievably still intact, but the fires raged on deep in the forest.

Shula gathered the elders of the order of the Sukras together, forty members in all; their quest: to put out the fires. They swept above the treetops with the authority of the powers from within and willed the fires to cease.

The aftermath was a destruction they had never encountered before on Venus. Trees uprooted. Trees burned to nothing. Green grass turned to black. The whole scene was devastation, yet the castle had been protected—not a stone unturned.

Everyone gathered at the castle for guidance, terrified for the future of Venus. As they turned up steadily over a short period of time, it became certain that they had the protection of Elyon. The damage to their wings would soon be restored with the powers of regeneration they possessed.

The elf king and queen entered the great hall, happy to see their people safe. Not even the grand paintings on the walls had moved during the quake. Some sat exhausted, while others stood in anticipation of what would happen next. The king beckoned Shula forth to speak on his behalf, for his grief lay heavily upon his heart.

Shula began to address the court. "We must all remember the words of Elyon and be in awe of his protection. Did he not say to measure carefully in your mind when you see these predicted signs? Then you will know that it is almost the time when he will visit the world—all worlds—once again. No doubt these things will increase in intensity, as they will on our sister planet, Earth. But Elyon will have compassion upon your souls if you stay pure in heart. We have become more susceptible in these last days due to our imperfect state, which is deteriorating fast. The enemy now has access to our hearts and our minds more than ever before. I beg you, DO NOT LET HIM IN. Be on your guard at all times. Search the Scrolls of Old and the Manuscripts of New, and you will be kept safe. Remember to help one another, and love your brother as you like to be loved yourself. Amen."

Everyone stood up and spoke in a chorus of unity: "Amen."

The Paristan stood tall, the flaming swords shining brightly in their guards at their sides; ready to be warriors for Elyon and His people.

The elf king spoke at last, encouraged by Shula's words. "We must restore what is ours and work together to bring relief to those who have lost their homes. If necessary, we must share our homes with those who have suffered loss, destroyed by this planet's natural disaster. Rest now, and the next dawn, we will inspect the damages before we prepare to travel west to the Valley of the Queens, where we hope to join Celestial and the Seraphim."

The Limnades

The forest's enchantment had been lost. With the sun blocked out, the gloom settled upon its shoulders like a dark veil of death. Calvor tried to think of Shula's words, but the empty chasm inside his soul stole the flavor of her wisdom from his heart. He walked alone in search of the path that would lead him to the Alpseid nymphs. He wanted to make sure they had not been hurt.

He was almost sure he had arrived at the same place he had once connected with, but there was no sign of the nymphs. The grass was black, and smoke filled his nostrils. He sat down, coughing and spluttering, afraid of letting his thoughts engage the possibility of the Alpseids' total destruction, vulnerable little beings that they were. He glimpsed a movement in the corner of his eye. He rubbed his eyes and turned around to see a tall, elegant girl lying close by on the ground. He cautiously crept forward, afraid she could be a ghul. Her eyes were shut, her long eyelashes casting shadows over her beautiful, pale skin tarnished by the soot; her white, flowing dress was ripped and soiled, but her beauty was still apparent, her slim, lithe body intact.

Calvor thought twice. He was afraid. Should I help her? Is she of the Devata?

He went against his better judgment and carefully swept her into his arms. He had not walked very far, stumbling over areas of broken earth, when he noticed her eyelashes fluttering. He set her down on a now-rare soft mound of untouched grass and lay her head across his lap in the shade of an old oak tree. The tree had showed its strength; its long, snakelike roots, embedded deep into the ground, had kept it from the vengeance of the unrelenting quake. Her eyes opened, but she did not speak. Calvor gently asked her where she had come from, but still no answer. To his horror, tears of blood ran down her delicately sculptured cheeks. He wiped them away gently with the dew from a leaf from the ground and picked her up.

"Worry not, whoever you are. I will take care of you just as I was taken care of by the Alpseid nymphs."

She did not answer. She merely closed her eyes once again. She was as light as a feather in his arms.

It was not far before he stumbled upon Larina, one of the nymphs who had saved his life. Larina flew up to the level of his eyes. She was a beautiful little Alpseid nymph, everything so perfectly formed for one so small—one elf's hand in height, blue eyes, and silvery-blue hair. Calvor was not aware that since she had lost her perfect state, she was known to exhibit jealousy and possessive tendencies. She whispered in his ear in her tiny voice asking him why he carried a Limnade away from her body of water—she would surely die.

Calvor wanted to know more about the Limnades. He knew only that they were nymphs of the water. Larina reluctantly led him to the others of her kind. It was evident to Calvor that she was not in the same spirit that she had been in the last time he had met her. Her off hand approach he put down to the hardship they had undergone during the tremors. Calvor walked in silence, Larina flying close to him, soberly taking in the ravaged forest. The songs of the birds had all but disappeared, and the ground was now uneven, having been ripped open by the quake in parts. The Alpseid nymphs were, of course, distraught with the destruction of their glens and groves, but at the same time, they were humbly happy to be alive. They too were surprised to see Calvor with a Limnade in his arms.

Their leader, Ossieta, explained more about her precarious position away from her body of water. "By daylight, the Limnades nymphs are but swans that morph into beautiful maidens when the sun sets. Alas, when the sun rises, if they do not return to their body of water, they will surely die. Her body of water must be polluted to cause her dying state before sunrise. If you can get her back to her source, we can see what the problem is and hopefully save her life."

Calvor asked the way, and the Alpseid nymphs willingly showed him which direction to go in. Larina and Ossieta accompanied him, although Larina did not look pleased at all. Calvor was too focused to ask why at that point. They flew, carrying the Limnade nymph to the River Castra, which ran through the edge of the forest eastward toward the coast.

They expected pollution caused by the catastrophe they had just endured, but what they saw chilled them to the bone. The stream had turned blood red. Calvor's face changed color—white with fear. Every living creature floated along with the rapid current. Other nymphs' bodies floated past, some strewn on the embankment, soaked in bright red blood—no one had been spared.

Afraid, Ossieta spoke in earnest. "We must get away from here. There is nothing we can do for them now. It is our duty to try to save the life of the nymph in your arms while we can, before it is too late...though I feel sure her fate is sealed, Calvor."

Calvor had been rendered speechless. He searched out his voice; it came as a whisper. "I tried to speak to her when she opened her eyes, but she did not answer. What can we do?" He looked down at her beautiful face.

Larina stood in stony silence.

"We must go in search of another body of water before sunrise and just hope she can adapt to it. Limnades do not like to leave the body of water that is their birthright; we can only hope and pray that she will adapt quickly to waters unknown to her—and, of course, will she be accepted by the nymphs of the watery deep that we first come upon?"

Calvor did not like what he was hearing at all. "We have no other choice. We will find out soon enough."

"Yes. Come, we cannot delay any longer," said Ossieta; she fluttered her tiny wings and headed toward the Castle of Alvor. "There we can look at a map of the forest for the nearest body of water that may not have been affected."

Calvor followed, carrying the nymph in his arms.

The king and queen of Alvor were distraught to hear the news. They laid the Limnade carefully on a soft, silk-cushioned sofa. The map gave them a clear picture of the River Harpina, which ran through the southern part of the Forest of Alvor, slightly east. It did not connect to the river they had encountered on the east coast.

Kisseiai joined Calvor and the Alpseid nymphs in order to help carry the Limnade nymph to the River Harpina, southeast of the Forest of Alvor. Larina flew at great speed with them in cold silence. The green-eyed monster had captured her soul unwittingly.

Exhausted by their journey, they reached the water's edge, and, sure enough, the water was not contaminated, or so it

244

seemed. The sun had started to rise as they placed the Limnade's body in the water. Her body floated out in the gentle morning current. The sun rose slowly, but nothing seemed to be happening as they waited with bated breath.

Calvor cried out, "Oh, no...please, Elyon, don't let her die...please...I will serve You all of my days and obey Your every command, but don't let her die!"

Kisseiai put her arm around him to comfort him. Larina could not hold herself back anymore as jealousy welled up inside of her. She began to tug at Kisseiai's hair from behind as hard as her small body would let her. Kisseiai cried out. "Ouch, what is the matter with you?"

Ossieta was just about to chastise her when Calvor shouted, this time with joy, "Glory be to Elyon."

Larina and Ossieta looked toward the river, and in the near distance, a beautiful swan elegantly swam away.

∞

Chapter 21

The Kingdom of Semiramis

Castle of Alvor...

Astoria did not attempt to take Patience with her to visit the underwater Kingdom of Semiramis after her last unpleasant encounter, so it was agreed that she would stay with the elf king and queen at the palace in expectation of her father's return. The elf king and queen and the Order of the Sukras had made a unanimous decision that someone had to check that all was well with the merfolk on account of their own experiences with the natural forces of the planet at ground level.

Shula picked out two of the Paristan to accompany Astoria, Corsica, and Shaloma. Calendula listened closely to their conversation and asked for permission to join them. Shula, knowing that Calendula had once lived in the underwater realm, thought it would be a good thing for him to help them. He knew the ocean kingdom very well.

The following day, the stealthy white horses of the Paristan rode at great speed east, toward the border of Castra. The clashing of their golden hooves creating sparks of fire with every step. The heat was stupefying, and the burden of what they might find in the wake of the destructive power of the quake lay heavily upon them.

Great trees stood bare and silent with tangled boughs and withered leaves. The smoke-filled air began to settle, casting a somber gray cast across the land. Yes, the once-beautiful land had changed like never before; a great sadness filled their hearts as they reached the river of Ossiana on the east coast of Cushara before Castra.

The horses reared at the sight of the great blackbirds soaring over the polluted river, full from a plentiful feast. The current was swift and treacherous, and the banks were high. Astoria spoke. "Look, Leviathan makes our planet waste and distorts its surface. None of us are immune as Venus mourns and fades away. Because we have changed the ordinance of things and broken the everlasting covenant, the curse has devoured our planet and left us desolate."

In the baking daylight, only where the rock pool lay behind the cascading waterfall was the air cool and moist. Droplets of cool waters clung to their warm skin. They passed under, relieved from the soaring heat that pervaded the air. Calendula led them to a cave. It looked inviting in its mystery. Inside, the air was misty and cool. With a frisson of unease, they carefully passed through.

Astoria's curiosity began to rival her fear as she found her eyes wandering among the murals on the rocky surfaces. Faded paintings of old, encompassing a celestial host of angels and Cherubim, could be seen in the flickering light of the torches burning brightly.

"I never knew this place existed," said Astoria, pleased to see such a vision of light amid the darkness of recent events. Calendula smiled, but there was sadness behind the gesture. They continued to follow him until the rocks gleamed as if they were wet.

Calendula began to dismount. "Here we must leave our horses. The sea is no place for them."

He halted under the shadow of a nearby rock. They could hear the turbulence of the sea beyond as Calendula placed his right hand upon the huge rock face, chanting Elvish words of supernatural power. The rock disappeared from sight before them, leading them into the heart of the Semiramis realm. Utter chaos abounded. The Golden Kingdom was in turmoil. Their homes had been destroyed, and some of the merfolk had been missing since the catastrophe. Calendula stumbled upon Mercy, the mermaid involved in the Pearl of Wisdom scandal. Her heart was heavy with grief; she could not find her daughter amid the turmoil. Astoria soothed her soul. "We are here to help you in any way we can. We will look for your daughter, but please do tell us of Princess Shakira and Prince Ovid. Are they safe?"

"Yes, I believe they are, but I have not seen them myself. I have heard that the Golden Palace still stands solid in its former grandeur and that the prince and princess are safe within its walls. The bottom of the ocean broke forth into sections, causing chaos and destruction to our realm. Homes have been destroyed, but the most chilling thing is that the creatures of the eerie deep have been propelled into our world, and we are afraid of what they may be capable of. We are not safe anymore. What if they find my daughter?" Mercy began to weep.

Astoria placed her arms around Mercy. "I am sure Elyon will keep her safe, as you have proved to be a worthy subject to this kingdom. Come. We will go to Shakira and then search for your daughter."

They passed through the undulating water, which was visibly corrupted with the debris of uprooted plants and murky waters from the depths of the ocean, stirred and shaken by the slight movement of the plate tectonics now rendered vulnerable by nature itself. The ocean floor had been pulled down, one plate of the lithosphere beneath another, forming a deep ocean trench beneath their underwater city. Merfolk swam in different directions in a state of shock, their once-beautiful city now in ruins. Their young clung to their elders in fear of the marauding scavengers eager to feed upon their fishy torso, a delicious delicacy for the creatures of the deep.

Small fish swam in droves swiftly past them as they entered the Golden Palace domain. Coral weed waved ghostly patterns in their path. There, unbelievably, stood the gleaming palace in the distance, a dull glow amid the dark, gloomy waters. Even the pillars and arches leading up to the steps were stoically unmoved by the disaster that had befallen the beautiful Kingdom of Semiramis.

Calendula prepared the way forward through the myriad of sea creatures and corals, some dead, floating among the debris surrounding them, others fighting for their existence. He turned to look at Astoria. Her mouth was stretched wide open, forming a scream, but the muscles of her throat had locked tight—no sound escaped as she pointed to the creature that lay beyond, heading for Calendula.

Shaloma had drawn her sword from its hilt, followed by Corsica. Calendula caught sight of a great black shadow looming ominously above him. He turned around swiftly against the force of the water to find the huge jaws and sharp white teeth of an undefined creature in pursuit of him.

Astoria's terror-stricken features were vivid, the horror clear in her eyes as a second creature of immense proportions entered their vicinity. She froze in terror. Calendula battled against the first creature, dagger in hand. His Elvin strength was apparent in the power of his movements against the underlying current. He mounted the creature and rode it as he would his horse, stabbing his sharp dagger into its back numerous times, a stream of blood following its path.

The creature's photophore lashed against Calendula in an attempt to dislodge him from his precarious position, but Calendula held on, sinking his dagger many times into the creature's head. Blood spewed out intermittently, coloring the surrounding water a nasty dark red.

Meanwhile, Shaloma and Corsica battled against the second, larger creature, which was serpent-like with a large, heavy jaw. A long tongue flicked out from its mouth, threatening to swallow them up like flies. Its long, large-girthed body was covered in sharp, horny protrusions as its tail lashed backward and forward, striking Astoria with an almighty thud. She tried to pull herself free from the creature's torso as her body was thrown in all directions with the swoop of its tail. Shaloma came to her rescue, pulling her free from the grip of the horny protrusions. Unable to attend to Astoria's wounds, Shaloma returned to battle alongside Corsica, plunging her sword into the eye of the beast. At that very moment, Corsica struck its heart with her sword, and the beast finally floated away in a trail of blue blood.

They immediately turned to Calendula to find that he had disappeared. There was no evidence of the creature's death; it too had disappeared from view. Astoria looked around, desperately clutching her side as she swam with one arm. Shaloma grabbed her other arm and gently pulled her back toward her.

"It is no use, Astoria. We have lost Calendula to the treacherous creature of the ocean. We must go on without him. Our only relief in this is his return to the blessed realm, where the shadow of death is no more."

The thought of not seeing Calendula again pierced Astoria's heart acutely, but she knew he would be at peace. He would not have to suffer the times of darkness and despair yet to take place on their planet. This was only the beginning! Her mind raced with the prophecies she had been made aware of. She needed to prepare her people for things to come and make sure Roberto did the same for his people on Earth.

They entered the Golden Gates of the Palace of Semiramis with a broken spirit and found solace in Shakira and Ovid's company. Shakira administered a healing potion used frequently by the merfolk to Astoria's wound and spoke gently. "We must gather our people to the palace, as many as we can fit in these walls. All are in danger from these predators of the deep, and we are sure of the presence of the Selkies—a great threat to our young ones in particular. We are most grateful for your assistance and very sad for your loss. You must stay and rest this night before you return—and return you must, for your own people need you in the absence of Celestial and Rusalka. How is Patience this day?"

Astoria sighed. "She is well, Princess, but of course she is fearful for her father the longer he is away."

"Of course she is! You must reassure her as much as you can when you return."

"Yes, Princess, I must show her the way to help her people

250

back on Earth. She has a great role to play in Elyon's kingdom for someone so young, but she has been chosen. And who are we to question the one who knows all?"

Shakira held Astoria's hand. "You speak words of wisdom, my dear friend. Now, get some rest in order for your wound to heal; there is much to be done." She gripped the golden carved armrests of her throne with an unease of what the future kingdom would be like in their now-treacherous ocean.

The night, so callous in its indifference, offered no comfort to Astoria. She closed her eyes, and the tears streamed unrelentingly down her lovely face. Thunder growled overhead on the distant shore. The darkness closed in like a dark veil, and sleep became elusive. She could not cope with the whirl of thoughts washing through her brain, revelations of deep and secret things that she could not make sense of.

She gently wakened Shaloma and Corsica from their slumber. "Sorry to break your time of rest, but until the day breaks and the shadow flees, I cannot stay here and wonder about our loved ones. We must return; please understand."

Shaloma and Corsica obediently followed Astoria from the palace back to shore, swimming through the still darkness of the deep waters to the undulating, inky-black waters of the surface, lapping gently against the rocks. They mounted their horses with heavy hearts, slowly retreating from the caves of Semiramis. Leading Calendula's horse to safety, their only thoughts were of their loving friend who had served them so well. They would surely miss him. How many more loved ones would they lose before they destroyed Dracon?

∞

Chapter 22

The Dungeons

The Castle of Syrtis...

It was dark and murky in the windowless dungeons. Admixture of damp earth and sweaty bodies permeated the enclosed atmosphere. All of Orion's seething anger melted away in the knowledge that Nastacia was still alive. His thoughts had been as dark as his surroundings, but now, a glimmer of light had fallen upon him, and his main concern was to escape from the hell-hole he found himself in and journey to the Fortress of Deimos, in the Valles Marineris region, south of Syrtis, in order to rescue his true love from the hands of Dracon.

He had managed to break free of his chains by the sheer force of his renewed strength. The air was thick with unease. The Draconian warriors and Martian hybrids waited with bated breath for his next move. His plan was to attack the Xanthurus guard when their food was brought to them, take the keys, and unleash the other prisoners. They would fight their way through to the exit of the castle. Then his fellow prisoners could go their own way, and he would go his.

It sounded simple, but the Draconian warriors were not so sure they could fight all the Xanthurus guards because they were comparatively small in numbers. They could see his point, however; they had nothing to lose. A swift death was better than the alternative—a slow, prolonged, painful death that Dracon would wield upon them. Could they trust this angel? Why would he help them? They could always slaughter him later, they supposed.

Orion's eyes darted toward the iron gates as he heard the clanking of keys. He lowered his head and slumped against the wall with a false air of defeat, giving the impression that he was still in chains. The Xanthurus bent down, placing the scraps of uncooked flesh near to his feet. Orion almost heaved at the stench of the meat.

The Draconian that had previously mocked him cursed the Xanthurus from behind, as planned. Turning round, the Xanthurus erupted like a volcano, spewing forth curses and his seething wrath. "You dare to speak to—"

Orion lunged forward, throwing a heavy blow with his iron like fist into the stomach of the Xanthurus.

The Xanthurus lost his balance for a split second and then recovered, letting out a mighty snarl. His eyes blazed bright red in frenzied rage as he pulled his sword from its sheath. Baring his fangs, he swung the blade a few times, feeling the weight of it. Then, using both hands, he swung back-handed, aiming for Orion's heart.

Orion ducked and rolled swiftly to the side of the Xanthurus, grabbing hold of his feet in a vise-like grip. The Xanthurus lost his balance, falling heavily to the ground. His sword clattered on the stone floor nearby, gleaming in the darkness. The prisoners began to chant in favor of Orion's defeat. The Xanthurus crawled toward his sword, which was lying close to his feet. Orion seized it and quickly sliced through the Xanthurus's tail before he had chance to stand upright again. His eyes flashed with a cold intelligence and a simmering ferocity. Blood dripped from his mouth onto his lips and chin as he pulled himself up from the floor, slowly aware of his defeat.

At that point, Orion plunged the sword straight into the Xanthurus's heart. He let go of it and watched the Xanthurus fall forward to the floor, pushing the sword deeper, through the other side of his torso. Blue blood flowed freely from the tail and the wound in his heart, spreading like viscous ink around his body.

The prisoners cheered silently, waving their fists in the air. Towering above the fallen body, he pushed it over onto its back and placed a foot firmly down, released his sword from the Xanthurus's chest, and wiped the blade on part of the black cape that was not covered in blood.

Orion used the keys to free the prisoners who shared his cell and beckoned them to follow him. Shadows cast by the flickering light of the burning torches on both sides of the stone walls gave undesired evidence of their escape as they cautiously found their way through the dark stone tunnels. They had not gotten very far when two Xanthurus guards leaped out of the dark recesses, fangs bared, red eyes glowing, ready for mortal combat, outnumbered by eleven to two.

Orion shot up into the air above the enemy and spiraled down behind them, aiming a blow to the back of the head, giving no chance for defense. The blade broke through the Xanthurus's skull in one fell swoop. He dropped to his knees without a sound and then to the floor with a loud thud. Turning toward the other Xanthurus, Orion was relieved to find him strewn across the floor, his familiar inky blue blood drenching his clothes; the Draconian warriors had recovered his sword and his spiky iron ball and chain.

Raised spears and blades flashed in the light ahead, promising death.

"There are too many," shouted one Draconian. "We can't stand against them."

"We can stand against them, and WE WILL stand against them, together as one. Give it all you have; this is your only chance. Fight to the death." Orion propelled forward. His mighty wings unfurled, forming a spreading canopy of blinding light.

The ranks of the Xanthurus fought against the blinding light. Wisps of red-colored breath laced the hot air. Suddenly, a storm of sparks flew high, the clash of iron upon bronze. Orion noticed the bridge ahead without railings on either side, a black chasm below. "Over the bridge! He cried "Push them over the side of the bridge."

254

One by one, the Xanthurus plunged down into the great void, taking with them the Draconians who had spurred Orion's escape. He had no time to despair of such a loss of life, but his revenge became ever stronger. All were slain. Then, out of the darkness, a horde of fellow creatures with red, glowing eyes appeared at the far side of the bridge. It was difficult to tell how many at first glance. The unity of chanting increased to a high crescendo, their shields held high in readiness for their intended slaughter.

Orion did not retreat. He led the prisoners, a canopy of white light before them as they crossed over the narrow bridge. Wild cries broke out. The smell of burning flesh was in the air and the distant cries of tortured souls. The shadow of death was upon them. A great weight of horror and doubt fell upon Orion. The thought occurred to him that as an angel warrior of imperfect state, he did not have the backup of Elyon anymore. Perhaps he would fail—it would not be just himself he was failing; what of the other souls and Nastacia?

No. The negative spirit must die. He said aloud, "If it is the last thing I do, I must lead these people to freedom and save Nastacia." His spirit lifted. He raised his wings high, tall and proud, crying out in a loud, thunderous voice, slicing through one Xanthurus warrior after another, decapitating and hacking off their tails with his trusted gleaming golden blade.

The Draconian warriors fought well. The fighting ceased; Xanthurus corpses covered the ground.

"Come. We must find our way out. All is not over yet," Orion reminded them, following a crooked path broken up by small pools of murky water, tiny bubbles coming up formed by the hot cauldron beneath, the underground furnace burning furiously day and night. The rocky cave walls were wet, the atmosphere steamy; droplets of warm water dripped down from above.

Orion thought back to an angel he had once known, Paimon, now one of the fallen Seraphim, the Serophoth. He had heard of Paimon's position in the Abyss—as master of the fiery furnace of the third Loka, master of infernal ceremonies. His supernatural force was to cure and inflict disease, torture, cure, and then torture again. He could not comprehend that an angel of the Lord of Hosts could contemplate such an evil existence. He suspected that Paimon influenced all torture in the universe, and thus, his presence in such a place as these infernal chambers would not be unusual. A shiver ran down his spine. The need to escape speedily was becoming more desperate.

Suddenly, a great shadow of a winged beast descended upon them. Its fiery wolverine orbs shone gold in the darkness. Orion recognized the grand marquis of the bottomless pit, an angel who was once of the order of the domination's, his former beauty desecrated with the merging shape of a wolf, the wings of a gryphon, and the tail of a black serpent.

At first sight, the Draconian warriors crouched back in fear. Orion stood before the great and mighty winged beast, three times the size of himself. "Marchocias, you do not frighten me! I damn you back to hell, where you belong."

Orion's wings unfurled once again; his brightness took Marchocias by surprise. He covered his eyes for a moment. It had been a long time since he had looked upon such holy light, but he slowly became aware that this light was not as bright as it should be. He smiled wryly to himself. This was going to be a lot easier than he had thought; Elyon had obviously deserted Orion, and he was fast becoming one of the Serophoth. He remembered his own glowing light dying as he changed to the creature he had become. He laughed a mighty roaring laugh that filled the dark cavern, echoing through the vast cavernous structure.

"I know what you are thinking, Marchocias, but I am not finished yet, and I will kill you. You are nothing but an abomination to all life itself, and Elyon will have the last laugh, you can be sure of that. To kill me is nothing, for I am finished anyway—no way will I become like you. I would rather die."

The dark beast, its shape huge and threatening, leaped into the air, beating its hideous wings in a heavy flapping motion. Before Orion had time to move out of its way, Marchocias came crashing down upon Orion, attacking like a wild animal. A loud mighty roar escaped from its large jaws, and its thick, sharp talons sank deep into his flesh, drawing blood. Unglorified...concealed in darkness, Orion gasped for breath. With one last ounce of strength, he struggled up to his feet, taking one last thrust of his sword into Marchocias's chest.

He fell backward momentarily but soon recovered, his great shadow looming above, threateningly poised for another attack. The wound seemed to have no impact at all, as Marchocias gave out another mighty roar and lunged forward with greater ferocity. He knocked Orion's sword out of his grip in one swift motion. By now, Orion was alone; the Draconian warriors had made a hasty retreat. Suddenly, Orion's eyes rolled upward, replaced by fiery orbs of flashing light. The bright light came pouring out as shafts of holy brightness, illuminating the cavern.

Marchocias was blinded by the holy light. Foaming and frothing at the mouth in terror, he flew like a hunted animal. Orion felt his body dissolve in to nothingness, along with his doubts and fears...all outside sensations drifted away...Orion had gone!

Chapter 23

Celestial's Trail Through Phebus And The Ring of Fire

Mars...

The smoky blur of the forest of Asan was lost in a deeper blackness that was already reaching the coastal tip of Phebus, beyond the mountainous range of Arcas on the east coast.

At the crest of the ridge, Roberto stopped to catch his breath. The fearful din of the tempest reached his ears as the wind blew his hair into a chaotic mess. He scanned his surroundings from the top of the lofty cliffs, surveying the turbulent black sea, greatly relieved that there was no necessity to cross such a tempestuous ocean.

The others caught up to him. "Come, Roberto. Don't stand too close to the edge. The wind is gaining from the north." Rusalka pulled him back safely to join them. "We must find shelter before the storm really takes hold."

There was a distant sound of thunder carried on the rising wind. Streaks of electric light headed in all directions, lighting up the black sky. They found a sheltered spot in the cave by the shore, overlooking the ocean, high enough not to be swallowed up by the gigantic waves of the turbulent sea furiously bashing against the rocks below.

Unexpectedly, the clouds were ripped apart by a sudden flash of spectacular lightning striking the surface of the raging ocean. The waves rose higher and higher. Corsivo stood at the edge of the cave entrance, viewing the amazing spectacle with awe, the others preferring to seek sanctuary within the inner walls of the cliff-side.

A tremendous bolt of thunder crashed through the air, almost knocking Corsivo from his precarious position. He used his wings to steady himself. The black sea heaved and rolled, churning, the waves now crashing fiercely against the cliff-side. The moon slid behind the clouds; the night was deep.

In the distance, Corsivo noticed a black shape in the darkness riding the waves like a horse. *Am I seeing things?* He looked closer, gripping the rocks tightly as the wind tried fervently to rip him from his shelter, the rain lashing with full force against his skin.

Suddenly, the shape grew larger, emerging high above the sea...the shape of a woman dressed in a black, flowing cloak, larger than life, illuminated by a green incandescent glow...moving quickly toward him. Her long, scrawny fingers splayed out like an animal's claw...the elongated fingernails discharging lightning from their tips as the sound of thunder crashed all around them.

The others came to see if Corsivo was OK. Struggling against the force of the wind, they saw the colossal, evil black figure. Her long white hair, blowing wild in the blustering wind, stood out in contrast to the dark sky. Her grotesque features moving ever nearer, she let out an almighty shrieking sound.

Brabantia shouted, her voice almost lost in the hurricane, "It is the harbinger of storms! Celestial, what can we do? She will most assuredly suck us into the sea."

At that moment, Ilk was sucked into the air, his small wings flapping in desperation as he was propelled forward toward the storm maker. "Argh...hhhhh...help...someone help...me...eeee!" His small voice was lost in the riot of the hurricane.

Sections of the sea began to rise in swirls of white-silvery

259

water spinning round like small cyclones. The storm maker's dark-black-and-green tentacles began to lash out from beneath the black cloak, growing longer...and longer, beckoning Ilk into the depths of darkness...down into the abyss.

Ilk could not bear it. His heart leaped into his mouth, or so he thought. He let out a scream from the depths of his soul, and his life passed before him in one quick moment. He realized with utter mortification that he was going to die—for sure this time. His pulse began to pound in his ears.

Corsivo hesitated no more. He threw himself off the edge of the cliff, exploding in a burst of wings. Celestial and the other angels followed him, their wings flashing, garments glowing, throwing a rainbow of colors everywhere. They flapped their mighty wings, fighting against the powerful wind.

The harbinger of storms rose higher and larger, tall and threatening. Thunder and lightning filled the sky, and the sea roared in unison.

Like glimmering comets held high with highly charged feathered wings, the angels soared around the storm maker, forming a circle of fiery light, striking with great force. As mighty warrior angels together in unity with Elyon, their power exceeded that of the powers of nature.

The grotesque being began to shrink, her form changing rapidly. Rancid breath poured out of her large mouth with each labored rasping; her tentacles lashed backward and forward in desperation. The others watched from a distance as the harbinger of storms disappeared slowly into the darkness.

The wind ceased. The thunder and lightning stopped, and the sea became unusually still. A strange calmness filled the land, as though there had been no storm at all.

A ripple of movement came from below. There, on the surface of the waters, was Ilk, fluttering his wings madly in an attempt to keep above the waters. Corsivo swooped down, picked him up swiftly, and flew back to their safe haven.

In a graceful, fiery spiral, the angels drifted down, and their shimmering wings gently closed.

"Well done, Corsivo. Your decision to react immediately was valiant. You are truly one to be counted on." Mikael threw his arm around Corsivo, appreciative that his brother was now a mighty warrior angel host of Elyon.

Gabriel also showed his respect, and the others praised Elyon for the angel's safe return. Roberto was in awe of what he had witnessed; it rendered him speechless. Ilk could not stop trembling. "Do you realize how close to death I was?...phew...I nearly died; do you realize that? I can't believe I am here at all. That is the closest I have ever got to dying...do you realize that? You may not have had me, Your Majesty. Do you realize—?"

"Yes, the realization of such a fate is ours, Ilk, and we are ever grateful that you are safe now. You will always be safe with us; do not doubt it." Celestial stroked his curly red locks in an attempt to calm him down.

Night still reigned, but all was peaceful, at least for the present. It was a lot to ask for on Mars, particularly in the region of Phebus, but they took the opportunity to rest until dawn. Roberto could not sleep. He felt too strung up with the events of the day. He could not even sit still. In order not to keep anyone else from sleeping, he made his way deeper into the cave, taking care not to wander too far, aware of the dangers of his unnatural surroundings. The interior was well lit by slow-burning torches set on iron stands. The air was heavy, warm, and still filled with a hushed malevolence. He had not gotten very far when he heard a gentle movement behind him. He swiftly turned around and came face to face with Rusalka.

"Rusalka, you should be resting, not following me!"

Rusalka looked straight into Roberto's warm brown eyes. There was a sad fascination about him. She felt the urge to care for him, hold him close, and lull him to a peaceful place, where she had been born—a place serene and beautiful beyond compare. She did not want Roberto to experience the fate of the humankind. "You must not go anywhere alone on this planet, Roberto. You need our protection. Can you not rest? Why do you look so sad?"

261

Roberto looked down for a moment. "I am not sad, Rusalka. I am worried about Patience. She is on another planet, and I have no idea if she is OK. I feel that I have let her down not being there for her. I just hope she understands."

Rusalka put her hand tenderly upon his shoulder. "Patience is in good hands with Astoria and the king and queen of Alvor. She is a special girl with wisdom beyond her years, and Elyon will protect her. Fear not; our return is imminent. You will soon be reunited with your daughter."

Roberto looked back into her eyes and felt lost, as if he were drowning in an ocean, deep...deep into the recesses of her soul.

She felt his desire and looked fleetingly away. Her heart fluttered; she felt breathless. *What is this feeling? This could not be....* He looked so young and innocent, yet wise at the same time. His face came slowly toward hers...their eyes locked, the key of desire ready to be opened.

His hands slipped around her tiny waist, drawing her close in his warm embrace. The waves of his desire lapped at her soul; she was lost in the moment. Her lips parted in anticipation, and she closed her eyes. Roberto was just about to kiss her soft lips when suddenly, her heart lurched unexpectedly and her eyes sprung open. Tears spilled down her cheeks as she slowly backed away in horror. She understood the significance of what had nearly happened, and she fell to the ground, muttering words in an unknown language.

Roberto was distraught; her reaction baffled him. He knelt beside Rusalka, begging her forgiveness, though he was not at all sure that he had done anything to hurt her. "Please go away, Roberto...please." She continued to speak words beyond his comprehension.

He did not go far but sat contemplating what had just happened. His heart grew heavy. He did not understand why he of all people had been used as a vessel for Elyon's purposes. What would Elyon think of him now that he had fallen in love with one of His holy angels? He wanted forgiveness, but he could not stop loving her. Yes, he had to admit to himself, he loved her. Would

Elyon understand?

He crept back quietly to the place where he had left her and slid behind a rock nearby. He saw her in all of her heavenly glory, clad all in white from head to toe with a golden crown of many jewels. A halo of shining light shone forth from her. He felt the serenity, the utter peace, and he sat silently...silently waiting for her return.

He knew without a doubt that he could not take her away from such wonder; he had nothing better to offer her. His love for her would not be enough; for her to become a mortal would surely not bring her the peace and contentment that Elyon gave her. He watched closely as her apparel transformed into Elvin state once again. The white light that had surrounded her all but disappeared. She looked up to see that Roberto had stepped out from behind some rocks nearby.

Roberto slowly approached her. "Do not fear me, Rusalka. I understand you. I will not even try to take you away from a life so precious. I...I love you too much for that. It would eat away at my spirit if I did such a thing. I know you love me; that's enough for me."

"Yes, Roberto, I do love you, but I will never leave our Lord of Hosts. You mean more to me than my own life, but the soul wanders everywhere seeking rest, at last returning to Elyon. An immortal soul, by its very nature, cannot find what it needs anywhere save in Elyon himself. I am sorry I cannot be in two places, but that is my sacrifice for my love of my creator. I owe Him everything, and as one of the Seraphim, I cannot live without full allegiance to Him. I am so sorry." A tear of sadness ran down her cheek. "Please understand He would not punish me directly for becoming a mere mortal, but I would lose so much that it would be impossible to bear...forgive me, Roberto."

Roberto wiped away her tears tenderly, then, stepping back, he held out his hand. "Come. We must not give this another thought; we must get back to Venus. I too want to serve Elyon and bring an end to the evil of Dracon and, more importantly, Leviathan."

Rusalka smiled and slipped her hand into his. "He who seeks death in these times will live life to the full in time to come. Worry not for the physical, for the spiritual remains forever for those in favor of our Redeemer. Embrace spiritual life—a living spring, ever flowing, fed from Heaven. No matter how dry this universe gets, this living fountain in the heart will never cease to flow." Rusalka's face shone with a serene joy as they made their way back to the others. It was not what Roberto wanted to hear right there and then, but he understood what she was trying to tell him: his earthly life was a mere shadow of the life to come, and Rusalka was evidence of that.

At the rising of the sun, Celestial was the first to awaken. She immediately felt the presence of something hostile and violent, something that would slaughter the innocent without remorse. Striving to quell her nausea, she alerted the others to her fears. "We must move with speed. This coast is treacherous; there is reason for its name, the Ring of Fire. Fire devours completely, and the evil here is far beyond anything you have experienced as a man, Roberto."

"I have seen enough for a life-time already. I am with you on that, for sure."

The sun was dim, finding its way through the cloudy sky in fleeting moments. Soft, silvery drizzle soaked them as they made their way southeast toward Castra. Roberto forged ahead, deliberately keeping his distance from Rusalka in an effort to keep his mind on their quest to return to Venus—and Patience. It weighed heavily upon his heart that he needed to work much harder on his relationship with his precious daughter, a gift from the mighty Elyon. He would be faithful and honor his responsibility—this he promised to his Almighty Redeemer.

The next three days they went on, the land was silent in its desolation, and by evening of the fourth day, they headed toward the forest region of Phebus near the east shore, where they chose to rest among the shaded trees. They searched for food in the surrounding woods and made a fire to dry off their sodden clothes.

Roberto had not gone very far in search of food when he happened upon a beautiful young man. His thick, shiny, dark hair fell around his bronzed, well-built shoulders. He was wearing very little in the way of garments, and his blue eyes, bright with youthful vibrancy, stared back at him.

"Can I help you?" Roberto did not know why he asked such a question when he was not of these parts and this younger man could probably help him. He looked amiable enough.

The young man smiled warmly. "I am sure you can be of assistance to me. Are you alone, or do you have company?"

Roberto felt a little concerned as to whether or not he should introduce this stranger to the others.

"Do not worry; I mean no harm. I have not had the company of good people for a very long time. It is difficult to find anyone of good character in these parts, but I am the forest keeper, and you must be careful. There are evil and dangerous beasts that dwell in this forest. The dark Elvin live under the very ground you are stood upon and will bring you menace. But I can protect you and show you where to go and where not to go."

Robert wanted to believe him and decided that he seemed a safe bet, although how he survived alone in such dangerous territory he could not conceive.

"Follow me. I have friends close by; I will take you to meet them. What is your name?"

"My name is Scallion."

"I am so pleased to meet you, Scallion. We are lost in these parts. I am Roberto from Planet Earth."

"I thought there was something different about you. I have never met mankind before, but I have heard rumors that it is good to seek your kind in the world that you live in and to live among them. Why are you here?"

Roberto explained briefly all that had transpired in a short space of time, turning his life upside down. Scallion was intrigued and excited to meet his friends. Roberto noticed the shadows changing and the rapid approach of night. It would be dark soon; he hastened his return to the spot he where had left the others

265

sitting around the crackling fire. They were eating their fill when Roberto returned with Scallion.

"We were just talking about searching for you, Roberto. You gave us a fright. We thought you had been gone for too long," said Brabantia, slightly annoyed.

"I am sorry I made you anxious, but I stumbled upon the keeper of this forest. This is Scallion, and he says he can help us find direction and would be glad of our company."

Scallion sat down among them as they offered him food. But Celestial did not feel sure of him; there was a nagging doubt that he may not be all that he seemed. Rusalka shared her thoughts but did not voice them.

After they had rested, had their fill of food, and dried off their garments, it was time to move on with the help of Scallion. He proved to be a good guide and a congenial companion through the region of dread and dark enchantment.

By the end of the first day, it was apparent that he had begun to take particular interest in the Paristan warrior Serepha. He stayed by her side, chatting in a very disarming manner. Serepha seemed enchanted by his singular attention, and her large, gray-blue eyes shone with admiration—pools of delight, for he could tell an exciting tale of great bravery and good swordsmanship. She told him of the flaming swords of the Paristan and the warriors back on Venus in animated enthusiasm.

Cava sidled alongside Corsivo. Many years of oppression and prejudices had taught her to be wary. "I may be wrong, but I don't like the way Scallion is charming Serepha. It will bring nothing but trouble. I don't trust him."

Corsivo glanced over at Scallion, who was lost in conversation with Serepha. "Hm...mmm. I am not at all sure myself, but I wouldn't like to say until I am sure, if you know what I mean."

"Yes, I know what you mean. But if no one says anything, it might be too late."

Nebula overheard their conversation. "I too think of this creature, whoever he really is, as something or someone different than he portrays among us. His presence leaves me feeling

266

uneasy, yet he is certainly keeping us from other unknown dangers that I think could be far more menacing than he seems to be. I can sense that we must be careful of his every move."

Corsivo did not reply, but he could see Cava and Nebula's point. He would talk it over with Celestial when he got the chance to be alone with her.

Two more days passed, and they reached the edge of the forest unharmed and without any attacks. They were thankful to Scallion for his expertise and protection. All seemed to have warmed to his good-natured spirit except Cava, who displayed a cold demeanor around him.

The edge of the forest was flanked to the east and to the south with mountain ranges. "Here is where I must leave you, my good friends. I hope the rest of your journey is a pleasant one."

Nebula was just about to check herself for her suspicious mind when he said his good-byes to everyone. Then, last of all, he turned to Serepha. His eyes poured into her soul, reaching deep within, stirring her emotions. Her eyes locked onto his for but one moment, and she felt the pull strongly...so strong she could not ignore it...so strong that she succumbed to the call of his heart. She tried to pull away, but she could not. He turned to leave, suddenly confident that she was under his spell and would follow him willingly.

Celestial grabbed hold of Serepha's arm. "Do not follow him, Serepha. You don't know him, and your place is not with him."

Serepha shook herself free violently. "No...leave me alone. My place is with him. I know he is my destiny. I am sure. Do not try to stop me!" She ran toward him at great speed as he turned around to welcome her into his arms. He picked her up and swung her round exuberantly, shouting to the others, "Make no mistake; I will take care of her."

Before the others could do anything about it, they had disappeared into the thick forest without a trace. Celestial spoke gravely. "I am afraid we have lost Serepha to the dark side. It was probably the Master of Deceit who planned to snatch her from under us all along. We will have to be more diligent in whom we trust. I am filled with sorrow for my blindness."

Nebula placed her arm gently on Celestial's shoulder. "You were not alone in your blindness, Your Majesty. I think I can honestly speak for all of us, more or less. We too felt uneasy about him but dared not voice it, for if we had been wrong, we would have lost a good guide through the dangerous forest."

Gabriel admitted feeling the same way. "I tried to justify myself with the fact that it would have been more dangerous to us all if we did not trust him. And that still could be the case, for more of us could be lost rather than one of our party."

"Yes. Therefore, we have made the right decision. Let us not worry about it anymore and get out of this forsaken land before we all lose our lives." Cava turned on her heels, grabbed hold of Corsivo's hand, and dragged him forward.

They all followed in silence, lost in their own thoughts. The atmosphere grew uneasy among them as they marched toward Castra wondering what would happen to Serepha.

Chapter 24

Return To The Castle of Alvor

Venus...

A sound woke Patience in the dark of night—a soft bang, then a brief scraping, the source unidentifiable. She sat straight up in the grand four-poster bed of the castle's bedchamber, instantly alert. Through the large, graceful, arched window, a full moon sailed the sky. She stared into the darkness with wide, attentive eyes adjusting to the shadows cast across the vast, regal room. It still seemed so strange to have sight, and there were times she preferred the darkness.

She looked toward the window once again and noticed a dark shape nearby. Had she seen it there before? She wasn't sure. It looked like...could it be...Wishbone...but he was statue still...it could be him; he wasn't by her side!

At first she was rigid, frightened to move, until her eyes adjusted as she stared into the darkness. She was almost sure it was Wishbone. She slowly rolled to the edge of the bed, pulled the covers back, and swung her legs round to climb carefully and quietly off the high mattress onto the marble platform and down a small step. She crept quietly along the beautifully ornate tiled floor in her bare feet toward the window, trying not to startle Wishbone...and, sure enough, as she came closer...it was him, gazing through the window as though he were in some sort of trance. She had never seen him so still, yet he was awake. She wondered what was wrong with him. It didn't make sense. It was

269

not dog-like behavior at all. She felt concerned for him.

"Wishbone!" Patience whispered, kneeling by his side. But he did not move immediately. "Come on, boy...what is it? What can you see?" She tentatively stroked his shiny coat.

The dog whimpered. Moving slightly this time, he made a frightened sound and backed away from the window, growling low in his throat. Then he hesitated, took two steps backward, looking pleadingly at Patience, and then came toward her, half wagging his tail. He began to lick her chin.

"Oh, Wishbone, you're drooling all over me." A rivulet of thick saliva dribbled down her arm and down her nightgown.

"I'll tell you what. I will throw on some clothes, and we will go out into the gardens to see what's troubling you. It is probably nothing, and I can't sleep now. Thanks to YOU, I am wide awake."

Wishbone glanced at her and then busily sniffed along the base of the door, whimpering softly.

"OK, OK, I am coming." She lit a candle kept in a glass goblet on the dressing table and made her way through the dark corridors of the gilded castle to the west side—the servant's entrance—followed by Wishbone. Twisting the key in the lock, she quietly pulled open the large, heavy wooden door.

Hesitantly, Wishbone followed her outside. "Come, boy, it's all right." With a little encouragement, he moved to her side. "Good boy." She hugged him lovingly. Suddenly getting a whiff of something that displeased him, Wishbone sneezed twice, shaking his head so hard that his ears flapped loudly. Then he backed away, snuffling and whimpering at the same time.

"What is it, boy?" Patience grabbed hold of his collar and bent down by his side, listening carefully to the far-distant sounds. The dark shapes of the trees were swaying, even though there was no wind in the stillness of the night. She had only wandered a short distance. Looking back at the castle, she noticed how bleak it looked in the dark—dull and gray, nothing like its former glory of golden turrets and sparkling towers. A shiver ran down her spine. Perhaps she should return before evil found her.

The darkness outside hung onto its secret. Patience still had no idea what had held Wishbone's attention so powerfully. Wishbone sat down and howled in anguish at the moon. She looked at the tree-lined forest in the distance; she could hear a low moaning sound coming from its depths, but she could see very little in the darkness. Motionless, she stood in an agony of suspense, wondering what would appear.

Why am I torturing myself so? She felt glued to the spot. Her head swiveled to the right and to the left as she tried to view everything around her. The atmosphere was highly charged. She felt her neck tingle as though a cold breath had passed over her. Her heart beat wildly; Wishbone growled yet again in the back of his throat and then whimpered in fear. She could hear mingled voices...soft whisperings coming from the forest beyond, coming closer...and closer still.

Patience finally spun round on her heels and ran back to the castle's entrance, followed by a very frightened Wishbone. All of a sudden, the soft ground gave way beneath her, and she found herself falling...falling...down and down in a shower of earth and twigs. Thud! She reached the bottom of a hollow space. The tree debris beneath her was quite soft, much to her relief. She felt dazed by the sudden shock as she took in her new surroundings.

Wishbone was not with her...she was alone. The voices from above came suddenly tumbling down toward her in a ribbon trail of soft whisperings that began to get louder and louder. She could see the distant light above from the pale, silvery moon and hear the sound of Wishbone barking in desperation. She tried to shout up to him, but her voice was lost in the ever-increasing sound of the faceless voices.

She felt sick with worry. How was she going to get out? She placed her hands over her ears. The voices were driving her mad; she couldn't think straight. Her eyes adjusted to the darkness, and she noticed a path to the right. She certainly could not climb upward—it was too far—so she decided to follow the only path available.

The path consisted of impacted earth and tangled roots with thousands of tiny white bulbous eyes peeking through at her. The

271

voices continued to follow her. Her heart hammered against her ribs. She tried not to look at the eyes as she made her way through the passage. The voices came louder and louder in her ears. Mutterings of evil filled the chasm, and she began to feel weak and faint.

She felt her way through, not giving a thought to the eyes anymore. It was only when she lost her balance and slightly pushed against the wall to steady herself that she accidently squashed one. Blood began to drop to the ground like teardrops, first from the one she had flattened and then a rush of never-ending tears from all of them, forming a river of crimson blood that swept Patience off her feet. Patience prayed fervently for it all to end. "Please, someone...help me..."

∞

Wishbone licked her face; Patience woke up with a start. She saw Wishbone on her bed, and her eyes searched the room for any evidence of last night's escapade. The sun shone brightly through the arched window. Stroking Wishbone, his tail wagging wildly, she then got out of bed and dressed quickly. She noticed a few scratches and bruises on her arms and legs, which puzzled her. Was last night a dream or was it real? She decided she would rather believe that it was most certainly a nightmare. After all, she may have gotten the scratches previously but had not noticed them until now. *Yes, that's what happened*, she reassured herself.

The castle was silent except for the servants starting their morning chores. Patience wandered about with Wishbone on her tail, simply strolling through the great halls, which were covered in large, beautiful, gilt-framed pictures of the Elvin clan. Everything seemed normal...at least as normal as things could be following all that had happened recently on Venus. The forest was not the same enchanted forest anymore; that was for sure.

Another hall lay across the way, in shadow, facing east. They made their way to the end of the corridor and walked up a great many stairs that wound around and around until they reached the top of the palace's tower. Patience opened the door of a small room facing north. There were shelves overflowing with books and a small entrance with more steps leading to the floor above, and a door that opened out to an observation point at the top of the tower.

Patience scoured the land as far as her human capacity could see. She heard the sound of the voices again caught up in the wind, whispering softly in her ears: "There is no escape. Now that you are here, you will never see your home again...you will be mine, as your father is now mine."

She shuddered in the cool breeze, turned away from the distant sight of the forest, and quickly traced her steps back down to where she had come from. An awful dread had settled upon her that she could not shake off. What if it was true? What could she do about it? Who was it that was speaking to her?

Later that night, she dined with the king and queen of Alvor in the high-ceilinged main dining room. She felt lost sitting at such a grand table, usually set for forty or more but this night set only for three. The long table was majestically laid with a silver dinner service and a myriad of white beeswax candles in fanciful crystal candelabras that glittered softly. Beautiful, low, clustered snow-white flower displays ran the full length among a swath of swirling ivy and silvery cob-web's dripping in dew. Tempting platters, piled high with exotic fruits and cakes, and unknown dishes under porcelain lids lay before her, but she felt too sick to enjoy such a spectacular feast. Her greatest comfort was that Wishbone was allowed to sit at her feet. Haunting music wafted from the gallery above, stirring her emotions even more. She realized how homesick she felt, and she longed for her father to return, if he was going to return at all. She had begun to have doubts. She played with her food on the plate in silence, half listening to the conversation between the king and queen.

She was just about to ask if they would pardon her when the door flung open abruptly. Astoria, Shaloma, and Corsica entered the room, quite obviously perturbed by something.

The king sat them down and ordered food and drink to be brought before them.

"How did the Kingdom of Semiramis fare against the attack of the forces of nature upon our planet? Please tell us of what you saw."

Astoria welled up with tears. "I am sad to convey the news of our Elvin brother Calendula. He is no more of this universe. But then, we must remember that he is in a better place, a place far beyond our imagination, a place of peace and eternal joy."

"Yes, that is the way to look upon the loss of such a loved one as Calendula. It is something we must all remember—and thus not favor our lives of this day, but only what we can do for our Almighty to save the souls of others before it is too late."

Astoria continued to tell the king of all that they had witnessed in the underworld of the mighty ocean of Semiramis, and they agreed that they must take a part in helping their people reclaim their planet. The king was distraught about the message Astoria had brought back.

"At this time, we have yet to know the true knowledge of the dangers that we may encounter now that we have been rendered weak and desolate in the sight of other realms. Other beings will most assuredly come, and we must be ready to fight any battle that comes our way to save Venus and all that is good among us."

Patience had been listening to all that was said; every word crushed any hope of ever seeing her father again. She began to sob loudly. She could not take any more of this talk of desolation. Astoria remembered Patience at last; she had been so immersed in her tales of woe that she had forgotten their little human visitor.

She stood up and walked purposefully toward Patience's seat. Pulling Patience up into her embrace, she spoke words of peace over the child. "You have only been hearing words of woe, my dear child, but you must not take heed. For wherever there is wickedness, there is also goodness. Dwell on the good things and dismiss the wicked, for your world is but an illusion when it comes to wicked works. They cannot prevail against the Almighty

One, so fear not. For light will always prevail over dark, and if you remember this, you will be a wise girl of your time. If you fight the fight as if you are going to win, you will win in the end because your master wins always. This life is but a preparation for the one to come—a transient path to everlasting life. Come; we will look at the Vessel of Truth to reassure you of your father's position."

Astoria bowed to the king and queen, pardoning her leave. Pulling Patience forward with true determination, she walked through the corridors and the great halls, up some winding steps on the east side of the castle, to Astoria's temporary bedroom chamber.

The Vessel of Truth stood in the center of a small, round, highly polished, ornate table in the middle of the large round room. The room was heavily curtained all around its high walls in rich purple velvet, and the black-and-gold wrought-iron bed was positioned in the middle of the room, its four ornate posts dressed in floating silvery gossamer.

Torches of light flickered beautifully from the walls, casting a peaceful light across the room. Patience could hear the songs of angels gently floating in unanimous sounds of joy and peace, and the Vessel of Truth began to add a brighter glow to the room, throwing out serene beams of hypnotic light that brought Patience to a place of peace...a peace that surpassed circumstance, a peace that only Elyon, the Elite One, could give.

Astoria consulted the Vessel of Truth. Patience sat by her side, watching, waiting to see what would be revealed. Serepha came into focus. She was in the ocean of the polar region of Mars; at first glimpse, Astoria did not recognize her. She was undergoing some form of transformation. Her face was shedding her skin as it burst forth, revealing the skin of some reptile creature beneath. It did not take long before Astoria understood the situation. The Vessel revealed the true state of events: the meeting with the Selkie named Scallion and the deceiving of her soul.

Astoria explained what had happened to Serepha as Patience hung on to her every word.

"A selkie can only stay human for a short period of time, and I

275

am not at all sure how long that usually is. But I do know that while he is in human form, he will search for and make an attempt to lure some unsuspecting female into his own world. If he is successful, he takes her to his underworld habitation in the great ocean of the Polar Regions, where he keeps her in chains and treats her with cruelty as a punishment for his return to the evil selkie state he so hates. Eventually, she becomes bitter and spiteful and reluctantly transforms into an evil selkie herself, intent on revenge for her fate. I am afraid this is the fate that Serepha has fallen into blindly, and that is why we must be alert at all times."

Patience looked worried again. Astoria pointed at the waters of the Vessel of Truth. "Look, there is your father—safe and sound. They are heading toward Castra. It will not be long before they return, my dear child. You must worry not."

"I am so glad you're here, Astoria. Some very strange things have been happening to me. I think that's why I felt so scared for my father. I have heard whisperings...voices telling me that I will never return home and that my father will not return to me. I was so afraid that I prayed for help."

"Then you did the right thing. Leviathan will use any delusional way to make you doubt. He will feed your mind with tales of destruction and send his consorts to lead you along the path of desolation. Keep your mind strong, for he is desperate to take you over and make you his own in a place so dark you will never bear it. Keep to the light no matter what it takes, and you will be protected. Do you understand me, Patience? It is imperative that you do, for I can see Leviathan is seeking after your soul." Astoria's eyes glazed over. "He is out there seeking to destroy and devour...we must not allow this to happen."

"I will not let him have my soul...I won't...I just won't."

Astoria placed her arm around Patience. "That is the spirit, my child! Now go. Find Wishbone. Keep him by your side, for he is sensitive to the dark world and will alert you at these times when you need to arm yourself with holy incantations against the manipulations of the dark master who is making great effort to

276

control your mind. Keep strong!"

Astoria walked over to a dark, intricately carved wooden chest and opened its heavy lid, revealing its array of interesting contents. She pulled out a silver cross-dagger that had the combination of a dagger and a crucifix. She placed it carefully into Patience's hands.

"This was fashioned after the fall of Queen Nebula by Carthage to avenge the death of Kafa. No one knows how it was returned from Mars after Carthage died at the hands of the Devatas. It is a mystery. I want you to keep it with you always. Sleep with it under your pillow at night, for it is imbued with the Spirit of Holiness. The mere sight of it induces fear into the most powerful of evil sources. A direct stab to the heart will cause death of a most horrific kind, a disintegration of form followed by eternal torture."

"Wow. It's beautiful. Thanks, Astoria. I will keep it safe always by my side. At least while I am here"

Astoria looked in the chest once more, this time pulling out a beautiful rhinestone leather strap. "Here is its holder. Wear it around your waist."

Patience buckled it around her waist immediately.

"Do not be afraid of using it. Remember, you are not using it in your own power, so you need no instruction. Faith in the source of such a weapon is what counts."

Patience thanked Astoria once again and made her way down the hall to the dining room. She found Wishbone chewing merrily on a large bone under the table. The enormous room was empty, light streaming through the intricate stained-glass panes and filling the graceful room with warmth and brightness.

"Wishbone, come, boy...come." Patience patted her leg as she spoke. "Can you tear yourself away from that bone for a while? Here boy...we can go for a walk in the gardens. I promise we won't go near the forest. I too feel afraid of that place now. Look what I've got here. A special dagger to protect us; we don't need to fear now."

Wishbone looked up to her pleadingly, then down at his bone

as though it was a hard decision. Then, wagging his tail, he came from under the table and cocked his head to one side.

"Come on, then, boy!"

He thumped his tail against Patience's leg in agreement and followed Patience into the gardens.

Patience strolled through the grass, her bare feet cooling in the morning dew. She heard the note of a sun-bird in the distance, and everything felt suddenly vibrant. The emerald-green sun-bird, with golden wings, flitted from one tree to another, then, diving headfirst into the pale-pink petals of a large flower, it picked out a teeny-tiny flower fairy, no bigger than a thumbnail. Patience tried to capture the bird before it took flight, but her movement only added to its swift departure. She just hoped that the flower fairy was not lunch.

She wandered aimlessly, watching Wishbone chasing the red-and-blue dragonflies, sometimes in circles. Finally, she stopped to rest, stretching languorously across the soft green grass to the south of the castle, which had not been damaged too much by the earthquake.

She basked in the midday sun, feeling positive about the return of her father, shutting her eyes to the external world and listening to the sounds of the birds singing their pretty songs. Wishbone laid his large head on the ground, and they drifted into a light sleep, tired from the night before. Patience was still not sure whether her escapade had been real or not.

Wishbone awoke first with a bark, followed by Patience with a start. She felt dazed and still half asleep when she first heard the voice.

"Hi. I am so sorry to disturb you. My name is Iyesha. I live in here in this forest."

Patience rubbed her eyes and scanned the fairy creature that stood over her. She was about the same height as Patience and was dressed in the colors of the forest—pale, silvery greens and golden browns. Her hair, as golden as the sun, fell around her shoulders. Her luminous green eyes were full of desperation.

Patience made an effort to speak to her. "Hi. My name is

Patience."

Pulling herself up from her kneeling position, Patience looked suspiciously at the fairy of the forest. After all, she did not know which strangers to trust anymore.

The fairy appeared distraught for some reason. "Please, can you help me? I have dropped my birth ring in the pool of reflections back there in the forest. I am not a water fairy. If I swim down in the waters, I will lose my wings and most assuredly will never return to land again to be with my kinfolk. That will not happen to you because you are not a fairy. You could swim to the bottom and find it for me."

Patience felt sorry for the fairy. She knew what it was like to lose a family member. Wishbone looked hesitant and took a pace backward, whimpering slightly, his tail between his legs.

The fairy pleaded with her. "Please help me. My folks will be so annoyed with me. Without my birth ring, any clan can take me away and claim me as their own."

Patience chose to ignore Wishbone's reluctance. "Show me the way to this pool. Is it deep?"

"Oh…thank you, fair maiden. It is not deep at all. It is a mysterious and magical place and can be hard to find at times because it shifts from place to place, never in the same spot twice. To find it, you must have a pure heart and a kind and gentle spirit and courage to pursue it."

Patience and Wishbone followed Iyesha into the great forest of Alvor, the very place they had previously wished to keep away from. The moment they entered, all seemed well—no whisperings of impending doom or dark, brooding gloom—and Patience began to relax a little as they walked under the canopies of high trees, their leaves swaying slightly in the midday breeze.

As they walked deeper into the forest, they followed a narrow, winding path covered in fallen leaves and branches, many trees laid across the ground, torn from their roots, withered, twisted, and tangled. The forest had sadly lost its former glory from the earthquake. There was an atmosphere of quiet desolation, as if everyone had left the place. No birds filled the trees with songs of joy. Not a fairy, elf, or even a nymph could be found as they trampled through the debris.

They eventually came upon a large, still, blue-water pool, illuminated with bright light that stood out in contrast to the disenchanted forest. Large, beautiful white lilies floated on the surface. Patience peeped over the edge and saw a reflection of herself in the clear water.

"You will need to go in to its depths to find my ring. You know I cannot!"

Wishbone began to bark furiously. Patience looked at him and then looked at the fairy. She did not know what to do. The pool seemed OK, especially as the fairy had said that only the pure of heart could find it, but it sure looked deeper than she had expected.

The fairy began to cry. "Please, you are my only chance."

Patience took pity on her. She took off her outer garments and gingerly dipped her toes in the water; it felt quite warm. The water reflected her trembling limbs in its stillness. Bravely, she took a deep breath and plunged into the watery depths, immediately drawn down by a fierce undertow. She squinted through the water, expecting to see fish and any other creature that might habit the pond…but she saw nothing.

The deeper she swam, the blacker it became until she could see no more. She looked above, wondering how far down she had come; she could see no light penetrating through from the surface. A chill crept up her spine. The water turned icy cold. Spinning around, she found herself encircled with dark-purple-and-green, luminous weed-like protrusions grabbing at her, twisting themselves around her small body. She tried to fight her way loose, gasping for air; her death came closer with every moment's lack of air.

And then she remembered the dagger in her belt. Her arms were bound at the shoulders by the slimy substance; its protrusions speedily grew by the second. She kicked and wriggled in an attempt to break free, and as they slithered around her neck, she managed to grab hold of the dagger and pull it out of its sheath. It was impossible to hack at the sea-like weed from the position she was in, but just as Astoria had told her, the sight of the dagger caused it to recoil in disgust and fear, releasing Patience from its stranglehold. The projectile apparition disappeared with the sound of piercing screams.

Patience replaced the dagger and swam furiously, arms and legs flailing with great determination to reach the surface with little air left in her lungs. Her head popped up out of the water, and she gasped for air, coughing and spluttering. Wishbone barked loudly, wagging his tail backward and forward in anticipation, glad to see Patience return from the watery deep.

She swam the last few yards to the poolside; a gray gloom had crossed the forest once again. She grabbed onto the grassy verge and pulled herself wearily out of the water, gasping for breath. She sat for a moment, looking at the pool of reflections; it was now gray and murky, and the fairy was nowhere to be seen. It was perhaps just as well, for she had not retrieved the ring. Though the evening had promised to be bright and clear, it now grew quickly dark under a low, oppressive shroud.

She looked reluctantly back at the pond, and, to her surprise, it had vanished from sight. Could I have moved away at all without realizing it? No…no, *I couldn't have. My clothes lie there on the ground as before!*

Patience shivered, feeling a coldness that penetrated her bones. She did not know what was real anymore. Slowly, she dressed in her outer garments, feeling so tired she could hardly move; her limbs felt like lumps of lead. Wishbone whimpered, walking backward and forward like a mad dog.

"What is it now, Wishbone? Are you going mad too? We really need to get home, but I feel so…so tired I don't think I can make it, I must rest…I'll just lie down for a short while."

She rested her head upon Wishbone's belly as he lay down beside her, and they drifted off into a light sleep.

She was halfway between sleep and consciousness when she heard the sound of a baby crying nearby. It had grown darker and darker; only floating orbs of light lit up the forest, and an eerie silence pervaded the atmosphere. Her awareness slowly revived as she sat up to listen harder. It seemed so wrong that the only sound to be heard was the distressing sound of a baby's cry of despair.

Patience dragged herself up, still feeling the damp cold in her tired body. "Come on, Wishbone. We must find this child."

Wishbone gave her a look of dismay, but she chose to ignore it. They crept along, following the direction of the sound, searching all around for the source. The dog sniffed along the ground, his ears alert, wisps of fear showing in his eyes.

Patience was the first to spot it. The baby lay wrapped in linen on the ground beneath a gnarled oak tree. The tree had lost its leaves and stood still in its bleak deadness. Patience picked the baby up tenderly. It was a beautiful baby boy; his chubby red cheeks and Cherub-like lips were appealing even to Wishbone. He excitedly wagged his tail and rubbed up against Patience's leg.

"Yes, boy, I know. He's lovely, isn't he? He surely must have a mother around here somewhere. He is too well fed and cared for not to. Unless she has been harmed or taken away. We must take him back with us and see what Astoria has to say. Come on. Boy, it is getting too dark, and I'm afraid of what lurks in this place."

Of course, Patience did not need to give him much encouragement on that matter. He hated the forest. He knew somehow that they were lost. The baby had stopped crying for the present, much to Patience's relief; she held him closely as they tramped through the fallen leaves, twigs, and debris of the damaged forest.

The growing presence of evil was all encompassing. Eyes gleamed in the darkness...Patience could hear a frantic flapping of wings above. She quickened her steps, her heart beating wildly, Wishbone whimpering, his tail between his legs.

Patience's imagination ran wild, and terror filled her soul.

"I must not be afraid...I must not be afraid. It is all an illusion...definitely not real...no, not real."

She stumbled over some stones in her path and fell to the ground with an almighty thud. In her effort to keep the baby safe in her arms, she landed awkwardly. A searing pain ran through

282

her ankle.

"Oh...no...that's just what I need, Wishbone. I think I have strained or broken my ankle. You are going to have to get me help, boy. Go, boy...go."

Wishbone could hear the flapping of wings and the strange noises of creatures unknown. He took three steps forward, then three steps back toward Patience, whimpering all the time.

"I am sorry, boy...but you must go...you are our only chance...get me help, please."

Wishbone knew he had to go. He set off at great speed, leaving Patience to cradle the baby in the dark.

She began to sing softly in an attempt to forget about the pain in her ankle. She leaned against the stump of a broken tree and felt the warmth of the baby next to her. She closed her eyes for a fleeting moment and opened them again, just as quickly feeling a sudden change in atmosphere for the worse. A horrid, sulfurous smell filled her nostrils. She screamed in disgust as she looked at the baby, who was...

She threw the bundle as far away as she possibly could. She could not believe what she saw; the baby was now a grotesque creature with yellow, bulbous eyes protruding from its gnarled face, its stench overpowering.

She was so shocked by the transition that she was not prepared for the creature to attack. A piercing sound came forth from its throat as it rushed forward and placed its long, sinewy hands around Patience's neck. Foaming and frothing, wailing and hissing, it tried to squeeze the life out of Patience's earthly body. Striving to quell her nausea as she choked, gasping for air, Patience pulled the holy cross-dagger from her belt and plunged it through the back of the creature, right through its heart.

The creature disintegrated, dissolved in a puff of smoke.

Patience clutched her throat, gasping for air, taking long, deliberate breaths. She looked at her dagger on the ground beside her and realized how grateful she was to be in possession of such a great weapon. She replaced it into her belt and hoped that she would be rescued before any other evil pursued her. She acknowledged the fact that she had been misled by Leviathan once again. *What will Astoria think? How could I be so stupid?*

∞

Chapter 25

The Fortress of Deimos

Mars...

Thoughts of revenge were the only consolation for Nastacia. She had been called to stand before the throne of Dracon immediately. *What will he want from me this time?* Thoughts of murder entered her mind. *Twisted by his greed and lust for power. Who knows what he and his gruesome army will do next? How can I ever escape?*

The windowless corridors in the fortress were dimly illuminated by widely spaced candles. Nastacia walked with steely determination through the dark, winding passages. She would not allow her imagination to run wild. She heard the cries of unknown creatures in the dark recesses, screaming from the stone walls. *No...I will not allow Leviathan to suck me into his powerful snare.*

As she approached Dracon's throne room, the large iron doors opened independently. Gowned in royal purple and scarlet, her head held high, her flame-red hair falling wildly over her shoulders, she marched purposefully toward Dracon's throne. The look on her face said clearly that she would not grovel or show any fear in his presence.

Dracon appeared bemused by her audacious behavior; a sardonic grin crossed his features as she curtsied begrudgingly before him. Bowing had never come naturally to her at the best of times, but to bow before one so repugnant was more than she could bear. Hate and loathing swelled up inside of her; she felt she would burst with the pain of it.

Tension filled the air. The Xanthurus waited for Dracon to explode with anger, but to their surprise, he stood up from his mighty throne and took one slow step after another until he towered above her prostrated head. Nastacia could smell his pungent odor as he placed a long finger ending in a thick, curved talon under her delicate chin and lifted up her head to penetrate her eyes.

Her emerald-green eyes flashed back at him with stubborn hatred. He let go of her chin; a loud, roaring laugh escaped from his throat. The stone foundations and walls shook, and the Xanthurus bowed down in fear of his next reaction. Nastacia covered her ears, finding it difficult not to fall to the ground faint-hearted. Her ears felt as if they were bleeding. She held herself in check and stood haughtily before him. Rubbing his chin thoughtfully, his white, bulbous, lizard-like eyes darting speedily from side to side, Dracon looked her up and down with a glint of amusement.

"You know...you do please me, my queen. You cannot hide your fear from me; it is leaking from your every pore. I can feel and taste it; so...oo delicious." His long, thin forked tongue lashed forward, tasting her salty, glistening skin.

Nastacia froze to the spot, her expression of pure revulsion apparent to all. Dracon returned to his throne. His expression turned to one of distaste. He could feel her pure hatred of him, and for some reason—he could not explain why—he wanted her to come to him willingly. Never before had he felt this way. It perturbed him.

"Go...go back to your chamber for now and prepare for a feast at sunset. Bathe in the incense of desire. You will please me yet again, my queen, but remember this: don't indulge your ego at the expense of your soul. Your soul will burn in hell!"

Nastacia picked up her skirt, turned on her heels, and almost ran out of the hall; a myriad of eyes watching her until she disappeared from view. She had only walked a short distance

286

when she stumbled and fell to the ground, aware of the horror of her situation. She began to sob relentlessly, untroubled by a serpent that slithered across her feet.

A voice in the shadows told her to hush. Taking a deep breath, she searched in the dimly lit corridor for the owner of the voice.

"Come. Follow me; I can help you."

Nastacia, glad to hear a friendly voice but wary of its intentions, took a few steps farther and peered at the figure looming in the shadows. The piercing blood-red eyes stared out from under the black-hooded cloak.

Nastacia recovered her voice. "Why would you, a Xanthurus, want to help me? Is it some trick you play?"

"Believe what you will, but your alternative is not exactly wonderful, is it?"

Nastacia looked behind to make sure no one had followed her. It ran through her mind that Dracon could be testing her loyalty to him. She hesitated for a moment and then relented. "You are right. I have not much to lose, for I am doomed anyway."

"Come, then. Follow me."

She followed the female Xanthurus through many passages that gradually became darker and darker. Making her way cautiously with only the light from the fire torch that the Xanthurus held in front of them, she felt a shuddering of her soul holding on to life. The atmosphere grew dark and dank; an eerie silence greeted them. Nastacia stumbled over something on the ground. Picking herself up onto one knee, she adjusted to the darkness surrounding her. The Xanthurus held the torch above her so that she could clearly see the bones covering the ground and rocky surfaces.

"Do not worry. They are dead...just dry bones left to rot."

"Who are they?" Nastacia shuddered as the Xanthurus lent her a hand to get up.

"That is not of your concern right now. Come; we must get out before we are discovered missing."

Nastacia stepped gingerly among the human bones, which pressed around her ankles in the ochre dimness. "What is in this for you?"

"You cannot believe that I could have a heart? It is true...I have my own motive for helping you. I want to come with you back to your planet. I am not loyal to Dracon or anyone on this planet. I had a position in Dracon's army once, but Egor had it in for me and plotted to have me killed as a traitor. I could have been one of these skeletons, but I hid. I hid well. It has been difficult, but these parts are only used to dump the dead, and I have lived with the stench for long enough with no company—even a Xanthurus has feelings, you know."

"That may be so for you, but I don't see it in general. The rat race is known to be evil and beyond redemption."

"You think I am beyond redemption?"

"No...I mean...well, of course not."

"Then I will help you escape, and you will lead me to freedom. I cannot have freedom on this planet. Dracon will hunt me down relentlessly like a wild animal."

The smell of death surrounded them. Nastacia began to understand firsthand what the Xanthurus had meant; it was blocking her throat...she was choking. She held her nose, trying to breathe from her throat only, but it seemed impossible. Coughing and spluttering, she fell to the ground. The Xanthurus picked up her small frame and placed her over her shoulders as though she were but a feather of a bird.

Time was of the essence. It would not be long before Dracon would find out that Nastacia was missing. They needed to reach Phebus by sunset. The passage led them to a rocky cave that gave way to an opening. They climbed through, the Xanthurus pulling Nastacia up and above the rocky surface. She gasped with relief, covering her eyes until they adjusted to the natural sunlight she had so missed.

"Come. We have no time to mess about. Fly if you must, but, of course, I can only walk."

"No. I will walk beside you unless the terrain becomes impossible for me."

They clambered over the rocks and crags, the hot wind rising

288

as the afternoon faded. Swirls of pink-and-orange dust encircled them, restricting their visibility. How long will it be before Dracon's venomous army hunts us down in deathly pursuit? Will we make it to the border on time?

∞

Chapter 26

The Portal

Mars...

Celestial and her troupe rode upon the back of a raw wind blowing from the east of Phebus, their wings a blurred flurry of jewels across the dark sky. The air was still filled with a heavy malevolence as they fast approached the portal of Castra, the invisible gates to Venus.

Roberto grasped tightly onto Mikael's central wings, his arms growing ever weary. He felt himself in the grip of irresistible forces sweeping toward an unknown destiny, and the dangers this time were not only invisible but beyond human comprehension.

It did not take long for Ilk's confidence to wane once more either; his mind filled with trepidation and panic. He doubted their return to Venus. They were so close to the possibility of escape, but he could feel it—feel it strongly. Something dark and sinister was close at hand yet again.

They continued silently in their relentless journey to freedom. Far below, the terrain, savage and forsaken, was a series of monstrous shapes that loomed menacingly at them. Only the light from the wings of the heavenly hosts pierced the darkness that engulfed them.

They veered toward the east shore in a flurry of flapping wings, approaching the valley, leading to the path of escape. And there—skulking in the distance, a sea of demons stood before them. Myriads of glowing yellow eyes peeped out of the darkness as the sky became filled with the shadows of evil.

Celestial turned in the night sky to face the others. "Speak holy incantations against these spiritual hosts of wickedness. Stick together. If we are united in love, they will not harm us." Foaming and frothing, wailing and hissing, the vile creatures unfurled their wings and flew in circles around them. Ilk shrieked in terror. Corsivo leaped forward, and, making a blinding sweep with his sword, he de-winged a demon, followed by another and another, one after the other.

Gabriel shot up out of their midst, a shower of demons following him. He soared higher and higher, spinning his flaming sword above his head, forming a circle of fiery light. He burned bright with the heat of fire, consumed with righteousness, vanquishing them with blinding light and his mighty golden sword. The ugly Devatas squirmed and wailed at the sight of his mighty bright light and fell from the sky at great speed.

Four black-horned flying beasts surrounded Mikael. Roberto slipped from his wings and fell rapidly through the air, praying holy incantations as one of the horned beasts clapped his bony hand down on his head, hissing and gnashing its teeth. Roberto felt its claws sink into his flesh, and his life passed before him.

Rusalka saw his plight. With a burst of brilliant wings, she transformed into a heavenly being and swooped down beside him, her blinding light growing brighter and brighter. She released Roberto from the grip of the horned abomination, watching it freeze in silence and trepidation. Roberto discerned their weakness. They were nothing against the power of Elyon's mighty warriors, and he began to feel in safe hands once again.

The heavenly warriors moved through the ranks of Devatas like blurring scythes until all that was left of them was a trail of sulfurous fumes floating through the air. They felt the presence of the Lord of Hosts, and a welcome calm filled the atmosphere.

At last they floated silently down to the valley below. Roberto fell softly to the ground; his bones ached to put as much distance as possible between himself and the desecrated place of torture he had found himself in. He jumped up and hastened toward the golden gates of freedom as though fangs were snapping at his heels.

The others followed him. All were ready to return to Venus at last; their journey had been a difficult one. Nebula was overcome with the thought of return to her once-beautiful kingdom, where she had reigned in peaceful bliss until that awful day she had lost her son. Her heart still yearned for her husband and her son, but she had much to be thankful for in her return to Elyon and his future purpose for her on Venus.

Corsivo gripped Cava's hand. Tears sprung unwillingly to her eyes. "Cava, do not be afraid! Venus is a new beginning for you, a better life than you have ever known. You only have to surrender to Elyon."

Cava looked at him with grateful affection; she choked suddenly upon her thoughts and looked away. She was almost certain she had only to submit, and a world of wonder and beauty would lie beyond. The path was in herself, not to be found in external things. She just needed to believe—not even know all the answers. Then there would be no more stumbling through darkness not knowing what horrors the next day would bring. She wanted to accept, surrender her soul, but something—maybe some stubborn part of her—resisted. She wished she could be like Corsivo, so damn sure of everything.

Their relief was short lived. As they approached the golden gates slowly, tension filled the air. Darkness fell over them once again. A crawling cloud of evil was coming.

A tremendously loud flapping of dark wings emerged in front of them. Leviathan's looming stature touched ground, burning orbs of fire pouring from his eye sockets. His clawed hand pointed long, black talons in their direction.

"Thought you could escape me, did you? I must admit you have come far. I thought your death would have come so much sooner. I am honored to have the privilege personally to put an end to your silly little revolt against all that is mine."

Ilk hid his face behind Nebula, standing at the rear. He could not look at the leader of the Serophoth. Celestial stepped forward, wings spread wide, followed by Corsivo, Mikael, and Gabriel. Brabantia stood in front of Roberto, Rusalka, and Nebula, extending her arms in an attempt to hold them back and protect them.

"We have not come this far to allow you to be the source of our death. Our Master is greater than you, and you know this to be true. Why do you even question it?" Celestial held her head up high and began to chant words in an unknown language.

Leviathan's wrath grew mighty at such words. He suddenly roused six powerful demon beasts with a sweep of his wing, and they gathered before him in an instant. His wings snapped downward, and he shot into the air, commanding the beasts to devour them all. And then he disappeared in the clouds, leaving them to their unnatural fate.

The beasts snarled, jaws opened wide, fangs protruded past their chins. Larger than the manticore itself, they circled round them, ready to pounce at any moment. Celestial shot up above them, spreading her glorified wings. Corsivo grabbed hold of Ilk and followed Celestial toward the dark, clouded sky. Feather-light tremors ran through Brabantia's scalp; her limbs began to shake wildly as her torso ripped open from head to toe, swiftly changing form from woman to beast; her pale-blond hair bristled, and a low, growling noise escaped her lips as she drew them back to bare her fangs, eyes wild, her senses sharpened.

And at that moment, a pale crescent moon appeared on the horizon. The other angels stayed by Brabantia's side. Rusalka swiftly lifted Roberto, shooting up high above the evil beasts. Nebula followed her but was only capable of flying low; her wings had not yet fully recovered from her years of trauma in Dracon's dungeons.

Swirling and hovering in a flock of blinding light, the angels above encircled the beasts. Gabriel roared a command and drew his sword. It flashed like lightning in the darkness. With a mighty burst of his wings, he thrust his sword forward into the side of one of the beasts, pulled it straight out, and immediately wielded

293

it forward once again with an almighty force. In a flourish of red glowing blades, Gabriel and Mikael fought with fervor alongside Corsivo. Flashing fangs and razor-sharp claws relentlessly pursued them.

Celestial and Corsivo descended, trailing a brilliant arc of light across the inky-blue sky. Just as one of the beasts leaped into the air in pursuit of Nebula, Corsivo snapped his wings into action and shot downward at great speed, hurling his sword like a fiery spear at the beast. The beast fell to the ground with an almighty thud, and a thunderous roar escaped from its throat, ending abruptly in a choked gargle. One by one, the beasts were defeated. Brabantia's white fangs flashed as she ripped at their hind legs, ferociously exuding a manic calm at the same time Celestial cut through the pack with a blinding light.

At last, the beasts lay bloody and defeated before them. Celestial strode forward toward the portal. "It is time to return. Come; let us enter the golden gates before any more evil comes our way."

Everyone wearily followed Celestial to the gates, but no one knew the truth of what they were about to return to on Venus except for Celestial. She had been given insight; her true purpose on Venus was about to begin. Her thoughts weighed heavily upon her heart. *He is out there like a roaring lion seeking to devour. No more will we be safe on Venus until Leviathan and his hordes are destroyed once and for all...that time is fast approaching!*

Observing a trail leading into the woods, the Xanthurus and Nastacia broke off the path leading them into the cool embrace of the trees. They stopped to rest for a while. Nastacia's green eyes shone brightly with exhilaration at the thought of escape.

"Don't get too hopeful. Dracon will have sent his army after us by now. We must be canny about our direction. It is a good idea to keep to the edge of the forest and travel first to Phebus. They will think we would take the shorter routes."

Nastacia shuddered at the thought of being captured by Dracon once more. "If he comes near me again, I swear I will kill him!"

The Xanthurus laughed. "You speak words of a mighty warrior, my girl. You are no match for him. He will crush your tiny bones with one hand."

Nastacia looked away in disgust. If only this were a dream and she could wake up from the horror of it. But it wasn't a dream, and she could not get away from the guilt of Orion's death; the awareness given by the heart was too strong. It was an injustice she had caused, and she desired revenge for the futile death of a man so loyal, even though his loyalty was misplaced. It was her fault that his standing with Elyon had been ruined, and there was no going back to Elyon now. The knowledge of not being part of the wholeness would remain forever within her soul like a stone in the pit of her stomach dragging her down.

She would have to return to Venus and confess to Celestial all that had happened because of her lack of loyalty and obedience. She would much rather die with forgiveness than be murdered at the hands of evil. Whichever way she looked at it, she knew she was doomed. She hoped that divine light would shine upon the abomination of her undesired master, Leviathan. The time would come, she felt sure of it.

She looked up at the Xanthurus, who was scratching at the ground in pursuit of some little bugs to eat. Nastacia squirmed. There was no way she could eat such horrible creatures, alive and wriggling. She drank some sap from a tree and nibbled on some berries.

"What will you do on Venus?" Nastacia sucked the sweet juice of the red berries from her fingers. "I am not so sure you will be welcome there."

"Welcome or not, I will be in a better place than this, don't you think?"

"I am not at all sure you will like it."

"Well, I will have you, at least, to help me when I get there."

"I will, of course, help you, for you have helped me. But I am not sure that I will be that welcome anymore either. You don't know what I have done."

"And neither do I care. You don't know what I have done. Let's just be glad that we both want something better for ourselves."

"What is your name?" Nastacia offered the Xanthurus some berries.

"Rattana...hmm. Thanks, these are good. I have never tried these before."

"Well, it is providence that we have come together. There is a better chance of escape with two of us. We must stick together and get out of here as soon as possible. Come, let us not waste time. Let us go."

Wisps of dark mist coiled around them in the bleakness of night. Conspicuous against the gloomy surroundings, a slender, iridescent, bright-green snake slithered past their feet, as yellowy-green as an unripe lemon. They kept a straight line to the edge of the forest; suddenly it became apparent that a recent fire had passed through. Burned skeletons of trees blackened the landscape as far as the eye could see. It was unnaturally still and eerily quiet.

The Xanthurus's lips tightened. She gave Nastacia an anxious glance. "There is no shelter here; we are very exposed. I suggest we make our way out of the forest to the valley beyond. We will take cover at the edge of the plain. There is a series of rocks flanked to the south and the east by mountain ranges. We should be safe there."

Nastacia's voice sounded thin and unconvincing to her own ears. "You know best. Lead the way."

She turned around suddenly, her expression one of absolute terror. "Did you hear that?"Into Nastacia's mind several images rushed at once, images of a place she never wanted to enter again. The growling sound came closer. There was no mistaking the sound of Oze.

"I cannot hear anything but the whisperings of the night. Come, we must depart from here before Dracon finds us."

296

Nastacia sidled up closer to the Xanthurus, quickening her pace. The growling sound followed close behind her heels, and although she could not see him, she could feel his presence close at hand. A sense of desolation and abandonment overtook her, but she did not speak of it. They journeyed on in silence.

Chapter 27

The Wrath

Mars...

The walls shook. The mighty roar of Dracon's anger filled the throne chamber. Fraught with conflicting emotions—desire for vengeance and desire for the avenged one—he paced the vast hall, commanding Egor to find Nastacia and bring her back without harming a hair on her head.

"But, My Lord, forgive me for what I am about to suggest—it is in your best interest. Would it not be wise for us to destroy her? She has no loyalty to you. She has even threatened to kill you."

Dracon flung his cape around furiously, erupting like a volcano, his eyes rapidly darting from side to side, his skin crimson red. "How dare you question my judgment? Did I ask for your advice? What sort of fool are you?" His voice filled the chamber, shaking the ceiling so hard that a crack ran through from one side to the other in one thunderous blow. Everyone present bowed low.

Egor prostrated himself before his feet, head touching the floor. "If My Lord would allow me to explain...I only want what is best for my master." His pulse began to pound in his ears.

"Then you will fetch her back in one piece. I will decide her fate on her return. Do you think you are capable of that?"

"Of course, Master. It will be done."

Egor left the throne chamber intent on obeying Dracon's command. He was aware that Nastacia must have had help to escape from the fortress, but who would do such a thing? He could not comprehend it.

He gathered the Xanthurus troops immediately; there was no time to waste. He was hoping she had not gone far. The forest of Asan would be the first place to explore, and he wanted to arrive there in daylight. *The little viper; I will find her and fill her with fear of return.* His heart brimming with hatred, he set off to search for Nastacia.

∞

A biting gust of wind broke through the quiet in the forsaken tundra lands of the Phebus Region. Rattana pointed to the strangely shaped rocks in the distance. "That is where we are heading...not far now."

Nastacia felt a renewed surge of energy at the sight of the rocks—a place of safety while they rested. The mountainous region ahead loomed majestically above the plains, embedded in coverts of feather moss. A howling wind slowed their pace.

The sound of growling had disappeared, but the presence was still strong. Nastacia was sure she was being watched by Leviathan's leopard beast. She was afraid, but it had been her dreams and her longings that had gotten her into trouble, and she deserved her fate. She would show courage in diversity. Her life had to be worth something, and now she knew what that something was: she had to kill Dracon. She would return when the time was right and fulfill her ambition. Tears formed on her lashes at the thought of Orion. He had been her only true friend; how she wished he were here now by her side. She blinked away her tears with true determined thoughts of revenge.

On they trudged to the weird melody of the wind; it seemed like a never-ending path of rocky ground until they stumbled upon an opening in the rock side. They edged inside carefully, weighing up the surroundings. After several minutes, the blackness gave way to a faint glow where daylight filtered through an opening in the rocks above.

"Any refuge is better than none. We shall rest here for a while. It seems safe enough, and they won't find us hidden in these caves. We can sleep in turns."

Nastacia needed sleep badly, and Rattana could see that. Taking pity on her, she took the first watch.

She scanned her surroundings carefully, wondering what creatures might inhabit the caves. If her geography was right, these were the mountain ranges of Phebus, and many a tale had reached her ears of the beasts of the Polar Regions. It was an area she had not cared to journey through before. But their options were few, and all directions brought mighty challenges, with death knocking at the door. She thought of Nastacia—a plucky little fairy; she would give her due for that. For one so small, she certainly displayed courage and determination. She actually quite liked her.

Wisps of dark mist coiled lazily around the walls as dusk approached, turning the cave into a growing darkness. Rattana became aware, deep down, of faint stirrings. Slowly, slowly, hardly discernible at first, a blue, corona-like illuminated mist entered the cavern, replacing the blackness with light. A sweet aroma filled the chasm, and light pulsed all around. Nastacia did not stir from her slumber.

A voice, soft and sweet, swirled around the Xanthurus, a voice with no face. She felt the utter beauty of something she could not comprehend...something so pure she could not look upon it. She felt unclean for the first time in her life; she covered her eyes with an all-consuming shame. The voice uttered words of hope and protection, of love and peace. Rattana had never felt such strong emotions and fell to the ground, sobbing like a child.

Nastacia awoke to the sound of her cries. The mist had all but gone, and the darkness prevailed. A star could be seen in the distant opening above and Nastacia could feel the presence of peace for the first time on her journey through darkness.

She walked over to the Xanthurus and patted her arched back, careful not to catch herself on the jagged central spines. "It is going to be OK. We will get to Venus, and you will get your heart's desire. Unlike me, you have not known the way and the truth and the light. You have stumbled in the darkness. Now the light has been revealed to you; it is your choice now. I am happy for you. For me, it is too late. I knew what I was doing, and I must now put things right. I will help you to stay in the light."

The Xanthurus stood up wearily. "I am not sure what you are talking about. Something has happened to me, for sure, but I don't understand it."

"You will...in time."

"Well, as soon as dawn returns, we must carry on northeast to the coastline, the Ring of Fire, and we are going to need protection there. I have been assured of it from an unknown source. Whoever it was pierced my heart with such pain for the path I have walked all my life, and I need to find a way of changing this feeling of utter remorse. This is not our nature, and I am not sure I like it at all."

Nastacia smiled. "Welcome to my world. You have been given a conscience. It is a difficult journey, but you will be glad of it; you will see. I wish I had listened to my inner voice. I would be safe and at peace by now instead of in pain and turmoil, anchoring for Dracon's death at the sacrifice of my own. Let me be a lesson to you. Heed what I tell you, and you will be saved."

The Xanthurus looked at Nastacia through new eyes. She knew the fairy meant her passionate words. She had actually found a friend in someone she thought she could never relate to. *How strange life can be!*

The Abyss

At the gates of hell, tension filled the air as the beasts of Leviathan approached the first Loka of the abyss. They had returned to join the hordes of the Devata awaiting the imminent return of their master. Like swarms of bats, the evil Devata clung to the fiery red walls, hissing in frantic conversation. Hot, sulfurous tar dripped from their sinewy bodies and black, membranous, jagged wings. Many shifting, fiery, red-gold, bulbous eyes pierced the darkness, watching...waiting...hissing words of foreboding.

The smoke of their torment ascended from the fire that proceeded from their mouths, and they gnawed at their tongues from the pain of their long-forgotten souls.

Suddenly, a dark shadow loomed above, like that of an immense black hawk. Feeling the presence of their master, they braced themselves—hair bristled on their arms, necks, and backs. They froze in silent respect and homage. A dark and crawling cloud of evil had returned to his lair.

Leviathan's black leathery wings snapped shut in twos as he landed with a thud on a large, red-hot piece of rock. The Devatas wrapped their wings around themselves in terror, dropping in hundreds from the high rocky surfaces to the ground to prostrate themselves before him. Fire poured from his eyes. His veins bulged with the rush of blood to his forehead as his form began to change from the half-human form of rippling muscles, the legacy of his former beauty, to the grotesque monster he really was.

His face, no longer flesh and blood, transformed into the ivory bone of a skeleton; his cheekbones jutted out unnaturally like horny protrusions, his nose in the center, a grotesque orifice. His fangs, much larger than before, lay bare in his gaunt, bony jaws. Red, bulbous eyeballs protruded severely from his orbital openings. His body became a scrawny skeleton of sinewy flesh; two black serpents formed his protuberant tongue, hissing forth proclamations of evil destruction.

Leviathan's rage poured from his being like streaks of lightning; his minions' black wings quivered in the darkness below. Even Oze and his other beasts of high station trembled at his mighty rage. Celestial and her entourage had returned to Venus under the protection of Elyon, and Leviathan was by no means amused. Nastacia had escaped from the hands of Dracon and must be stopped before she returns to Elyon.

Fire burned furiously all around them. "She is mine. See to it that she does not return to Venus, since you have failed already with the Seraphim, you useless fools! I will not be thwarted." He howled loudly with destructive intent. "See to it that you do not let me down. My patience is worn, and I will be victorious."

Like a sea of unrelenting bats, flying aloft and rampant, his vile followers, goaded by rage and conspiracy and reckless indignation, let out an eerie wail that filled the chasm with evil. Grabbing the air with violent, desperate wings, they fled from Leviathan's presence filled with hatred, death, and despair.

The depths of hell were consumed with the fires of eternal torment. The fear of Leviathan prevailed!

∞

Chapter 28

Return To Venus

The moon cast a gentle, pearly luster upon the land of Castra; they found shelter among the trees waiting for the sun to reveal its precious light. Celestial took a long, deep breath, taking in the uneasy atmosphere. She felt an undesired change upon Venus. The fields below were completely covered by the waters that overflowed from the river Ossiana. As the moon drifted across the sky, the valley became a plain of rippling silver, the streams and rivulets a gossamer web of sparkling streaks of lustrous light. What seemed catastrophic to the Venusians, Cava deemed utterly beautiful—a more wonderful sight than she had ever seen.

As soon as the sun began to rise, they moved out from under the cover of the trees, making their way down a rock-strewn path. The Ossiana River flowed to the eastern Cushara coastline into the Semiramis Ocean. Since it flowed too fast to cross, they flew the breadth of the river and landed on the grassy slopes beyond. Not far in the distance was a welcome sight—the forest of Alvor, but all did not appear well. Celestial reckoned that two dawns would pass, and then they would be guests at last in the castle of Alvor with the king and queen.

Roberto could not contain his excitement at seeing his daughter. He had come close to never seeing her again when death seemed the only outcome, and now he was back on Venus; he thanked Celestial for her almighty protection—or *should it be Elyon I am to thank?*

Brabantia felt great sorrow for losing Serepha to an unknown world where she had been sucked into the horrors of a Selkie life. She looked forward to returning to the Cau-Cas Caves, quite unaware of the fate of her fellow warriors. All were relieved to be back but did not know the tribulations yet to come on this once-safe planet.

The sky cleared, and the sun's piercing rays rose above the hills, bathing them in welcome warmth, producing a false sense of security. All, for a pleasant moment, seemed normal. They chatted excitedly about their return to their loved ones.

As they spoke of familiar things, Cava had the overall sense of not belonging. She was aware that not only did she not have a loved one to return to, but she was an alien. An all-encompassing sadness filled her heart. She looked different, and she was different. *How on earth will I fit in, and what will Corsivo ever see in me?*

The day had passed without incident so far, but the realization that their land had been ravaged by natural disaster became more and more apparent. They traveled in silence. The sound of falling water, the roaring rumble of the majestic Cushara Falls could be heard close by, a curtain of muddy spray descending from above. Seven waterfalls, arranged in the shape of a horseshoe, one hundred meters high, falling in cascades, had lost their former glory. What had once been something of extraordinary beauty—turquoise waters surrounded by a majestic, leafy, tropical rainforest—was now strewn with debris of all kinds, a vast mud bath lying at the bottom of the raging falls.

In the distance, the thick smog danced around the impressive mountain peaks of Cushara, surrounded by an unrelenting silence. By midday, it was raining hard, slowing their progress and dampening their spirits. Their entrance to the former enchanted forest was one of despair for what had once been. The ground was soaked as the rain continued to pour; beneath the cool cedars, it was gloomy and cold. The ground beneath their feet heaved upward as though the dead were trying to escape.

Cava turned to Celestial with suspicious eyes. Corsivo read it as confusion sidling up to her, "What are you thinking, Cava?"

"Why do you ask?"

He felt a little uneasy. "You look confused."

"Would you not be...I was told Venus was a planet of great beauty, peace, and tranquility. It seems a bit lacking in that area, don't you think? Something terrible has happened here, and everyone is struck by a certain silence—or have you not noticed?"

"I am unsure of this land also. Remember, I lived on Mars like you, Cava. The difference is I trust Celestial, and we will find out what has occurred here when she is ready."

"Suit yourself. I'm going to ask her now."

Cava stepped out in front of Celestial. "Before we go any farther, I want some answers. What has happened to this beautiful planet you promised? It sure does not look or feel like a safe place to me. And to think I risked my life to get here too."

Corsivo sighed. "When will you ever learn Cava? The world does not revolve around you!"

Ilk fluttered his wings in indignation.

Celestial held up her hands. "It is OK, Corsivo. Cava does not understand our ways. Can a mortal be right in front of Elyon? I think not...even in his angels he puts no trust; his wisdom cannot grow without seeking the truth for himself. Cava needs to find her own way in her own passing of time. Such is the way of mortals. It would be good to remember that Elyon crushes with the one hand and heals with the other, but at the end, he redeems his chosen ones from the grip of Leviathan and his makers of storms, earthquakes, and desolate destruction."

Rusalka loved to hear the wisdom of Celestial's words, spoken like the floating, silvery notes of the Aegle harps. Such words were a comfort amid the gloom of evil snares. The Paristan horses rode on bravely, carrying the weary Nebula and Roberto, the thick mist swirling around their legs and gnarled, dead trees in their path.

It occurred to Cava that she may have been a little too harsh in her manner earlier in the day. Corsivo had kept his distance since she had spoken to Celestial. She began to panic. What if she had no friends in this new, uncertain world? Where would she go? She could not return to Mars now, and she hated this feeling of deep sentiment she had felt since her acquaintance with Corsivo. She had promised herself at the brutal death of her parents at Dracon's hands that she would never allow herself to form such attachments. Encapsulating her heart, she had always managed to feel nothing more than esteem or transient friendship. She could guard her heart from the pain of such an alliance. Why did she care what Corsivo felt about her? But she did—and that was the problem she now faced. She cared very much. Rekindled memories that were best forgotten invaded her open mind.

The rain stopped, and the sun half appeared through a gauze of clouds. The sight of the castle's spires rose up out of the mist, a most welcome sight to behold for the worn-out travelers. An urgency to arrive as quickly as possible to the castle as a place of grateful refuge spurred them on in their exhausted state.

∞

Chapter 29

The Forest of Alvor

Venus...

Patience ran joyfully into her father's open arms, relieved that he had returned safely. Wishbone joined in the reunion, jumping up and down and barking in excitement, almost knocking Roberto over as he blinked away his weariness.

"Don't forget me!" a little voice chirped up from behind. Ilk's small wings flapped rapidly. His golden-red curls bounced, and his deep-blue eyes grew wide with anticipation.

"How could I?" Patience laughed. "You know, Ilk, I have even missed your chatter, believe it or not."

Everyone laughed for a fleeting moment, the king, queen, and Astoria so relieved to see them...but a heavy melancholy pervaded their souls. Grave matters needed to be discussed. What would their future be in this now-ravaged land, in a realm where nature was its throne? How long before they would have to battle the forces of Dracon's mighty army?

That night, the clouds covered the moon, and the rain lashed against the window panes as the lanterns flickered in the castle's corridors. Sleep did not come easily to Roberto. He sat in the corner of his bedchamber with nothing but his thoughts, thoughts of Rusalka...thoughts of his daughter and of things to come. A pale, vaporous moon filtered light into the room, but the shadows were deep.

Maybe it was the onset of hysteria, a combination of fear and exhaustion. He closed his eyes firmly and tried not to think of it. Compelled to open them once again, this time, sure of what he saw floating in the void, there she was in his chamber, draped in wispy silk...ghostlike, yet she appeared so tangible. He remembered her, the scent of her; the color of her eyes like the deepest ocean, her rosebud lips and her long slim fingers—there was no mistake; it was Marissa. She moved toward him as if sensing his confusion, whispering his name in a soothing, almost hypnotic voice, softly...softly.

Roberto reached out longingly. He did not see her move from the other side of the room, but she knelt before him at the side of the bed, and, gently holding his hand, she kissed it lovingly. Roberto closed his eyes momentarily with the thrill of her touch—a touch he had longed for day after day. He opened his eyes to look upon her soft features once again. He brought his other hand tenderly forward to touch her face.

"Is it really you, Marissa? Oh, how I have missed your beautiful smile and the quirky things you used to do that made me laugh and brought life to my soul, Marissa...Marissa."

Slowly raising her hands to her own face, she began to fade away until she was yet again no more than a sweet memory. He felt that feeling that had become part of his existence of late. He could not decipher the difference between his dream world and reality. In this state of confusion, he drifted into a light, troubled sleep.

A little later, his eyes snapped open once again. Anxiously looking around the room, he searched for answers. He had seen her again; of that he was sure...had he been awake or sleeping? He could not say. She had appeared exactly the same as when he had first set eyes on her, but this time, there had been an uncharacteristic evil countenance about her. She had looked straight through him with dark fire in her eyes.

A feeling of resignation forced its claws into his heart. He quickly pushed his thoughts away, feeling a sudden urge to leave the room. He pulled himself up from the bed. There was a lassitude to his steps and a feeling of fuzziness inside his head, and the air inside the castle seemed heavy. He thought he noticed the shadows in the room perceptibly deepen, the temperature decline rapidly. He shivered, bracing himself and half turning his head, not wanting to look but feeling compelled to confirm his suspicion that she was still in the room watching him. He reached the heavy oak door, felt for the handle in the dark, and twisted it clockwise to open it...it would not turn...he tried once more...it seemed stuck. He began to panic; the hairs on the back of his neck stood on end. He felt her presence behind him—a slow, deliberate movement, feet dragging across the floor, and the sound of air being sucked in and exhaled, a slow, even respiration like the sound of the last rasps of life from disintegrated lungs. He dared not look around, desperately trying to turn the handle. The sound moved closer. Roberto rattled the handle in complete fear and frustration. This time, he heard the click of metal as he turned the knob and the door opened.

He lurched out into the dimly lit hallway, slamming the door behind him. He thought he saw the handle move, but he didn't hang around to find out. Instead, he ran down the hallway to the nearest flight of stairs and almost flew down the winding staircase, his right hand steadying him as he sped quickly and quietly down the creaking steps. He looked back for one moment; blinking rapidly...he thought he could see her again at the top of the stairs looking down at him. Her features began to change slowly. First, her lovely green eyes glazed over with a look of pure madness. Roberto watched in horror, rooted to the spot. Then she opened her mouth slowly until it grew to a gaping hole almost the size of her petite face, and an almighty, deafening, screeching sound emanated from it.

Roberto could not look upon the pitiful creature any longer and turned away, not quite believing what he had seen. *Is it my imagination?* He studied his hands, surprised at their trembling state. Never had he felt fear and such a mixture of emotion, so intense, so all consuming...he had to crouch down; his stomach felt as if a red-hot poker had been thrust into it. He held on to his gut for a short while, not daring to look back. The pain subsided, and he recalled what he had witnessed. *It could not be my Marissa—not this unspeakable creature. She was too good a person to endure such a fate as this. No...I will not accept that.*

He reached the large silver doors leading to the living room. Cautiously, he pushed open the doors, which were slightly ajar, and he peered inside. The room was in darkness, as he had expected. The heavy drapes were still pulled back, and the moonlight filtered through the large lattice windows. There was nothing amiss though, nothing out of place and no sign of life except that he noticed that someone had lit the fire with kindling and recently chopped logs. Roberto looked back through the doors, fearful of seeing her again. He bit on his lower lip, scanning the room once more. He walked across the stone floor toward the largest window and looked into the darkness of the glade. The moon provided enough light to see as far as the dark edges of the surrounding forest. Roberto leaned closer to the window; his breath misted the glass partition. He wiped the mist away with his sleeve and looked carefully into the distance. The glass clouded once more. Again, he rubbed forcefully with the palm of his hand. He saw a spectacle of vivid, flickering halos of lights dancing in the shadows—tiny, glittering orbs weaving in and out of the tree branches, their movements exquisitely synchronized.

Suddenly, they moved out of the forest and seemed to be flying toward the castle. Roberto did not want to scare them away, so he sat quietly in the shadows...waiting to see if they would appear inside the castle walls. When he raised his head again to look about the darkness of the room, with just the flickering of the fire providing any light, he saw the twinkling phenomena flying around the room, and the sound of the tiny tubular bells filled his ears. He held his breath in case he frightened them away. Like luminescent butterflies, they flitted here and there, but their shape was too indistinct to make out.

His gaze became intent. Finally, a female form settled on a small table nearby, standing still long enough for him to gaze upon her tiny, perfectly formed limbs, and he was dazzled with her beauty and perfect form for one so small. She did not seem to notice him. Then, other female fey came and joined her. They began to dance in a circle, each miniscule movement exquisitely performed. Roberto moved slowly toward the dancing fairies, his breath held tightly still. He felt that his breathing could blow them over, they were so teeny and their wings so paper thin and delicate, shimmering all the colors of the rainbow. He felt so honored to look upon a spectacle so rare and wonderful.

But then he suddenly felt an all-consuming need to cough. He tried to stop it, but the more he tried, the more he could not contain it. No sooner had he made a sound than the fairies took one look at him, and they were gone.

Roberto wrestled with his unruly thoughts and emotions for the rest of the night. He sat there, still, gathering his senses. He shut his eyes and raised his hands to cover them, struggling to make sense of everything until he finally succumbed to exhaustion as he felt the warmth from the fire wrap itself around his tired body. He drifted into a dream state once again, but this time, it was a peaceful one.

The next morning, Roberto said nothing of his apparition or the astral phenomena to Celestial or any of the others, and they set out in a mist that blurred the treetops, entering a region of dread and dark enchantment. The forest of Alvor had become unpredictable; there were moments of enchantment, flickers of light in the darkness, soon followed by the spirit of evil gloom.

On horseback, Patience nervously followed her father, bending her head forward to avoid the hanging foliage of the dense forest. She endeavored to bury the trepid feelings in a deep corner of her mind, glad at least to travel with her father by her side. She loosened the skin she held around her shoulders and took a swig of the refreshing water. She replaced the cap and returned the skin to its place, then carefully fingered the sheathed dagger Astoria had given to her. Wishbone stayed close to her horse, the hairs along his spine bristling visibly. Silence reigned between them; only the sound of the horses' hooves striking against the uneven ground could be heard.

Rusalka carried her bow and arrow and Brabantia the Paristan sword, but Celestial's hand did not throb with the promise of battle—the time would come soon enough. Nebula and Cava rode with them, side by side, relieved in the knowledge that Mikael, Corsivo, and Gabriel had flown ahead to prepare the way. Ilk chose to stay close to Celestial crossing the undulating contours of a land he knew so well, a land transformed by the wrath of nature itself at the hands of an evil source.

The mountains rose up like sentinels through the mist in the distance. The birds' echoes could be heard across the windswept valley as they approached the perimeter of the Light of Hope, which surrounded the Hanging Gardens of Sukra. Sentinels had been strategically placed at the four gateways, north, south, east, and west. A white owl flew above them. It was about an hour before dawn.

Soft music came steeling out of the fading darkness, subtle but permeating, like the fragrance of jasmine. The moon shone like crystal with a heart of fire, and the living trees entwined together, forming an arched gateway to paradise.

Unlike the land they had traveled across, the gardens had been untouched by the recent quake. Immediately as they passed through the archway, peace and serenity encompassed them. In the guarded gardens of white light, nothing was faded, nothing withered, for every stone and water was hallowed from the river of life.

The sun rapidly began to set, painting the sky pink and gold. Nebula's focus turned to a stream of cool, clear water nearby. Water fairies floated along on bits of fallen branches and leaves. She felt her heart flutter with delight and was rendered breathless at the beauty that surrounded them. The sun was now pouring through the trees, giving the floor a golden glow as it shone through the rich foliage. They slowly passed by the river, where crystal waters shimmered like glass.

"Now, this is what I call beautiful...it's awesome," Cava shouted at the top of her voice, dancing around with utter excitement. She even grabbed hold of Ilk, sweeping him off his feet and planting a kiss on his unexpecting cheek.

Ilk wiped his face with his hand. "Yuk...don't do that again, Cava. You wet me. You're as bad as Wishbone. Why does everyone want to wet me? What have I done?"

They all laughed. Nebula sidled alongside Celestial, cutting into the laughter. "This place is touched by the hand of Elyon. It is a relief to enter such a hallowed place in these dark times. I am so honored to walk by your side, Your Majesty. There are no words to express such feelings of deep appreciation for rescuing me from a fate worse than death itself."

Celestial turned to Nebula with sparkling eyes. "It is not I you owe your life to. It is true that you are loved by me also, but it is our Eternal Master who redeemed you from such a cruel fate because of His love for you. He knows the workings of your heart, Nebula, and He will make you a mighty queen once more, even mightier than before. You will rule in a time of great tribulation, but you will stand strong and lead not only your nation but many nations in the InterWorlds to victory. No more the palace of peace but a mighty warrior queen, you will see the enemy fall at your feet and beg for mercy."

Celestial turned to face the others. "Yes, it is most certainly comforting to return to this hallowed place, but we must alert ourselves to the knowledge that the spiritual climate on this planet has changed beyond anything we have encountered before. Many battles were fought in the ancient days; however, the battles that now lie before us are not of flesh and blood but of principalities and powers beyond these worlds."

A profusion of pink-and-mauve flowers greeted them on their winding path, leading to the foot of the mountain of hope. A cut-crystal stairway wound its way up, carved into the mountainside. Too weary to climb, those without wings hitched a ride to the summit, up high into the clouds, to the crystal palace of Sukra.

The crystal palace itself was much more spectacular than Nebula had imagined. They walked through the pillared halls into an antechamber, where they were greeted warmly by fairies dressed in white-and-silver tunics that flowed to their tiny feet, garlands of sweet jasmine adorning their hair.

314

After they had freshened themselves from their long journey, they met in the vast dining hall. Twelve slender columns of pure crystal held the ceiling aloft, twelve splendid crystal-and-silver chandeliers cast a rainbow of glittering light across the inlaid mother-of-pearl and ivory walls, reflecting from the columns. Along the two opposite sides, gilded daybeds draped in floating gossamer lined the base of the high walls, covered in white silk and adorned in oyster-pink and silver cushions, fringed in silver threads. Glorious melodic music, softly played on silver harps, filled the air with inviting serenity, fit for a queen's return. Refreshments had been set out on the long crystal dining table— bowls of exotic, fragrant fruits; colorful vegetables of unusual varieties; small cupcakes intricately decorated; and jugs of the sweetest white wine made from the prolific grapes of Sukra.

Their appetite was suddenly voracious at the sight and smell of such fine fare, and they ate until they could eat no more, in the flickering light of the tall white candles held up in star-shaped crystal holders surrounded by white blossoms and the greenest of leaves.

Following the feast, Celestial pardoned her immediate departure from their company. A suspicion struck her the moment she had stepped foot in the Crystal Palace and it was growing stronger and stronger. *Where is Nastacia?*

She passed through marble halls and perfumed corridors lined with flickering candles in search of Nastacia, asking all who passed her way as to the whereabouts of both Nastacia and Orion. Her suspicion was well founded—no one had seen them for some time. She contemplated the splendor and magnificence, the wealth and the luxury of her surroundings and all that Nastacia coveted. To what avail would it be for a fairy to gain her planet but to lose her soul?

The west wing of the palace consisted of three stories. On the ground floor, a large, pillared hall of many mirrors opened up through a graceful arch into a vast, open courtyard surrounded by impressive marble pillars. A grand marble-and-glass staircase, the walls lined with mirrors from top to bottom, led to two upper floors containing the apartment chambers of Celestial's most honored staff and Nastacia's large and magnificently furnished room.

There was no sign of Nastacia and no indication of where she might be. All sorts of conjectures and speculations passed through Celestial's mind. She was most surely prey to mingled hope and alarm; conflicting emotions stirred within her. Strange visions began to oppress her. It was imperative that she seek the wisdom of Elyon in the most sacred of chambers, the inner sanctuary—the secret chamber of the Silver Temple of Immortality.

Chapter 30

Nastacia's Return

Venus...

The hour of sunrise was now rapidly approaching. Celestial had gone alone for the night to the temple in search of the ever-trusted wisdom of the wise and powerful counselor, Elyon; ominous visions of an unwelcome kind had invaded her mind.

In the meantime, two beings seated themselves by the crystal waters in the gardens of Sukra contemplating their next course of action. Calm and beautiful lay the waters at that moment beneath the silvery moon—as if no evil existed under its pearly luster. Throughout the night, Nastacia had wandered up and down the grassy verge, uneasy and restless. While Rattus had slept under the cool canopy of the evergreens, Nastacia encountered a dark figure passing by in the distance...no mortal shape. The shape had drawn steadily nearer...nearer.

She stood still, unable to move a limb, and, as the figure came closer, she was taken aback to see the shape of a man. *Who could be wandering around these gardens at such a time as this? Surely everyone would be staying close to one another in these treacherous times.* She noticed his features were handsome and his eyes of dazzling beauty, the whites of his eyes shining brightly in contrast to his deep-blue irises, but his glance was penetrating and cold, and his countenance terrifying. His attire was that of men-folk; she could not comprehend his nature.

The man's piercing gaze penetrated her soul. With an uncomfortable shift of stance, Nastacia looked down at her dress, which was filthy and full of debris, evidence of a journey most fierce. She lifted her head, stared straight back into his beautiful yet foreboding eyes, and responded in a petulant tone, "What is it you want from me?"

His countenance softened slightly as he spoke charming words of seduction. "I offer you words of solace. I know all the mysteries of the female heart. How satisfied are you with your life's desires and all that you have acquired? Here you are in a garden so full of beauty, where nature is tamed by a sacred hand and the abundance of life's means surround you, eternal summers and peaceful reveries, yet your heart is full of woe and the peace you desire is so far removed from your soul."

Nastacia looked wistfully into the distance. "This I know: these are not words of solace, sir. They are true nevertheless, but what can you possibly offer me that can give me such peace—peace that surpasses all circumstance? What mortal can offer this? You certainly mean to make fun of me?"

"I am no mere mortal, and everything you desire will be yours if you do all that I ask. Celestial is searching you out to destroy you. Do not listen to her words of forgiveness, for my taste can discern the unsavory. Her words are of sweetness and light, but her intent is of bitter waters hidden behind the kindness of her actions. You must destroy her before she destroys you. Dracon is not your enemy. He will assist you to accomplish your sovereignty on this planet. You will be the Queen of Venus as you have so long desired."

Nastacia felt uneasy. Every hair on her body stood on end. "Who are you that speak such powerful words into my life? You turn words of wisdom into sorrow and shame. Get behind me, viper. Your words are of a desperate one, which are as the wind."

No sooner had Nastacia spoken such bold words than the man's beauty melted away like a moth. Nastacia's face turned deathly pale through the violence of her inward fears. There, in front of her, stood the leader of the Serophoth, Leviathan himself. Lightning flashed forth from his orbital orifices; his fearful countenance expressed a malign rage and all-consuming hatred. Spreading his powerful wings, he thrust forward his clawed hand and repeated words of destruction upon Nastacia, and, as he faded, his curses caught in the wind of change, filling the sacred garden with wicked intent.

Nastacia fell to her knees and looked up to the countless stars lighting up the heavenly floor. "Oh, Almighty One, please spare me. Let him be put to shame and dishonor—he who seeks to suck my life from me. The words of his mouth are deceit; please take me under the shadow of your wing. I will guard my ways from now on, My Lord, for innumerable evils have surrounded me. I know I did not carefully consider my destiny, and your adversary became my master through selfish pursuit of what did not belong to me. The yoke of my transgressions were woven together by his hands—the hands of the evil one." She dared not speak of his name. "Oh Lord, look at my affliction, for the enemy is exalted because of my own transgressions. For these things I cry out. Only you can restore my life now, but I despair that I deserve for you to do to me as I have done to Orion." The thought of Orion hit her stomach like a fist; she would have given anything to bring him back, but not through the power of Leviathan, no...*NEVER will I go down the path of evil pursuit again!*

No sooner had Nastacia said this to herself than her mind instantly wandered. But one never knows what one will do in the future, for the path of truth can be hard to bear sometimes, and sometimes it is hard to define what is right and what is wrong. *What if he is right? I could still be queen, and everyone would revere me...no...no...no...you evil beast...you are playing with my mind!*

Nastacia experienced undefined emotions, switching from one pattern of thought to another until she felt like screaming. She held her hands tightly to either side of her head, trying to silence the battle inside her mind as she walked back to where Rattus lay under the cedar tree. Rattus was unaware of all that Nastacia had experienced; the rigors of the journey had taken their toll, and she still lay sleeping when Nastacia returned. She woke her gently, not wanting to alarm her.

"Come, Rattus. We must continue to the palace. You can rest there."

The air was sultry and still, the garden unusually hushed. No animal moved or made a sound, no leaf stirred. Rattus got to her feet slowly, and they made their way to the winding steps cut out at the bottom of the mountain of hope.

∞

Nastacia entered the great hall of the Crystal Palace unannounced, followed by the looming figure of Rattus. A sudden silence swept across the banquet as everyone turned to see the Xanthurus with Nastacia. Rusalka moved forward to greet them with a warm smile upon her face. No one else moved. Nastacia cleared her throat, holding her head high defiantly. "You need not worry, Rusalka. Rattus will not harm anyone. She comes in peace. I would not be here if it weren't for her. I owe her a great deal."

Rusalka held out her hand to Nastacia. "Come, join us. You must be weary and in need of sustenance, my dear child. You too, Rattus, are welcome to eat at our table."

Nastacia walked unhurriedly to the great banquet table, uncomfortable with the silence and the stares. Still holding her head up high although she was feeling very vulnerable, she pulled out one of the high-backed ivory chairs, opting to sit at the back end of the long table. Rattus followed, choosing to stand rather than sit on chairs too small for her large frame.

The silence broke loose into incessant whisperings. Nastacia shifted nervously in her seat, wondering how much they knew of her plight. She picked at the feast, knowing everyone was carefully watching and weighing her up. Rattus, on the other hand, dived in hungrily, her manners leaving much to be desired. *Well, what could one expect from the Xanthurus?*

320

Nastacia noticed that Celestial was not present. A wave of panic passed through her. "Where is Celestial? No harm has befallen her in my absence, has it?"

Rusalka and Astoria looked at each other before Rusalka spoke. "She is safe and prepared for all she must do to save our people, and that is all you need to know."

Nastacia detected an accusation in the tone of Rusalka's voice but chose to ignore it. "I am so relieved. I have been beside myself with worry, as you can well imagine." Nastacia looked down, playing with her food on the silver platter; she shifted nervously in her chair.

Ilk could not help himself. "Don't you think we don't know what you have been up to. You should know better than that, Nastacia. We aren't fools, you know. I mean to say...where is Orion? What has befallen him? You must tell us...you must."

"That's enough, Ilk!" Rusalka cut him short, got up, and walked to the back of Nastacia's seat, placing her hands gently on her shoulders. "Nastacia does not need a character assassination. I am sure she has been through pain and anguish on the path she has chosen for herself. Is that not true, Nastacia?"

Nastacia cleared her throat and looked down at her plate. "Yes," she said in a quiet voice, feeling very ashamed and uncomfortable in the silence that surrounded her. An emotion of deep sadness and remorse engulfed her.

"We need to pull together. Our future on this planet is uncertain, but we must not give up. The wicked ones are ready to draw their swords and bend their bows in readiness for the kill, and we must be prepared for action. Evil is about to shower upon our beloved land. As for us Elves, the songs of our bows must be played once more like never before, yet this is only the beginning of things to come. The silver cord has broken the physical, and the astral will connect as if the forces of the universe were being called together to coalesce their powers in one mighty blow," said Rusalka, her eyes revealing a soul full of answers and a story yet untold.

"Our allegiance on Venus now falls upon the reinstatement of our beloved monarch, Queen Nebula, and all that she brings to this land from high places."

Nebula, knowing her duty, did not protest but kept silent while whispered voices filled the great hall.

"How will this affect Earth, Rusalka?" Roberto cast his mind back to Edwina. He had hardly given her a thought of late. He suddenly felt ashamed of how he had treated one so faithful to his endeavors. All the work he had thrown himself into for many years now seemed so insignificant.

"It is a question of great importance to the human race, and that is why you are here, Roberto."

She gave Patience a quick glance before letting her cool blue eyes settle on Roberto. There was a note of tenderness in her voice.

"Yours is such a cursed planet. And you particularly are the last of a dying generation that Leviathan wants so much to protect—the Children of the Wrath."

Roberto's hairs rose on his skin as a mounting sense of doom returned. His heart thumped loudly against his chest. "I don't understand...I know that I am subject to some generational curse that has been so obvious. But what on earth has that go to do with Leviathan, and what are the Children of the Wrath?"

"This is why you must be strong, Roberto. Patience must bear no children until the curse is lifted. Your ancestors lead all the way back to the Children of the Wrath, born of fallen angels, the Serophoth, who became the children of Leviathan after they turned against Elyon and were cast down to the abyss. They dwelt for a short time among the daughters of men, bearing their children—giants named the Nephilim."

Rusalka saw the look of fear in his eyes. "Yes." She looked straight into Roberto's fearful eyes. "These are grave words of utter despair for me to impart to one so precious to me. I have been so afraid to tell you that you are a descendant of Leviathan himself, Roberto—father of the Serophoth."

Patience did not understand, but she could feel the tension in the air. She looked at her father and just wanted to go over and

322

hug him, but somehow, she felt glued to the ground she stood on.

They had all gathered around Rusalka in the inner courtyard, which was open to the restless, changing movement of the clouds, surrounded by verdant foliage and the sound of softly flowing water from the many fountains.

"How can that be?" Roberto could not take it all in, holding his head in his hands.

Rusalka walked over to him and put her hand on his weary shoulder. "I know this is a great burden to bear, Roberto, but there is so much at stake. The generational curse must be severed, and only you and Patience can do this—with our help, of course. While the curse remains, the Serophoth still have the power to infiltrate Earth and cause havoc to the nations. By breaking the curse, you will free Patience's children from the curse, and mankind will be free from the influence of the Serophoth. It is in their best interest to keep Patience alive and continue their line and access to Earth itself. So, you see, your life is important to Leviathan. He will preserve it at any cost, but he will make you all suffer because he hates the power you have over his presence on Earth. Elyon cut off their ability to take daughters of men themselves, but they would think nothing of making sure Patience bore many of their cursed children using anyone available to fulfill their purpose."

The swish of his own blood coursed through his veins, and he suddenly felt a great determination and strength surge within. He would not allow Patience to pay the price of being born of the evil generation of his forefathers. It had to stop now, and mankind had to be relieved of such untamed evil.

"I see that our eyes are being enlightened that we may know the mysteries of the eternal ages."

Rusalka smiled. "I see you are learning our language well, Roberto."

"Yes...very different from the subject of light-curve photometry and analysis upon the much-debated binary asteroids and their formations, which I have been absorbed with for some time. I still find all of these spiritual phenomena above my comprehension, even though they are staring me in the face. But you can be sure that I will protect my daughter and my people no matter what it takes. Remember, death was once my friend, but not anymore, thanks to you. So we will fight to the end."

"Celestial wasn't sure if you would be up to the challenge at first. But I always had faith in you, Roberto, and I know you will not fail to do and become who you were meant to be from the days not so long ago in your mother's womb. In place of your forefathers will come your sons, whom Elyon will appoint as princes upon the earth and forge a mighty nation to conquer the evil one. Generations that follow will speak of your name upon their lips."

"If I am not ready now, I never will be! I have no choice in the matter; it has been thrust upon me. But rest assured I am determined to fulfill my purpose. Forgive me for repeating myself; it is why I am still alive, although I wished for death for so long, and death has no fear for me. Patience is my main concern now."

Patience rose from her seat and walked to her father's side. "I am with you, Father, to the end. I have realized the pain you went through and hold no grudge anymore. You don't have to sacrifice your life for me. I need you, Father, and I was so mean to Edwina. I feel a cad now. I hope she is OK and will forgive me."

Roberto put his arms around her. "No need to worry, Patience. We have great angels on our side and Elyon himself. We must stay strong and have faith in our survival and end this wretched curse placed upon us and our children to come. Dry your eyes and let me see that plucky girl I have grown to hold so dear to my heart."

Roberto cast his mind back to Edwina. Poor Edwina—she had put up with a lot for them and was always loyal and keen to meet their needs. Looking back, he felt very guilty too about the way he had taken her for granted and had not even given a thought as to how difficult it must have been for her at times. He would have to make it up to her when he returned.

Rusalka smiled. "Your father speaks words of wisdom, Patience. Come, we must all rest and prepare a gathering of all the people in readiness for battle against this evil that pervades our planets."

∞

Chapter 31

The Wrath of Dracon

Mars...

A river of boiling blood and fire ran through the depths of the Castle of Syrtis; the eternal inferno burned ferociously night and day. The Xanthurus had been ordered to have their weapons of mass destruction sharpened and gleaming, ready for battle.

"No weapon must be left out. I will have my revenge, and soon." Dracon's voice boomed above the banging of steel upon steel and the screeching chatter of the Xanthurus, his large frame casting shadows across the cavernous walls.

The Xanthurus work came to a standstill. Their large, looming figures became silent. In the evil hole of destructive intent, they cowered before their master, watching his cruel eyes darting from side to side. *Whom will he pick on today to* punish? Thought Egor, who stood by his side as he eyed his fellow creatures up and down, wondering how such a powerful race had come to this. He did not have time to think long; Dracon pointed to a female Xanthurus too near for comfort.

"You—bow down at my feet and kiss them."

"Yes, My Lord," she said in a small, squeaky voice that did not match her stature. She fell heavily on her back haunches, and, kneeling before Dracon, she tentatively bent her head down toward his feet. Quicker than the eye could see, Dracon's bony fangs came erect in the pale roof of his mouth. Drops of venom sparkled on their needle points as he bit into her shoulder, sinking rapidly through the tough hide of the Xanthurus skin.

A shrill cry escaped her mouth, echoing through the cavern walls and reaching the sky. It was followed by a deep silence all around except for the sullen lye gurgling beneath the boiling waters of the sulfuric lake and the flickering of the raging flames of the forge.

All knew her fate. To be bitten by Dracon meant a slow, painful death.

"This is what happens to those who disobey me. Back to work—if you know what is good for you. Filth, you are nothing more than the dirt under my foot." Dracon pushed her aside and turned around swiftly with a swish of his cape. The Xanthurus recognized that the punished one had done no wrong. It was just Dracon's way to assuage his anger; his rage had been growing stronger by the hour.

The flicker of flaming torches ran down each side of the increasing incline, which led to a large metal door. Dracon passed through it into his chambers and slammed the door shut; the bars of iron fell into place with a loud clanging sound.

He paced the room, festering with a single spirit of fierce and evil intent. The color of his skin had turned an intense red. How did Celestial get away...and that evil witch Nastacia too? Celestial was not as weak as I thought without Shimm-rae...if only I had destroyed the little tyke. I need to get to Venus somehow—find a Venusian who has ventured on Mars. I captured Nebula, but even she escaped. As for Nastacia, I will kill her as soon as I get my hands on her...she will die for her defiance, along with thousands of others who dare come up against me...the MIGHTY DRACON. Yes, I will be far superior to my father. He got soft in his ripe old age and wanted a peaceful existence, but not me. I am hungry with the need for power...the power of the universe. And then there's Earth...yes...Earth...how I would like to conquer that planet before the hands of Elyon can bring it back to its distant beauty.

He banged his fist hard against the stone wall.

"I will kill Celestial and Nastacia when I get my hands on them."

∞

Chapter 32

The Gathering

Venus...

The time had come...order needed to be returned from the chaos that had crept over the land. Celestial proclaimed an imminent gathering of all Venusians and every living creature who would participate in the challenge of elimination of evil.

The gathering took place in the sacred gardens of the Silver Fortress of Solitude—still a haven of beauty and protection amid the devastation surrounding it. Already, many had lost their lives during the natural disasters that had befallen the planet at the hands of the evil one.

Celestial hovered before the vast crowd, radiating an intense luminosity, a golden light that shone forth from her transparent skin, creating a golden nimbus around her. The crowd stood transfixed, utterly disarmed by the celestial spectacle. Beside her stood Gabriel, Mikael, and Corsivo with ilk, who sat on his shoulder, and to the rear sat forty Elves of Sukra, Rusalka, Nebula, Astoria, and Nastacia. Roberto, Patience, and Wishbone took their places with Cava at the front of the crowd, surrounded by the Paristan warriors on either side.

Patience had to avert her eyes. Since the recovery of her eyesight, her eyes had been sensitive to any bright light, and the light before her was the brightest she had ever seen, even emanating from Celestial.

Celestial's crystal-clear voice echoed throughout the sacred gardens, reaching the perimeters. This time she spoke earnestly of things to come, and there was none of the usual serenity in her voice.

"How should we meet the evil that threatens our planet? Consider and incline your ears. The song of the sword and the bow has now been sung as a symbol of military light. The wicked ones have drawn their swords and bent their bows in readiness for the kill. So gird your sword and sharpen your arrows. Let each one of you have your horse by the bridle. Follow and charge the enemy. Drink of the wrath of Elyon. For, have we not been forewarned that spiritual warfare will continue until all kingdoms of the universe have returned to their rightful owner...as it once was?"

Silence fell upon the crowd. Not a sound could be heard except the hypnotic voice of Celestial and her words of battle.

"Fear not. It is not the end. It is the beginning of things to come. Our heritage will change. A new planet will be born from the dark energy of our universe, and there we will prosper and multiply until the days of the New Age and the secret of Elyon, yet to be revealed. Therefore, go prepare, be vigilant, and have faith. Our mighty women of valor have joined the angels—mighty women, trained for battle, who can handle sword and spear. They will shake the kingdom of darkness; they serve none other than the King of Kings. They fight until there is no battle to fight. From the very beginning of time, there has been a spiritual battle for your souls. Leviathan, the Dark Prince, has pulled as many as he can down into a dark and eternal pit of damnation, and he wants to take you into bondage. Do not allow him to take your soul."

In the blink of an eye, she was gone. The crowd dispersed, heavily in thought, many knowing that what their queen had spoken would come true. But there were those among them who had long been changed due to the infiltration of the sprites taking over their fairy auras. They were unsettled by the words of hope and glory that Celestial spoke—after all, words were powerful, and many a word came true! They took it upon themselves to have their own little gathering and devised a plan to thwart Celestial and her army of angels, fairies, and Elves from assured victory.

Draconians could not pass through the portal of Venus of their own volition, but it was possible for a Venusian to bring them through. They planned to visit Mars imminently; they had a tale to tell. Dracon would look up to them with praise, for they had something that he could not have by himself—yes, if they gave access to Venus, he could take over, and they could join him as his loyal servants. A high reward would be theirs.

Aria rubbed her hands with glee. She too had once been a Venusian beauty, but greed had shown a way for other sprites of ill virtue to win over her soul, and now she dared not even glance in the mirror to see what she had become. She wanted revenge—sweet revenge—and many others who had come upon the same fate would gladly follow her path.

It was as if the forces of the universe were being called together to coalesce their powers in one mighty blow. The discord of Leviathan raged through the land like a malignant cancer, infiltrating the utter perfection of what once had been beautiful beyond compare.

$$\infty$$

The day was gray. A vast blanket of clouds filled the sky, covering the sun and dissipating its glory. The forest seemed very still. No call of the birdsong or sounds of enchantment filled the air. Even the trees, not just mindless stalks growing out of the earth, stood still in anticipation.

Celestial and the others had returned to the Crystal Palace to prepare for the battle ahead. No one knew exactly when the time would come, but it was imminent—there was no doubt of that. Ilk was afraid, very afraid, and Patience felt his fear too, adding to her own despair of what might be. After all, this could be the end

331

for all of them.

Rusalka sat with Patience and Roberto, trying to reassure them. It was true that they now had some idea of what they were up against, even Roberto, but even he knew it was going to be more than he had encountered so far. That was enough to induce utter fear to the core of him, but he needed to reassure Patience and tried not to show his rising anxiety.

They were deep in discussion when it happened—every window in the palace hall suddenly imploded. Millions of shimmering fragments and shards of glass flew through the air as a mighty gust of wind roared through the openings, violently shaking the heavy chandeliers. Ilk flew to Corsivo and buried himself under his mighty wings, his whole body trembling. Patience let out a piercing scream that reached the rooftops. Roberto threw himself over her to protect her from the explosion of glass. The angels had to brace themselves against its power. The others held on tightly to anything strong and stable they could lay hands on. It was an ill wind that roared through the hall. Lightning flashed, followed by a thunderous roar that shook the very foundations.

Celestial's voice could be heard faintly above the desolate sound. "It has begun. Be aware that there are those whose teeth are swords and whose fangs are knives."

No sooner had she uttered words of warning than legions of dark floating forms filled the expanse. A fluid multitude of grossly misshapen shapes that amalgamated to create more substantial configurations swarmed all around them. They began to emerge, ever growing, their ragged, nebulous arms reaching out. It was impossible to tell how many there were. Their countenances told of eternal misery and depravity. Their figures were not solid...amorphous, subtly shifting, merging together as one black blanket of dark matter and then separating again, forming discerning black shadows depicting death.

Even the wind could not dispel the malodor they brought with them. Their wicked eyes gleamed in anticipation as they gathered around. A jagged bolt of lightning split the air and struck the palace, forming a huge crack across the ceiling, followed by the incessant, immense roar of thunder rolling across the malevolent sky.

At first, Roberto was too shocked to move or speak. He could do no more than watch as the sinister apparitions moved closer, with grasping, indistinct arms. A cold sensation ran down his spine; for several heartbeats, he could not move, could barely even breathe. Letting go of Patience and placing his hands to his throat, he felt himself choking on the sulfurous atmosphere. The great hall was a maelstrom of activity and sounds, and, momentarily, he noticed that there was no sign of the angels or Rusalka. He then took one look at Wishbone cowering underneath the long, large table and swiftly let go of his own throat, grabbed hold of Patience's hand, and pulled her under the table with him.

Patience, resigned to her father's lead, was unable to take in what was happening. Alas, the entities followed them...swarming under from every angle, they came to claim their lives and their souls. Patience huddled up close between her father and Wishbone, holding on to them. She looked at her father with fear in her eyes.

"Close your eyes, Patience. Please close your eyes and keep them closed, no matter what you hear. Trust me!"

At that moment, an immense, jagged bolt of lightning hit the black Devata; this time, it did not come from the sky but from the hand of Celestial and the other angels. The entities screamed such a piercing, screeching noise that Roberto and Patience had to put their hands over their ears. The pain was terrible, like a red-hot poker being pushed through to the brain. More bolts of lightning came from all sides until the screeching reached a peak and the pain was so intense that Roberto could not see.

A benevolent hand touched his side, and he immediately felt the pressure release from his brain. A calm, gentle voice broke through the screeching sound, a voice that could be heard despite the chaos. "Remember what I taught you. Think of them as nothing but an illusion."

Roberto could smell the odor of something so terrifying in his presence...so malevolent...sucking away all the good air...he could feel its breath touching his skin on the back of his neck. He could not open his eyes...he dared not open his eyes. He froze.

He heard the voice softly speaking again, as though it were coming from within his own head. "Face your fear with victory. Listen to the voice of your soul. Do not believe that evil could prevail over good. That is not the way of Elyon."

Roberto held on to Patience, tightly keeping his hands over her eyes. His ears felt as if they were bleeding, and his head felt as if it were going to burst, but he held his breath, knowing he had to concentrate deeply on the words of the softly spoken voice and its truth amid the maelstrom.

Lightning struck the black hordes once again. Wishbone yelped pathetically. Then the sound of the screeching stopped abruptly. Roberto's eyes opened grudgingly. He was so relieved to find Rusalka kneeling by his side, and the darkness had all but gone. Just the faint smell of sulfur remained, and utter silence ensued. Only the soft voices of those he was well acquainted with filled the air once again.

"Come—they have gone. You are safe now."

A moment of eerie stillness followed. Rusalka placed her hand on Roberto's shoulder and for just one moment felt the acute pain he was feeling. Taking a sharp intake of breath and swiftly removing her hands, she searched his heavily laden eyes. The others came forward to comfort Patience and Wishbone as they climbed out from under the table, shaking uncontrollably. Wishbone winced quietly. Ilk fluttered his little wings and settled on Wishbone's back, holding on tightly and listening hard for any signs of the return of the Devata. Nothing could comfort him at this time; he was aware that this was only the beginning. Oh, yes, I am well aware. I just want to disappear off the face of Venus. Thank Elyon we have Celestial to protect us.

He tried to appear brave. "You have nothing to worry about, Wishbone. They don't stand a chance against us. Believe me, we will have them running away from us soon. You'll see." Ilk laughed nervously.

Wishbone stayed close to Patience, his tail between his legs.

Celestial glanced at Roberto. "We must get out of here before Leviathan or Dracon send more of their armies. That was just the start of the things that will befall us, and they will be grouping together to form a powerful army as never before. They know we are a force to be reckoned with—have we not got the backing of Elyon? So they will be well prepared."

They immediately packed everything they needed for the journey east. Rusalka was a little worried for the Earth people; they seemed so exhausted, particularly Roberto. Their journey through the palace gardens was easy enough, but they did not expect the changes they would encounter beyond. It was too dangerous for them to take to the skies, so they thrashed through bramble and rough undergrowth, sustaining tears to their clothes, scratches and cuts to their arms and legs. Falling, rising, never stopping, cruel branches grabbing out at them. Lashings from this branch, scrapes from another, shadowy sightings, none of which, mercifully, disclosed themselves properly.

Eventually, they reached the end of the wooded area, and a great field as green as seaweed opened up before them. At last, a respite from the forest, no branches or unsightly things to stall their journey.

Roberto leaned against an enormous oak tree on the edge of the wood. Its gnarled bark conjured up images of grotesque, twisted beings trapped in eternal torture, each of its thick, long branches ready and waiting to grab anything that may pass by. Who knew what lived inside the trunk, deep in the channels of the bark of the standing people, as Ilk called them. Anything seemed possible to him now.

"We will take rest here." Celestial could see the exhaustion etched on Roberto's face as he thankfully slid down, leaning against the tree.

He felt his tongue cleave to the roof of his mouth and began to pour the remains of his water-skin down his throat urgently. Patience watched him spilling the residue down his chin. Roberto looked up at her from his crouching position and held out the skin for Patience to drink from.

"It's OK, Papa. I think your need is more than mine right now; you finish it. I have already finished mine."

"No, you must drink more. You will need it." Roberto watched her drink the remaining water with relish. He thought how she would never have drunk water as if her life depended on it before. As a child, she had never liked water—would not touch it unless it was diluted with fruit juice. Everything they had in their past life, they had taken so much for granted. He understood that her world had changed so significantly that she must have felt beyond her years. The child had gone—been snatched away from her so quickly, it was beyond comprehension. He wondered how he would have survived so great a challenge at such a vulnerable age. Her life had a purpose beyond human recognition, and that fate was soon to unfold. It was on her young shoulders to maybe even sacrifice herself for the sake of mankind. He dared not think of such a cost. He was determined to save her from the Serophoth and their darkest angel, even if it meant his own death. He shuddered at the thought of his ancestry.

Patience walked back to Wishbone and nuzzled into him. She knew she did not need him the same anymore, but she would never want to be without her loyal friend, and he needed her now—how things had changed in such a short time.

Ilk sat on Wishbone's back, a position he seemed to have taken a liking to, leaning down on his elbows, head in hands, while Celestial and Brabantia surveyed the region carefully. All seemed peaceful for now—in fact, it was uncannily so.

Brabantia scanned the field once again with her sharp eyesight. A savory scent filled the air; she spied a mammal of some sort in the distance. Without warning, she leaped into the air head first, bursting out of her skin with a sharp tearing sound. Her clothes and armor fell to the floor intact. One second it was Brabantia the warrior diving into the air, and then it was the magnificent silver beast charging through the field.

Ilk flew up into the air, flapping his tiny wings in earnest.

336

"Where is Brabantia going? Has she seen something? Oh, no...it could be them Devata again...we...we must hide back in the woods...bury ourselves underground or something...come on...come on." He grabbed hold of Patience's hand and pulled hard, almost propelling her forward.

"Don't panic, Ilk. I am sure Brabantia would have said had it been anything of that nature. Maybe she has spied us some food. We could do with something to eat. I'm starving."

Ilk let go of Patience but did not feel fully reassured by her words, convinced that they were still being hunted. But he tried to hide his fear with mirth. "Yes. My tummy thinks my throat is cut."

Patience laughed. "You remembered, you funny little thing."

"Hey, we'll have none of that, my dear. I happen to have a good memory, you know. People just underestimate me, that's all. I will have you know that I—"

Patience stepped in before they all got a lecture on Ilk's ever-expanding knowledge. "It's OK, Ilk. I know you are brilliant. Really I do."

"Well, I wouldn't go as far as to say that. But I am well read, and I have had the best teachers, and anyways..." Ilk rambled on, not even noticing that everyone had switched off to all he had to say.

Meanwhile, Brabantia sprinted across the land at great speed. Her superhuman strength, speed, and senses, far beyond those of wolves and men, brought about a speedy return that consequently presented them with a hearty supper.

They made a campfire to roast the sweet meat and ate silently until their hunger had been satisfied and they ready for the continuing journey to the forest of Alvor. Everyone rested in the pale glow of the moon. Their first intention was to find fresh water to fill their skins.

Roberto stood up and walked toward the great oak tree again. He ran his hands along the rough surface of the bark, wondering what stories the old tree could tell. Rusalka crept up behind him. He felt her presence, prompting him to turn around and search

337

out her eyes.

"I know what lies heavy on your mind, Roberto."

He placed his hand around her tiny waist, pulled her toward him tenderly, and gently kissed her soft lips.

For one moment in time, Rusalka relented and returned his kiss with fervor.

"Oh Rusalka...Rusalka...if only you could be mine...I would do anything...whatever it takes."

Rusalka pulled back in fear, pushing Roberto away from her. "You don't know what you are saying, Roberto. This should never have happened. I am so sorry. Please forgive me...forgive me." Rusalka turned her back on him and walked swiftly back to the group, leaving Roberto bewildered and uncertain. She found Celestial awake, sitting beside a tree.

Rusalka walked toward her and sat beside her without saying a word.

"What is it that weighs so heavily upon my sister's heart?"

Rusalka felt ashamed to speak of her actions, but she knew that someone much more important than even Celestial knew every little thing about her—could count every hair on her head.

"Do not look upon the human traits you have acquired, Rusalka. For worry not, they are as fleeting as striving after the wind, but your celestial being is eternal."

Tears ran down her cheeks like tiny diamond droplets. She held out her hands to her face, caught the sparkling gems in her open hand, and stared at them with wonder. She looked at Celestial for answers. How could she cry? She was an angel of the Seraphim—not human; her tears were not even those of a mortal. "Am I becoming a mortal?"

"I cannot give you the answers you so desire, Rusalka. You must find your own way, as is the way of all creatures great and small. And we are no exception. Rest now. We have the greatest journey of all at dawn."

When Roberto returned, Rusalka watched over him as he drifted off into a troubled sleep.

The thick leaves rustled in the night breeze, casting fluttering shadows that shifted around them. Rusalka watched the play of shadows and was surprised to find herself sleepy. Her head felt heavy. After a while, her eyelids drooped, and before long, she had drifted off into a world of dreams—a world unknown to angels.

The Seventh Loka of The Abyss

From Leviathan's mighty throne proceeded lightning and thundering and the voices of untold spirits. Thirteen lamps of fire burned before it. Legions of living creatures full of eyes in front and back, all with six wings each and eyes glowing red as fire, prostrated themselves before the throne.

Their master had returned. His body, as vapor wrapped in a black cloak, drifted down to be seated before his accursed minions. Flames burned on the soles of their feet as they cried out in misery for the attention of their master.

The Seventh Loka was the lowest part of hell, a desert of flaming sand. A lake of boiling blood and fire named the Phlegethon encircled the abyss as a ring of fire, shooting arrows at the fallen ones who emerged higher out of the mouth of the river than each was allowed. The river was patrolled by the guards of hell, the Medellion.

The bottomless pit was as black as a moonless sky, lit only by torches of fire. The locusts prepared for battle, their wings reverberating through the ravine like a myriad of hornets ready to attack when their king, the angel of death, gave the order. Out of their mouths came fire and brimstone.

At the blast of the breath of their master's nostrils, they prostrated themselves even lower, cowering under his mighty rule, afraid of his dark mood. Serpents slithered on the ground, hoods flared open, and feathery black tongues flickered backward and forward, but the legions could not see them, for their fear of their master rendered them insane.

Leviathan the Devourer spoke with the voice of thunder. His foreboding shadow fell across the legions as he gave authority for the imminent battle. A yellowish, curling mist filled the ravine, turning and drifting, and the sound of flapping wings was as the sound of a myriad of chariots and horses running to battle as the fiery gates of hell opened wide.

The Serophoth, followed by their legions, ascended from the fiery pit, the heavens calling out for battle once more. Venus was their destination, and no one was to be spared.

$$\infty$$

Roberto opened his eyes under the leafy canopy of the oak tree. He stared at the darkened sun, ringed by its glowing, gauzy corona. His thoughts were of the endless power that drives and rules all life on Earth, that blazing disc in the sky that all creatures great and small rely on to burn steadily without variation.

Celestial was the first to speak. "We aim to travel north to the Valley of the Wells at the Tenth Ridge. There we will find water to replenish our skins. Then we can continue our journey to the Temple of Immortality, where we will meet with the mighty Seraphim of the Sixth Heaven and the order of the Sukras to prepare for the attack of the Serophoth upon the Temple of Immortality."

Rusalka inclined her ear. "Your life will be in danger, my sister, for you have the Key of Dreams to the Sacred Chamber."

"This I know. But they cannot enter consecrated ground— death will befall them. They will need me to acquire the Sphere of the Secret of Immortality."

"We will not let that happen." Cava spoke defensively. "We will fight, and we will win. I will not let them destroy you, Celestial. I come from a line of mighty warriors, and you yourself said there is no one mightier than Elyon. Surely he will not let Leviathan prevail."

"It is nice to hear you speak such words of faith, Cava. It has been a long and arduous journey for you. I am honored that you want to protect me and the sphere that belongs to the Almighty One."

"I do, Your Majesty. You have taught me so much about truth and light, and I am out of the darkness because of you. If that means I have to fight to the death, at least now I am fighting for a good cause. I am ashamed that there was a time when I would kill at will."

Corsivo was listening intently. "I too feel the way you do, Cava. I will be fighting by your side." Cava smiled. She felt a warm, tingling sensation in her heart.

Brabantia led the way. She paused for a moment to catch her breath and gazed at the uphill terrain, calculating the most efficient way over the rocks without being easily spied. They picked their way carefully across the crevasses until they came upon the sixth ridge, where they decided to rest in order to give Patience and her father time to recover their breath.

There were rain clouds on the horizon. Patience had noticed her father's subdued mood. His silence unnerved her. Rusalka kept her distance, choosing to stay by Brabantia's side at the front of the party. Her face was radiant, but a kind of longing hovered in her eyes.

That sense of being watched still nagged at Roberto, and Ilk felt his unease, looking back every now and again to see if they were being followed. They finally reached the tenth ridge and made their way cautiously to the Valley of the Wells. They filled their skins.

"Here, let me do that for you." Roberto held his hand out to Patience.

"I can do it myself, Papa. I am not a child, and I am not blind, in case you had not noticed."

Roberto was a little stunned by her candor. "Yes...er...of course...I am sorry. I only wanted to help."

"Oh, no...I am sorry too, Papa. I'm just so tired. I didn't mean to snap at you. It's just that...well...you were never there for me

341

when I was blind, and sometimes I forget that you are here for me now. I suppose I have learned to be self-sufficient in many ways."

"Yes...I am sorry for that too."

"I know," she said, leaning over the wall to fill her own skin. Her father looked so dejected that she just wanted to put her arms around him. But it wasn't the right time, in front of everyone. And she was aware of their position—they were very exposed in the Valley of the Wells.

They gathered together to continue the journey to the Valley of the Queens in the Ossiana region, southwest of the forest of Alvor.

Patience searched out her father's eyes, "Why us, Papa?"

It was a question he kept asking himself. "I suppose there is no reason; it just is. I wish I understood myself, but I am a mere man. I realize, after a long life of study, I actually know nothing—yes, nothing—but I do know that I love you. You are all I have." His voice broke slightly as he spoke.

"You have Edwina too."

Roberto thought of Edwina. My...he hadn't given her a thought for so long. He hoped all was well with her back on Earth. She had been a loyal and good nanny and housekeeper, and even more than that, she had been a friend. She deserved more than the way he had sometimes dismissed her, and all she wanted to talk to him about, mostly, was Patience. He wished he could go back and start again, put everything right. He was sure many people felt that way.

Just as he was about to speak again, thunder began to rip through the sky. A burning-hot wind came from the south. Out of nowhere, hurtling toward them came a large beast and its rider. The beast was jet black with eyes of fire, its wings the span of six prone men. Its rider was garbed in a magnificent suit of armor the likes of which Roberto had never seen, every inch of his or her body covered in a golden, shimmering light. The weapon the rider wielded was no less impressive, a golden lance enchanted by a glimmering aura. The flying beast propelled itself forward at lightning speed.

Ilk took flight immediately and hid in the nearby well they had

342

just left behind.

Brabantia mounted her resplendent white steed, brandishing her trusty sword, which glowed amber like newly forged steel. She raised the sword with ease, and with obvious comfort of both weight and usage and with a mighty battle cry, "Eulalia," she plummeted toward the demonic force. The beast slammed into her steed with one of its mighty wings. Brabantia raised her sword once more as it burst into flame and began to shake as she uttered words of revenge to an incantation of the warriors of old... words so powerful that the ground below them shook.

With a final scream of battle, she sliced the flaming sword down through a large rock as though it were water. A cloud of dust obscured the light. Within a moment, the effect of her actions became clear—a host of flying beasts came forth from the sky. Even the wind held its breath. The angels joined forces with Brabantia, their swords immediately unsheathed.

The first wave of demonic forces disintegrated at the sight of the lightning emanating from the holy angels. The ones that followed seemed more resilient. Ilk popped his head over the top of the well, horrified at the vision before him. He was just about to return to his hiding place when he suddenly felt himself being carried through the air, caught in an enormous black leathery feathered wing, one very red eye looking straight at him. Ilk began to lash out wildly in a feeble attempt to free himself. The beast flapped its wings vigorously, plunging downward toward the valley below. Ilk screamed. He did not know which would be the worse fate: to be thrown and killed by the impact of hitting the ground at such a speed or to be gobbled up by this...travesty of nature brought from the chaos of hell. No, neither of them would do. "Help," he screamed, knowing his voice would probably not be heard above the maelstrom. He took a deep breath and closed his eyes with trepidation, ready to meet his maker.

Has it happened? Am I dead? I don't feel anything. He could not understand why they had taken so long to hit the ground. He opened one eye and then the other. There was Corsivo, beating his wings in circles around the beast of hell. Ilk watched him unsling the bow he carried on his back and shot an arrow into the center of the beast's head, right between the eyes. Ilk cheered Corsivo on, but he was soon rendered speechless when he saw the beast spitting out fire and black venom. He was not out of the firing line yet.

Corsivo knocked out another arrow and then another. As the beast began to turn toward him, he abandoned his arrow in favor of his sword. Raising it higher than the beast's wing, he sliced through its musculature. Then, in one swift movement, he grabbed Ilk by his little body and extricated him from the beast's limply falling wing, throwing Ilk onto his back. The de-winged creature hit the ground with a loud thud, its body burned out. A heap of black ash, blown away by the wind, was all that remained.

"Hold on tightly. It's not over yet."

Corsivo dipped and flew downward toward the black creatures that surrounded Mikael and Gabriel. Ilk held on for dear life, shutting his eyes tightly. He could not believe that he was still alive.

Meanwhile, in the valley below, Brabantia ran forward, leaped high, and landed on the back of one of the beasts as it soared upward. She grabbed the winged creature's neck and hung on tightly as it twisted and turned in an attempt to send her falling through the air.

Brabantia tugged hard at the wings until one tore free. She held on to its body as the creature's screams filled the air and blood and feathers fell to the ground. As it plummeted to the ground, Rusalka swooped down to her aid. Brabantia let go, grabbed hold of Rusalka's waist, and pulled herself up onto the angel's back.

Patience stayed close to Nebula; they had found refuge behind one of the wells in the valley. Roberto had told them to stay there until the fight was over. She crept slowly forward to take a peep around the edge of the well.

"Don't look, Patience!" Nebula tried to pull her back, but it was too late. Patience had just seen her father being carried away by one of the winged creatures. She screamed and ran out into the open.

"Papa...Papa...Someone help him, please."

Nebula ran after her and pulled her back toward the well.

"No. I must help him. I don't want to lose him." She fell to her knees and began to cry uncontrollably, her hands covering her face. Nebula pulled her to her feet, dragged her back to the safety of the well, and drew her to the ground, wrapping her arms tightly around her. She placed her head upon her shoulders and closed her weary eyes for just a moment. When she opened them, she froze solid at the sight before her—two large red eyes looming above her. The beast flared its nostrils and bared its huge orifice of gigantic fangs, which dripped saliva.

To Nebula's huge relief, Brabantia and Cava launched at the creature's rear end, and the beast turned from her pouring, out black venom and fire as it began its attack on Cava and Brabantia. They dodged its fiery display, but its claws ripped into Cava's flesh. She yelped and swung around, slamming her heavily ringed fist into its side. It staggered backward. Brabantia followed with a karate chop into its throat, crushing its larynx. The creature fell onto its side, but not before Brabantia had unsheathed her sword so quickly that it had not seen it as it fell helplessly onto the blade, which sank deep into the beast's heart. A whirlwind of strength and energy, it dropped like a stone, still gasping for air and writhing in pain. Then it lay still on top of Brabantia.

A hand touched Cava's shoulder and helped her to her feet—to the safety of the well. Nebula bathed her wound with water and wrapped the bleeding arm in a swath of material she had torn from Patience's dress. Cava gritted her teeth, turning pain into the pleasure of victory. She looked beyond the well, where the beast lay, to see if Brabantia was still there. But she could see no sign of her.

"Stay here. I must find Brabantia; she saved my life."

Nebula touched Cava's shoulder gently. "No...wait. Brabantia can look after herself. You need to rest that arm."

Cava reluctantly did as she was told until she heard

Brabantia's cry from beneath the beast.

"She is alive...under the corpse...we must help her."

This time, Nebula agreed, and the three of them came out of their hiding place to rescue Brabantia. They tried in unison to shift the beast, but its stature was too much for their strength to bear.

"We must get help. Are you OK, Brabantia?" Cava searched out her position underneath the great carcass.

Brabantia was chanting unknown words—words of fire and destruction. She held on tightly to her mighty sword. It had never let her down before, and she knew it would not let her down now. "Go back behind the well. The sword will set me free." Her voice was muffled, but they managed to make out her words.

It seemed a long period of time before they heard the sound of crackling fire. Patience pointed at the beast as it caught fire from within and burst into flames. The flames leaped higher and higher until nothing could be seen of warrior or beast. From this fire burst forth four streams of flames, spreading in four different directions—north, east, south, and west.

Cava was the first to speak as they looked on in horror. "Now...that is a great loss to all of us. She was a warrior like one I have never seen or may see again. I have learned so much from her. It is sad to lose one so great."

Nebula cast Cava a searching glance. "Have you not learned anything yet, Cava?"

Cava looked back at the fire consuming the beast and then back at Nebula with a deep frown upon her face. She was just about to ask her what she meant when she saw in the distance the rise of Brabantia from the depths of the raging fire, walking toward them, sword in hand and not a hair on her face or body harmed. She ran toward Brabantia with open arms, happy to be of assistance.

"I am so glad you are alive. I thought we had lost you for good."

Brabantia patted her on the back. "Thank you for your trust, Cava, but there is no time for dalliance. We must go and help the others."

346

Cava did not know what to make of it all. *Are they mocking me?* Now was not the time to dwell on such matters. She would find out later.

To the east of the mountain, the beast dragged Roberto through the black clouds, its talons deeply embedded in his garments. Roberto's hands closed around the protruding handle of his blade, but his eyes revealed that he was already aware of his fate. He attempted to unsheathe the blade, knowing he probably had only one chance to thrust it backward into the beast's chest. Its shape, huge and threatening, loomed above him. He took the knife in both hands, lifted it above his head, and threw it backward with as much force as he could possibly muster.

The knife missed, falling toward the ground. The beast let out an ear-splitting roar that almost deafened Roberto. Hot breath streamed from its nostrils. It seemed to be heading for the mountain peak, where the air seemed to tremble with darkness and a power so dreadful he did not dare look.

Corsivo beat his wings in circles in the higher atmosphere, waiting for his command from Mikael and Gabriel, both valiant angels of Elyon. They plunged down to the peak of the mountain, which lay to the southeast of the Valley of the Wells, and hid among the rocky summit. It had been transformed from a place of light to a dark and forbidding place, now the realm of demons and beasts.

The beast was not aware of their close proximity as it dropped Roberto carelessly into its nest. He landed on one of the two gigantic eggs lying adjacent to each other, eggs much bigger than he was. Roberto looked around at the dimensions of the beast's bed. *How am I ever going to get out of this before the beast returns? I will have to climb and hope for the best.* He slid down without inhibition, off the surface of the smooth egg to the floor of the nest. Grabbing hold of the unusual material it was made of—strings of soft metal all intertwined—he began to make the prodigious climb.

He had managed to get halfway up before he heard a loud

cracking sound from within the nest. He turned his head to look at the source of the noise, already having an idea of what was happening, and just as he had thought, one of the eggs had begun to hatch...first a leg, then a wing, followed by the head of the beast.

Roberto attempted to climb faster. He was aware that it was a newborn creature; nevertheless, it was still a creature of hell, and he needed to get out before it realized it had such a thing as an appetite.

He looked back as the beast broke free from the comfort of its egg. It appeared too large to be a newborn, furred and clawed, long of tooth, with glittering eyes looking straight in his direction. Then he heard the cracking sound of the second egg just as he was about to reach the top. The first beast made a chilling sound as it tried to make its way toward Roberto. He hung precariously over the rim of the nest, one foot dangling inside the death trap. The beast clawed at his leg, desperate to fill its yearning stomach. Roberto bashed at its claw with his bare hands, sending the creature into a spin that landed it on its back at the bottom of the structure. Its cry was deafening. Roberto almost felt sorry for its despair but soon got over his compassion at the sight of its quick recovery and swift climb back up toward him. He was not about to become a meal now, after all that he had been through. Without much thought, he took a gigantic leap down the other side of the nest, grabbing hold of the strips of protruding soft metal loops surrounding the structure, and climbed rapidly down to the bottom.

With a sigh of relief, he realized he had nature on his side. It became apparent that the beasts had not yet acquired the ability to fly—they did not follow him. However, the sound they were making was enough for the mother to hear and make an early return. He looked cautiously around the rocky surfaces and made his way through the crevasses to a small opening leading to an inner cave. The opening was just big enough for him to crawl through, assuring him some amount of safety for the present.

The cave was dark and damp, and Roberto had no idea where

it would lead. He felt the cold gripping his lithe body. He climbed through with dull endurance, varied by moments of uncontrollable sadness. More and more, he was becoming convinced that he would never see Patience again. He reflected on how much life had changed course, swept by the wind in uncharted territory. His main concern was for Patience, yet he also felt an unprecedented responsibility toward Venus and its inhabitants. How he had often prayed that death would come quickly. Now he wanted so much to hold on to every thread of life belonging to him. Despite the cold, he began to sweat profusely. The sweat flowing from his brow stung his bloodshot eyes. He searched for a way out of the labyrinth until, weary and worn, he could not remember the last time he had slept a full night. He found a smooth spot to rest his tired limbs and fell unwittingly into a deep slumber.

∞

Chapter 33

The Temple of Immortality

Venus...

For an immeasurable amount of time, all was confusion amid the battle. Then the realization that the Devata had retreated left them feeling triumphant despite their exhaustion. Everyone gathered together for the count. Luckily, they had rebanded without too much bloodshed.

Stung by a sudden recollection, Patience looked enquiringly at Celestial and then Rusalka. "MY FATHER...THEY HAVE MY FATHER!"

Not one of them seemed shocked by her revelation. Celestial placed her arms around her. "It will be our quest to find him, little one. Death will no more be their aim toward your father than to destroy me. He has too many answers they wish to learn. Come, we must not delay. Dracon and his mighty Xanthurus army will find a way of infiltrating the Temple of Immortality; we must gather there and prepare."

Patience could not bear the thought of leaving the vicinity where her father could still be found. "I will stay here and find him; I must...they may kill him. I don't mean to be disrespectful, Your Majesty, but how would you know what they would do to him? You told me yourself they have powers beyond human comprehension."

"Yes, my child. You are going to have to trust me once again, for I cannot leave you here at the mercy of Leviathan. It is you he wants, not your father. You must follow my instructions if you are to save both yourself and your father. This is your destiny. We all have a destiny, sometimes beyond our understanding. here shall you abide until your destiny is fulfilled. The time approaches for you and your people when the summers will be without flowers, the trees without fruit. Men will be weak and their laws unjust. Honor will count for nothing. Women will be shameless and children without obedience or natural affection. Their only comfort will be that the sun still shines until evening comes, and then the darkness begins. Certainly I would expect you to question my judgment, for you have free will."

Ilk flew close to Patience's face, his wings fluttering madly. "Our queen is right, you knows. We can't stay here. They may return, and this time, we might not be able to fight them off. I know he's your father and all that, but we have to think of ourselves. After all, what good would we be if we were dead—yes, DEAD?"He almost screamed out the last word.

"OK, Ilk. Don't get carried away," Corsivo said, shaking his head.

Rusalka looked upon Patience with compassion, feeling overcome with fear herself for the fate of the man she had come to hold so dear to her heart. But she knew blind faith had to be her path. "Celestial speaks words of wisdom with her tongue, Patience. We must comply."

Patience fell silent while she considered their bleak position, and reluctantly, she followed her companions once again, looking out across the valley below, the land now drowned in mist. They set off to the temple at great speed, not knowing what they would find when they at last arrived there.

∞

Aria

The journey for Aria and her followers proved to be more arduous than she had at first imagined. She had heard the wild stories of Mars and its inhabitants many times from the Aegle clan she had grown up with, but to her, ignorance was bliss. They were nothing more than stories told by those who had never set foot on the face of such a planet.

They had experienced a few unsavory characters along the way, which confirmed their belief that it was fortunate for them they had a story to tell—one that Dracon would want to hear. So they arrived safely at the Fortress of Deimos to be ushered into the great Draconian hall, where Dracon himself was seated on his large iron throne.

Aria was taken in alone as spokes-person for the group. The others had to wait outside in the dark corridors, which were tainted with the whisperings and evil mutterings of the Devata. The Xanthurus stood over them menacingly, watching their every move. They had never before experienced anything so dark and terrifying. Even in the recent catastrophic events of Venus, they had not witnessed such evil. Each one of them looked at the other, having an idea what the other was thinking, but no one dared speak. Fear possessed them, and the Xanthurus could smell it pouring out of their pores in anticipation of what could turn out to be a good meal if Dracon had a mind to destroy them.

Aria stared silently at the lizard man before her. He was surprisingly thin, she thought. His description had been correct in most details, but she had expected someone more ferocious. It was when he spoke that she changed her mind rapidly.

"What news do you have from Venus? I hope for your sake you have no connection to Nastacia."

His voice echoed alarmingly through the hall. Her first reaction was to fall to the ground and cover her ears. Dracon roared with laughter, making it even worse for her tender ears. Recovering herself as quickly as she had fallen, she pulled herself up onto her knees and bowed before him.

"STAND UP." Dracon was getting impatient, his skin transforming color from greenish gray to pink. His bulbous eyes flitted from side to side.

Nervously, Aria stood up suddenly, finding it hard to keep her balance at first. His voice had upset her equilibrium. She did hope that she was doing the right thing. For a fleeting moment, her blood ran cold at the thought of what she was about to do...but fleeting it was.

"There is a child."

"SPEAK UP WOMAN." Dracon's gray forked tongue flicked in and out.

Aria cleared her throat. "There is a child...a human girl...and it has come to my knowledge that the master you worship desires her for the purpose of beginning the process of breeding once again in order to father a new generation of Nephilim on Planet Earth. This can only be achieved with this girl, as she is the only living descendant of the forgotten race and carries their blood. The very day she gives birth to the child of Leviathan himself, the nation will begin its rebirth, just as Leviathan has planned."

Dracon's color immediately drained back to its former color. He felt a new surge of excitement. Things had been going badly for him of late, and this gave him a fresh opportunity to prevail once more.

"Is that so? How do I know you are telling me the truth? What is your name, you can tell so much from names?"

Aria spoke with more confidence as she suspected an excitement in his demeanor. "My name is Aria. I am of the Aegle faerie race, and I bring with me my followers. We do not like what is going on Venus and wish to make our own way to the path of truth."

"And what makes you think I can trust you? You have certainly risked your life coming here; I will give you that. Do you take me for a fool? After what happened with Nastacia—your superior, I may add—Do you think I could let you go back now?"

Aria felt her blood run cold in her veins. A Xanthurus guard who had been standing by the side of Dracon stepped forward.

"May I speak, Your Majesty?"

Dracon nodded his head but did not take his gaze away from Ulanda as he spoke. "Make it quick."

Egor shifted uncomfortably. "Did you not say so yourself, My Lord, that you wanted access to Venus? And this fairy can give you just that—a passage through the portal."

Dracon snapped his eyes, darting backward and forward animatedly. "I am well aware of that, you moron."

Egor bowed before him and returned to his place, knowing full well that he had pleased Dracon with his words of wisdom.

Dracon continued. "If what you have told me is true, then you will have no objection to giving me what I desire."

"Of course not, Your Majesty. Do you think for one minute that we would put our lives at risk unless we had something you desire? I may be small, but I am not that stupid. We only want what is right, and we know you will reward us well. I am sure of your great qualities, My Lord."

"Egor, have a meal prepared for our guests, and make them comfortable. We have plans to make."

Egor ushered Aria through the vast cavern and through the doors. Her followers had heard every word that Dracon had uttered, and it was with great relief that they were accompanied by Egor into another, smaller cavern, where they could relax and eat. Aria, however, found she could not eat. Her heart was still beating wildly at the thought of being at the mercy of Dracon, but it was too late now. She would have to take him to Venus.

∞

The way to the temple was etched into Brabantia's memory, and they found their way, easily crossing the suspended Bridge of Mercy to the temple gates. The bridge was flanked with highly decorative pointed arches and colonnades soaring high above, covered by intricately carved hammer beams. The foliage that had become part of the structure itself fell in swaths of monochromatic color that had replaced the emerald green.

They crossed slowly through the sweeping curves of the evocative, dark, and moody walled bridge in silence; all that could be heard was the thrum of the horses 'hooves echoing eerily through the chasm and the rustle of the thick leaves as the breeze blew through every opening. Cava watched the play of shadows with a thrill of danger that surprised her; the tiny hairs on the back of her neck stood up. Brabantia touched her trusty sword, bloodied from the heat of battle, and fought hard to stop the bile rising in her throat.

When they finally arrived at the monumental gateway leading to the golden colonized temple, everything seemed normal at first. Rusalka looked at Celestial to see if she was the only one who had noticed. No breeze bent the branches of the trees or set the flowers swaying. No animals moved in the gardens; no birds sang from the treetops. The place was caught in a web of darkness and slumber, but there was still light before the setting sun. As they approached cautiously, a drapery of swirling mist encircled the temple, and it stood clothed in mysterious black. No sentinel angels could be seen guarding the entrances.

Celestial looked beyond the temple. An unmoving, oppressive curtain of cloud hung over fields and hills, shutting out all sight of the sky. The mantle of evil was already present. Two huge black flying creatures flew past them in an ominous pair—birds of prophecy that appeared before warriors doomed to die in battle.

Rusalka shivered. Never before had she felt so vulnerable. She could only imagine how Patience must be feeling, choosing to stay close by her side. Ilk had already taken cover under the wing of Corsivo. The two had become attached lately, much to the dismay of Wishbone, who had rather liked his company. Wishbone whimpered lamely with his tail between his legs.

The black creatures had vanished by the time they reached the peripheral landing of the pillared temple. The massive golden columns drew the eye up through the atrium toward the ceiling, 590 feet above. The contours of the building produced a superb acoustic so remarkable that the breathing of someone standing in the middle could be heard as though the person were standing in close proximity.

They mounted the two spiral staircases, which curled precariously around each other in a double helix, reaching about two-thirds up the minaret. The vast place seemed abandoned.

Cava was the first to speak. "What's going on here? This ain't normal! I thought you said an army of angels would be here to protect us. There is no one here. We will be at the mercy of the Xanthurus, and believe me, that ain't good...no, no, no...it ain't good. We might as well say our good-byes now,' cause we don't stand a chance."

Ilk began to panic, fluttering his wings even faster than usual. "You just cannot say that Cava...what do you know? We have fought them before, have we not, Your Majesty? We can do it again, and at least this time we are in our own territory. I wish you wouldn't do that to us. You really are scaring me."

Cava laughed nervously. "Stay calm, little man. You're causing a draft with those little pearly wings of yours. Of course I mean it. You haven't had to fight an army of them before, and in case you have not noticed, we are a little out-numbered."

Celestial intervened. "We have no time for empty words or mirth. Come, let us walk into the main chamber and seek some clarity. I will leave you there while I visit the inner chamber to see what the spheres hold for us."

Brabantia placed her hand gently on Celestial's arm as she passed by. "Before you go, I feel compelled to ask you something, Celestial. Where is your crystal sword?" Brabantia had noticed for some time that it was missing, but because Celestial had not mentioned it, she had not had the nerve to delve into so private a matter. But she could not keep it to herself any longer.

"That, I fear, has fallen into the wrong hands."

Nastacia's ears pricked up, and her face reddened. She knew she must come clean. "It is true, Your Majesty. I hate to say it, but I took the sword and left it in that forsaken place, Mars. I hate to think whose hands it is in now. I beg your forgiveness for my vanity to think I could outsmart you and to even desire such a thing."

"You have my forgiveness, Nastacia. My heart is warmed by your return, and the sword will find its own way back to me, its rightful owner. It was a gift from Elyon when he gave me the task of bringing Venus back to him."

Nastacia threw herself at the feet of her imperial master and murmured expressions of gratitude. But her heart sank within her; the pain of her betrayal and the hurt she had caused Orion weighed heavily upon her mind and marred her very existence. She could see what her vanity had caused, and she wanted so much to make amends somehow. She would have to wait for the right moment. Bitter memories resolved her decision to seek revenge to rid life of the evil Dracon. But for now, she dared not dwell on such matters. Nastacia was not such a fairy to be influenced by reflections so harrowing as the loss of Orion when the need to stay positive would spur her on.

Night fell swiftly upon them. The inner temple shimmered with firelight and candle flame, the flickering of which was the only sound that could be heard in the eerie silence of the night. Even Ilk and Wishbone were uncannily still.

Cava sat as though she did not have a care in the world, with one leg up on the large table as she broke the silence. "Where is this Paristan army of warriors you speak so much about, Brabantia? I don't see them running to join us in our hour of need."

"They will come. Have no fear."

"Oh...I don't fear death anyway." Cava tapped her long, fingernails on the golden table.

Ilk proved he was still alive, flapping his tiny wings frantically. "How could you say that, Cava? You know nothing about Brabantia and her warriors or what they are capable of. I for one trust them. No one has yet beat Brabantia in combat, which is why all the warriors who have any ambition to be champions come to be trained by her. They handle their weapons with great dexterity. They fight in single combat and know all the moves." Ilk put his fists up in an attempt to show them what he was describing. "Blow to blow, shield to shield, sword to sword. Bet you couldn't beat them!"

Everyone laughed at Ilk's rendition of a warrior in battle; it looked so comical in one so small. "And don't forget, they can shape change into the fiercest wolves you can imagine. Yes, I am glad they are on my side, and so should you, believe me. I knows what I am talking about. I have seen them fight often, yes, I have, and—"

"OK, little man, you win. But I think we will need more that the Paristan warriors against Dracon's mighty army; believe that." Cava gave him a cocky glance, which did not go down well with Ilk, as he lunged forward and pulled on her hair.

Rusalka grabbed hold of him and extricated him from Cava's hair, while all Cava could do was laugh. "It does not become you—this behavior, Cava. You are just making things worse for everyone."

"I'm sorry. I'm just trying to lighten the mood."

"Well, it's not working," said Corsivo. "It's not the way, Cava."

"Well, I hope you are right, little man, for all your sakes."

Corsivo had been listening carefully to what Cava had been saying. "I think you are just as afraid as any of us, Cava, but you need to have more faith."

Cava knitted her brows in consternation. "It's all right for you to say, Corsivo. You are an angel now, and certain powers have been bestowed upon you."

"I will protect those more vulnerable than I am, rest assured."

"I don't need protection. I am quite capable of handling myself."

"That's what we all think until the time comes when something is greater and more powerful than we are. Beware of your pride, Cava."

Rusalka held her hands in the air. "Sh...sh...sh. I can hear something."

Everyone fell silent. At first, the sound was faint—crashing hooves and flapping wings in the distance.

Ilk jumped up into the air, beating his wings more than ever before. "It's THEM. They're coming again, probably with the Xanthurus this time. Heavenly places! Help us...argh...argh...hide, Wishbone." Ilk mounted Wishbone, placing his tiny arms around his neck as far as he could manage with his short, stubby arms. Wishbone made a choking sound as he dived underneath the octagonal-shaped golden table.

The sound grew louder. Ilk froze in anticipation. Brabantia began gathering weapons from every place she could find, swords, battle axes, knives, bows and arrows—anything and everything that would be useful to fight the enemy. The others joined her.

She urged them down some sweeping steps into a maze of corridors. Moonlight filtered through the arched windows, highlighting the sleeping stone figures on the sarcophagus, creating a mirage of peace and tranquility in the vaulted space. The whole structure had a ghost-like appearance to it, set against the moonlit sky almost as if it were only partially there, existing in this world and another world simultaneously.

The sound of horses' hooves and the battering of wings rang heavily in the distance. They gathered together in the Chamber of Sukra, a multi-level maze with winding passages leading to halls, libraries, and galleries where fine murals proclaimed the power of Elyon. Through a passage in one of the floors that led down a labyrinthine maze of steps to the consecrated Inner Chamber of the Secret of Immortality, a place that only Celestial had ever entered, opened by the Key of Dreams, Celestial prostrated herself among the spheres, her tongue like a flame speaking the language of angels.

The great doors of the main hall flung open. Ilk took a deep breath, closed his eyes, and began to pray. The Xanthurus, led by Dracon and Egor, surged into a gallop, forelegs reaching forward with a loud, thumping sound, crashing through the temple's maze of corridors.

Patience's heart beat rapidly at the approaching sound of the enemy. Keeping close to Rusalka, she wrapped her fingers firmly around the handle of the precious knife that Astoria had given to

359

her.

Rusalka whispered in her ear, "Whatever you do, stay close to me at all times."

Dracon shouted a battle cry that echoed throughout the great, high ceilings.

At that moment, just as Cava was about to speak, the door in the floor of the chamber they had taken refuge in flew open, revealing an auroral spectrum of tiny orbs of light flitting around in a luminescent frisson of iridescent rainbow colors, followed by the wondrous sight of Celestial's open wings generating intense bright light and suffused energy, so utterly bright that Roberto and Patience felt compelled to cover their eyes. Then followed peals of thunder and sounds and flashes of lightning, the thick stone walls cracked from top to bottom on all sides, and the ground began to quake.

Slowly, the temple began to fall down, stone by stone, just as it had been erected stone by stone many moons ago. Dracon instructed his army to retreat at once, swiftly leading them to the nearest exit. The Xanthurus, scared of their fate, ran like frightened animals, their massive hands and feet scrambling over dead and alive bodies of their own race, fighting one another in a desperate attempt to save themselves from the mighty structure crumbling above and around them. For a moment in time, they had forgotten the quest, and survival became their intention.

Meanwhile, Celestial hovered above those she desired to protect, so that not one stone fell upon them, until all that remained of the temple was the inner chamber standing erect among the rubble. The Xanthurus and Dracon had disappeared from sight, and a serene calmness filled the void.

"Phew."Ilk climbed from under Corsivo's wing. "That was close!"

"Yes...too close for comfort."Cava winked at Ilk.

"We are still not in a position to be flippant, Cava."

Celestial had returned to her former self. "It would be of value for you to listen to Rusalka, Cava. Our enemy is still nearby and waiting only for the opportunity to return and enter the sacred chamber that now stands alone amid this unholy destruction. Come, we must find a place of refuge, that I may keep you all safe for my return to the inner sanctuary and protect all that is Elyon's."

Weariness over came Patience and Wishbone as they traveled north through the dense forests toward the deep lakes that surrounded Mount Avian, situated at the border of Castra, south of the portal.

Mount Avian was the highest mountain on Venus, reaching up into the heavens. The summit had never been seen, and its lowest point plunged into the depths of the Semiramis Ocean on the Cushara coastline. The planet's tallest waterfall glinted among the trees.

A distant thrum became a roar when they stepped precariously into a multiplicity of watery amphitheaters. Angel's Throat boasted an unbroken wall of water curtaining across a 1,700 foot vista in a 270 degree arc. The whole length of the inland cliff face had water falling over it in a total of 270 cascades that unified in a single crescent, a breathtaking display of the power of nature and a reminder of the mighty supremacy of Elyon.

The group walked silently through the mist-shrouded ledges, where water vaporized and rainbows emerged from the spray. Brabantia suddenly felt new vigor fill her body as she took in a deep breath of the pure atmosphere they had entered. It seemed that Venus had become a place of extremes, a place of exquisite beauty or unimaginable horror, a place of peaceful tranquility tainted by an evil infiltration of alien terrain.

The vegetation that surrounded them was sweet and fulsome. "Let's rest here for a while and replenish our reserve." Brabantia pointed to a spot that would shelter them from the eyes of any intruder, a cave-like ledge behind the falling waters.

"I will leave you here in the capable hands of Rusalka and Brabantia, for my swift return to the inner chamber is vital." And as soon as Celestial had spoken her words of departure, she was gone.

Chapter 34

Leviathan

Roberto opened his eyes. Slowly, his mind clawed to the surface. A flicker of anxiety crawled up the back of his neck when he remembered where he was and what he was hiding from.

He felt perturbed by his dreams of Marissa's solemn cries of despair and pain. He immediately threw away the reflection, intent on finding his way out of the dark cave. Before long, the tunnel narrowed and plunged a few feet downward. Roberto climbed nimbly down to a bubbling lake of green, milky waters, and, drawing a deep breath, he closed his eyes as the warm, soothing water rushed over his head. He felt it flow into his nostrils, down his throat, and into his lungs, and then he pushed himself forcefully to the surface and took a gulp of air. His heart pumped strongly, and he hoped the way out would become clear, as he thought he could see a flicker of light in the distance.

Above soared a high ceiling of spectacular calcite and mineral formations, and the faint green of daylight grew closer in the shaft beyond, just strong enough to cast the walls of the passage entry into a silhouette. Roberto thought how he would love to float there for hours, weightless and relaxed, suspended in the void, all thoughts drained from his mind. He chided himself at once; there was no time for fanciful thoughts. He needed to get back to Patience before Leviathan got his hands on her. The thought made him shudder.

A whirlwind of newfound strength and energy possessed him, and he finally reached an opening that brought him out of the caves into the glaring sunlight where the waters turned to a twinkling sapphire blue. Roberto swam to the nearest dry land and dragged himself up onto the grassy verge. He lay there for a short while to recover his breathing, and then he heard the flapping of wings, large wings. A solid and forbidding mountain range of granite peaks loomed dark and majestic around him. He did not have a clue where he was or which way to go, but he was sure the beast had spied him.

His heart thumped in his chest. He could hear the rush of waterfalls in the distance, the sound of water pounding against rock. He followed the sound and took refuge among the lush vegetation. Again he heard the flapping of wings, but this time, it was the sound of numerous wings. Roberto scanned the sky, looking for the source of the increasing sound. The clouds began to part and melted away.

With an echoing roar, angels unlike any he had seen before came hurtling down from the brooding red sky and settled on the ground before him. Then, suddenly, an agile black figure dropped from the trees above; a torrent of air passed by. It swooped to the ground with a heavy thud.

Roberto shrank back into the foliage. He smelled a terrible odor of putrescence. Black shadows thickened and coalesced, taking on bat-like shapes that stood in the light of the sinking moon, featureless save for the dreadful eyes.

The black figure spoke—a guttural, rasping, croaking utterance. Indescribably menacing, it chilled Roberto to the bone. Beside him, on a metal leash, stood a creature of great proportions that had the appearance of an overgrown leopard. A low, guttural growl proceeded out of its mouth, and a ribbon of smoke streamed from its nostrils.

Roberto felt his heart sink with a feeling of utter desolation. All his senses were affected by the presence of the dark angel. His huge, leathery, bat-like wings were black against the silvery sky. Tilting forward, he pulled them close to his side, revealing his

363

rippling torso and long white talons.

"I am the morning star. I have in my hands life and death, but the sorrows of Sheol surround me day and night, and the snares of Elyon confront me." The dark angel moved a few steps closer to Roberto, smoke emerging from his nostrils and fire from his eyes.

"What do you want from me?" Roberto struggled not to show his fear.

"Do not play with me. You know what I want...and you will give her to me."

"Over my dead body...Elyon is my master, and He will protect her. You will never have her to breed your evil race once more."

"It's your lucky day this very day, for you are more useful to me alive than dead."

Leviathan opened his mighty wings, and a loud crack of thunder ripped through the sky, followed by lightning, "SEIZE HIM!"

Roberto attempted to run, but the speed of the Serophoth was beyond anything human. He had no choice but to allow himself to be taken to a place he could not imagine. He felt desolate and alone among the depravity of evil. Only Elyon himself could save him now.

Meanwhile, back at the Temple of Immortality on Venus, Celestial hid behind some trees. Dracon and a few of his Xanthurus army sat among the fallen stones. The Inner Chamber still stood solid against the desolation. Celestial looked with horror in her eyes at the broken bodies of the Cherub sentinels, no longer stone but flesh and blood...blood spilled carelessly on the ground. She felt a deep, all-consuming sorrow for the Cherubs she had loved so well. It was obvious that Dracon had not realized he would never be able to enter the consecrated chamber, for he would shrivel up and die. The spheres held no immortality for him.

She walked confidently from behind the tree into full view of Dracon and the Xanthurus. As she approached them, everything she touched as she passed by blossomed forth flowers of wondrous scent. She shone with lunar beauty shafts of light that pierced their darkened souls. Blood trickled from Dracon's nostrils, and his eyes glowed with a dreadful yearning mixed with an evil wrath. Her beauty could not escape him, but his hatred for everything she was consumed him.

Her melodious voice touched the treetops. "It is of no use, Dracon. You can never enter the Inner Chamber, for it will be your end with no beginning." Her pure white feathery wings opened wide, exposing the fairy fruits of the spirit, each tiny orb throwing out tremendous light that rendered Dracon and the Xanthurus temporarily blind.

She left them stumbling about in their own darkness, turning the long, golden Key of Dreams in the silver lock and entering the Sacred Chamber. Swiftly she closed the vast, arched silver doors on the outside world and took her place among the spheres to meditate, looking for the answers she so desired.

Dracon's wrath consumed him as he fell to his knees and let out a great roar of anger. Even the Xanthurus froze, holding their elongated hands over their ears.

"BREAK DOWN THE DOORS! I DON'T CARE HOW YOU DO IT. JUST DO IT."

His long white hair fell in wild tangles to his shoulders and his skin turned an alarming crimson as he spoke, grotesquely bulging eyes darting frantically from side to side. Egor had seen him in some major furies, but none so intense as this one. He immediately ordered his army to break down the doors.

The Xanthurus chose a large oak tree nearby to rip up from its roots, regrettably without a care for its inhabitants or the tree's spirit, the Nyadd. The branches fought back in horror, and the writhing roots encircled them, twisting and turning themselves around the Xanthurus's necks, squeezing the life out of each one of them. Thousands of tiny faeries and creatures of the bark pinched and bit into their flesh until they were covered in cuts from head to toe. Next, the sound of wailing developed into a chorus of woeful, dreadful despair that emanated from every tree. The Nyadd came forth, streaming out seamlessly from the trees, their tiny, handsome faces contorted with pain and fury. Before

365

long, seven of his army lay dead on the ground, increasing Dracon's fury to boiling point.

Anxious now, Egor sent forth ten more of his rat race to arrest the tree that had become grotesque, twisting, thrashing, living thing more dangerous than any beast or man.

"Have we not lost enough of our army for one day, oh master? Could we not close ranks and come back with more of your mighty warriors, My Lord?"

As soon as he had uttered such words of defeat, he knew he had made a mistake. Dracon would not accept defeat—it would always be his choice to fight to the death without thought of consequence.

"You will follow my orders. If all of you lay down on this alien ground this day, let it be so."

Dracon towered above Egor, his long, gangly arms folded tightly across his chest. His all-consuming rage was evident—his long, gray tongue flickered in and out at will, and the color of his skin turned an even darker shade of red. Egor obeyed, sending more and more of the Xanthurus until the tree was finally defeated by twenty of them, battered and torn. The weary worn sat on their haunches while those who had watched in horror yanked the vast piece of wood from the ground and carried it forward at great speed in an attempt to break down the doors of the Sacred Inner Chamber.

Time and time again they tried to break down the barriers between them and the Sphere of Immortality, but not even the slightest of movement came about. Suddenly, the sound of the trees swaying in the wind became apparent, and they could not ignore it. One tree after another began to violently rip its roots from the ground until the ground started to shake. Suddenly, they were surrounded by advancing roots making their way toward them at great speed.

Dracon let out a deafening roar above the eerie sound of the slithering roots. "WE WILL NOT BE DEFEATED."

Egor issued a command to fire a volley of arrows at the progressing trees. The Nyadd screamed out in horror as the

366

arrows pierced their souls, and they began to drop one by one to the ground. Shortly, only a few remained. As each tree was damaged the pain of the Nyadd increased just as each tree that died would bring about the death Of the Nyadd.

Dracon bent down to pick up one of the tiny, writhing creatures between his thumb and finger talons. He gazed at its tiny, perfect, humanlike form, the size of his smallest fingernail. All Nyadds were female, and her nakedness was partially covered with her long brown hair, which flowed to her ankles. She wriggled and fought against his grip, crying out desperately, her tiny voice hardly discernible. Her fate had already been decided; death was a certainty, but she did not relish the idea of satisfying a greedy Xanthurus appetite. It was enough to die a death of honor bestowed upon her through the end of life of her tree. Egor opened his large jaw wide revealing his long, pink tongue and sharp incisors. Dracon dropped her into the Xanthurus mouth, smiling with evil contentment at her uncomely expiry.

Egor snapped his jaw shut and chewed slowly to savor the delicacy Dracon had provided for him. The remaining Nyadds screamed violently, returning to their trees in the hope of survival.

"SET THEM ALIGHT. DESTROY THE FOREST."

Egor gave the Xanthurus orders to burn down the forest before the forest devoured them. No sooner had the fire been lit than a warm breeze blew in from the south, causing it to spread rapidly. The trees marched forward, many of them already ablaze. Dracon and his army left the burning forest and its shrieking spirits behind in search of a safe place until the fire had faded.

The Nyadds burned and squealed harrowingly. The smell of charred flesh and burning wood filled the air as the fire consumed everything in its path. The flames leaped high all around the Sacred Chamber of Immortality until finally they died down, leaving the forest and all that was in it nothing more than a memory of all that was—and yet, the Sacred Chamber of Immortality stood untouched by the scorching fingers of fire, shining in all its given glory, a bright light amid the darkness.

∞

Chapter 35

The Sacred Chamber of The Temple of Immortality

Venus...

The time had come. Celestial wandered through the suspended spheres of spectral glowing light. Each one had a message to tell of infinite wisdom from the eternal flame. A surge of power beyond anything she had ever encountered before filled her soul—she almost floated toward the entrance of the vast chamber. Once outside, she closed the heavy doors with the Key of Dreams and placed it around her slender neck for safekeeping. So dark was the air, so loud the cry of the wind that she did not at first notice the sheer destruction of the recent fire. Overhead, the sky was black and devoid of stars. A chill descended upon her skin.

Leviathan moved toward her soundlessly, drawing all the light into his being so only the dark remained. Eyes of fire flared to life and burned with unmistakable rage. He advanced menacingly toward Celestial. As powerful as she was, she felt a momentary fear that took her by surprise. Her thoughts were of what he had once been. She was transfixed by his steadily changing app-earance, from the almost beautiful dark- angel she had known to the most ugly, grotesque being she had ever laid eyes upon...that bared the true nature of his debauched soul.

She resolved to stand steadfast despite an inner voice telling her to flee. His boney orifices burned crimson with fire, and his voice was as empty as his soul. Fear was an emotion Celestial had conquered during the War of the Heavens, but seeing the archangel she had battled with so...so long ago gave her a flicker of that emotion once more, and now, his soul had taken on all that was dark and dire.

The ground she stood upon stole her strength and rooted her to the spot. Thunder roared from the heavens.

"BOW DOWN TO ME."

Fire emanated from his hollow mouth as he spoke. She kept silent. She would not. She could not. Feeling somewhat diminished in his presence, she nevertheless stood firm. He spoke louder this time. White lightning struck the ground nearby as he repeated his command. She bore down deep within to muster up the courage to deny him his wish.

"You know the power of the Mighty Flame. I will bow to no one other than the Almighty—Elyon."

The ground shook with his unspoken rage.

"I tell you this day, you will bow down to me. But it will be of your own free will. For now, it is enough for you to know that I have bound in chains someone precious to you and yours. So, you see, you will search me out - this much I know. My time is near when every living thing will worship me and bow down at my feet and beg for mercy."

Her most merciless foe stood before her, impatient and demanding, fearsome and deranged, but, for a fleeting moment, she felt pity for him. He was a mere shadow of what he had once been, a despicable image of all that was ugly and evil, a lost soul of darkness fallen from the everlasting light of the Eternals.

"You are snared by the words of your mouth. You are a pitiful soul, Leviathan. What made you choose a path so wretched? In the greatness of your folly, you shall go astray. You have profaned His crown in every possible way. You have cast it to the ground. Your house is the way to hell, descending into the chambers of death. There is no escape for you now. You are as helpless as a captive animal."

She cringed inwardly at her spoken words of truth, but her face stayed expressionless. She was all too aware of his manipulations and chose not to question him about whom he held captive. Leviathan let out a mighty roar that made the ground tremble beneath her feet.

"You will eat your words when I am universal leader. Your fate will be worse than death itself. You will be mine. Then we will see who is pitiful then.

Celestial closed her eyes at the sight of his overpowering wrath. Up above them, the skies thundered vociferously, and then a scattering of dark forms suddenly surrounded him, hovering cautiously, they themselves aware of Leviathan's dark rage. She kept her eyes closed so as not to look upon the abomination before her, and a bright, serene light radiated from her in the midst of the maelstrom.

"You are not what you see yourself to be."

Leviathan wavered in and out of a solid form as she spoke.

"You are no longer as powerful a Serophoth as you once were. Look at yourself. You can't even keep your solid shape anymore. How long do you think it will be before your powers are as the wind, having passed by for a short visit—then gone forever?"

The nearness of his evil chilled her to the bone. The darkness enshrouded her, and, beyond her control, she began to shiver violently. Leviathan let out a sneering laugh, a sound so raw it made her recoil. She caught her breath, staggering a little as she tried to control her emotions. The wind howled, whipping at Leviathan's robes. He began to retreat slowly, his laughter caught in the wind, his burning eyes still fixed on her shaking form. She strived to stand firm against the strong force of the prevailing wind, but the strength of it beat her down to the ground. She looked up one more time, steadying her position, her fingers digging into the soil, her hair and feathered wings flapping wildly. He was fading slowly enough for her to look into his featureless orbs, and now the fire had gone from them, and all that was left was the hatred inside. Not just for her alone but for every living thing.

Leviathan vanished with the swiftness of a shadow exposed to light, leaving only an acrid smell lingering in the air. Then, abruptly, the sky grew calm. The wind died down, and all was quiet once more. The valley was empty of movement and sound, and the wall of mist that had gathered began to lift. It was then that Celestial noticed the ravaged forest beyond the clearing. She rose to her feet, wearily drained of strength and spirit. The trees had been burned mercilessly. Her heart felt burdened by the fate of the Nyadd, those elemental spirits of the trees that had lost their souls for eternity, for the death of an elemental was final and without question. She thought of Dracon and her enemies, and her soul cried out for blood.

∞

When the dawn set alight the sky, she made her way to Angel's Throat, cautiously aware that around every corner lurked danger. Her thoughts were of Roberto. It was most assuredly he whom Leviathan held in chains. She feared that Dracon had not been idle while he lingered in the Valley of the Queens. The fire had passed through the forest there, leaving no blade of green; brown, withered tree stumps remained. There would be no end to his destruction of Venus if she did not act swiftly. She flew steadily on the low, whispering breeze, her fairy spirits surrounding her beating wings, their glittering light subdued so as not to catch attention. She felt their position was too naked, but she needed to return to the others speedily before Dracon or Leviathan found their hiding place. Without her, they were all vulnerable.

Dusk came early, followed by a starless night. She saw no sign of anyone as she approached the summit of the mountain. Just the sound of the cascading waters could be heard. The sound was more melodious to her ears than the songs of men, more melodious at that moment than even the songs of the merfolk, but never could they be more euphonious than the resonances of the Eternals—oh, how she longed for that sound, so sacred and

372

serene. She landed on the cliff top and picked her way along the rocky summit until she found the cave behind the waterfall where she had left the others to fend for themselves. Her sudden appearance filled them with amazing joy. Ilk flapped his pearly gray wings until he was out of breath, and even Cava gave a rare and heartening smile.

Rusalka stepped forward, her hands held out to Celestial. "We were beginning to concern ourselves for your plight, My Queen. It is so good to see you return to us unharmed, but you look weary from your travels. Sit for a while and tell us all that you have seen and heard."

Celestial sat down. She did not wish to tell them of her encounter with Leviathan or his revelation regarding Roberto. Instead, she told them not to fear for what they did not know or understand. Brabantia brought her a silver goblet of refreshing cool water, and, bending down on one knee before her, she placed it carefully in her delicate white hands. Celestial fingered the cup and took a grateful sip of the rejuvenating liquid, closing her eyes for a fleeting moment.

They sat huddled together, talking in low, mournful tones. Venus had become a mere shadow of what it had once been. How could such a planet, chosen above all others by Elyon, ever experience such tragedy? Had Elyon abandoned her? And what had become of Roberto? Respectfully they waited, all eyes upon her sweet face, which belied the wisdom of her eternal life. She opened her eyes and spoke as though she were in a trance, looking at them but not seeing them.

"Darkness has spread like a disease from one world to another, the subtle corruption of pure hearts of creatures both great and small. Oh, how it makes my heart weep."

Beyond the shelter of the cave, the sound of the wind rose sharply, and a blinding light filled the sanctum. Suddenly the blade of Brabantia's sword glowed hot with flames. She had drawn the sword and was holding it high above her head.

"The tides of fate are flowing beyond our expectations, and we must prepare for battle. Let us move forth and join forces with our sisters of the Paristan, our angel warriors, and all who desire to shame our enemies and glorify the name of Elyon and the Eternals. Come, follow me. We must make haste and be victors against this all-consuming destruction that belongs to the angel of death. Those destined to die by the sword will die by the sword; those destined to die by the hands of Elyon will die a cursed death."

Ilk flew up into the air, flapping his tiny wings in earnest. All color had drained from his face. "What are you going to do, Your Majesty, without the crystal sword?" He covered his face dramatically with his hands, then, pulling them away as swiftly as he had placed them there, he continued. "We are most definitely doomed. Oh, what can we do? We need to find it...and we need to find it now. Oh, my dear, we will be destroyed without it. How could you, Nastacia? This is all your fault. We would have had the sword had it not been for your foolish behavior."

Cava rolled her eyes and gave Ilk a disapproving look, then shifted her gaze rapidly to Nastacia and back to Ilk. Nastacia froze. Her body trembled slightly. Tears sprang to her eyes and spilled over, running down her cheeks. She felt sick to the stomach as she remembered what she had done, and she had not even told them how she had led Orion to an untimely death. She shuddered as she thought of the implications of Leviathan or Dracon laying their hands upon the sacred sword.

Celestial gently placed her hand on Nastacia's arm. "It is not for us to make judgment, Ilk. Nastacia has a battle of her own to win, and we can only help her on her journey to a place of inner peace."

Nastacia covered her eyes with her hands. Her body racked convulsively as she tried to suppress her sobbing. Ilk could not take it upon himself to comfort her, but Rusalka stepped forward and held her in her arms until the tears subsided.

"Your pain shows your heart-felt repentance, dear one. You must fight your battle and win. Come, we must all be strong in the midst of oppression."

Patience spoke out suddenly. "What of my father, Your

Majesty? Have you any news about him? Please tell me what you know. I would rather hear the worst than live in hope of seeing him again."

Celestial's expression did not change. "Be anxious for nothing, my child. With a pure heart, nothing will be denied you...but alas, the journey is written in stone."

Patience did not know what to make of Celestial's words. The sadness in her eyes prompted Ilk to put his little chubby arms around her neck and give her a comforting hug. Wishbone followed his action by licking her face. Patience managed a half-hearted smile, warmed by their affection, but deep in her heart, she could not stop worrying about the fate of her father.

Cava rolled her eyes again. "We are never going to get anywhere with all this mushy stuff. I say we go now and meet our enemy."

Corsivo gave Cava an ironic smile. He really thought she had a lot to learn about the nature of others, but he could not help liking her boldness and courage at times.

Celestial climbed down from the mountain summit with renewed strength and took flight, enveloped in her own radiance. Such was her brilliance that they could see neither the sun nor the stars above nor the land below. They followed without question, knowing that all she said was true and unalterable.

Patience nestled among the warm feathers of Gabriel as he took flight on the wind. She was aloft and felt safe for the moment, triumphant over the terrors of the night that lay below. She thought of her father and how she missed him now that they had become so close, but she was determined to believe that he would be safe in the hands of Elyon somewhere, waiting to see her again.

They flew high into the clouds for a while and then descended slowly, carving around mountain passes, along stony ridges and past jagged peaks.

Finally, they came to a vast gorge. Celestial took a look over the edge of the precipice and then glided into the cavity, followed by the others. White wings, spread wide, hovered gently down, set aside by the darkness. Celestial was the first to spot something moving among the shadowed rocks below. It was hardly discernible in the murky distance to any but the Eternals—furred and clawed, ten times larger than any horse or its like, long of tooth and with flashing eyes, its wings the span of six prone men, a beast pitch black with eyes of copper. Its head, with gorgon-like tresses, lifted upward toward the descending angels, and its eyes gleamed with anticipation.

Corsivo propelled forward at lightning speed, overtaking Celestial's position, beating his wings in circles in the higher air while he unslung the bow he carried on his back and knocked an arrow into it. Then he gave the command, and Mikael and Gabriel, as valiant as Corsivo, threw themselves down, plunging into the depths of the canyon, where the beast waited with bated breath. Corsivo and his companions flew in circles around the hungry beast, taunting it with their spears. It reared and spewed fire and black venom, revealing its elongated, gray, two-forked tongue. Mikael let fly another arrow and knocked another, ready for release. Corsivo found himself staring into a palisade of sharp-edged teeth, into the glistening, crimson cavern of an eager mouth. If it hadn't have been for Gabriel's sharp action, he may have found out more about that enormous cavern all set to devour him.

Mikael had climbed the beast's back, tugging hard at the gorgon-like protrusions, which seemed to have a life of their own, throwing him from side to side. Meanwhile, Gabriel shot an arrow into the beast's left eye, followed by one into the right, rendering it blind. With a guttural cry, it reared back on its hind legs, breathing sporadically and swaying from side to side. The angels finished off their attack together until black matter seeped out onto the ground, where the beast found the hiding place for its monstrous soul.

Patience watched in awe at the mastery of the angels she had come to hold so close to her heart. Rusalka held her tightly.

"Here, the orderly laws of nature do not apply anymore. The shapes and behaviors of many living things here on Venus have

376

changed so that we recognize these creatures no more. Stay very close to us, my child, for we know not what we are dealing with any longer."

Ilk held on to Rusalka's wings. "Perhaps we should think of moving planets. A voice came down the wind that there is another planet not so far from here that is not even inhabited. We could go there and start afresh. Yes, I think we should go at once. What do you think, Patience? I bet you would agree with me...after we have found your father, of course. I wouldn't—"

Rusalka smiled at him. "The easy path is not always the path of victory, as you will one day see, young Ilk."

"Oh, I know you speak words of wisdom, Rusalka. I know you speak words of truth, but sometimes you may get it wrong..."

Taking no notice of Ilk's ramblings, Celestial gathered everyone together. "You have fought well, warriors of Elyon."

Corsivo stepped forward. "Thank you for saving my skin back there, Gabriel. I am most grateful."

Corsivo didn't see the look of astonishment and then anger that crossed Gabriel's face. He was hidden in the shadows of the rocky overhang. "I would have done it for anyone, Corsivo; make no mistake."

"Point taken brother...I did not mean to make out that I am different or of more importance than any other being, but it proves we are a team, does it not?"

Gabriel did not smile, but Corsivo held out his hand in friendship anyway. For a moment, Gabriel stiffened. He was clearly stunned. Then he reluctantly shook the proffered hand.

Cava chipped in, "It's about time you two made friends. What is your problem, Gabriel? Manticore got your tongue?" She laughed out load.

Gabriel gave her a hostile glance. He had not taken to Cava from the beginning, and he could now see why.

Celestial stopped the banter. "One who has knowledge and no faith is as one who is lost, Gabriel."

Gabriel remained quiet as he gathered his weapons. He hated his position. He felt he had failed Celestial the day she was taken from Venus, and now she had Corsivo at her disposal, who it seemed, could do no wrong. His thoughts were enmeshed in how he could prove himself a mighty warrior again—and not just by saving Corsivo's skin. Perhaps he should have let him die. Gabriel chided himself for such a thought—he was an angel, was he not? How could he even think such a thing? He gave Corsivo a furtive glance, feeling suddenly guilty, and hated him even more for making him think such evil thoughts. He sighed heavily as he followed the party leaving the heights of the gorge west to the banks of the river Vasawati.

Meanwhile, in the subterranean labyrinths of the Castle Syrtis in the Syrtis Major region of Mars, Roberto lay on the cold, dank floor, starved of food and water. Leviathan had led him into the hands of Dracon, who incarcerated him in an attempt to lure his enemies away from the hallowed places of Venus.

Roberto shuddered at the thought of the implications if Leviathan were to lay his hands upon his most precious daughter. Over his dead body could he allow such a thing to happen. He felt sick to the stomach as he tried to recall her sweet face and eyes so full of innocence, a deep sea-green. He smiled to himself at the thought of her sheer determination and tenacity, much like that of her mother. He was scared, more afraid than he had ever been in his short life so far. He had to escape—and soon.

Chapter 36

A Battle Most Fierce

Venus...

Vasawati was a wide river, and the simplest way to cross would have been to fly across its expanse. But dawn had broken with its orange hues, and they needed to travel low, hidden from the eyes of the lofty ones. The air was very still except for the sound of rushing waters and the far cry of some creature in terrible distress. Celestial lifted up her arms and spread out her hands toward the undulating waters in a gesture to summon the spirits of the river for added protection. Her wings spread open, sparkling like a multitude of glittering diamonds gleaming against the indigo sky. She seemed to grow in size and stature.

Patience gazed from behind her hands covering her face from the brilliant spectacle. She suddenly felt very small and diminutive. What looked like brilliantly colored butterflies with shimmering, membranous, gold-and-silver wings hovered just above the surface of the water, wavering like candle flames. Then, one by one, they rose up like streams of water, twisting up into the air and suddenly diving down back under the surface of the watery deep. Peeking through her fingers, Patience couldn't believe her eyes as the waters began to part, forming a wall at either side, creating a pathway for them to walk through. The water nymphs stood like sentinels, holding back the pillars of swirling water as Celestial and her party passed through safely to the other side.

"Well, I never thought I'd see the day when even the rivers obey an angel's command." Cava was more impressed by Celestial's power than ever. She began to see she was more than just any angel, and she felt honored to be part of her quest to save Venus.

Ilk jumped on the bandwagon. "Yes, I told you, Cava, and you would not listen. Our Majesty is an archangel of the Seraphim sent personally by Elyon himself. And I might add that I am her messenger. I think you forget that sometimes; you should be nicer to me...you should. Anyways, I always knew she could part waters 'cause I know she can do anything, and—"

"I get the picture, little man. For goodness' sake, do you ever give it a rest?"

Patience turned around. "Look!" she cried, and they turned back, lifting their tired eyes to the river as the waters joined forces once again as though they had never parted.

They journeyed on until dusk, into the gathering night, until the first sign of sunrise. A bitter chill came into the air. The mountains in the distance were shrouded in a dense mist. As they approached the Valley of Aloha, the clouds began to part and melted away, and a bird caroled to meet the dawn. The Silver Fortress dazzled, standing tall and proud in the distance. Its soaring heights, delicate stonework, and well-lit interiors encouraged a lifting of the eyes toward the heavens. The sudden change of atmosphere was greeted with an appreciative delight, for nothing had changed in the hallowed gardens of the fortress, still a haven of beauty and tranquility amid the maelstrom of changing atmosphere that surrounded it.

There was an endlessly long moment of reverent silence as the party stepped foot on the hallowed ground. The warmth of the sun upon their skin delighted their hearts. They could hear the sweet-throated birds sing in the branches, and all around were trees in blossom and blushing flowers. The trees were tall, and the branches were far sweeping. A silvery stream ran past, breaking on the banks in a milky-white foam.

Cava was the first to speak. "This can't be real! How can this be?"

Ilk flew in front of her. "Of course it's real. It's always been the same on hallowed ground. Don't you know anything, Cava?" He folded his arms as though he had got one over her and gave a wide smirk.

Cava was annoyed with him once again. "Well, of course, Ilk. You know everything…I forgot…silly me! As these lands are your birthright, I would expect you to have knowledge of these parts. I am a Draconian—or have you forgotten?"

Patience interrupted."Please do not fall out when we are so privileged to be here. Who cares who knows what? Is it not more important that we savor this moment of peace before the enemy finds us and destroys us?"

"Words well spoken, Patience. The enchantment of Venus flickers in and out like the balance of human life itself, precarious as unchartered waters. But here, for now, everything remains constant, the tides of change will affect all regions on this planet…it is only a matter of time." Celestial pointed toward the fortress. "Take heed…the angels await us."

As they approached the entrance, two angels stood sentry, on either side of the gates. They radiated an intense luminosity, a golden light that shone from their transparent skin, creating a golden nimbus around them. The gates opened immediately. The angels did not speak or turn their heads to greet them but stood silent in their intent to guard the fortress.

Celestial led the way through the vast arched entrance to a vaulted space. The sunlight filtered through the many arched windows, creating a serene, peaceful focus that highlighted the gleaming white stones of the central tower. The central tower was flanked by two adjoining towers incorporating gothic-style, multi-storied windows of epic scale. The sweeping curves of the walls, smooth, with textures from the verdant, sparkling, silvery-green foliage, integrated nature into the sacred structure. Great carvings of angels stood tall and comforting among displays of large blooming lilies. The sound of trickling waters from the many decorative fountains and waterspouts could be heard among the chorus of singing angels. All seemed peaceful on the surface, as though they were oblivious of the world outside. But Celestial knew better, whispering unknown words to one of the angels.

The angel led them toward a staircase that preceded a long, vast, lit hallway lined with long elegant windows on one side and mirrored walls on the other. At the end of the hallway were the largest arched mirrored doors that Patience had ever seen. The doors seemed to open themselves when Celestial stood before them, and the sight before Patience's and Cava's eyes caused them to take cover behind Rusalka and Brabantia.

Tall and elegant stood the Seraphim...radiating an intense luminosity that lit up the vast hall. Multiple wings shrouded their tapered bodies as they seemed to float on air. A fine, ethereal music echoed through the structure; heavenly music that worked on the senses. They stood transfixed, utterly disarmed by the celestial sight. Even Corsivo, who had become one of them, had never yet seen such a manifestation. It was a sight that Patience knew would be burned on her mind forever.

The chorus of sublime music stopped suddenly, as Celestial had been followed in by the Paristan, the King and Queen of Alvor, the Order of the Sukras, and other Elves and Aegle fey. Outside the fortress, numerous Venusians gathered in the gardens and around the mountain floor, ready to hear what Celestial had to say.

Queen Celestial in all her serene beauty, floated gently upon the silver throne; surrounded by Corsivo, Gabriel, and Mikael. Thereafter, the trumpets were sounded, and a tense silence fell upon the buzzing crowd. In a solemn hush, all eyes were turned toward Celestial. She spoke of fierce things with a gentle voice.

"Give ear to my words. Hear my voice plainly, for I have much to tell. Here we take cover from the tempest, but the eyes of those who see will not be dimmed, and the ears of those who listen will not be sealed. On the land of my people, beyond this sanctuary, have come up thorns and briers. Even on the palaces of the joyous city, our towers and our lofty places have become ruins.

"Behind the shadows of great rocks in a weary land our people hide. We must protect our land and our beloved ones. This sacred place will be our haven no longer. We will go forth and set our path through the portal to the trail of Asan, and we must search out the dwelling places of Dracon and his armies and destroy his kingdom of evil intent. You must deliver yourselves from the hand of the hunter before he hunts you down, shedding innocent blood. Go prepare. When the sun sinks low and the way is dark, we will make our way to the portal. All who wish to follow my path raise your hands to the heavens. Those who do not will stay here and wait our return."

The Paristan and the Seraphim raised their hands without hesitation, followed by the Order of the Sukra and many others in the crowd. Celestial scanned the hall. "So be it!" Throwing her cloak around her shoulders, she disappeared into the air.

The crowd dispersed slowly, some with fire in their hearts, ready for the fight ahead; others with heavy hearts, afraid of what might be. Rusalka had noticed Patience raise her hand freely, although Ilk had not. She made her way toward them, pushing through the crowd.

"Patience...Patience!"

Patience could only just hear her voice among the excited chatter. She turned around swiftly, spotted Rusalka in the distance, and made her way toward her, followed by Wishbone and Ilk. Wishbone, a little fraught with the commotion, kept rubbing himself up to her for attention, almost knocking her over.

"It's OK, boy. It's OK. Calm down...everything will be fine."

Ilk fluttered his little wings, vying for attention. Patience felt more than a little nervous. In fact, if she were to tell the truth, she felt terrified.

Rusalka grabbed hold of her hand. "Come, child. I will take you somewhere quiet that I may speak with you and be heard."

Dragging Patience gently through the assembly, she led her to a small, inviting chamber and closed the door tightly behind them. The candles flickered from all corners of the room, and through the open, gracefully arched windows.

383

The brilliance of the stars pierced the cloudless clarity of the crisp atmosphere. "Patience...how can I put this? You cannot possibly go with us to Mars. It is far too dangerous—and I do not wish for you to be fearful, but it is you Leviathan wants. It is imperative that you stay here. It is for now the safest place on Venus, and it is our responsibility as the Seraphim and the Order to keep you safe."

"But I must go with you. I want to find my father, and I don't want to be left alone. I will be more scared without you here."

Ilk stepped in. "I will stay with you, Patience. You know I will. I will protect you...or will you protect me?" He scratched his head. "I suppose we can protect each other, can't we? And, of course, we have Wishbone. He will protect both of us."Then, taking one look at Wishbone's trembling frame, he continued. "Er...perhaps not. Well, we can all try to protect each other. Three is better than one, and we are safe here, anyways, aren't we, Rusalka? And—"

"Yes Ilk. You need not worry; you can stay also. You will have Astoria, Nastacia, and the king and queen of Elvor and the Seraphim guards of the fortress to keep you all safe. So worry not what may or may not happen."

"Then we shall pray for you, Rusalka. Please bring back my papa. I am so worried for his safety. The longer he is away, the more I fear that I have lost him forever."

Ilk flew into the air, flapping his pearly wings. Then, taking a deep breath, adrenaline running high, he said, "Oh, Patience, do not speak of such things. We must speak optimistic words against the black, negative thoughts that that the dirty rotten Serophoth Leviathan would like to plant in our heads...that vile, destructive, ugly, low-life, vermin creature of—"

Patience laughed a little. "Well Ilk, that's a bit like the pot calling the kettle black. You see, it's usually you who is negative. But I will forgive you 'cause I know your heart is good and you mean well."

Ilk flapped. "Yes, of course I mean well. Why wouldn't I mean well? For goodness' sake, I am your friend, and I like to think you are mine, Patience. I would be very upset if you weren't. I have always—"

"I know, Ilk. I know. We are friends, you silly little cherub." And she leaned forward and gave him a kiss on his forehead.

Ilk blushed but showed his moment of pleasure in her kindness. And then, to his surprise, Wishbone tried to lick him.

"Hey, steady, Wishbone. I like you, old chap, but I don't need a shower. Had one this morning. Bathed in the fresh dew...much better than your saliva. No offense meant, of course."

Rusalka was amused but had greater concerns on her mind. "I will leave you here for now. I must join Celestial and the others for our preparations. I bid you good day, and if I don't see you before the journey, I look forward to my return. And I will bring your father back with me—this I pledge to you with all my heart." She embraced Patience with a warm feeling of pure love and then grabbed her cloak, flung it around her shoulders, and strode across the room with a fiery passion for all that she must now do.

The Dungeons, Castle of Syrtis

Deep down in the hostile enclaves of the Castle of Syrtis in the Major Syrtis Region, the air was warm and heavy with the scent of damp earth and rotting flesh. Roberto looked down at his ripped clothes, which revealed his bare torso. His hair had grown long, hanging around his wide shoulders. He had crossed seas and lakes and mighty rivers and traversed vast plains, gaping gorges, sheer cliffs, tundra, and dangerous forests. He had encountered strange and wondrous creatures, fearsome beasts, and dark entities, but all that was etched upon his mind was the beauty of Venus, Rusalka, and his daughter's safety.

Panic struck him! As he frowned, trying to filter through his memories, he could recall nothing of Earth, yet he knew he was human. He tried hard to think back, but he could only think of

Venus and Mars. No grip had earthly things on him any longer; gone were all his earthly cares. He needed to remember where he had come from, but the harder he tried, the more unnerved he felt.

His spirit took refuge in the fact that he was still alive, and his thoughts returned to Patience. His mind swirled, and although he could not remember Earth itself, he was aware of his ancestry, which was like a prison from which there was no escape. And now he was incarcerated deep down within the dungeons of the Castle of Syrtis. He sifted through the ruins of his past life in the far corners of his mind. He should have paid more attention and protected Patience from the evil that had tormented her dreams, the evil that had become a reality. He should have listened— something he realized he had not been good at, and the cost was too much to bear. He hit his fist against the wall; the heavy chains rattled against the cold, uneven stone wall. She needed his protection, and he couldn't give it! He was in the hands of a highly skilled predator, and he was so tired, his mind full of thoughts piled up like bricks, he couldn't think clearly. He needed sleep to clear his head, if only for a few moments…

Roberto slumped to the floor, his body aching and stiff, perspiration beaded on his eyebrows. He felt dizzy, and his head was throbbing…his eyes were heavy, and darkness surrounded him. He observed a movement in the blackness. He thought he was alone. He froze still and listened, staring out into the expanse to witness more movement. Nothing stirred.

He dared not breathe, in case he disturbed whoever it was…for a time, he lay awake. It made no difference whether he opened his eyes or not; the darkness was impenetrable. He must have dozed off; he awoke abruptly to the sound of someone breathing very close to his face. He jumped up, horrified to see the face of Marissa once again, glowing in the dark. He blinked twice to make sure of what he saw. She gave him a look of empathy, her fingers reaching out to stroke his brow. Fear tightened a noose around his neck as his world swam back into focus. He studied her sea-green eyes as she searched his countenance, and for one sweet

386

moment, he remembered her as she once was. He reached out to hold her tendered hand, only to find it crumbling to dust as he grasped the frail fingers, the ashy remnants of what once was predestined to decay. Her whole body fell to the floor in a heap of dust and then blew away as though she had never existed.

Roberto felt like screaming. His hands covered his face, and his body rocked backward and forward. Forcing down his panic, he considered his options. He shuddered at the thought of the implications of Leviathan's intent if he were to lay hands on his daughter. *Over my dead body will I let that happen!* He felt sick to the stomach remembering her sweet face and eyes, so innocent, a watery, pale green, and he smiled at the thought of her determination and tenacity, much like that of her mother. He was scared, more afraid than ever before...he had to escape, and soon.

Through a crimson haze of his own pounding blood, Roberto could see the silhouette of a figure crouched down in the corner of the dungeon...no sign of movement, not even the sound of breathing. Time stood still in the boundless space between moments. He cleared his throat nervously, petrified in the knowledge that someone or something was crouching down in the recesses of the dungeon. Something unmoving...then the thing started to move slightly out from the darkest shadows toward a small circle of hazy light that shone from a gap in the high ceiling above.

Roberto could only make out an indistinct shape, a black outline of something very tall and painfully thin. He tried to close his eyes and will away the vision. *Is it Marissa?* He could not bear the thought! His teeth began to chatter uncontrollably. Then...from its crouching posture, the figure began to unfold, revealing its full stature and spindly legs, its grotesque head protruding from hunched shoulders. He could hardly make out its face, so battered and swollen it was. Twisting into an expression that might have been pleading, its lipless mouth stretched out to speak, revealing its long, sharp fangs and a thick, gray tongue.

"Please don't be afraid of me!"

Roberto was startled at the power of the female voice that

erupted from the creature. He stood up tall and straight. "Who are you?"

"I am Freja, lizard-woman...wife of Ulus, murdered brother of Dracon."

"Why are you here in this forsaken place? How come I have only just noticed you here?"

With stiffened limbs, Freja limped even closer, and Roberto noticed the extent of her injuries. He could see she was of no threat to him however great in stature she was. "Come sit by my side and tell all." He gently patted the ground beside him.

Freja sat down slowly, in obvious pain. She took a deep breath before she spoke. "Dracon is my brother-in-law. He murdered his brother because he was in line for the throne after the death of Perilous the Great. In contrast to Dracon, Ulus was the most-wise of lizard men, benevolent and a great master of the sword. But he was thwarted by the trickery of Dracon." Freja swallowed heavily. Roberto placed his hand on her shoulder. "Take your time, Freja...you have obviously suffered much."

"I bore Ulus a child, a lizard boy. We named him Fire, for his hair was as red as his crimson skin when he cried." A tear ran down her face as she told Roberto his fate.

"Dracon took his life also! He robbed me of everything dear to me and placed me in the dungeons to dwell upon my loss. The Xanthurus guards give me a beating every now and again to make me aware that I am still alive. This time, they placed me here with you while you were sleeping, but I have no idea why. There are many dungeons and cells down here full of criminals and innocent creatures alike. Why you have been placed here by yourself, I have no idea either."She winced in pain on movement.

"I am so sorry for your suffering, Freja. I too have suffered at the hands of Dracon, and I have a daughter to save before he gets his murderous hands on her. I must get out of here. Will you come with me?"

"I will try, but I have had no strength to even think of such a thing."

"You must rest for a while until we find the right moment."

388

"Thank you for your kind words. What species are you, and why have you been incarcerated?"

"Have you got all night? I think it better you rest, and I will tell you all about me when you are feeling a little stronger."

"OK. It's so nice to speak to someone again. I have not uttered one word since the death of my family a long time ago. Thank you for your kindness."

Roberto helped Freja lie down. "Sleep, Freja...and I will keep watch so that you can rest peacefully."

At last she slept. Roberto stared into the darkness, listening to the steady breathing of the lizard-woman. Fluttering shadows shifted around the dungeon, filling the cavern with menace. The darkness that pervaded at times seemed to last longer than the period of one night; he had no means of measuring the passing of time. For a while, he sat perfectly still in the dark silence, trying to make sense of all things until sleep caught up with him and his eyes grew heavy, pulling him down into the depths of his dream-world.

The Battle at Deimos

How far Celestial and her party had traveled they could not tell. The mutterings of the watchful enemy were all around them as a reminder of the hostile land they traversed and the peril that waited mercilessly around every corner. The ground passing beneath them changed from leaf-littered forest to murky, green bog and lichen-covered rock. The air grew steadily colder, and snow began to fall—first in large, star-shaped flakes, then in a veil of sparkling white drops that blinded their vision. The journey ended at the foot of some mountains with an opening large enough for them to crawl through for shelter. It was a solid, forbidding range of gray granite peaks, one layering upon the last like sleeping sentinels against the gray sky. Ice-capped pinnacles

389

rose over snowy valleys, and the wind howled in the distance.

Within its dark confines, they laid down their weapons and kindled a burning-hot fire to warm their extremities. Cava spoke out in the silence, blowing into her hands. "You've never experienced this on Venus, have you?" She smirked.

"No, we have not, Cava. You are right, and that is why we have not brought the Aegle faerie with us—for these temperatures would almost certainly not be conducive to their gentle structure."

"Then how come Nastacia came here?" Cava said with a quizzical glance.

Celestial had been listening to the conversation. "Nastacia is different from all other Aegle faeries. Her father was not of the Aegle."

"Of course, that leads me to ask who her father was."

Rusalka's eyes met Celestial's in her silence.

Celestial stood tall and serene. "It is not for any one of us to divulge the secrets of her birthing. It is for her and her alone to find out, for she is in the dark as much as you yourself, Cava."

"Oh, I see. I am intrigued now and will not be satisfied until I find out," Cava said in a groaning mumble.

Corsivo looked at Cava and sighed, shaking his head from side to side.

"What...what have I said wrong?" She studied Corsivo and then Celestial.

Celestial replied in a faint but steady voice. "It is not good to consider one-self to be wise in one's own eyes, Cava. Come eat of my bread and forsake foolishness and live. A talebearer reveals secrets, but a fool's mouth is his destruction."

Rusalka looked down, revealing her despair for the ways of mortals, knowing the eyes of Elyon were in every place, and he who restrains his lips is wise. "We must pray to our Lord of Hosts—oh, how my soul longs for His court, my heart and my flesh cry out to Him. Oh, Elyon, Illustrious One, make our enemies like the swirling dust that is blown away by the wind. Give us strength so that we may lie down and our sleep be sweet, that we may not see the range of their cruelties, which are great. They satisfy themselves with the flesh of all that is good and throw them to the vile beasts whose hunger never subsides. Strengthen our resolve and make us mighty in the eyes of our enemy. Amen."

"Amen!" They all spoke out in a loud voice in unison—all except Cava, who gently whispered beneath her breath with the realization of her doubts.

When the fire had burned to ashes and all that remained was a heavy darkness, they strived to continue their journey, venturing out once again into the terrain of the northern border of Deimos, where the boundaries were as elusive and changeable as the beings themselves—sometimes visible, sometimes not, and, even more confusingly, visible to some and not to others. They passed hidden caves and pits amid the arid pink wilderness and Draconians of great size and loathsome habits who preyed upon mortals.

Rusalka abruptly stopped still, eyes closed.

"What is it, Rusalka?" Celestial put her hand out for all to halt immediately.

"Dracon is gathering his army; and I can see he has left the Castle of Syrtis in the Syrtis Major Region. They are making their way to the Fortress of Deimos now and will more than likely reach their position by dawn—before we arrive there."

Celestial gathered her thoughts swiftly. "Then we must be prepared to battle as soon as we swoop down into the valley of Deimos. Come, follow my trail."

Rusalka spoke quietly to Celestial as they walked cautiously over the rough terrain. "You must be warned of the dangers we face and be aware of those who especially wish you harm, my queen. There appeared to me a vast army, mainly made up of the Xanthurus, but there were two of the Serophoth there, taller than any I have ever seen. Their faces shone like gold and their eyes like burning lamps, and fire came forth from their mouths. Their dress had the appearance of feathers, but they were black as night, as is usual. But they had another set of wings that shone gold, and their feet were the color of dark grapes, and in their voices a promise of paradise…I almost felt that they had changed. What does it all mean?"

Celestial did not seem surprised at all by what Rusalka had seen. "I have always known the way of the Dark One, Rusalka. Do not believe what you see. Believe only in the power of Elyon. Leviathan is the master of lies. As you yourself know, he comes with the hot breath of a sun-baked desert and with all that is exotic and colorful. So beware that he does not entice your senses and inflame your base desires. Fear not, my sister, if you be not swayed by the deceit of the wicked one."

For a moment, Rusalka felt ashamed of her feelings. A flicker of doubt passed her soul; she was not used to such feelings. *What is wrong with me?*

As the day drew in, the naked trees darkened and loomed. Scuttlings and cracklings, mutterings and growls, grew louder. The Paristans' horses grew distressed. Brabantia's horse reared and showed the whites of its eyes. Frustrated, Brabantia swung her mount this way and that, seeking out its angst. Nothing was yet apparent. They had cleared the forest, which stood dark and foreboding behind them. A wind lifted the wings of the angels and the winged-horses, filling them with buoyancy, and there followed peals of thunder and sounds of flashing lightning.

And then, out of the darkness, they were rushing swiftly toward them! Some black as night, huge, ill defined, semi-human, and altogether evil and abominable. They were conscious of a profane smell and blood-curdling cries. Then they were followed by the Xanthurus army coming at them in their thousands.

Cava cried out, sword in hand, "Let's kill them before they slaughter us."

Celestial rose up before them, growing larger and larger, until her countenance was ten times their own. Her brilliance shone forth, a blinding light over the valley before them. Her hand held high the Sword of Truth, the tip of which began to glow an emerald green—a dazzling, radiant green. Within seconds, the advance guard of the verminous Xanthurus army was moving forward like a wave, flowing over the hills and valleys. Before they had time to think, the Xanthurus stood all around them, slithering and squeaking, their fur matted with river water. Hungry eyes glinted for vengeance. The air was filled with restless scratching and their high, thin, incessant squeaking. The creatures were all around them now, thrusting their quivering whiskered snouts, scenting them like carrion. Heads raised high, they showed their long, yellow incisors, and the stench of the promise of death poured out from their mouths.

One leaped through the air at Brabantia, and the others moved closer. The packs were converging in the distance from all directions, with the Serophoth and the Draconians marching forward. The first cries of panic splintered into shrieks of agony as one angel was ripped apart, fingers clawing blindly at the deadly creatures.

Brabantia and the others tore through the army, hacking off their heads one by one, the Paristan fighting each one with two swords, the second ablaze with the flame of the Paristan. The angels flew forward in a cacophony of thrashing wings, the icy air tearing at their throats. With blood-red eyes and gaping mouths, with flaming nostrils and sharp claws, other hideous creatures came forth, their teeth like knives.

Celestial hovered above the only light in the midnight sky. Unlike Venus, there was no place of natural light shining from the heavens. The avenging angel's skin shone pure and luminous against the indigo background, mercurial and elusive.

The two Serophoth swooped down from above and settled on the ground beneath Celestial, deep in the valley. Such was the heat from their malevolence that the ground beneath their feet began to smolder. Then, not far from where they stood, the ground suddenly began to open slowly into a dark chasm, and out of the crevices rose an army of monstrous creatures, breathing fire, slithering and crawling out of the gates of hell.

Swooping down, the Serophoth engaged in battle against the Seraphim, sinking their horny talons into their pure flesh. Corsivo and Mikael fought valiantly with no letup, their swords slashing through the air at the speed of sound. Celestial scanned the horizon, and, as if the sun had risen in the night sky, the darkness opened. Pure white rays broke through from the heavens, flooding the place with divine light like beams of light emanating from the sun. A blizzard of warrior angels came forth, gliding down in spirals of celestial light, their wings stretched outward. Light pulsed all around the valley, forming a hedge of angels with raised swords—a flurry of fiery blades. They began to chant a language of angels, their voices shaking both the heavens and the land they stood on. The enemy grew stronger in numbers, and Dracon's wrath grew deadlier.

Meanwhile, one of the Xanthurus had cornered Gabriel. The Xanthurus's gleaming red eyes bored into his soul, its mouth wet with spittle, jaws open wide with a deep snarl, baring his sharp fangs. Gabriel confronted his attacker, ready with sword, moving from side to side. The hybrid tensed its muscles—Gabriel could not tell whether it was a he or a she; they all looked the same to him, and probably the female was just as menacing as the male. As the beast moved forward slightly, he moved back, his heel touching something solid behind him. He did not dare take his eyes away from his assailant. The Xanthurus snarled. Gabriel could hear snickering all around him and occasionally caught glimpses of flitting forms. He stumbled over the stony rock behind him, falling to the ground and losing his sword. It landed on the ground too far away for him to grab it in time. The Xanthurus's bulging red eyes stared down into his eyes, his large, rat-like foot pushing down into his chest. And then, in one undertaking, he dug his talons into Gabriel's eyes, gouging them from their sockets.

Gabriel screamed out in agonized pain, holding his hands over his face, blood pouring from his orifices. The Xanthurus was just about to finish him off when Corsivo threw a dagger into the Xanthurus's back. He turned round to see where it had come from just as Corsivo swept down from above, decapitating the Xanthurus in one swift movement.

Corsivo grabbed hold of Gabriel, throwing him over his shoulder. He took him to a safe place and laid him on the ground.

"I can't see!" cried Gabriel. "The rat took my eyes...he took my eyes!"

Corsivo could not stand his despair. "I hate to leave you like this, Gabriel, but the others need my help. You must stay here, and I will come back for you."

"Why...why would you come back for me? I have not been a friend at all."

Corsivo ripped a piece of cloth from his loincloth and secured it around Gabriel's eyes to stop the bleeding. "I will be back.... don't move...then I will know where to find you. Everything will be OK."

Corsivo took one more look at him in all his misery and reluctantly left him to return to the battle-field. In the far distance, at the foot of some cliffs, Brabantia's heart was beating so quickly she thought it would burst from her chest. The Xanthurus's teeth clenched as he thrust forward his sword, pushing her backward. Brabantia's strength declined with each of the vermin's blows, which only served to make him bolder. She had slain too many to count that night, and her body grew weary. The Xanthurus hacked ever more violently; the clash of steel upon steel caused vibrations to shoot through her entire body. She could barely block each savage blow. Even her trusty sword had lost its enchantment, and she was too weak to shape change.

Now she found herself retreating backward, up the slippery rocky incline, with each swing. Her only hope was that with her speed and her aim, she might hack off his tail, which would give her an advantage. Steel hit steel with such a force that sparks flew high, and before she had a chance to strike the next blow, the Xanthurus unleashed an almighty strike that sent her sword flying through the air and over the cliff edge.

She was glued to the spot momentarily. The Xanthurus's large frame loomed threateningly over her, his hot breath streaming from his nostrils. His arrogance was such that he made no move to strike immediately. He simply stood over her, sword raised, poised to finish her.

At the last second, Mikael came up from behind the Xanthurus before the steel sliced through Brabantia's torso. And in one swift motion, he hacked off the Xanthurus's tail.

The Xanthurus dropped his sword and swayed from side to side. Brabantia quickly rolled over to the sword, grabbed it, and flung it mercilessly into the Xanthurus's heart. By this time, Corsivo was in battle with two more of the Xanthurus, and Brabantia joined him in combat until they too had been slain.

The grotesque beast showed its sharp, yellow fangs with the clear intent of ripping out Cava's throat. She leaped aside as the beast lurched forward with thorny fingers that clutched and curled. She unslung her sword from its sheath facing the beast, sword in one hand dagger in the other. She had practiced combat all her life, and, for once, she was grateful for her training. She had become a master of the sword and the knife out of necessity rather than desire.

A rumble issued forth from deep within the beast's cavernous throat. Its huge form lurched forward, swinging from side to side, its nostrils flaring. Without hesitation, she spun around in one continuous motion, slicing through the beast's torso with the silver blade. The beast snarled as blood sprang from a gaping wound in its abdomen, and it fell to the floor with a great thud. It had only time to rise again when the sword cut the air with a hissing sound as it angled at the beast's neck. With a hideous shriek, the beast grabbed hold of the blade, blood spurting from its clawed fist from a gash that cut to the bone. The beast snapped the blade in two, and in an instant, Cava felt her feet leave the ground. The force of the beast's violent assault sent her hurtling through the air, spinning as she smashed into the nearby rocks.

Cava fell to the ground gasping, the wind forced from her lungs. She struggled to regain her breath as she watched the beast weigh her up from the distance between them. The beast reared ferociously, ready for the kill. Cava watched thankfully as Corsivo came out of nowhere, moving too fast for the beast to check its momentum. He spun the wounded beast into the air and smashed it down with such great strength and power that the ground sank beneath it on impact. As its eyes closed, its form

396

began to change—first to a winged Serophoth and then to nothing as it disintegrated to dust of the ground, blown away by the prevalent winds.

Corsivo laid down his sword to pick up Cava. "Are you OK?"

Cava brushed herself down. "Of course...I am fine. I would have gotten him myself, anyhow."

Corsivo smiled. "Of course you would, but it's always nice to have a little help."

Corsivo picked up his sword with a half-smile and threw it to Cava. "You are going to need this."

She grabbed hold of it, looking straight into his soft blue eyes. "What about you?"

Corsivo took flight and looked down at her from the air. "I don't need any sword, Cava. Your need is greater than mine." He flew off into the dark, starless sky, lit up only by the Seraphim in battle.

Lightning ripped through the darkness, thunder roared, and the waves of the sea pitched high in the distance. Steel hit steel ceaselessly, a series of wild attacks unleashed from the creatures of the abyss. Many of the Xanthurus and Draconians had already been slaughtered.

Celestial surveyed the battlefield through superhuman eyes. Flaming missiles propelled forward, cutting through the sky like meteors, igniting terror. "The Seraphim fought well, and Corsivo proved his allegiance...but now is the time to end this battle most fierce and rid ourselves of the enemy."

Celestial moved so fast that no being could detect her amid the tumult. Lightning ripped through the darkness, and the thunder reverberated endlessly. The south wind grew hot. She knew what she had to do. The Key of Dreams had more power than Dracon had ever known, and now she would use it for its true purpose.

She flew low, at first at lightning speed, but as she neared the region of the great chasm in the ground below, she ascended above. The stars of the night sky revealed themselves as she dashed through the darkness. Celestial spread her mighty wings, growing in stature. Those on land looked up toward the awesome display of scintillating light in the black sky. The radiant light began to spread out in a three-dimensional form, spouting incantations that boomed across the expanse toward the gates of hell.

The gates of hell in the bowels of the ground opened wide once again, and the creatures that had escaped formed dark shadows that coalesced and rose up in a spiraling tornado of scaly-serpent-like-bodies...the Devata...relegated back to the depths of the abyss .swallowed up in the deep subterranean Lokas, where light never shone and pain and suffering abounded. Their howls came to a crescendo...then silence!

The stars disappeared from the skies. Celestial took the Key of Dreams from around her neck, locked the gates of hell firmly shut, and placed the key carefully once more around her neck. The Draconians and the Xanthurus that remained wandered aimlessly, wounded and in despair. There was no sign of Dracon. Celestial made her way to the Fortress of Deimos alone. Her blade grew hot with the flames of revenge.

The fortress rose high into the heavens, dark and foreboding. Celestial scaled the high walls that surrounded the upper tower. She spied a Xanthurus guard at the entrance, and, taking him by surprise, she thrust her flaming sword through his spiked back into his upper chest. The vermin soldier fell to the floor with a dull sound. She entered through the iron doors with ease, as if they were made of paper, such had her strength become.

At last she came upon her enemy sitting, eating as though no battle had even begun, so arrogant was he in his victory. His neck snapped round at her presence. Startled, he shoved away from his table and rose, standing nine feet tall. At the sight of Celestial, Dracon's rage unleashed. His heartbeat quickened, and his blue blood coursed through his veins as if it had a mind of its own, empowering his every muscle with unnatural strength. His monstrous reptilian eyes shone with a terrible ferocity, darting backward and forward wildly, and his ashen green skin turned a deep, deep crimson.

He moved in, fangs flashing menacingly, his weapon ready for the kill. She could smell the acrid smell of blood from his open mouth as he licked his lips with anticipation. "I will taste your flesh at last and then drink in your blood at sunrise."

Night had closed down in a black mantle that threatened them all. At first, only the light from the burning torches remained, casting shadows across the chamber. And then the avenging angel bathed him in her purifying radiance, her eyes momentarily closed.

For a split second, Dracon faltered with an intense urge to succumb to her heavenly charms. Swiftly gathering his resolve, he lunged forward to attack Celestial. So pervasive was their presence in the room that even the tiniest of creatures below scuttled off in all directions, afraid of the wrath they saw. His rank odor filled her nostrils as she hovered above him, her form larger than he had ever seen, her sword on fire.

"Your time has ended, Dracon. Revenge is mine." Her voice no longer resembled the serene nature of her angelic form. It had become resonant and more powerful than Dracon's.

Dracon tried not to show his fear. "Such a mission of revenge can only fail. A body without a soul cannot die. Find the soul, then you can destroy the being." Then he let out a loud, uncontrollable laughter that shook the ground and the walls of the fortress.

But even his anger was no defense against the avenging angel. She lifted her sword, imbued with the fire of everlasting death, and slammed it full throttle through Dracon's heart.

Dracon let out a terrifying screeching sound and clutched at the sword stuck in his chest, which burned through his hands slowly. In one swift motion he pulled the blade out and allowed it to fall to the floor at his feet. He tried to stem the seeping blue blood from his wound, and a flash of horror passed over his face. He looked down at the sword. It had made contact with the icy-cold of the floor, the fusion of which brought about a ring of fire that now surrounded him. A high-pitched sound emanated from his vocal cords.

Celestial watched as smoke rose, carrying to her the aroma of seared flesh, the smell of sweet revenge—but for one moment,

399

she felt a flicker of sadness for his futile life.

"Your soul has bowed down to the dust of the ground…clung to the depths of Sheol. It could have been so different. You could not see that Elyon alone spreads out the heavens and treads the waves of the sea—He who created life and death, in whose hands is the sovereignty…you fool."

From her vantage point, she observed his slow death. Lightning struck once more from above, then silence followed, except for the crackling fire that consumed the fortress and its tower for all to see.

Celestial returned to the battlefield to round up her army. "Victory is ours…Eulalia!" She exclaimed.

All were weary and ready to go home, but they knew it was not yet over. Dracon had been slaughtered, but where was Leviathan?

Rusalka was the first to speak. "A vision most vivid has passed my mind, Celestial. Lord Bellucci is being held captive in no other than the dungeons of the Castle of Syrtis. We must make our way there and release him. The Xanthurus are guarding him, and they will be none the wiser of Dracon's death. We must meet the Naga as promised and destroy the rest of the Xanthurus army gathered at the castle Syrtis. They will not believe us that Dracon is deceased."

Celestial knew as much. "Yes. We will travel northeast and take some rest on the way to ease the pain of our injured ones. Make all preparations necessary for the journey. With favoring winds, we shall fly east."

The Paristan army had been ordered to go straight to the Castle of Syrtis and wait for the others to join them after they had collected the Naga. They gathered their weapons and once again set off on a journey through the trail that would bring them to the castle Syrtis. They stumbled on through the dark hours of the night in weary silence, hearing nothing but the icy wind hissing in their ears.

The night had given way to sunrise. But the terrain turned more treacherous, and there was no distinct path for them to follow. The sound of flapping wings rose and fell in steady cadence, and it seemed that they had been flying for a long time before they found a place to shelter among some craggy rocks in the middle of nowhere. The shadows slid out of every crevice in those rocks. They seemed alive, almost an entity in themselves.

They began to climb, working their way through the footholds until they reached a break in the rocks. They climbed across the opening and beyond, where they found themselves standing on a rise that overlooked a sun-baked, barren, rocky valley that stretched on and on with no letup.

Cava was the first to hear the sound coming from the rocks. "Sh...sh...can you hear that?" She looked at Corsivo and then at Celestial.

"I heard it!" said Brabantia.

"Me too," chipped in Mikael.

Gabriel held on tightly to his arm. "What is it?"

"Who knows the spirit of this desolate place?" Celestial tried to make light of it because they needed rest and this was the only place of shelter from the relentless sun for miles. She led them down the other side of the rocky incline, and, sure enough, there was that sound again. It was a wailing sound, low and insistent, seeping through the rocks.

"We will take our refuge here." Celestial sat down to encourage the others to do so.

"We can't stay here. Listen to it! It could be dangerous for us to rest here. I for one say we head south a little and then venture east." Cava was adamant.

"If that is what you want to do, Cava, you go alone. Gabriel needs rest, and we will give him water."

Cava paced up and down. "But there is no water. Look around you; it is as dry as any desert in these parts."

401

"We will stay. You may leave if you wish."

Cava was hungry and thirsty and in no mood for an argument. She picked up her things, muttering to herself, and stormed off, walking southward.

Corsivo followed her. "Cava...please...come back. You should know by now to follow the path of the wise ones!"

"Please leave me alone, Corsivo. You have no idea of my beginnings or my life before. Leave me in peace. I can't stand the moaning rocks, anyway. They sound pitiful. I have just had enough of everything."

"But you are in no state of peace. You are at war with none other than yourself, Cava."

Cava marched on, not looking at him. "What do you care, anyway? You have made your mark; you have been chosen. I am glad for you, Corsivo. You deserve it. You are an angel of honor, and you have proved that to us all. Even Gabriel sees it!"

"I wish him no harm."

"I know that, and so does he. He feels inferior to you since he let Celestial down, but that's not your fault, Corsivo."

Corsivo grabbed Cava's hand. "Stop...please, stop."

Cava stopped for a moment and gazed up into his pleading eyes with uncertainty. Then she pulled away from him. "I want to do what is right, Corsivo, but my mind is a whirl! I have loved some of the things I have encountered in this new world beyond my imagining, but I feel that I don't fit. How can I be comparable to the likes of Rusalka, Astoria, or even Brabantia? This world is beyond me. It has so much more meaning. It means so much more thought and understanding than I have ever had connection with. Don't you see? I am...I am a Draconian. I have known nothing but survival and combat."

It was then that Corsivo noticed the cut on the palm of her hand, her crimson-red blood dripping slowly to the ground. Cava pulled away her hand and covered the small wound with her other hand. "It's nothing, only a scratch."

Corsivo recalled the warm, metallic taste of blood...and for a moment in time forgot who he had become. A darkness shone from deep within his eyes, from the recesses of his soul, as he ran his strong, beautiful hands across Cava's alarmed face. He grabbed her hand and licked the fresh blood from the seeping wound, and, with an all-consuming desire to devour her there and then, he let out a ferocious roar that did not belong to his Seraphim nature.

Cava recoiled in fear and struggled to free her hand from his prolonged tight grip, knowing it was useless. His body, with hard-core muscle and superhuman strength, brought her to her knees and pinned her arms back, trapping her against the rough surface of the ground. The moon cast its pearly glow, lighting up her silvery skin. Her eyes grew wide with fear as she lay beneath his merciless strength, aware of some inner struggle within him. She looked up into his darkened, burning eyes. Her breath caught in her throat as his hand closed over the nape of her neck in an unbreakable grip. Cava froze...her feelings and emotions crowded in until she felt overwhelmed, choking out her words, reaching out to ease the contorted lines on his face. "Corsivo...you are not that depraved beast anymore. Look at me...I am Cava...your friend."

Corsivo inhaled deeply, raging with hunger; the beast inside him roared for release. She held herself still, aware of their combined heartbeats, the blood pulsing in their veins simultaneously. Corsivo's realization hit like a fist in his stomach. He saw the expression on Cava's face. He let go of her suddenly and stood for an instant, looking down at her petite form—a rare, precious creature that needed his help, not this cruel intention he had forced upon her. He held out a hand to help her to her feet.

She was reluctant at first. He had turned on her, and she had never expected that. She had trusted him and only him. She was afraid; her emotions swirled as her immediate response was to defend herself or flee, but she knew that it was no use. Her power and strength was no match to his. She gazed enquiringly into his pleading eyes and grabbed hold of his proffered hand.

He was furious with himself, trying to make some sense of it all. Lifting her small face up to his with his large hands, he looked penetratingly into her dark, liquid eyes.

"You are the one person I want to protect, Cava...but you won't allow me. You insist upon your own independence so fiercely. All others lean upon my strength, which I have been bestowed so benevolently, yet you seek to help me dismiss such an honor. I am so sorry, Cava...truly I am. Will you ever trust me again? I thought the beast had gone forever, but now I know I must keep him in check."

Cava's demeanor changed suddenly, and she spoke softly. "You are of the Eternals now, radiant and wondrous. You are blessed as the servant and warrior of Elyon the Great. You are beautiful, Corsivo!" No sooner had she given her speech than she recoiled, ashamed of her words. She turned from Corsivo and walked on speedily.

"Wait...please...wait, Cava!" Corsivo grabbed her arm once more, but Cava broke loose and marched ahead, not willing to listen, afraid of the swirling emotions held tightly within.

Corsivo sighed heavily and turned away in despair. He took the route back to the others, who were crowded together behind the rocky incline. Although the terrain suggested intense heat, nightfall had brought the temperature down considerably, so they had kindled a warm, inviting fire. Corsivo joined them, sitting around the hot, leaping flames, focused on Cava. He felt her pain as deeply as if it were his own, for he had been in that place of isolation, and he had been fortunate enough to be rescued. *How could I have betrayed her trust? And now she is gone!*

Rusalka passed Corsivo a bowl of food, gazing into his troubled soul. "Eat, Corsivo. Worry not for the fate of Cava; it takes time to turn sorrow into wisdom. She will return." She smiled and turned to fill the remaining bowls with the steaming stew.

Miraculously, Celestial had conjured up refreshments. They had soon eaten, and the waters of life had been provided despite the barren land on which they traveled. The fire died down to dust embers, and the dawn was greeted by the sun, shining endlessly hot and arid, across the valley of Megiddo. They left the moaning rocks and flew relentlessly over the dry, forgotten land until they reached the Syrtis Major region, which changed rapidly to the blustery, icy winds of the Polar Regions.

As they entered the mouth of the caves of Syrtis, a heavy darkness descended upon them. The rising passageway beyond glowed with burning torches. There was an overpowering, unpleasant odor. Brabantia ran her fingers across the blood-tainted, rough rocky walls and then turned to Celestial. The recognition of what may be struck her like lightning.

Celestial spoke. "Cannot my taste discern the unsavory?"

"Yes, there has been blood-shed here, Your Majesty, and not so long ago."

Mikael pointed to a long, shiny, black, snake-like torso covered in some rocks in the distance.

"What is it?" Gabriel felt his direction along the cave wall precariously, picking his way over the unyielding surface. "What has happened here? Where are the Naga? Someone tell me what is going on, please!"

Corsivo joined Mikael in an effort to lift the rocks from the carcass.

Brabantia gently guided Gabriel forward. "It looks as though someone or something got here before us, Gabriel, and I am not sure if the Naga have taken flight. There is bloodshed for sure."

"Oh, that's terrible. If only we had gotten here earlier, we may have been able to save them."

"Yes...if only," Brabantia said in a whisper, hardly able to contain her despair. The cave became dark and stifling; wisps of smoke curled in the air. The sounds of their movements echoed back as they slowly descended down a deep shaft, pausing for a moment at a sloping loge directly below the cave mouth, which led to a narrow tunnel that plunged deeper and deeper into the subterranean recesses of the caves. They had not reached the dwelling place of the Naga when they came upon the reality of their plight. The deeper caves had been flooded, completely subject to the tides. A frown disturbed the smoothness of Mikael's forehead. "How could this have happened? And in such a short space of time? I do not understand!"

405

Looking down from the ridge, where they teetered on the edge, Brabantia held on to Gabriel. "What...what is it? I can hear the swirling of angry waters," he said.

"Yes, Gabriel. The caves are flooded, and there is an extremely dangerous black vortex below us, like a giant bathtub drain sucking down gallons of water. We need to get out of here, and quickly."

No sooner had Brabantia finished speaking than Gabriel lost his footing on the unstable edge of the precipice and went spiraling down swiftly toward the swirling maelstrom. Before he had time to set his wings in motion, he plunged into the violent vortex, which sucked him down and down. He fought drastically to swim to the surface, but the force of the waters was too much for his impaired strength. He was just about to abandon hope...his lungs feeling as if they were going to explode...when he felt himself being dragged upward with a ferocious power struggle between the forces of nature and the might of angels. Corsivo's power was tested to the limit, but his resolve was greater than it had ever been. Celestial and the others looked below in horror at the flurry of beating membranous wings and swirling, hostile, turbulent waters, willing Corsivo to rescue Gabriel and himself.

Finally, Corsivo dragged Gabriel up from the tumult, gasping for breath, thrashing his heavily water-soaked wings through the air. Mikael flew down to help them. Once they had reached the ledge, Celestial and Mikael grabbed hold of Gabriel firmly to steady his position. Corsivo sat for a moment, his breathing labored. He looked down at the rapidly rising, swirling waters below. "We must get out of here...and quickly."

Gabriel had recovered his breath but had been rendered speechless. His thoughts were not the thoughts of a pure Eternal anymore, and he could not understand his confusion. His thoughts were of vengeance, but...*Why? Why would I wish that Corsivo had drowned when he risked life to save me?* He felt so ashamed of his feelings; he wished he could whip them into submission, but however much he tried, he could not, and a deep self-hatred clawed itself into his heart.

They found their way back through one of the many passages until they could see a glimmer of light ahead. Following the light into a large cavern with a ceiling lost in its height, Brabantia gasped at the massacred bodies of the Naga strewn across the ground from one side to the other. Corsivo held his breath tight, filled with an all-consuming passion for vengeance. They cut through, stumbling over the dead bodies lying useless in pools of fresh blood. The slaughter had been recent, and no one had been spared, or so it seemed. Rusalka felt a tear run down her cheek. She did not care for such a human emotion, but in this case, she was glad of it. She wanted to feel sorrow for this unfortunate race.

With considerable trepidation, they reached an exit that led them through a long, narrow, winding passage. The roar of water behind them rang noisily in their ears as a reminder that they needed to find a way out speedily.

The passage opened up to a large chamber that claimed the remains of what had once been the dwelling place of the Naga. Tables and chairs lay overturned, some broken into pieces. Debris of all kinds had been left strewn across the ground—crockery, weapons, tapestries, and treasures of old lay among the blooded bodies of the Naga, some staring flatly from their eyes, others with no eyes to stare from. The stench was overwhelming. They passed through in reverent silence, climbing over the devastation of what should have been their alliance in the destruction of evil. When they finally reached an opening in the cavern, they spotted light in the distance…the light grew steadily as they climbed farther upward. The rocks around them were numerous, with the sounds of running subterranean rivers and seething lava pipes all around. Then, looming over them from an upper ridge, was the darkened figure of a hybrid serpent, blue-black like a raven, her hair wild about her face, as though blown by a tempest. From behind that face came forth many faces attached to one body, with undulating, electric-blue, gorgon-like tresses, followed by a huge, wet-looking, black, uncoiled tail.

"Hydra!" Celestial held out her hands. "Hydra…your eyes

407

speak of unspeakable horrors...we are so regretful that our return was not without delay."

Hydra moved toward them, gripping the surface of the rocks, thrusting her body from side to side in a smooth, undulating movement, her heads shifting backward and forward. Translucent serpent shapes formed a poisonous curtain across the entrance and above the deeper reaches of the cave. The creatures hissed from the dark recesses, below the faint glimmer of light from above. Hydra began a long, slow continuous hiss, like that of a venomous snake prepared to strike. Her eyes glowed with malicious intent, and her fangs gleamed in the darkness. The hiss coming from each of her many throats was a promise of merciless revenge.

Brabantia caressed the silver handle of her sword. The sound of the torrid waters could be heard drawing ever closer. Celestial grew in stature, her light shining brightly for Hydra to see. She spoke in a gentle manner.

"Do not think we know nothing of your pain and sorrow, Hydra. We are not your enemies, though they who have murdered your loved ones are still out there and revenge is surely your own. Be sure Dracon is no more, and those who have served him at the Castle of Syrtis deserve to be punished. Let us help you to this end."

Hydra hissed, her voice thick with wrath. "I want revenge! She who is without darkness will help me, and I will be forever in her debt."

No sooner had her dulcet tones been heard than the transparent vipers slithered away among the rocky crevices in a cacophony of hissing noises that eerily filled the chasm. The way became clear for them to ascend the deep, narrow passages, following a path that wound along the edge of the precipice toward the source of the light above. Celestial shrank back to her normal size, her shimmering wings gently closing, and Hydra led the way out of the cave to greet the light of day.

Outside, the atmosphere was peaceful but restless and alive with strangeness all around. They traveled by foot across the forsaken tundra. A biting gust of wind broke through the quiet, whipping the drifted piles of snow from the surrounding mountains. Their path brought them at last to an opening cut through the wall of trees like an archway. The trees grew to a very great height and did not divide from one another until close to the top. It grew darker and darker, only the flash of moonlight shining through the spaces between the canopy of trees swaying madly in the wind. A short way ahead, the gloomy, sinister Castle of Syrtis stood, a colossal monolith, a dark shape against the lighter darkness. They made their way through fallen, crumbling leaves and other debris that had collected. Dead birds of Heaven lay on the rotting mulch beneath their feet, pale bones showing through decaying plumage.

Chapter 37

The Castle Syrtis

Mars...

Advancing along the rear of the castle, facing west, they found their way in through an opening in the ground. A flicker of light from within the depths of the tunnel caught Brabantia's attention. At first, the source of the illumination remained obscure. Brabantia guided them closer to the light, hoping to reveal a way into the dungeons. The tunnel was dark and stifling; menacing shadows danced in the distance. The light grew steadily until they reached the end of the tunnel, and then voices could be heard nearby—squeaky, rat-like sounds. Brabantia held out her arm to bring them to a halt.

"Sh... sh...guards!" She peeped cautiously around the corner.

"Mikael, Corsivo, follow me. Everyone else stay here."

Corsivo and Mikael followed Brabantia, remaining as close to the wall as possible so as not to be seen. Suddenly Brabantia screamed out "Attack!"

Without hesitation or doubt, Brabantia drew her silver blade from its scabbard, dashed forward, and turned a sharp left into the adjacent tunnel, Mikael and Corsivo floating steadily by her side. The guards were taken by surprise but quickly recovered, ready to defend themselves. They moved in, fangs flashing angrily, weapons held ready. Brabantia could smell the acrid odor

410

of blood from the mouth of the Xanthurus as her blazing silver blade, glowing like newly forged steel, clashed with the vermin's bronze sword. Her vermeil armor glittered in the torchlight. The Xanthurus's eyes had the appearance of death; those glassy, red, bead-like eyes did not move in any direction. His long snout and gnashing fangs hovered threateningly above her as he carried on beating at Brabantia's sword. The Xanthurus gave Brabantia a murderous glare, at which she aimed such a blow that her sword shattered at the hilt. Angrily, she realized she had no other option but to shape change. The Xanthurus leaped forward, ready to thrust his sword into her heart, but he landed awkwardly on the ground, as she had moved so swiftly his eyes had not seen it. He quickly turned around in wonder as the wolf snarled showing his long, sharp canines dripping with thick saliva.

"Where the hell did you come from?"

The wolf encircled him, growling from deep within. Before the Xanthurus had time to get up, the wolf whirled in mid-air and sprang upon him, jaws wide, head low, ripping flesh with incredible power. The Xanthurus struggled to get a good angle to fight the wolf off, but his realization quickly became that death was a sure thing.

Brabantia licked the blood from her lipless jaw, turning to scan her position in the flickering light of the burning torches. The stone walls gave off a ghostly luminescence in the darkness, and an odor reached her nostrils, a necrotic scent tinged with the smell of damp earth. The dancing shadows had an odd pattern to them, leaping shadows of dense black. Corsivo and Mikael had slain the other two Xanthurus guards and returned to find the white wolf that they were familiar with shaking her shaggy head, held low, until she leaped gracefully into the air, becoming particles of shimmering dust that coalesced and reshaped, wondrously appearing once again as the Paristan warrior she was.

Celestial and the others had joined them, and the narrow tunnel led them at last to an opening cut through the cave wall like an archway. It grew darker and darker as they walked through and approached two tunnels branching off in different directions.

"Which should we take, Rusalka?" Brabantia whispered cautiously.

Rusalka closed her eyes for a moment and then opened them sharply, like one who had seen something quite shocking. "The one to the left leads us to the dungeons where Roberto is held, but we must pass through the fires of hell and torment first."

"Take the lead, Rusalka and Brabantia...we will follow." Celestial commanded them forward.

Corsivo held on to Gabriel, guiding him into the tunnel. At first, Gabriel grasped hold of him with both hands. He could feel the soft earth below his feet, and the awareness of his vulnerability enraged him. He pulled his arm away from Corsivo's grip.

"I can manage!" he spat quietly with contempt at Corsivo.

"I am only trying to help you, Gabriel. The terrain is dangerous, my brother."

Gabriel muttered under his breath. "It's all right for you to be so generous of spirit, Corsivo. Everything just falls neatly into place for you. Overnight you became a sensation—loved by all, everyone's savior—and what sort of life did you lead before we came upon you that fateful day? A life of depravity and sin! I have lived an eternity in the sacred heavens of Elyon before I was sent to Venus. I deserve more than this. I am a true Eternal—not some fake who thinks he can make up for all the evil he has bestowed upon others."

Celestial placed her hand across his mouth. "Sh...sh...that's more than enough, Gabriel. Good and evil can become entwined, and speeches of a desperate one are as the wind. Be careful not to lose your soul to the power of the wicked one."

Gabriel's entire body prickled. He knew her powerful words were words of the all-wise and all-knowing, so he reluctantly allowed Corsivo to lead him through the winding tunnel, his soul hot with anger and envy that he knew he must somehow crush. The flames from the torches placed high above their heads leaped high, casting macabre shadows in their path, the darkness

412

carrying disturbing vibrations—the cry of a desperate one, the high-pitched screech of the Xanthurus, and the unknown screams of violent distress echoing through the great stone walls as they crawled deeper and deeper down into the abysmal depths of the castle.

Suddenly, from each stone that lay on the ground before them, rose a trembling, swaying pillar of flame, and in each glowing flame, a spirit writhed screaming in terror. Gabriel winced at the high-pitched sound and covered his ears with both hands, letting go of Corsivo. "What is it? Who's there? I can't bear it!"

Corsivo laid a hand on his arm, and Celestial spoke above the tortured sounds. "They are the lost souls of Syrtis coming forth to warn us of the danger of what lies ahead. They are to be pitied, for they are damned for eternity to burn in hell, and hell has no fury like that of Elyon when His mighty rage is unleashed. And unleashed it shall be when the time comes."

Rusalka shivered. "Come. We are approaching the torture chamber; the Xanthurus will be armed and ready for combat. We must fight to the death." She noticed the weapons that hung on the walls. From the notches on the blades, it was clear that the weapons had seen recent combat and spilled the blood of many.

The tunnel opened into a large mausoleum. The smell of decaying bodies in the tombs and the mold growing on the stones hung heavily in the damp air. Water dripped incessantly from the high ceilings and ran in rivulets down the gray walls. All was dark and silent as they passed through the huge chamber, scanning every corner for movement of any sort. The only source of light was an opening some distance away, which they followed, creeping cautiously past the crypts. The stone figures of Draconian royalty lay covered in bat excrement and other dubious debris, which they did not care to explore at any length. Brabantia guided them slowly through, her eyes fixed on even the deepest of shadows.

They finally reached the source of the light, which carried them past a maze of paths deep within the subterranean castle until they arrived at the entrance of a downward-sloping cave. At first, they heard a low moan as the atmosphere became more and more stifling. The interior was dark, with only a few burning torches to light the cavern. The moaning sound grew louder and louder, until it reached howling point. The sound of perpetual incantations, mixed with the horror of violent screams, came from the other side of a huge, heavy wooden door. Brabantia took one look at Mikael, and without so much as a word spoken, they ran forward in unison and pushed the door open.

The intense heat hit them instantly; flames leaped high, twisting, dancing…seething like boiling magma in a volcano, wanting to escape, needing an explosive release. The lake of fire ran a great expanse through the colossal cavern, the ceiling lost in its height. Spilled innards raised a ripe aroma.

The Xanthurus ceased chanting immediately, their malevolent red eyes focused intently upon the intrusion. Then the long-prolonged screech arrived, the cry of war known to all as the Xanthurus.

Brabantia and the Eternals leaped swiftly into action, unleashing a series of wild attacks. Fiery arrows spun like sparks showered from a hot fire. Brabantia seized a battle-ax from the castle wall and swung it backward and forward, hacking off the tails of as many of the enemy as she possibly could. Their cries and the sound of steel upon steel filled the chasm, and the heat soared oppressively.

Finally, Brabantia came face to face with Egor, Dracon's right-hand man. She recognized him immediately. His eyes were dark red, sunken, feral, revealing the violence within. She recoiled at his slavering aperture as he drew back his lipless mouth, revealing his strong, yellowing canines. He swung a lethal-looking iron weapon held on a chain from side to side, watching her fixedly. He easily parried her first advance. She anticipated his move and swung the axe in her left hand so swiftly that Egor looked down in disbelief at his weapon arm lying in a pool of blood on the ground below.

Egor screeched harrowingly and then dropped to his knees with a heavy thud. Brabantia was just about to finish him off when another of his vermin army attacked her from behind, wielding his axe into her side. She reeled momentarily, her mail seeping blood down her right side, and then she turned to see the small eyes glowing red in his gigantic skull. Leaping gracefully, she flung herself onto the Xanthurus's back, seizing his head and twisting his neck in one violent motion. He fell to the ground with a heavy crash, Brabantia still holding on to him to soften her landing.

Egor had recovered enough to seek the kill, having stemmed the bleeding of his wound. He spun his head round, his fangs extended, his eyes full of revenge, and then he swung the deadly weapon toward Brabantia. The sharp, lethal spikes sank deep into her skin, ripping into her flesh. Brabantia shouted out with gritted teeth, "Dracon is dead, you moron. You are nothing without him."

The Xanthurus swung his weapon once again, more ferociously than the first time. "You lie...you evil witch." The iron spikes struck her skin again, tearing away her blooded chainmail."The rest of your army has also been defeated in the valley of Deimos. You are alone, and you will all perish. Such is your fate!"

She forced herself up. The power of each thrust threw her back. The look of victory on his face infuriated her, but she felt too weak to shape change.

Egor pounced upon her, ripping through her armor, feeling the flesh tear away under the pressure of his powerful talons. She dropped to the floor. Her wounds were deep; her dark-crimson blood poured freely. Then Egor bit into her throat like the rabid animal he was and drank her blood as it spurted from her throat like a fountain, until he had robbed her of her last breath.

Egor turned triumphantly until he realized he had come face to face with the wrath of the mighty warrior Mikael. Mikael's stature had grown, and his eyes, soft and as blue as the sky, had turned into inky black orbs; his pure, white, feathery wings were now a fiery red. Fear clawed at Egor. He had never witnessed the rage of an Eternal Warrior, and his blood chilled in anticipation of death. Mikael thrust his sword through Egor's heart with such a cry of

415

extreme rage that the cavern shook, bringing down tumbling rocks from all sides. Egor let out a terrifying screeching sound, clutching at the sword still stuck in his heaving chest. In one swift movement, he pulled out the sword and let it fall to the ground. He tried to stem the bleeding with his remaining hand, and a flash of horror passed over his face. Mikael picked up the bloodied sword, sliced off his head, and held it up as a trophy for all the Xanthurus army to see.

The Eternals fought with a new vigor at the loss of their loved one, and Brabantia's corpse for a while became lost in the confusion of flaming arrows, smoke, and flapping wings. Despite the vermin's efforts, the Eternals and the Paristan shed muscle and flesh until copious amounts of black, inky blood had been spilled, until there was nothing left but blood and bones beneath their relentless onslaught—until the battle had been won and victory was theirs. But a great sadness filled their hearts as they knelt beside Brabantia's still body and closed her lifeless eyes once and for all. The Paristan warriors wept. Their only wish was to take her body back with them though impossible.

"She was a great warrior!" Mikael said, holding his emotions in check.

Celestial placed her hand on his arm. "A great warrior's end is not this way. Elyon will see to it. It is only the end of Brabantia as we know her!"

"She will be greatly missed by us all." Corsivo glanced at Celestial, wiping the sweat from his forehead, but his thoughts were immediately overtaken by the whereabouts of Cava and her safety.

Rusalka rose to her feet, her face wet with tears. "Come. We must find Roberto and get out of this place. It is the heart of darkness; one could lose one's soul in this desolate existence of vile decay and destruction of all that is pure and noble."

Smoke rose from the inferno, carrying the intoxicating aroma of seared flesh and the terrible sounds of the accursed souls forced to embrace the eternal flames crying out harrowingly from the lake of fire. Celestial steered them over the massacred slain toward a high bridge that was suspended precariously over the maelstrom of the fiery pit.

"Now is the time to return to your truest form, Rusalka. Your wings will be your savior; we must fly over this bridge. It is too dangerous to cross by foot."

Celestial, Corsivo, Gabriel, and Mikael waited for Rusalka to transform. She closed her eyes.

"I can't." Opening her eyes, she looked at Celestial in despair. "I can't do it. I have no energy left; I feel so weak. What is happening to me?"

"Despair not, Rusalka! Corsivo will carry you over, and Mikael will help Gabriel. A place such as this is enough to deplete even the strength of Eternals. Your strength will return soon enough. Remember Him...before the silver cord loosed or the golden bowl hath broken...the spirit returns to He who gave it."

Rusalka sighed heavily. She did not feel sure anymore about the way she felt; she had changed. It had been slow and insidious, but nevertheless, she felt different. She could even feel the emotions of mere mortals. And what was this feeling she had for Roberto that consumed her soul beyond recognition? And now she could not summon her Seraphim being—the being she now wanted to embrace more than anything else she desired...or did she? What was this doubt? She could not understand it. Such confusion of thought had never been hers to ponder!

They could feel the intense heat rising from below, through every fiber of their feathery wings, and the sound of the pitiful souls rose higher and higher, echoing eerily through the vast cavern. Then, suddenly, rising up from the mouth of the furnace, a fiery beast of great stature with three heads, each the size of a lion ascended gradually upward, teeth and eyes flashing like knives. Its black eyes smoldered an eerie red, and it drew its breath up into the air, and it immediately became a threatening flame darting toward them, followed by another and another. The white heat of his black rage poured forth with violent intention, all three heads breathing fire simultaneously.

Gabriel shouted out hopelessly. "What now, Your Majesty?

417

How I hate to rely upon the gallantry of my brothers to protect me! What is down there?" He held on to Celestial tightly.

Corsivo placed his hand on Gabriel's shoulder. "I know, Gabriel I don't think now is the time to discuss it, do you, brother?"At that point, Corsivo dived downward toward the gargantuan beast, amid the orange-and-red tongues of fire waiting to consume him, and Mikael followed swiftly.

Celestial turned to Gabriel, speaking in silvery tongues among the tumultuous clamor. "See with more than your eyes. Let discipline and control be your master."

Gabriel took a deep breath and reached within himself to feel the power of his master once more and leaped from the protection of Celestial to fight as a warrior for his queen, as was his duty as a Seraphim of Elyon.

The beast sucked the air from the cave, leaving Rusalka and Celestial breathless. It let out an ear-splitting roar that came from all three jaws, its armor of scales black as tar. Gabriel thrashed out blindly with his sword, slicing through the air at random until he felt his blade sink into something close. The beast roared loader, and its fury raged forth. Gabriel grew bolder, thrusting his sword farther forward, unsure of how close he was to the beast. The jaw of one of its heads opened wide—so wide that Gabriel had stepped into the chasm, surrounded by gnashing teeth. Corsivo saw Gabriel's position and quickly jumped into the chasm with him.

"Thrust your sword downward, right where you stand, Gabriel." Corsivo threw his sword through the jaw of the beast with the power of angels, and it shot up into its brain. Gabriel stuck his sword downward piercing the beast's throat. The beast let out a great roar, and, with a weak, gurgling sound, it toppled over, blood bubbling from every orifice. The beast fell backward into the depths of the fiery lake and disappeared as quickly as it had risen.

The angel warriors floated back to Celestial and Rusalka triumphantly. "I see my guard has returned to his rightful place." Celestial smiled warmly.

Gabriel touched his eyes with his fingertips. "My eyes...my eyes. I can see...my eyes have been restored." He looked at Celestial. "Thank you, my queen...thank you so much. How can I ever repay you"

Celestial smiled once more. "Don't thank me, Gabriel. The power to heal yourself was always there."

Corsivo patted Gabriel on the back. "You were brave, my brother." Then he turned away to seek their way through the tunnels down into the dungeons.

Descending the castle's dark underground tunnels, they uncovered an aperture in the cave-like floor with a winding set of stone steps, each one smooth and shiny with immeasurable use. Rusalka felt a sudden, overwhelming rush of heat through her body at the prospect of finding Roberto alive. The image of his face appeared in her mind. Soon she would be with him once again, and the tension grew. She could feel it in her tightened muscles. *Why does the thought of him frighten me so?*

Chapter 38

Escape From Mars

A sudden noise roused Roberto from his slumber. Holding his breath, he listened suspiciously.

"What is it?" Freja pushed herself up stiffly to have a look.

They both sat upright, trying to make out what the sound was in the distance. It was footsteps, light and airy, unlike like the footsteps of the Xanthurus. Roberto jumped to his feet, fully aware now, his drowsiness startled away. He waited, his eyes fixed firmly on evidence of any movement in the darkness that surrounded them. Freja had managed to pull herself to her feet, standing a full nine feet tall, towering above Roberto. He glanced up at Freja, and, lamely but loudly, he said, "Anyone out there?"

No answer. He felt suddenly afraid. Maybe it was the Serophoth, or, even worse, Leviathan himself!

He looked at Freja again and could see by the expression on her face that she was thinking something along the same lines. They had no time to discern who—someone or something approached the cell...and forcefully drew back the heavy bolt after turning the key in the lock. Roberto had never felt so relieved in his whole life when he witnessed the radiant aura of the Eternals light up the dank, dark dungeons like a holy place.

"We are free, Freja. These are the Seraphim, holy angels of light. We are safe at last."

An intense, dazzling flood of lightness filled the cell. Roberto and Freja covered their eyes, so bright was the light. And although the shadowy corners remained, the light shone forth. Rusalka floated gracefully before him, keen to free him from the chains that bound. Celestial immediately spoke powerful words of freedom that broke the iron cuffs from both Roberto's and Freja's hands and feet, and Rusalka noticed that Roberto had pulled at his chains so much that his wrists and ankles were raw and bloody. He blinked rapidly, and, as the bleariness cleared, he realized who stood next to him. His stomach clenched tightly; his pulse raced erratically. He wanted so much to touch her hand, to feel her warm skin. He felt momentarily exhilarated, joyous, and yet...all too aware of the dangers that surrounded them. He saw her smile, and even as it filled his emptiness, there was desperation in his voice.

"Rusalka!" Her name slipped easily from his weary lips. Rusalka's compassion ran freely beyond any reasoning at the sound of his voice, and she leaned forward without hesitation, licking his wounds with her healing tongue. Her black hair swung, glossy, flowing from her shoulders, adorned with tiny diamond stars, and he could smell the sweet perfume of her presence. He had not noticed she had the wings of angels, he was so consumed with the passion of his love for her. With her face so close to his, her breath warm on his cheek like some warm, sweet scent, he felt a warm flush course through his veins, and his heart began to quicken even faster. He remembered her beauty but had forgotten how potent it was.

Rusalka slowly looked away from him, feeling uncomfortable under his intense gaze. Everyone watched in awe, aware of the electricity between a mortal and an Eternal—nothing good could come of it.

Celestial broke the spell."Come...we must reclaim what is ours...it will be redeemed. Our land will not perish, but be aware: the time will come when the Seraphim will battle with the Serophoth, and that will be the battle of all time. Until that time, many kingdoms will arise in one place after another, and great tribulations will occur beyond our imaginings. Fear not; Elyon will guide the path of the Seraphim until His time comes to rule all dominiums, and only then will peace be restored. Consider carefully, Roberto By no means is your work done. It has just begun!"

Roberto perceived the weight of her words and received them with a heavy heart. He just wanted to wipe away the misery contained within the stone walls of the castle. He had lost all sense of time itself and now only knew that when the sun rose, it was day, and when it set, it was night, which then brought about its own curse. *When will it all end?*

Freja helped them find a way out of the castle without much hardship, and Rusalka healed her wounds. She had much to thank them for and would return to Venus with them, for she had no interest in staying in a land where peace and love had been lost, with nothing but a future of uncertainty remaining there.

The cold air hit Roberto instantly, refreshing him and clearing the awful smell of decay and mustiness that had filled his nostrils in the castle walls. He heard the voice of his soul, the voice of wisdom untold, and knew in his heart what he had to do when he returned to Venus. The pale crescent moon appeared on the horizon like a specter. Life on Mars would never be the same. For some, it would be a blessing, but for others, a curse as yet unknown.

Return to Venus

Patience had almost given up hope of seeing her father again. Astoria and Nebula had tried to comfort her in his absence, even teaching her to play the harp of angels, so magical and sweet in the sound of every note. The change upon Venus lay heavily upon the hearts of the Venusians, and even the faery seemed to have lost their sparkle. Patience wished that she could do something to help, but it was far beyond her capacity to help those whom she depended on for her own survival.

Nastacia had not been the same since her return to Venus, often babbling incoherently like one gone mad, her green eyes blazing with hell-hot anger. Wishbone had taken to hiding from her every time she came anywhere near them, and they had been

422

banished from leaving the fortress because of the known and the unknown dangers that had filled the land.

She just wanted to go home—that place she had once hated seemed so far away, yet she missed the security and the warmth and comfort of Edwina. Yes, she realized how much Edwina had meant to her, and she knew she was safe in the arms of her nanny. If only she could see her again. And this time, she would be nice to her and show her that she appreciated everything that she did for her. One thing she had noticed was that her nightmares had ceased recently, replaced by dreams of hope and light and the beauty of angels. She was at least grateful for that.

She wandered aimlessly that day around the fortress chambers, followed by Wishbone and Ilk. Ilk had become a constant companion. Sometimes she was glad of his company, but other times, she felt she wanted to strangle him because of his incessant chatter. Even Wishbone behaved as though he were deaf.

"Ilk! Will you ever stop talking? Do you realize you're doing my head in sometimes?"

Ilk folded his little chubby arms and fluttered his pearly gray wings. "How rude, Patience! I never thought you could be that rude. I thought you had patience, as your name suggests. I am obviously very wrong. Well...I don't believe it...I will just have to leave you alone for a while, and then you will see you need me..." and he just walked off, muttering to himself quietly.

Patience sighed heavily and turned to Wishbone. "I've done it now. He will probably not forgive me. Well...Wishbone, don't look at me like that. At least you don't have to answer him all the time, and you can just switch off...oh...I just give up around here."

Patience waltzed off to be by herself. She walked slowly down some long, winding steps, and when she was halfway down, she heard a commotion in the hallway. She crept down slowly, listening to decipher what it was about. Then she heard the voice of her father, plain and certain. She flew down the rest of the stairs as fast as her tiny feet would take her.

"Papa...Papa! It's really you! I thought we wouldn't see each other again. I can't believe you're safe, and you have returned."

Roberto threw his arms around her and hugged her tightly. "Patience...my beautiful daughter!" He stepped back. "Let me look at you...it's so good to see you and know that you are safe. I have worried myself sick thinking about you."

"Well here I am, and we are both safe. It's a miracle, Papa, after all we have been through."

"Yes...yes, it is! But we have had angels on our side, thankfully!"

"Oh...Papa...I am so happy to see you."

Rusalka curiously watched their reunion. She was joyous to see their display of true affection, but there was a nagging feeling inside that she was about to lose a loved one. *What is this love that bonds me so tightly to this mortal? It is not the love of angels or heavenly things!* She left the company in search of solace, to make sense of her feelings...something she could not put into words and something that was not of her nature. She walked around the circular walls, which were held up by columns of silver-gray marble, and marveled at the beauty of such a structure. She came to the great painting of Celestial, Archangel of the Seraphim. It covered a large surface of one wall, lifelike and majestic. Her silver eyes gleamed and seemed to stare back at her. She sensed that the picture was delving deep into her soul, as though it were Celestial herself reading her thoughts. She turned away, ashamed of what Celestial might see. Her loyalties had become divided. She was neither hot nor cold in the eyes of the Eternal One; He would spew her out as though she were distasteful if she were to return to the High Heavens as *the thing* she had become, neither Elvin nor Seraphim nor mortal being—a little of all three, maybe? She could not decipher. The confusion had to be stopped; she had to find a way back or change completely into someone mortal among strangers. She walked with airy steps away from the painting and then picked up her wings slowly and gently, flying upward toward the expanse of the high ceiling and out through an open window into the night air.

Roberto searched the fortress, hoping to find her. But no one

424

had seen her for some time, and the night grew darker. All who stayed within the fortress's walls chose to take refuge in restful sleep, but Roberto could not rest, at least not until he had seen Rusalka.

He walked out into the fortress gardens, and the candle flames wavered in the wind as he passed by. The darkness itself seemed to have a voice, whispers here and whispers there, as though he were being watched from a distance. He had not gone very far when he spotted Rusalka in the distance and followed her in the deep cover of the woods. At first she did not notice him, but his foot broke a twig with a loud crack.

She turned instantly. "Lord Bellucci, are you following me?" She smiled a wry smile.

"Not exactly. I was just out walking and saw you in the distance." Roberto felt a little uncomfortable and a smile did not travel to his eyes, but he still persisted in his endeavor to walk with her. "You know it is dangerous for you to be walking alone in the forest at this dark hour!"

Rusalka stopped for a moment, observing his obvious concerned expression. "I have nothing to fear more than myself...and you."

Roberto felt the weight of her words. "You don't need to fear me, Rusalka. I will not harm you. I will only do as you wish." He fell to his knees and held her tiny, soft hand in his and gently kissed her velvet skin. Rusalka's heart raced frantically. She averted her eyes so that he could not see the wishes of her heart. Her stomach clenched, and with eyes wild with fear, she cried out frantically. "Stop...Roberto...stop." There was desperation in her voice. "Roberto." His name was a plea. She closed her eyes. "Roberto, please. I beg of you. I cannot become as mortal man."

Roberto insisted. "You can if you so desire, Rusalka; you know you can! The earth, the sky, the wind, and the water, and, of course, my love will serve you well."

Rusalka stared down into his face, reading the passion of his desires. Her eyes chastised him. "Would you have me live in eternal darkness when you are gone? For although I will have the body of a mortal, the feelings of a mortal...my immortality will prevail."

Roberto sprang up from his knees and placed his hands around her tiny waist, pulling her close to him, his face inches away from her slightly open mouth. She made a supreme effort to keep herself in control, pulling herself back from him, turning her face away from his alluring eyes. Roberto lifted her chin with gentle fingers and guided her eyes to meet his own. "You are the most beautiful being I have ever laid eyes upon and the most remarkable woman I have ever encountered, and I can't leave you behind when I go back to Earth. You must come with me. Please, Rusalka?"

Her body was tense. "Please do not ask this of me. I would be such a disappointment to my maker; I owe Him so much. No...I can't do it, Roberto. I can't do it! I don't know who I am anymore!"

The strength of angels broke her free from his grip, and she spun around in a circular movement until her wings took flight and she soared up above the forest trees, up and away until she was out of sight. Roberto stared at the crescent moon in the indigo sky, sighed heavily, and retraced his steps back to the fortress. He thought of dwelling with ease beyond the dominium of time and the glories of becoming part of an enchanted world, the fabulous unearthly beings that had touched his soul beyond his wildest dreams, and he thought of Rusalka. He understood how such superior beings would express amusement at the ways of men and their perpetual striving after the wind until their short life drifts away by the ravages of time. He thought of the magnitude of the gulf that divided this world that had become momentarily his own and the world of his origin. He knew it was time to think of earthly things once more and be the man he was meant to be—and, most of all, to protect his daughter from the Serophoth. The Nephilim must never be born again of fallen angels and the daughters of men. His daughter, Patience, must never be allowed to be that vessel. He would make it is life's vocation to prevent such a fate from befalling her and the generations that followed.

426

Roberto returned to the fortress that night, but sleep eluded him and dawn broke another day to face the reality of his position. Roberto requested an audience with Celestial, and the answer came swiftly back by messenger, little Ilk himself.

"Hi, little fellow. It's good to see such a familiar face! I believe you have entertained Patience and Wishbone in my absence, and for that I thank you. We will always remember you."

Ilk flapped his wings backward and forward like a fan in motion. "You sound as though you are leaving us, Lord Bellucci! Surely you aren't leaving just yet. We have much to do in the renewal of our planet, and we will need your help. I am sure of it. You must see our queen. She does wish to speak to you, but I am sure it is not about your departure. I certainly don't want you to go just yet. Please, you must—"

Roberto tried to calm him down a little. "I must go sometime, Ilk, but maybe not yet. Let us see what Celestial has to say on the matter, shall we?"

"OK...OK...you gave me a fright then...phew...I would miss Patience and Wishbone if you left. I have become very, very attached to them, you see, and...not that I am not attached to you, of course...but—"

Roberto was beginning to lose his patience. "Yes, erm...I must go now...see you later, little fellow."

Roberto entered the circular hall in the middle of the fortress, passing the columns adorned by the softest of light, like celestial spheres throwing off iridescent reflections across the mirrored floor. Sculptures of angels created from pearls of transparent clarity, whose edges were trimmed with dewdrops, stood in the great emblematic area of the court. And there, in all her splendor, sat Celestial, Archangel of the Seraphim, on the silver throne of thrones. Her diaphanous white robe flowed in silk ripples to the ground, a brilliant light emanating from every fiber of her being. Roberto averted his eyes as he walked furtively toward the throne, and, as he approached her, she allowed her brightness to dim considerably in order to engage with him. His heart beat wildly in awe.

427

A soft, cool breath stole in, bearing a perfume so potent and sweet, and a silvery voice spoke of things to come. Her speech was low, hypnotic, her eyes mesmerizing. "As the seed that is sown dies and arises again, so is the fate of Venus. We will break our bows and cut our spears into pieces. The dark, reddened skies will grow light and azure blue once again, and new life will spring forth across the planet. The fertile green valley's will return as quickly as they had gone, first in the south and then to the east, rapidly spreading to the north and the west. Every tree will grow tall and strong. New cities will be built on verdant land, where our children of Venus will live and thrive. Our queen of hearts will rule once more. This I tell you this day."

Roberto cleared his throat. "What will become of you, Your Majesty, when Nebula sits on your throne?"

"It was never my throne. I came only for a season, and now I must return whence I came until such a time when all angels of light and dark will clash swords with no mercy and the evil one is no more."

"What must I do now?"

"Elyon's favor is toward a wise servant, Roberto. Your visitation has preserved our spirit, and for that we are truly grateful, all of us here on Venus. Songs will be sung of your bravery throughout our land. You will not be forgotten...now and for always. It is now time to return to the place where you were born and face up to the ancestry you have been unfortunate to be a part of. You must protect Patience, and all your generations to come must be sheltered from the wrath of Leviathan. He will never give up his quest to bring forth children from the daughters of men, and until the time comes when he will be destroyed once and for all, he must never produce the Nephilim, as he once accomplished. The Nephilim of old were strong and mighty, and if they grew in numbers as a vast nation once more, then it would be the end of men—and that is not the way of Elyon."

"I will do all you say, Celestial. I have learned a great many things on this planet, wisdom and understanding beyond words. It is with great sadness I leave you, this planet, and everyone I

428

have grown to care for. Before, my heart was dead, and now, I am alive. I have come to appreciate the love I feel for my daughter, and she has come to appreciate me. I can only thank you for all that you have done for us. There is only one thing I wish to ask of you, Celestial."

"Pray...ask what you desire from me."

Roberto cleared his throat once again. "My desire is to take Rusalka with me back to Earth. She would be good for Patience and could help me protect her from the forces beyond my control."

Celestial smiled. "I understand the ways of men. The human aura is full of passion. This can be your downfall, or it can be your strength. Your feelings betray you, Roberto. Ah...love...the love of mortals! I know it is powerful and hard to resist, but Rusalka must make up her own mind on this matter. She has free will, as we all have. Surely you have discussed this with her at some point of your journey?"

"Well...yes, Your Majesty, but she keeps avoiding the subject."

"Then she is not ready, and you must give her time. She would be sacrificing so much to follow her heart in this affair; thus, it is a decision one must not make hastily. There will be no going back for her."

"I see."

"However, all is not lost regarding this subject. Hope is eternal."

"I understand, Your Majesty. But if I return to Earth, I will never see her again."

"No man can be certain of the future of anything—only the passing of time. Go now. Prepare for your journey, and you will do well to remember: all things desired are nothing compared to the value of the wisdom of Elyon."

And then she was gone! Roberto left the hall feeling sad about the possibility of never looking upon the face of Celestial or Rusalka again, or even of walking through the enchanted places of Venus. *What do I remember of earthly things? Not much! And Corsivo, Mikael, and even Gabriel...I will miss them all.* The air was heavy with the scent of jasmine, and the lute brought forth the plaintive cry peculiar to the instrument. He thought of Rusalka and her lily-like beauty and the radiant nimbus of tiny, fluttering beings that made up her irresistible aura, each one delicate and perfectly formed, like tiny miniatures of her. The Seraphim! Irrepressible beings of flame and energy, and his beloved was one of them. *How could I possibly have thought that she could embrace earthly things? I had to be mad to harbor such desires.* He would have to be strong in his endeavor to overcome his feelings, but he would never give up hope.

CHAPTER 39

Castillo Di Duomo

"Unseen powers shape the lives of mortal man"

Edwina threw open the door of Patience's bedroom anxiously. "I have been calling you for the last fifteen minutes, Patience. Why are you ignoring me? You have an appointment at the hospital in one hour, and you have to get washed and dressed yet; never mind the fact I have prepared your breakfast and it is going cold!"

Patience pulled down the duvet on her bed, bleary-eyed. She had known she was going back to Earth, but she had not realized it would be so sudden. And she had not even had a chance to say good-bye to anyone. Edwina was busily opening the curtains and muttering to herself. *Is she aware that we have been away? I remember vaguely someone telling me that to those back on Earth, it would be as though we hadn't been away—and maybe that's for the best. How would we explain where we have been, and who would believe us anyway?*

Her surroundings seemed so strange to her. After all, her first sight had been of another world—a world so far apart from all of this that she was seeing for the first time. Wishbone ran to her side as she stepped down from her four-poster bed. She grabbed his ears, fondly staring straight into his knowing eyes, and kissed him on his wet nose. They shared a secret that Edwina would not believe.

"I have laid out your clothes, Patience. Please be quick. I don't want to be late. Dr. Edwards is a busy man, as you know, and we

431

don't want him complaining to your father, do we now?"

Patience smiled; Edwina had not changed. She was grateful that some things had stayed the same.

"Don't worry, Edwina. I will be as quick as I can." Patience rushed toward her clothes lying on the table near her en-suite bathroom, picked them up, and flew into her changing room so speedily that Edwina was startled by her compliance and ease of transit.

"Are you OK, Patience?"

"Yes, of course. I won't be long!"

Wishbone followed Edwina downstairs, his appetite ready to be satisfied. Edwina always gave him a good meal, and it was comforting to know that this morning would be no different now that they were home.

"Wishbone! You know you must wait for Patience. I will feed you when you come back down. Go on...go on, boy. Look, it will still be here when you get back."

Wishbone could smell the aroma of a juicy steak. "Go on, boy. Go fetch Patience."

Wishbone barked; then, wagging his tail and drooling all the way up the stairs, he met Patience at the top with Roberto by her side. "Come, boy. Let's all go for breakfast." Patience grabbed hold of his harness and took it off. "I won't be needing that anymore."

Wishbone wagged his tail enthusiastically. Patience was in awe of the many portraits of her ancestry on the walls as they walked down the sweeping staircase, and the elaborate decorations of her family home. It all seemed a little surreal to her.

Edwina looked suspicious when Roberto walked into the breakfast room together with Patience and showed her to her seat, then sat himself down by her side.

"To what do we owe this pleasure, Roberto? I had not been informed you were joining us for breakfast. What would you like? I am in a bit of a rush this morning; I have to take Patience to hospital, but I can make you something quick. A slice of toast or some cereal, maybe?"

"That won't be necessary, Edwina, but thank you anyway. I

432

have taken the liberty of canceling the doctor's appointment. I do hope you don't mind?"

Edwina was alarmed. "But, Roberto, it is her annual check!" As she spoke, she watched Patience get up off her chair and walk to the kitchen sink with her dish and rinse it.

"What is going on here? Will someone kindly explain?" She looked at Patience and then at Roberto quizzically.

"I am sorry, Edwina. I can only tell you that Patience has got her sight back, and things are going to be different around here. Isn't that so, Patience?"

"Yes, Papa."

Edwina sensed a change in the relationship between Patience and Roberto, and she was trying to make sense of it all. "Well, sorry if I seem a little confused. It seems to me that you went to bed last night, and you have come down this morning as two different people. Patience can see, and, Roberto, you look so different. I don't know how to explain it, but you seem so close. Yet you have hardly said a nice word to each other for the past year—that I can remember, anyway. So what is going on?"

Roberto pushed his chair away from the large breakfast table and got up. Edwina noticed the look in his warm brown eyes, as if a shadow of darkness had been lifted from his soul. "Please don't ask why or what, when and where, because I don't think anyone will believe what has happened to us. But I can say it is for the best, Edwina, and we still want you to stay with us. Patience needs you, and...well, I do too. Maybe in time, we will be able to tell you about things that must be kept secret. Time will tell all."

Patience laughed. "You sound just like Celestial when you speak like that, Papa."

Edwina quickly picked up on the name. "Who is Celestial?"

Patience glanced at her father with an apologetic expression on her face. Roberto put his arm around her. "As I said, Edwina, we can't give you the answers right now. I can only ask you to trust us. You have been with this family from the beginning, and we are in your debt for all that you have done for us, especially for your care of Patience."

433

"Yes, Edwina. I am so grateful for everything you have done for me, and I promise to be more helpful to you."

Edwina looked as though she could have been knocked down with a feather. Her watery blue eyes welled up, and the tears came flowing down her cheeks. Wishbone almost knocked her over trying to lick her face and probably would have done so had not Roberto taken control of the situation. They all began to laugh together for the first time. Patience offered Edwina a handkerchief.

"Thank you, Patience. I am so happy you have your eyesight, but you seem so familiar with it...I really don't understand. I think I am finally going mad!"

Roberto laughed again. "I am not sure if you are or I am, but at least we are friends. And whatever we have to go through in the future, we are in it together. We think of you as family now, Edwina."

That night, Edwina went to bed with a wonderful feeling of joy in her heart. She did not know what to make of it all, but it felt good to be finally accepted as one of the family, and even more so to be acknowledged by Roberto—the lovely Roberto; what had happened to him? Whatever it was, she was ecstatic at his remarkable change. And Patience—well, *who would have thought it?*

Roberto and Patience found it difficult at first getting used to earthly things once more, but it wasn't long before their time on Venus had almost been forgotten. Roberto made a big effort to spend time with Edwina and Patience, and they enjoyed the long summer together picnicking, boating along the river, dining out in stylish places, and generally socializing with friends and family. Patience felt happy her dreams had come true. She worked hard at her piano, and a career as a master solo pianist became inevitable. Roberto was proud of her achievements and enjoyed her company as she developed into a charming young woman, but it was never far from the back of his mind the danger she could be in if the Serophoth got close to her. He tried to explain to Edwina all about their "dreams," as he put it, but he was not sure she understood the full implications or whether she even believed in such a reality as other worlds and other beings beyond anything man has seen or encountered. But he had! And he knew the horrors of the abyss and all its evil.

A shudder ran down his spine. Edwina placed a hand over his. "What is it, Roberto? You look pale."

"It's nothing! Something just walked over my grave; that's all."

∞

Winter crept in slowly. The castle started to take on a brooding element once again. The summer months had brought the place alive with singing birds and canopies of scented flowers. Edwina had filled every room with freshly cut flowers, and the sun had shone brightly through the many large windows. All that was dark and dismal had been forgotten. But now, the thick walls felt cold and required extensive heating to bring back any warmth at all in its many vast rooms.

Patience was out walking on the grounds, with only her footsteps for company. She pulled her scarf securely around her neck as the wind almost whipped it from her shoulders. Rubbing her hands together in an endeavor to create some heat, she focused on the keep in the not-so-far distance. High up in the blackest part of the tower, inside the arched stone window...something moved. Was it a trick of the light coming in from the first signs of the silvery moon, or was it...

She turned swiftly, and her chest tightened as her stomach leaped over in a summersault. *No...it can't be!* She could not think of it. She looked back once more, but it had gone. Perhaps her imagination was getting the best of her—and after what she had seen, was it any wonder? She thought of all those years ago, when she had been to a place that time forgot...a place of unimaginable tales. *Was it all just a dream, or was it as real as my father remembered?*

She quickened her steps until she was running. The moon

shone bright, and the thick leaves rustled in the wind. Dancing shadows had an odd pattern about them, filling the night with untold menace. When she reached the castle entrance, she quickly shut the heavy, creaking door behind her and slid the bolts urgently in place. Still gasping for breath, she turned around to see her father standing there in the warm glow of the candlelight. His eyes looked dark...alarmingly so.

"Where have you been at this hour, Patience? You know I have forbidden you to walk these grounds alone, especially at night."

"I am sorry, Papa. I got carried away and lost all thought of time. And before I knew it, the sun had gone down. And it happened so quickly, it seemed unreal."

Roberto helped her take off her coat. "I only say this for your own good. I don't want to spoil your freedom, Patience, but you know what may pursue you, and you need constant protection. I love you, and I will not let any harm come to you. You are a special young woman, and you must take good care of yourself and be vigilant."

Patience did not dare tell her father of the feeling she had felt out there in the dark, or the movement she had seen in the keep. "Yes, Papa. I will be more careful in future. You have my word."

His voice softened. "Good. Then I will say goodnight, sweetness. I have a long day tomorrow. I am giving a speech at the university, so I am going to retire with a nightcap. See you in the morning."

"Goodnight, Papa!" Patience leaned over to give him a peck on the cheek. She did love him so for his concern, even though it was irksome at times.

She wandered up the winding staircase and along the west wing to her bedroom, aware that she was dragging her feet; a great heaviness had descended upon her. Wishbone was waiting for her; he always liked to sleep in her room, and Roberto was all for it—extra protection and all of that, he said.

Her bedroom was of vast proportions for just one person. It opened into a smaller turret room, perfectly round. She entered the circular room and looked through its long arched window

436

into the darkness of the night. The moon hung low in the indigo sky, its dimensions much larger than usual, and the wind wailed like a crying child. Tracing her steps back to the high-ceilinged room, she shivered uncontrollably. The nights were drawing in, and she needed to wear something warm for bed. How she hated cold feet. She searched her drawers for the pink fluffy bed socks that Edwina had bought her the Christmas before. Wishbone seemed a little unsettled and in need of her attention more than usual. "Go to your bed, Wishbone...go on...I am tired. I need sleep."

He reluctantly obeyed, his tail held between his legs. "Anyone would think I neglected you, silly dog. You know you're my best friend and always will be." Patience leaned over to turn out the light and snuggled under her goose-down duvet to escape the cold.

Sleep came speedily, a great escape from the sudden feelings of unease that had found her that night. Wishbone too was deep in slumber. Then it happened. Wishbone growled deeply within his throat but did not move from his bed. *Is it a dream, or is it real?* Patience could not discern her state of being anymore. Time stood still in the boundless space between moments. She lay trapped, frozen to the spot, petrified in the realization that someone or something stood waiting in the shadows of her room. Something unmoving, with an aura so chilling it froze her heart. Was it...could it be...HIM?

Patience clutched the duvet under her chin. The thing moved slightly in the shadows. Patience stared wide-eyed into the darkness. She could only make out an indistinct shape, a black silhouette of something very tall and menacing. She felt the familiarity of its odor, which floated in the air.

Suddenly, the figure moved forward, closing the distance between them. Other shapes moved at his feet. Then she saw his face move out of the shadows. With a silent gasp, a gulping breath, she could not believe her eyes. A most beautiful male angel stood over her with a smile so beguiling it took her breath away. She was mesmerized by his beauty, his perfect features, and his golden, toned physique. His long chestnut hair shone with golden strands that complemented his liquid golden eyes, and his feathery wings shone gold and silver. Patience was rooted to the spot until he held out his hand to her. Mesmerized, she placed hers in his and slowly sat up in her bed. The angel picked her up easily into his arms and flew out of the window into the cold night. Wishbone dared not move, surrounded by the black creatures that had once turned him into a frog. He lay in his bed, rooted to the spot. Not a sound escaped him.

The next morning, Patience awoke to the sound of pouring rain tapping incessantly on her windows. A cold wind blew through an open window in the turret room. She climbed out of bed and searched for her slippers. The drapes from the arched window were blowing wildly, and the window banged against the wooden frame. Wishbone followed her every move, whimpering for some unknown reason. Patience closed the window and fixed the lock. "It's OK, Wishbone. It's only the wind."

She remembered her dream vividly. At least it was a beautiful dream, a dream of love and a promise of things to come. She would keep it to herself, so happy that the nightmares of her youth were a thing of the past since her return home.

It had started off a nightmare, she supposed, with that awful, foreboding feeling that always accompanied such dreams, but ended up with passion and romance she had yet to encounter in her own life. He had been so handsome and benevolent. She felt a nice shiver run through her body. Oh, how she hoped to dream about him again.

That day, she felt on top of the world and played her piano with dedication and passion. Edwina commented on her mood. "You seem very pleased with yourself today, Patience. Is there anything you're not telling me? If I did not know any better, I would say you have the look of someone who has been ensnared by a thing called love."

Patience laughed. "I wish! Now, if dreams come true—which I know they can—then you never know, Edwina."

Edwina laughed once more, leaving Patience to her work in

438

peace. "Oh, before I leave, Roberto and I would like you to join us for dinner tonight. Is that OK with you, Patience?"

"I would love to. See you later."

Roberto returned home that evening. Dinner was prepared, and as soon as he had settled in and changed, ready to dine, he made his way through the winding corridors and down the sweeping staircase to the main dining room. He wanted to celebrate. Life was good, and he wanted to show Edwina and Patience that he admired the part they had played in his contentment.

Patience came down in a turquoise-blue chiffon dress with her hair pulled back in a chignon—looking very much the lady of the castle, Roberto thought. Her eyes shone, and she had an air of lightness and frivolity about her that evening. Edwina had certainly made an effort, wearing a black, silk, beaded evening dress, with her long auburn hair flowing loose around her bare shoulders. Roberto saw her in a different light somehow that evening. He had never really noticed her obvious beauty. Of course, she could never have the beauty of angels, but that was too much to ask of mortals. But for a mortal, she was pretty special.

The night went well. Roberto talked of Patience's future as heir to the castle and of Edwina's certain place as part of the family. "I have a surprise for you both."

Edwina was the first to speak. "Oh. Please pray tell, Roberto. You know I can't stand the suspense."

Patience giggled slightly. "Yes, come on, Papa. What is it?"

"I have two tickets here for a trip around Europe for two very special ladies, and you will be going next week."

Patience put down her knife and fork. "Papa...that's wonderful and very kind of you, but I have concerts in the next two months. It's out of the question!"

"You will go, Patience, and you will go with Edwina."

Edwina did not know what to say. She was very flattered that he would do such a thing for her and Patience but did not really want to go without Roberto.

439

"Why must we go, Papa?"

Roberto cleared his throat and averted his eyes. "I have a foreboding feeling about this place at present, and I can't get rid of it, Patience. You know I have a connection with another world. Well...images and visions have been haunting me these past few nights once more, and I want to make sure you are safe. Have you had any visions, Patience? What about the other night when I saw you in the hallway? Had you seen anything? You seemed scared."

Patience looked down. "I have had dreams...but not necessarily bad ones. His face was beautiful...an angel who visits me in the middle of the night." Her voice became soft and wistful as she spoke of the angel of her dreams. "He is so youthful. His eyes sparkle like crystal, and he illuminates the darkness as brightly as a thousand lights. He comes to me full of hopes and promises. He can only be from the heavens—a heavenly creature that watches over me."

Roberto felt the sudden heat flush through his body. "Stop this, Patience. He is not what you think! This angel of light could be the very Serophoth that desires your participation in the creation of the Nephilim."

"No, Papa...he can't be...he is too perfect and beautiful—beyond compare with any of the angels we have seen."

Edwina frowned. She did not understand any of this talk, but she knew Roberto was passionate enough to believe it himself, and it was better to be safe than sorry. "We must listen to your father, Patience. He would only act in your best interest, and you know that."

"OK. I will pack my things and cancel the concerts, but why can you not come with us, Papa?"

"There is much to do here for me. The castle does not run by itself, and it is not I who is in danger, Patience. I would just feel better if you return in summer when the castle seems so much safer."

Patience yielded to her father's wishes. Edwina sympathized with his urgency to keep Patience safe—although safe from what, she did not understand. It all seemed so far-fetched, but she had to admit to an uneasy feeling about the castle that she could not explain. She excused herself on the pretense of feeling tired so that Patience could have some time alone with her father.

"You never speak of Venus much, Father. I miss its enchantment and the mystical beings that make the heart soar. You miss Rusalka, don't you?"

Roberto glanced at Patience, then looked down, fiddling with his hands. "Yes, I do, but I don't miss the evil that we encountered, and I am afraid of it following us here. That is why I want you to go away for a while. This castle, however dear to me, holds the curse of our ancestry, and that is what I fear. Is it a porthole for Leviathan to reach you?"

"I do not feel his presence, Papa. I am sure it will be OK. e have the protection of the Eternals, but I will go away for a while if it makes you relax. I don't want to see that worried look etched on your brow, as it is right now."

Patience walked over to him and kissed him on his head. "I too am tired, so goodnight, Father, and try not to worry. I love you."

"I love you too, Patience. Much more than you know. Have a good, refreshing sleep, and we will make arrangements in the morning for your journey."

"OK, Papa."

Wishbone followed Patience up the long, winding stairs and along the hallway to the east wing. A fire had been lit, and a golden light flickered across the room. Sleep eluded her that night, her mind a whirl about the beautiful angel and her father's concerns. She did not know what to think. Wishbone slept soundly at the foot of her bed, and the fire died down slowly, leaving only the glowing ashes in the hearth.

Her angel came once again on that night, beautiful and dazzling. He gazed at her with those crystal azure eyes that melted her heart. *Am I asleep or awake?* He swept her up in his arms as if she were a feather, weightless as air, flew through the arched window in the turret, and soared high in the dark sky among the vivid, twinkling stars of Heaven.

Then everything seemed like a blur. She could not remember

that eternal moment in space between flying high and lying back in her bed, the room dark and cold. She looked up with fear at the huge, grotesque figure hovering over her. *Where is my beautiful angel?* She could barely breathe; evil washed over her. Then it unfurled its heavy wings and departed at great speed.

Patience's heart pounded, and she swallowed a sob. She struggled to cry for help, but no sound escaped her lips. She shivered, trembling visibly. Around the room moved dark figures, things that defied the eye's attempt at recognition. Then she found herself looking up into the face of...could it be?- the face of her mother. She lifted her hands up to touch her face, a beauty so pure it lit up the room and cut through the darkness. Softly...with a voice of many whispers...she spoke words of comfort. She leaned close to Patience so that she was inches away from her face. Patience felt for one moment the love of a mother, so complete it hurt. Her eyes felt heavy with exhaustion, and she shut them for a second in time.

When she opened them again, she saw a hint of silver-blue shimmer flicker from the image of her mother, and before her eyes, she disintegrated into fragments of iridescent light that quickly disappeared into the darkness. All was quiet except the faint snoring of Wishbone. Patience lay there, afraid to move...afraid to sleep. *Am I asleep?*

Meanwhile, in his own bedroom, far away from Patience, Roberto tossed fitfully. For a while, he lay silent, attempting to sleep, but sleep eluded him. He found the images of Rusalka, so incisively etched in his mind, were becoming less distinct, more diffused, with each passing day, and he found it disconcerting. He had to accept that love was a giving thing, and to love Rusalka entailed acceptance that she belonged to the living Eternal One, where she would find the peace that would elude her living among mortals.

The embers flickered with a soft golden glow as the fire died down in the hearth.

The wind had an electric quality that night. Roberto had noticed the consistent hum when he shut one of the windows before getting into his large mahogany four-poster bed. Something did not seem right—thunder bolted from the night sky, followed by bright flashes of light, and the rushing wind indicated something ominous approaching the castle, getting closer by the minute. Roberto tossed and turned in his bed.

He sensed it—the approach of evil. It was near, and he was afraid to define it...afraid to accept it.

Suddenly, his door slammed open, and a shadow loomed black in the doorway. Roberto's stomach turned over as though its intention were to leap from his body. He was rooted to the spot. He formed the name of the leader of the Serophoth on his lips. "Leviathan!"

Thunder struck violently, and an evil, leering grin stretched out across the dark angel's face.

"IT IS DONE!"

He left those evil words hanging heavily in the air. Then, he was gone. The wind howled outside, and Roberto knew what he had to do. No man, woman, or child would ever be safe again until the seed of Leviathan was destroyed.

The End

∞

To follow...

InterWorlds

The Rise of the Nephilim

Printed in Poland
by Amazon Fulfillment
Poland Sp. z o.o., Wrocław

53973649R00268